A PILGRIMAGE TO MURDER

A PILGRIMAGE TO MURDER

Paul Doherty

Severn House Large Print
London & New York

This first large print edition published 2017
in Great Britain and the USA by
SEVERN HOUSE PUBLISHERS LTD of
19 Cedar Road, Sutton, Surrey, England, SM2 5DA.
First world regular print edition published 2016 by
Crème de la Crime Ltd, an imprint of
Severn House Publishers Ltd.

British Library Cataloguing in Publication Data
A CIP catalogue record for this title is available from the British Library.

ISBN-13: 9780727895844

Severn House Publishers support the Forest Stewardship Council™
[FSC™], the leading international forest certification organisation. All
our titles that are printed on FSC certified paper carry the FSC logo.

Typeset by Palimpsest Book Production Ltd.,
Falkirk, Stirlingshire, Scotland.
Printed and bound in Great Britain by
T J International, Padstow, Cornwall.

To Emma and Kelly, beloved daughters
of our very good friends
Marc and Christine Freeman
Kindest regards and best wishes,

Paul Doherty

Historical Note

By the late summer of 1381 the Great Revolt was over. The peasant armies which had occupied London had fled back into the surrounding shires. The Day of the Great Slaughter had dawned and the lords were determined to impose retribution on their rebellious tenants. London had quickly recovered, the powerful merchants eager to make up for what they had lost during the days of blood. Old rivalries, both in the city and the court, begun to surface once again. Murder, in all its forms, made its presence felt, even on holy pilgrimage to Canterbury . . .

Historical Note

Part One

Azrael: the Four-faced, Four-winged Angel of the Abyss

'Strangulation!'

Athelstan, Dominican friar and parish priest of St Erconwald's in Southwark, moved his ave beads from one hand to the other.

'Strangulation,' he repeated, 'is mentioned in the Book of Tobit, where it describes how the Archangel Raphael chased a demon to Alexandria and strangled it there.' He crouched down beside the corpse of John Finchley, a minor clerk who used to work in the great, grey bulk of Newgate prison. A handsome young man in life, even pretty featured, Finchley had been transformed into a hideously gruesome spectacle by the wire-like garrotte string wrapped tightly around his throat. The clerk's face was almost blue-black, eyes popping, his stained, swollen tongue thrust between yellowing teeth and thickening lips. The shock of death had loosened both bowel and bladder and the stench was noisome. Athelstan tried to ignore this as he whispered the 'I confess' on behalf of the dead man before delivering swift absolution. The church taught that in many deaths the soul could linger for

1

some considerable time close to the corpse, its lifetime place. Not all souls moved directly into the light, so the souls of the dead could still be absolved of sin.

'And the young woman?' Sir John Cranston, Lord High Coroner of London, tapped Athelstan gently on the shoulder and pointed to Felicia Kempton who, caught swiftly and savagely by death, lay in the corner of the room as if gently placed there after the assassin had finished with the garrotte string around her once smooth, unwrinkled throat. Athelstan moved across, swiftly administered the last rites then stood up.

Cranston had remained just within the doorway, his beaver hat off, and his plump, cheery white face, even the thick white hair, moustache and beard, seemed to bristle with good humour. Cranston's ever-dancing light-blue eyes were full of merriment. Swathed in his usual bottle-green cloak under which he concealed the ever-full, miraculous wineskin, the coroner exuded *Pax et Bonum* to the world and its wife. Athelstan knew the reason why. The Great Revolt had been crushed, the King's peace ruthlessly enforced, and Sir John Cranston, or 'Merry Jack' as he referred to himself, was about to be reunited with his buxom wife the Lady Maude, his twin sons the Poppets, Francis and Stephen, not to mention his wolfhounds, Gog and Magog, and all the other members of the Cranston household. Some months earlier Cranston had removed his nearest and dearest from the city and placed them in the green fastness of the countryside behind the high curtain wall of a fortified manor

2

where they were instructed to remain until the great tumult in the city was resolved.

'Time passes, time changes,' Athelstan declared, 'but murder never rests.' The friar gestured around the small solar of Simon Mephan's narrow house in Milk Street, not far from the bustling markets of Cheapside. 'Murder does not reckon time,' he continued, 'or wait for this or that. The Great Revolt may be crushed but the nightmare phantoms and the mocking ghosts will not leave us in peace . . .'

Athelstan paused as Cranston's burly bailiff Flaxwith, along with his constant companion Samson, whom Cranston secretly called 'the ugliest mastiff in the kingdom', a judgement which in all truth Athelstan could not contradict, came clattering down the stairs. Flaxwith hurriedly whispered in Cranston's ear.

'Yes, yes,' the coroner agreed. 'Brother, shall we bring Mephan's corpse down?'

'No, I need to view it as it is.' Athelstan and Cranston followed Flaxwith back up the narrow stairs and into the bedchamber which stood to the right of the stairwell. Simon Mephan, an elderly man, sat slumped over his chancery desk.

'He is dead as a nail,' announced the dark-featured physician. Cranston closed the bedchamber door behind him, and the physician, Limut, wiped his hands on a napkin and threw it on the desk. 'I have examined Simon most carefully.' Athelstan caught the slight accent of another tongue and wondered if Limut was French or Spanish. 'Indeed,' the man continued, 'I know Master Simon very well. I am his family's physician, as

3

I am for other notable households in Farringdon ward. I have, like the good Lord, scrutinised his bowels and his heart.' The physician smiled slightly at his own joke. 'The very humours of the man.'

'In which case, Master Physician, what is the cause of death?' Athelstan enquired. 'How was he murdered?'

The physician, lips all pursed, wrinkled his nose and studied the little Dominican from head to toe, as if memorising every detail of this friar: dark-eyed, his olive-skinned face cleanly shaved; the black and white robe he wore rather shabby, and bound by a piece of frayed cord; scuffed but stout, thick-soled sandals on his bare feet. The Dominican held Limut's gaze, his full lips slightly parted as if on the verge of a smile, large eyes unblinking in their stare. Athelstan was vigorously threading a set of ave beads through his surprisingly long fingers, but he paused at the sudden booming of a bell.

'The hanging bell,' Cranston declared. 'They are taking the condemned from Newgate to the gallows over Tyburn stream.'

'And someone else,' Athelstan murmured, still holding the physician's gaze, 'will be making that same journey for the nightmare here. Now, my friend,' Athelstan's face creased into a smile as he pointed at the dead man slumped in his chair, 'is that murder?'

'Yes and no,' the physician replied. 'The young man and woman downstairs were garrotted, and expertly so.' He paused as Cranston made sure the door behind him was shut and went over to sit on the bed.

4

'Look.' The physician walked around the desk and tilted Mephan's head back so Athelstan and Cranston could more clearly see the half-open mouth, the glassy-eyed dead stare and the highly discoloured facial skin, especially around the mouth and jaw. 'To put it succinctly,' Limut explained, 'Simon Mephan died of heart failure. His heart just gave way which,' he let his hand drop, 'is perfectly understandable. Master Mephan's heart was not strong; he was becoming more frail and weak by the month. The shock of what happened downstairs . . .' The physician shrugged and pulled a face.

'Yes, just what did happen downstairs? Sir John, Master Limut, bear with me.' Athelstan crossed to the door and turned. 'Master Physician, might I know your first name?'

'Giole.' The physician smiled. 'It's Spanish. I am from Castile.' Athelstan stared at the physician, a neat, precise man, clean-shaven, his black hair combed back and clasped in a tail behind his head. Giole sported a silver ring in one earlobe, and jewels glistened on his wrist and fingers. He was dressed soberly, though Athelstan suspected the dark robes were of pure wool and the supple boots of the finest Cordovan leather. Limut smiled at Athelstan's close scrutiny. 'Brother?'

Athelstan raised a hand. 'I am sorry, Giole, but looking at you, I see a reflection of myself.' He walked over, hand outstretched, and the physician clasped it warmly.

'Yes, Brother, there is a likeness, I agree. You must meet my wife Beatrice, my son Felipe and daughter Maria. I am sure they will agree there is a likeness between us.'

'There certainly is!' Cranston chortled from where he sat on the bed cradling the miraculous wineskin. He unstoppered it, took a generous mouthful and encouraged the physician to do likewise.

Athelstan refused, beckoning both men to follow him. They went downstairs and into the solar guarded by Flaxwith, Samson and one of the other bailiffs. Athelstan walked into the chamber and stared around. Everything seemed to be in place, no disturbance or disarray. Cups, flagons and goblets, all polished and clean, stood on a small, gleaming table. The white rope matting on the floor was in place and Athelstan could detect no recent stains. The lock on the money box or tally casket, however, had been smashed, its concave lid thrown back. This was the only other sign that hideous violence had taken place – that and the two corpses sprawled gruesome and grisly in their agonising death throes. Athelstan pinched his nose at the foul smell.

'Have the corpses moved as soon as possible. Well, Sir John, Master Giole, how did this occur? What do we know?'

'From what I understand,' Cranston replied, 'a neighbour leaving for the Jesus mass at St Mary Le Bow noticed the lanternhorn outside had not been lit and the front door was off the latch. An honest, God-fearing woman, I know her well. She came in and saw this horror, then she raised the alarm. The hue and cry were proclaimed

6

and the sheriff's men summoned, then they sent messages to me and for Master Giole.'

'I arrived with my son Felipe,' the physician explained, 'and we met Sir John, who said he had sent for you, Athelstan.'

'Every man's death is significant, Sir John, but why were you summoned?'

'Mephan is – was – a senior clerk in the Secret Chancery of my Lord of Gaunt. He worked for Thibault, Gaunt's Master of Secrets, whom we know so well. Now the revolt maybe crushed,' Cranston shook his head, 'but, following any fierce fire, embers still glow. In a word, the sheriff's men wondered, as I do, if this was the work of the Reapers.'

'Who?' Limut demanded.

'The Reapers,' Cranston repeated. 'Really, the Upright Men wearing a different hood and carrying a different banner. The Great Revolt is over. The Community of the Realm has been shattered and the Upright Men, its principal adherents, are dead, fleeing for their lives or imprisoned. The same goes for their street warriors the Earthworms. They are like ears of corn, shattered, crushed and dispersed to the four winds. The Reapers are the remnant, a so-called secret society composed of Upright Men and a few captains of the Earthworms.'

'Ah yes, I have heard of them,' said Athelstan. 'They write out proclamations and nail them to the doors of churches, full of threats and menaces.'

'True,' Cranston agreed. 'Their proclamations have even been pinned to the doors of the

7

Guildhall. The Upright Men are no longer interested in bringing about God's commonwealth or transforming London into the Holy City of the Apocalypse. They simply want revenge on all those who have crushed their dreams, defeated their levies and hanged and disembowelled their comrades. Mephan could be their victim. After all, he is in the retinue of Thibault, the regent's henchman and dark-souled companion. Consequently, if the Reapers do exist, perhaps they marked Mephan down for death whilst the other two were simply killed to silence them. And yet . . .'

'And yet what, Sir John?'

'Nothing for the moment, little monk.'

'Little friar, Sir John!'

'God be with you all,' Cranston retorted. 'But Athelstan, tell us why you have brought us down here.'

'Well,' said Athelstan. 'The front door was off its latch, not broken or damaged, true?' Cranston agreed. 'And no disturbance was heard?'

'None, little friar,' Cranston replied. 'Flaxwith has already made enquiries. Nobody heard or saw anything out of the ordinary.'

'What was the situation here?' Athelstan asked. 'I mean the household?'

'According to the local gossip, Felicia was the maid and John Finchley was Mephan's lodger, but he also acted as his private clerk or scribe. Others claim both were homosexual, that Simon loved young men. Isn't that true, physician?'

Limut pulled a face and spread his hands. 'Sir John, I know very little about my patient's

8

private life, and what I do know is of little interest to others.'

Cranston continued blithely, 'Finchley was dedicated to his master, I understand. Both he and Felicia lived here. Now, before I despatched Tiptoft to fetch you, I had a good look around, but I could find nothing in this narrow, rather plain house to explain these murders, how they occurred or why.'

'Quite so.' Athelstan crouched down beside the dead clerk. 'Here lies a young man, and there sprawls the corpse of a young woman. Both of them vigorous and strong, both garrotted. Their assassin used a piece of fine twine which he left around their necks. He probably carries such deadly strings in a purse on his belt. Now I believe that the assassin was known to his victims. He rapped on the door and was welcomed in.' Athelstan stood up. 'And that's when mystery descends like a mist. Look, Sir John, Master Giole. Two young people garrotted. Did they struggle or kick out? Upset furniture? Try and escape? Scream, shout?' Athelstan shook his head. 'There is not a shred of evidence that they did so.'

'Could they have been drugged?' Cranston queried. 'We have seen that happen before.'

'I smelt no wine on their breath,' the physician declared. 'Nor have I seen any used goblet, cup or jug of wine. Perhaps there might be something in the kitchen or, more probably, the garden – we should go there.'

'The assassin must have arrived before nightfall, before darkness descended. Look.' Athelstan picked up a candelabra; each of the spigots held a primed candle. 'These haven't even been lit.' He returned to the two victims and examined their fingers and wrists and scrutinised their clothing. 'It's true,' he sighed, 'no sign of resistance or struggle on either of them or around them. The breaking of that tally coffer is the only noticeable damage, or theft, to their property. Well, as far as we can establish.'

'Indeed, very clever,' Cranston commented. 'I suspect the assassin took coins but nothing which could be traced back.'

Athelstan, who'd glimpsed rings and bracelets on the dead Felicia, murmured his agreement. He rose, left the solar and went down a stone-paved passageway smelling of rosemary and thyme, which led into the kitchen with its adjoining buttery. The kitchen was clean: the fleshing table had been well scrubbed, and the small ovens either side of the mantled hearth had been swept as was the hearth itself. Herb pots had been filled with crushed plants and a vase on a ledge sported a few roses, whilst the horn-filled windows had been scrubbed clean of flies and other insects. Fire irons on the hearth were dust-free, polished and neatly arranged.

'A clean, tidy house.' Athelstan spoke over his shoulder to Cranston and the physician who had followed him in. Athelstan walked into the buttery: on its table was a leg of cured mustard-glazed ham, a pipe of Spanish wine, a platter of manchet bread rolls, a dish of spiced sauce and a bowl of chopped vegetables next to a tray with three goblets and a jug of white wine, all covered

10

by a fine linen cloth. 'They were preparing for their evening meal,' Athelstan murmured to himself.

'And given the weather, eating it outside,' the physician declared.

'We should go out there,' Athelstan suggested.

He walked across the scrubbed kitchen floor and out through the door leading to a fairly large garden: a perfect square bounded by the house, the other three sides being lined with bushes and trees, probably preserved from when that part of London was still farmland. The garden, like the rest of the house, was neat and orderly. The grassy plots and hedgerows were clipped, the customary three partitions into kitchen garden, flower bed and herb plot all clearly set out. The garden also boasted a small carp pond fringed with lilies and luxurious reeds as well as two garden bowers with flowers growing over the outside and comfortable turf seats within. Leaving Cranston and the physician chatting in the doorway, Athelstan walked across and stared down at the golden carp darting in ripples through the water.

'Athelstan! Athelstan!'

His name was called in a hoarse whisper. The friar started as the corpse of a magpie, a garrotte string wrapped around its throat, was tossed onto the paving before him.

'Be ye warned, Athelstan, be ye warned. Now and in the future.'

The friar shaded his eyes against the dazzle of the strengthening sun which cut through the foliage and bushes in sharp shafts of light, then he glimpsed it, a shadow darker than those thrown by the trees though using them to stay concealed. The sinister figure moved a little closer, becoming distinct enough for Athelstan to make out a black cloak, a cowl and a face mask as well as a small arbalest, primed and ready, its barbed bolt winched back.

'Sir John!' Athelstan yelled. He heard the click of the crossbow and the bolt whirled through the air to shatter against the wall of the house. Cranston shouted and lunged forward, the physician with him. Athelstan glanced back. He heard a crackling in the fringe of trees and realised his sinister visitor must have scaled the curtain wall and fled. Athelstan crouched down and picked up the feathery, soiled corpse of the magpie and showed it to Cranston. After he had briefly explained what he had seen and heard, he placed the magpie down on the grass, walked to the fringe of trees and then came back.

'Brother, if what you describe appeared last night to Mephan and his two companions, it would have caused consternation and panic.'

'I agree, Sir John,' Athelstan replied. 'The hue and cry would have been raised to shouts of "Harrow! Harrow!" I don't think Mephan's assassin appeared like that. So why return to bait us dressed so threateningly, acting so menacingly? Unless, of course, we are wrong and he did the same yesterday evening just before dark. Did he invade this garden then swiftly and silently strike at Finchley and Felicia? Was he interrupted by Simon Mephan who fled upstairs?

The attack and Mephan's flight were all too much for the old clerk and, in sudden terror, his heart gave way. All this is logical and possible, except for the reappearance of the assassin this morning in such circumstances.'

'Are you sure it was the assassin?' Physician Limut demanded.

'It must be,' Athelstan replied. 'The magpie, the garrotte string, the threat.' He picked up the magpie's corpse and studied it carefully. 'It was well tended, a young bird, perhaps easy to catch or trap in a lure or a snare, but why?' He recalled the warning, the crossbow bolt smashing against the wall, then he began to laugh.

'What is it, Brother?'

'The magpie.' Athelstan placed the corpse back on the grass. 'Notice its colouring, black and white, the same hue as a Dominican. Moreover, our order has been likened to a flock of magpies by the preachers who accuse us, in some cases most deservedly, of being magpies in human flesh with an eye for gold and all that glitters, whilst our work as members of the Holy Inquisition has also been compared to the depredations of marauding magpies.' Athelstan shook his head. 'But why warn me in such a way, eh? I have no wealth, and I certainly don't work for the Inquisition.'

'If it was the assassin,' the physician repeated.

'It must have been.' Cranston picked up the magpie's corpse and threw it into the bushes.

'I think it's time we revisited Mephan's bedchamber,' Athelstan declared and led the way up the steep stairs. Observing that the door to

13

Mephan's chamber had neither bolt nor lock, Athelstan believed that one of his conclusions was correct: Mephan had been truly terrified. Had he come down and seen the corpses or been there when one of them died, a swift but hideous death, the last thing Mephan expected to witness in his neat and orderly house? Athelstan paused and joined his hands together.

'I do wonder,' he said slowly, 'about that apparition in the garden just now. He must have been waiting for me. He must have expected me to go into the garden.'

'Well, that's fairly logical, Brother,' the coroner declared. 'Three hideous murders have occurred here. We are bound to make a sweep of the house and its garden. Perhaps it's just a matter of waiting. But why have you brought us up here again?'

'Well,' Athelstan replied, 'imagine that the assassin has entered the house. Yes? Mephan is busy in his bedchamber. Perhaps he hears a sound or a shout. He comes down those stairs and sees something which terrifies the life out of him. He turns and hastens back up the stairs in deep fear of his life. He does not feel well, the beginnings of a seizure. An old man and sickly, the flight up the stairs proves to be too much,' Athelstan waved his hand, 'and, God rest him, the poor man collapses and dies. What I can't understand is why he fled up steep steps into a bedchamber with no lock or bolt on the door. Why didn't he try and flee through the main door leading onto the street?'

'Perhaps it was locked and bolted,' Physician

Giole declared. 'Perhaps the key had been removed by the assassin.'

'Perhaps,' the friar replied. 'But I still think it is puzzling.' He walked around the bedchamber, then knelt beside the muniment chest near the chancery desk and lifted the lid.

'All gone,' Cranston sang out. 'We had a visitor very early on. Master Thibault, residing at the Guildhall, heard of Mephan's mysterious death and despatched Albinus his henchman to survey the property. Believe me, Brother, anything and everything of interest will be gone.'

Athelstan stared into the empty muniment chest and quietly agreed. Master Thibault, John of Gaunt's confidant in all matters politic, would have been quick to remove anything which could hurt either him or his cunning master, especially in these last days. The revolt was now well and truly crushed and the Commons and the Lords were beginning to demand answers to all sorts of questions about why the revolt had occurred, how it was managed, who did what, where and when.

'Oh yes,' Athelstan whispered, 'anything injurious would have been taken. But let me study Mephan.' He crossed behind the desk. The dead clerk slouched in the high-back chair, wedged against the edge of the desk. The surface in front of him was cleared of all scraps of parchment which, Athelstan concluded, would have been the work of Albinus, Thibault's eerie-looking messenger. Pushed away from the corpse was a book of the Gospel of St Luke, its heavily brocaded cover of red, gold and green ornamented

15

and decorated with Celtic and Greek symbols such as the Tree of Jesse and the Tau. Athelstan picked the book up, its pages yellow with age, opened up the first folio and read the inscription: '*Hic Simonis Liber* – This is Simon's book.' One page of the Gospels had been marked by a sharp-edged quill pen with a white bony point and a black feathered stem. The tip of the pen was tinged bright red. Athelstan checked the ink horn on its tray and found the same, a pot of blood-red ink. He believed both the quill pen and the ink horn had been recently used. He leafed through the pages of the Gospel and saw a phrase, two of its words being punctuated with red dots, '*Nomen nostrum est legio enim multi nos.*' The words '*legio*' and '*multi*' had been heavily under-scored with red ink. 'Our name is legion for we are many,' Athelstan translated. He studied the context of the line and realised the extract was from the account of how Jesus crossed the Sea of Galilee and landed amongst the Gesarenes. No sooner had he gone ashore than he had been confronted by a possessed man, so violent that he had broken free of his chains. Christ then exorcised the demon and, in accordance with the ritual, demanded that the devil possessing the man give his name. The reply '*Nomen nostrum est legio enim multi nos* – our name is legion for we are many' had apparently attracted Mephan's attention, but why? Was it connected to the murders? The friar closed the book and slipped it into his chancery satchel. The account of the exorcism reminded him of something similar demanding his attention at St Erconwald's.

'Brother?'

'My apologies, friends, I am daydreaming,' Athelstan confessed. 'But perhaps you could both assist me.' Both coroner and physician hastened to pull the corpse away from the desk. Athelstan crouched down and scrutinised the dead man's thick woollen robes and stubby, cold fingers. He detected spots and stains of red ink. Athelstan smiled to himself. He was now certain that those notes on the Book of the Gospel were the last thing that Mephan had done before he died, even when he was in the middle of that final deadly spasm, a message from the dead to the living.

'Sir John,' Athelstan got to his feet, 'I believe we are finished here. You have searched the house?'

'I have, and found nothing untoward. Even if there was something, I am sure it's been removed. Now, Brother, I need refreshment. Flaxwith can be trusted. The corpses will be moved to the death house at St Mary le Bow, and the chambers here and all their contents will be itemised and sealed.'

The physician came out of the shadows. He had been studying a decorated tapestry on the wall depicting a celestial battle between angels dressed like clerks, their golden hair curled and crimped, the jewel-encrusted silver chancery belts around their slim waists crammed with pouches for quills, ink horns, wax, pumice stones and other clerical necessities, and monkey soldiers wearing the garb of forest archers, Lincoln-green tunics and black leggings stretching

17

down to horned feet, their bat-like heads cowled in fur-trimmed hats.

'Master Giole?'

'A number of matters.' The physician took a deep breath. 'First, if you wish to break your fast, why not join me and Beatrice at our tavern, Amongst the Tombs? It stands near St Martin's in Ludgate close to the Bishop of London's palace.'

'You own a tavern, Master Giole?'

'My wife Beatrice runs it, assisted by my son Felipe and my daughter Maria. They hope to become members of the Vintner's Guild. We bought the tavern a few months before the outbreak of the revolt and had it refurbished. Being foreigners we kept our presence very discreet. Now the storm is over, I am told merry times have returned to London. We have opened and do good trade.' The physician's dark, handsome face eased into a smile. 'I am a master of physic. I ply my trade from the tavern, having sealed indentures with the aldermen and council of Farringdon ward to act as their physician – hence my presence here.'

Cranston smacked his lips. 'I have heard good things about your kitchens. But why the title, Amongst the Tombs?'

'Ah,' Limut laughed, 'because it is allegedly built over an ancient graveyard. The ancient ones of the ward claim the cellars are haunted by a host of hostile ghosts, vengeful spirits and other denizens of the dark.'

'And what do you think, learned physician?' Athelstan teased. 'Do the vindictive dead sit amongst the barrels of your cellar?'

18

'I doubt it.' The physician laughed. 'More a question of slithering rats, dripping casks and squeaking mice. But Domina Beatrice leads and instructs a veritable chorus of chefs and cooks. Moreover, I wish to discuss another matter with you.'

Athelstan plucked at the physician's sleeve. 'Master Giole, Sir John and I,' he glanced at the coroner, who nodded, 'would be honoured to sup with you. Indeed,' Athelstan continued in a rush, 'I have some other business I would like your help with. Rest assured, I shall pay.' He paused as Limut shook his head and raised a hand. 'I would usually ask for the help of Brother Philippe, Custos and principal physician at St Bartholomew's,' Athelstan added.

'I know Philippe,' Limut replied. 'I respect his reputation.'

'Too famous for his own good,' Athelstan agreed. 'His order has sent him to Glastonbury to recuperate and recover after the troubles here.'

Athelstan dared not meet Cranston's gaze. The friar certainly recalled the end of the troubles at Smithfield just outside St Bartholomew's. Sir John had struck at the rebel leader Wat Tyler and, in doing so, broken the spirit and will of the rebel army. Tyler had been grievously wounded and took refuge in St Bartholomew's, but the Lord High Coroner, full of fury, had dragged him out to the common scaffold, hacked off the rebel leader's head and placed it on a pole. 'Poor Philippe,' Athelstan murmured almost to himself. 'He worked at the very heart of the fury. Many of the wounded and dead were taken there.'

'And many of those dead were adjudged to be rebels and traitors,' Limut declared. 'They still discuss this in the taverns, how the King's men dragged the corpses from the death houses, with hooks through their noses and mouths, to be hacked and cut, decapitated and quartered before being displayed on London Bridge or above the city gates. I . . .' He broke off at a clamour from below: raised voices, people moving about, footsteps pounding on the stairs. Flaxwith, accompanied by a gasping Samson, tongue hanging out, jaws all slavering, came into the room. The mastiff immediately headed for Sir John, tail wagging, eyes all expectant. Cranston shooed it away as Flaxwith announced that three clerks, Matthew, Luke and John Gaddesden, had arrived from Westminster desirous of seeing Sir John and paying their respects to their master, Simon Mephan.

'The evangelists,' Cranston breathed, 'brothers, sons of Adrian Gaddesden, cordwainer and rope-maker to our noble regent John of Gaunt. Those clerks are the pillars of the Secret Chancery and are steeped in all the villainy that haunt of demons can create.'

'Sir John,' Athelstan retorted, 'you are too harsh!' The friar paused. 'You say three, Sir John, but there are four evangelists.'

'There used to be four brothers, but during the Great Revolt one of them, Mark, returned to the city on some secret errand from Gaunt and Master Thibault. He was caught out in the open,

20

recognised, seized and decapitated on the steps of the Conduit in Cheapside. Straw was stuffed into the dead man's maw before his head was poled on a stake near St Paul's Cross. The brothers mourn him . . .'

'And they are party to Thibault's conniving ways?'

'I am being truthful, Brother. The Commons would love to know what those three gentlemen do, though I suspect that will never happen. They and Mephan are Gaunt's liege men, his retainers, his coven, his servants in peace and war against all enemies both within and without. You have Gaunt, you have the evangelists and, of course, the bridge between them is Master Thibault.' Cranston drew a deep breath. 'Flaxwith,' the coroner jabbed a finger at the bailiff, 'you are scrupulously itemising this house and its contents?' Flaxwith murmured his agreement.

'And you have sheeted the two corpses below?'

'Yes, Sir John, we have laid them out in the shrouds we brought. We will seize a wheelbarrow and take them to St Mary le Bow.'

'Good. In which case,' Cranston turned back to Athelstan, 'we are finished here.' The friar nodded. 'Master Giole,' Cranston tapped the physician on the arm, 'have a further scrutiny of Mephan's corpse, help Flaxwith sheet it and we shall be with you very soon.'

With the physician's agreement ringing in their ears, both coroner and friar went down the stairs into the solar. Cranston snapped his fingers at the bailiff on guard, who bowed and left as the coroner turned to greet the men sitting on the stools and chairs. All three got to their feet, introductions were made, hands clasped and the kiss of peace exchanged. Cranston asked the clerks what they wanted; their reply was simple enough. They were grieving, curious and eager to pay their respects. Cranston explained that the corpses had yet to be released under his seal which, he declared, would likely be done by nightfall. After all, it was summer and burials had to be swift because of the heat.

As the clerks discussed the funeral arrangements and asked Cranston what had actually happened, Athelstan studied the three men closely. They were of a mature age, vigorous in manner. Athelstan reckoned Matthew, the eldest, must have reached his fortieth summer whilst his younger sibling, John, was probably no more than twenty-three years of age. Nevertheless, despite the age differences, all three clerks looked the same: auburn-haired, fresh-faced, clean-shaven. They came across as bland in appearance, voice, expression and gesture. Quietly spoken, yet, despite all this, sharp of wit and keen-eyed. Athelstan sensed that these clerks were very subtle and hid behind different masks which they donned to suit the occasion. They were not meant to stand out in a crowd. They were all dressed in padded, sleeveless tunics boasting the dark blue and gold heraldic devices of the Royal Chancery, their white shirts beneath were high-collared and spotlessly clean, and their black hose was and pushed into soft, low-heeled boots. All three wore the chancery ring on their left hand with a silver Lancastrian SS collar around their necks.

They listened politely to Cranston's explanation, shaking their heads and murmuring exclamations of surprise or brief prayers for Mephan's departed soul. These clerks were possessors of great secrets, and as Athelstan studied them, he recalled the stories about the Secret Chancery and the doings of the mysterious Star Chamber close to Westminster Hall. According to Cranston, Thibault and his coven had played a highly dangerous game during the Great Revolt. The Secret Chancery was an office or department within the royal enclosure but its loyalty was not so much to young Richard, but more to the Crown of England and its representative, the regent John of Gaunt. Men such as these made that distinction, and during the revolt which swept the city in a bloody storm, faithfully observed such a separation. Richard of England, apart from loyal councillors such as Cranston, had been left to his own devices as Gaunt, for God knows what reason, took an army north to the Scottish March. Some whispered what would now be regarded as heinous treason; that Gaunt hoped the rebels would sweep his royal nephew away in the murderous mayhem which would engulf the city. Once this had happened, Gaunt could return as the all-conquering hero, crush the rebels and take the crown for himself.

Thibault, Gaunt's principal henchman, was no better, having secretly withdrawn into the fastness of the formidable keep of Hedingham Castle in Essex. He had, however, made one concession, a great favour to Athelstan in return for the friar looking after Thibault's beloved daughter Isabella: Thibault had arranged the abduction of all the men from Athelstan's parish and kept them in comfortable confinement until the revolt was over. Athelstan's parishioners – the likes of Watkin the dung-collector, Pike the ditcher, Ranulf the rat-catcher and all the others of their conniving coven – had been staunch Upright Men, followers of the Great Community of the Realm, the Parliament of the Peasants. However, when the revolt collapsed, none of these men could be indicted for any crime at a time when indictments were flowing from the Chancery and King's Bench like snowflakes in a blizzard. Listening carefully to the clerks and how they worked with Mephan, as recently as yesterday, Athelstan realised that the crown, Gaunt in particular, was still pursing the rebels and anyone associated with them as ruthlessly and mercilessly as a starving wolf would its quarry.

Athelstan picked up a stool and came to sit beside Cranston. The clerks now lounged on chairs, stools or the top of chests.

Matthew, the eldest, turned to him. 'You are Athelstan? We have heard of you,' he made a face, 'and many of your parishioners.'

'I am sure you have,' Athelstan retorted, edging forward on his stool. 'And rest assured, I have heard about you gentlemen, but now I would like to learn a little more. They call you the evangelists?'

'Matthew, Mark, now sadly deceased, Luke and John,' the youngest replied, 'but you, as a priest, would know that.' Athelstan caught the sarcastic tinge.

'Oh, I live and I learn every day. My condolences on the death of your brother. So you three are all full blood kin?'

'We are the sons of Adrian Gaddesden,' Luke replied, 'and his lovely wife, our mother Margaret. Our father loaned my Lord of Gaunt generous sums when no other merchant would lift a finger to help. Isn't that true, Sir John?' Cranston quietly agreed. 'And we . . .' Luke was the largest of the brothers, his belly straining at the belt around his waist. He kept wetting his lips and, quick of eye, glanced around as if searching for something to drink. He was also highly nervous. Athelstan noticed a slight sheen on his forehead and he kept twisting his fingers. Now he was closer Athelstan realised all three brothers seemed unsettled. One of them, John, went to open his belt wallet as if to bring something out but then abruptly changed his mind.

'You were talking about your family?' Athelstan queried.

'There is not much to say,' Luke replied rather mockingly. 'My brothers and I were scholars at St Paul's and from there went to Stapleton Hall in Oxford, where we acquired both our bachelorship and our masters. My Lord of Gaunt and Master Thibault recruited us from the Exchequer of Receipt and appointed us to the courts of Chancery, then the Chancery itself.'

'And finally the inner sanctum?' Cranston

intervened. 'The Secret Chancery, the House of Whispers and the Mansion of Secrets?'

'If you say so, Sir John, and,' Matthew held up a hand, 'before you or Brother Athelstan ask, let me remind you we have taken a vow of secrecy, not to discuss the business of the Secret Chancery or the doings of the Star Chamber.'

'Of course,' Athelstan agreed. 'So now to Master Mephan's murder and that of his two . . .'

'Companions,' Luke intervened. 'Master Mephan's companions.'

'As you were,' Athelstan retorted, 'close colleagues and comrades. Yes?' He didn't wait for an answer. 'So who would murder him?'

'The Reapers. The Upright Men. The Earthworms. The Great Community of the Realm,' Luke spat back. 'All those treasonable, treacherous, hell-bound covens who plotted our total destruction and almost brought it about. Foul, sin-ridden souls who barbarously murdered our brother Mark. Mephan's death is revenge for the work we did in crushing their diabolical dreams to a bloody dust. Pig-souls, wolf-hearts, demonwitted . . .' Luke paused, wiping the spittle from his lips on the back of his hand. Matthew put a restraining hand on his brother's arm and smiled tactfully at the friar.

'Was Mephan threatened?' Athelstan asked.

Matthew opened his belt wallet and drew out a piece of fine twine. He handed it to Athelstan, who held it up against the light.

'The same cord used by the assassin,' he murmured. 'And what is this?' He shifted the cord through his fingers until he reached the

26

piece of hardened parchment pierced by a hole through which the twine had been threaded. Athelstan peered at the phrase, translating the Latin.

'Lord Azrael greets you.' Athelstan looked up sharply at Cranston's exclamation.

'I shall tell you later,' the coroner declared hurriedly, 'but not now.'

Athelstan held the garrotte string up, making the parchment medallion twist and turn. 'Azrael,' Athelstan repeated. 'The Angel of Death.'

'Simon received one yesterday,' Matthew said, 'as he was making his way out of mass to the Chancery.' He pulled a face. 'At the time we didn't realise its significance. We even thought we'd use the cord when we went bird-snaring across the moor around Perilous Pond near Old Street.'

'You snare birds?'

'Always have,' Matthew gabbled on. 'Anyway, today as we left our chambers near St Margaret's in Friday Street, a street urchin stopped us. He said a man had given him a coin to deliver these to us. He thrust three pouches into my hand and left. Each pouch – really just a dusty little leather sack – contained a cord and medallion similar to the one Simon received yesterday. It's a threat, isn't it, Brother Athelstan? We are in great danger for what we have done.'

Athelstan sensed the real panic of all three clerks. One of them might be able to hide it better than the other but they were all in mortal fear for their lives. Little wonder, these men had

27

exercised great power and were now set to pay for it.

'So Master Mephan received his yesterday as he left the Jesus mass?' Athelstan spoke quietly to divert and distract the clerks. 'And you received yours . . .?'

'About an hour ago on our way to Westminster. We decided to hurry here and seek Master Simon's advice.' Matthew shrugged. 'Then we heard the shocking news.' He put his face in his hands even as his brothers, clearly agitated, rose to their feet, unable to sit still with the fear coursing through them.

Athelstan plucked at Cranston's sleeve and they too got up. The friar hurried into the buttery, where he poured three goblets of wine. He stared around. Flaxwith and his bailiffs had sheeted and moved the corpses to the garden, and they were now busy sealing chests, caskets and coffers. Physician sat on a turf seat, lost in his own thoughts as he stared mournfully over the flower beds. Athelstan went over and assured him that he and Sir John would not be long, then he hurried back to the solar with the tray of goblets. Cranston had soothed the evangelists' fear, telling them that as long as they were prudent, they'd be safe. Athelstan distributed the wine goblets, and as he did so he established that all three clerks had been at home the previous evening. All bachelors, they'd only left their chambers to have supper at a nearby tavern, the Glory of Galilee. Further questioning elicited little of substance. The evangelists would say nothing about their work and could provide little information about

Mephan's murder or indeed the threats levelled against them.

'There's only Empson,' Matthew added as an afterthought. 'Roger Empson.'

'And?' Athelstan asked.

'He has disappeared.'

'Who is he?' Athelstan asked.

'Master Thibault's principal messenger and most trusted courier,' Cranston intervened. 'Before the revolt when my Lord of Gaunt went north to the Scottish March, Empson rode back and forth keeping both Gaunt and his henchmen fully appraised of what the other was doing.' Cranston took a generous swig from the miraculous wineskin. 'A good man, Empson. I can see why Thibault used him. Empson's also a skilled man-at-arms. He has to be. On a number of occasions he was attacked on the open road. If it comes to sword and dagger play, Empson could hold his own, be it out on the open heathland or some stinking Cheapside alleyway.'

'I agree.' John, the quietest of the evangelists, spoke up. 'Roger always carried documents safely, he is an excellent horseman. He was frightened too.'

'Of what?' Athelstan asked. Despite the warmth and light pouring through the solar window, the friar also felt the fear cloying the hearts of these men.

'Revenge,' Luke said. 'Roger often took messages not only to my Lord of Gaunt and Thibault but to commanders of the royal forces. He also laid indictments against those who attacked him.'

Athelstan sat down on a stool and stared at the evangelists. 'I am shocked,' he exclaimed. 'The revolt is over, it is crushed. It's the Upright Men who should be terrified, not leading clerks of the Royal Chancery. I can understand Master Thibault being wary, but why strike at you?'

'We've thought the same,' Matthew agreed. 'But surely, Brother Athelstan, it's a matter of logic. My Lord of Gaunt and Master Thibault are surrounded by guards, professionals, mercenaries. We have to go back to our ordinary lives. I cannot move amongst the stalls of Cheapside behind a screen of Hainault mercenaries.'

'Then what about Sir John?' Athelstan enquired. 'He crushed the rebels! Indeed, he executed one of their leaders.'

'It's different,' Matthew retorted, 'or I think it is. The Reapers see Sir John as a soldier, a loyal royal knight carrying out orders. He does not have, how can I put it, the personal vindictiveness of Master Thibault. Sir John was not responsible for the poll tax or all the other executions which led to the revolt.'

Athelstan got to his feet, ave beads slipping through his fingers.

'And what has happened to Roger Empson?'

'He disappeared about three days ago,' Matthew replied, 'though I understand he has been seen cowled and cloaked amongst the stalls of Cheapside. But he has gone into hiding. Why and where I cannot tell you.' Matthew spread his hands. 'We have to leave now. Brother Athelstan, we may have words with you on other matters, or rather Master Thibault will . . .'

30

A short while later, Physician Limut led Athelstan and Cranston out into Milk Street. Both he and the friar had to wait a short while outside the doorway as Cranston gave Flaxwith more instructions about the removal of the corpses to St Mary's and the sealing of the house and its contents. The coroner also informed the evangelists, who had followed them out, that they could pay their respects to Mephan and his two companions at St Mary le Bow after the Jesus mass the following morning. Athelstan and the physician engaged in desultory conversation, and Limut once again referred to some matter he wished to discuss with the friar. Eventually Cranston joined them, and the physician led his guests off through the surging crowds.

The weather was fine, the sun growing stronger. Londoners had poured out of their mildewed tenements to bask in the sun, do business or carry out any mischief they could. Athelstan felt uneasy as he often did when he first entered the crowded city streets. Yet he also sensed a change; the soul of London was commerce, bartering, buying and selling, be it human flesh or oranges from Seville. The Great Revolt was over, the rebels crushed and milled to nothing. The scaffolds might be heavy with cadavers, the lumbering execution carts and corpse barrows a common sight. The quartered remains of traitors, all tarred and bloodied, decorated a forest of stakes on every available gateway, but the revolt was definitely over. The city was desperate to repair as swiftly as possible the damage to buildings and, above all, to return to its usual frenetic trading. The rebels and their proclamations were now dismissed as part of a phantom dream, gone like a watch in the night. No longer did the Earthworms swarm through the Cheapside crowds, but instead the liveried, armoured retainers of the city council and the great lords, all buckled for war, swaggered along the runnels and alleyways.

The merchants and traders had returned, their stalls piled high with goods and produce; they were doing a bustling trade whilst the dusty air rang with the shouts and cries of apprentices touting for business. Market beadles and bailiffs patrolled carefully, their white canes of office ready to slice at any tinker, trader or itinerant cook who crept out from the needle-thin alleyways to ply their unlicensed trade. Pigs, cats and dogs roamed backwards and forwards. Half-naked children scurried over midden heaps, sending the vermin fleeing back to their holes. Whores in their bright yellow gowns and orange wigs, faces daubed white, red and black, scurried backwards and forwards across the thoroughfare, one hand holding a pomander, the other all gloved ready for some customer. Around these swirled the lords of the sewers, the barons of the gutter, the earls of the dagger and the bolt as well as the pimping pontiffs who looked after their shoals of whores as shepherds would their flocks of sheep.

A myriad of smells drifted; the foul, noxious fumes seeping from midden heaps and lay stalls mixing with the sweet fragrances of freshly baked bread, and ripe, bloody meat sizzling under different coatings of spiced vegetables. Cries, shouts, curses and prayers were raised. Accidents happened: wheelbarrows tipped and burst, baskets were dropped, barrels overturned, casks split. A dog was caught under the wheel of a cart, its dying screams drowned by the screech of bagpipes as bailiffs led a long line of doleful curfew-breakers down to the stocks. Soldiers and men-at-arms made their way through. Priests carrying the viaticum for the dying, hurried along mouthing their prayers as an altar boy raced before them, capped candle in one hand, tinkling bell in the other. Processions of the Blessed Sacrament, cloaked in thick mists of the sweetest incense, mingled with the drunken revelry of both wedding and funeral parties. Guests and mourners shoved and pushed whilst a corpse slipping from its bier nearly caused a riot.

Athelstan and his companions hurried up under the dark, forbidding mass of St Paul's, its spire packed with holy relics as a defence against lightning. Athelstan always thought the spire looked like a finger of accusation pointing towards heaven. They passed through the Shambles, which reeked of all the bloodied, fetid odours of the slaughter house. The fleshers' stalls were close to the grim, grey fastness of Newgate, a prison bulging with fortified gates, shuttered windows, crenellated walls, iron-studded doors and steel-barred portcullises. They reached the more peaceful area of St Andrew's and the tavern Amongst the Tombs, a square of grey ragstone wall pierced by a magnificent gateway on its southern side.

They entered its spacious cobbled yard and passed the stables and many outhouses into the tavern proper. Athelstan marvelled at the sheer elegance of the place. The large kitchen was well stocked; Athelstan glimpsed pipes of Spanish wine and cured legs of ham richly coated with a yellow mustard sauce. The taproom even had small, closet-like chambers where guests could sit and dine by themselves. The woodwork, beams, balustrades and furniture were of the finest oak and polished to a shimmer. No rushes lay strewn on the clean-swept floor, nothing but the finest rope matting. The walls were decorated with tapestries, fine square paintings and triptychs, all reflecting the theme of how wine gladdens the heart of men. It was still mid-morning and people were drifting in from the local churches to break their fast.

Cranston, at Athelstan's urging, asked for a private chamber. Physician Limut ushered them into a room at the rear of the tavern. Fine linen-wooden panelling covered its walls, and the polished floor was spread with turkey rugs. The room was well lit by a wide casement window, and fragranced not only by the delightful smells from the kitchens which stood nearby but also the heavy sweetness of dried herbs stored in pots placed around the room. The chamber boasted a table, two high stools, a chair and a bed, all cushioned and comfortable.

Once Cranston and Athelstan were settled, physician Limut brought in his family. Beatrice his wife was clearly proud of her Castilian heritage, lapsing into Spanish because she was so excited, as she confessed, 'at meeting the Lord High Coroner of London and the famous Dominican Athelstan'. A small, vigorous woman with a strong, slightly harsh face framed by black, wiry hair, Beatrice bustled back and forth, hands emphasising what she said as she delivered a spate of questions to her husband but hardly waited for an answer. Athelstan swiftly concluded that Lady Beatrice was the cornerstone of the family: her two children, Felipe and Maria, watched their mother with a benevolent expression. Felipe was in his early twenties, a sombre-faced, dark-haired young man, rather stony-featured with his unblinking eyes and stubborn mouth and chin. He was apparently very devoted to his sister Maria, a pretty, wide-eyed, black-haired woman of about eighteen summers. Slender and svelte, Maria talked with her expressive eyes and Athelstan imagined she could likely shift her mood in the blink of an eye.

Introductions were made, pleasantries exchanged. A tavern servant brought in dishes of spiced pear, plum and currant tart, figs in a cream sauce and a jug of the lightest white wine. Once Cranston and Athelstan began to eat, the physician ushered his family out then came and joined Cranston and Athelstan at the small table. Seating himself on one of the stools, he filled a goblet and sipped at it appreciatively.

'Brother Athelstan, I have a great favour to ask of you. As you may know, I travel the city, and as I do so, I pick up chatter here and there.'

'About me?'

'Certainly, and I have heard about your intended

35

pilgrimage to St Thomas a Becket's shrine in Canterbury. I understand you intend to leave St Erconwald's a week from today, on the eve of the Feast of Our Lady. You and your parish council are going to Becket's shrine to give thanks for the wellbeing of your congregation after the Great Revolt.' The physician drew a deep breath. 'Gossip also says, Sir John, that you are joining Brother Athelstan in his pilgrimage of thanksgiving as well as to meet the lovely Lady Maude at Canterbury after her long sojourn in the countryside.'

'And who,' Cranston asked laughingly, 'was the source of all this gossip? Though I have my suspicions.'

'You are correct, Sir John, both characters are well known to you. Leif, the one-legged beggar and his constant comrade and bosom friend, Rawbum. I have treated the latter for the hideous sores on his backside.'

'And he has only himself to blame; he was drunk and sat on a pan of bubbling fat.' Cranston shook his head in mock disbelief. 'Now he and Leif haunt my house of rest and refreshment . . .' He paused abruptly.

'At your favourite hostelry, the Lamb of God in Cheapside?' Giole smiled. 'You can mention that name in here, Sir John; competition is good for the soul.' He pushed back his stool. 'Now for that favour I mentioned: I would be most grateful if you would consider me and my family joining you. We too have a great deal to thank God, Our Lady and St Thomas for. We are foreign born, and foreigners were marked

36

down for destruction during the Great Revolt. I know what happened to those poor Flemings, both the merchants and the ladies of the night, hacked and hanged. We hid deep in the cellars during the terrors, but we all took a vow to make a pilgrimage to the great Spanish shrine at Santiago di Compostela if we were brought safely through the storm, but now that is impossible to carry out.' He smiled thinly. 'Accordingly, I went to the archdeacon's court, the Bishop of London's man. He has absolved us from our vows and said a pilgrimage to Canterbury would be a fitting replacement. If we travel there our vows would be fulfilled. We leave this tavern in the hands of a most skilled henchman and we would be very pleased to join you.'

'We cannot stop you,' Athelstan countered. 'The King's highway to Canterbury is free.'

'Yes, but would we be welcome with you?'

'Of course, Master Giole!' Athelstan clasped hands with the physician, as did Cranston.

'In which case,' the physician rose and sketched a bow, 'I shall leave you in peace.'

Once Giole had left, Athelstan heaved a deep sigh, blessed himself and watched Cranston clear the platters on the table before them.

'The news of our pilgrimage is spreading, Sir John. It's an excellent idea for many reasons,' Athelstan reflected. 'A journey through the English countryside at the height of summer to one of Europe's holiest shrines in one of this kingdom's loveliest cities . . . It will also be an opportunity to escape London, which, despite appearances, still feels the sharp pangs caused by the revolt and its brutal crushing. Master Giole and his family will be most welcome. They are jovial company. I wager the family are highly skilled cooks whilst our master physician could tend to any sickness or injury on the way.' The friar rubbed his hands in satisfaction. 'Yes, I think God is directing us. Now, to this present business, Sir John. I noticed that the name of the demon Azrael means something to you?'

'Yes, it certainly does.' Cranston drained his cup. 'Years ago when I fought in France, as you did – you and your brother Stephen-Francis . . .' Cranston paused. Secretly he wished he had not mentioned Athelstan's brother, but he had blurted it out before he could stop himself. Years ago, as a young man, Athelstan had run away to join the King's wars and had taken his younger brother with him. Stephen-Francis had been killed. The news had hastened the death of Athelstan's parents as well as prompting Athelstan's long journey to the Dominican order, his ordination as a priest and his appointment to the parish of St Erconwald's in Southwark. Prior Anselm of Blackfriars had, in his infinite wisdom, also ordered Athelstan to act as Sir John Cranston's secretarius; the coroner always prayed that this was now a pleasure rather than a burden. Cranston took a slurp from his miraculous wineskin and quickly studied his companion. The friar, however, resting his head in one hand, merely smiled faintly. 'I met men,' Cranston continued, 'so-called soldiers, knights, squires, men-at-arms, individuals who loved killing. They were not warriors but torturers, abusers of both the innocent and the vulnerable . . .'

'And we have found the same here in London,' Athelstan declared, pulling himself up. 'Many people commit murder out of fear, desperation, lust, avarice, sometimes even distorted love. Indeed, we are all guilty. At some time in our life we all kill our neighbour in our mind's eye, provoked by hatred, anger, jealousy or revenge . . .'

'Most learned one,' Cranston teased, 'I would agree.'

'Yet there are others who kill and fiercely enjoy it,' Athelstan continued, becoming quite animated. 'They perceive it as a craft, a pastime, something to be developed and cultivated as you and I would a garden plot. Only here the full blossom is hideous murder.' Athelstan paused to sip at his goblet of white wine then pushed it away and pulled a face. 'I do not like Rhenish,' he whispered. 'Now, in the murder of Simon Mephan and his companions, do you think it is a case of assassins who enjoy what they do?'

'I certainly do, little friar. Mephan's assassin enjoyed what he did. He sent a soul-chilling warning. He has done the same to the evangelists and now to you. Azrael deeply relishes what is about to happen.' Cranston moved his goblet away so as to rest against the table. 'And it is not the first time I have encountered him . . .'

Athelstan exclaimed in surprise. He stared around the small, comfortable chamber and repressed a shiver.

'We are spiritual beings,' he murmured. 'We

39

live in the metaphysical world of ideas. This certainly applies to the situation we are now in. Something dark and hideous has slipped into our lives. I am glad we are going on our pilgrimage to Canterbury; it will provide spiritual refreshment in so many ways.' Athelstan paused. 'No one knows this, Sir John, but you mentioned my brother Stephen-Francis. He was killed in France but I brought his corpse back on a war cog to Tilbury. I took it along the pilgrim's way, the route we will follow to Canterbury. I had his coffin buried at St Grace's priory, about four miles from our first resting place at the Sign of Hope. I think it would be good to visit his grave there, but that's for the future.

'Now, Sir John. Azrael will hunt us and we will hunt him. He may follow us to Canterbury or be waiting for us there, or here in the city, or Southwark when we return. We have to know our enemy. He can assume his chilling titles and issue dire warnings but he is still a man, not a demon, whilst we have the angels of light who will bring us God's grace in the coming confrontation. So, let us list what we know.

'First, Simon Mephan and the evangelists work in the Secret Chancery. God knows what mischief passed through their hands or what role they truly played in the suppression of the revolt. Secondly, Mephan receives a warning: a garrotte string with a makeshift medallion bearing the pointed message, "Lord Azrael greets you". Yesterday evening Azrael the demon, the Angel of Death, swept into that narrow house in Milk Street and annihilated three lives. Three souls despatched brutally and barbarously to judgement. No time to prepare. No shriving. No prayer. Thirdly, two of the deaths are certainly very mysterious – Finchley and Felicity are garrotted yet they do not appear to have resisted. Not a shred of evidence of a struggle, no stool overturned, and yet surely as someone is garrotted they must lash out with arm and leg? This does not appear to have happened. Nor is there any proof that they were drugged and, even if they were, the shock of the garrotte would have startled them into some activity.'

'Of course,' Cranston breathed, 'that solar should have looked like a taproom after a violent affray. Apart from the coffer being forced, there is no other sign of violence. Unless, of course, they were strangled elsewhere and the corpses brought to the solar.'

'It's possible,' Athelstan murmured. 'Yet there is no mark on the corpses. Anyway, fourthly, Master Mephan. He dies of a heart seizure. He is old, corpulent and weak-hearted. He was forced to flee up those stairs in great fear for his life. I do wonder why he retreated there and didn't seek refuge in the street. Did the assassin lock and bolt the front door? However, fifthly, before he dies Mephan opens that Book of Luke's Gospel and underscores two words of the phrase, "Our name is legion for we are many." The Latin words for "legion" and "many" are emphasised. Once he does this, Mephan places the quill pen, stained with red ink, between the pages of that Book of the Gospels. Undoubtedly he was sending a message. He was attracting our attention, or

41

that of any law officer, to what he had done, but why? I suggest that Simon Mephan died shortly afterwards, certainly before the assassin burst into his chamber. The murderer would rigorously inspect Mephan's corpse and leave. He would certainly make sure that Mephan was dead.

'Sixthly, Mephan's message, what does it really mean?' Athelstan patted his chancery satchel. 'I will certainly scrutinise it most carefully. Was Mephan trying to tell us that there was more than one assassin? Yet that is not what the verse means. The possessed man in Luke's gospel maintains he hosts an entire household of demons. Nevertheless, in the end, the Gesarene demoniac is, as scripture says, one man. Seventhly, why all this mummery, the mystery play, the ritual of warnings and threats? I agree with you that our assassin revels in all this drama and the power it gives him. He plays with his intended victim like a cat with its prey. Have you seen the like before?'

'Yes, I have.' Cranston took another generous swig from the miraculous wineskin and offered it to Athelstan, who refused, so the coroner put it back beneath his cloak and continued: 'It's interesting that he threatened you but not me. I wonder why. After all, I am the law officer, not you. You are a Dominican priest who also happens to be my clerk and secretarius. There is something rather singular about all this. We need to make careful enquiries.

'You know how certain items can spark a memory, Brother? I read all the returns the sheriffs make each quarter to the Exchequer.

Now and again amongst the dross I find a few grains of gold and silver. Usually malefactors, wolfsheads and outlaws who've decided to move from London to practise their villainy elsewhere. The sheriffs also summarise their income from the goods, chattels and moveables of those who died mysteriously yet violently, as well as the goods of those executed for crimes throughout their shire.' Cranston stroked his lower lip with a stubby finger. 'I am sure that I have come across some reference to mysterious murders by strangulation! Oh, and before you ask, Athelstan, the victim was not some tavern wench but a powerful merchant, and a message referring to Azrael was left on his corpse. Yes, now I recall!' The coroner sprang to his feet. 'I am certain such a murder occurred this year, certainly since the end of Lent, in Rochester. I am also equally assured there was a similar one in Colchester around the same time. But we will have to see. I need to reflect, make careful enquiries . . .'

'As well as prepare for Canterbury,' Athelstan replied, also getting to his feet. 'My good friend, the day draws on and Southwark beckons . . .'

Part Two
The Master of the Secret

Peter the Penniless, the self-confessed repentant miser and lover of gold, walked into the nave of St Erconwald's. He ignored the mystery play being staged in the entrance of the church and instead studied the ancient font, with its large stem and heavy bowl encrusted with mysterious Celtic signs. According to Mauger, the parish bell clerk and self-proclaimed chronicler of St Erconwald's, the baptismal font was hundreds of years older than the church which housed it. Mauger was certain that the font had been used by the great Erconwald when that famous Saxon bishop of London exercised real power throughout the city. Peter the Penniless, however, although he would have liked some holy water from the bowl to exorcise himself, decided to ignore it as well as the swirl of bodies engaged in the pageant around the font. He felt his hand grasped and turned to stare into the fear-filled face of his pretty young wife Amelia.

'Peter,' she begged, 'please come home.' She glanced back and beckoned their clerk Robert, who stood just within the church door, to join them.

'No, I must seek sanctuary,' Peter hissed. 'I need the sacred oils and the holy water. I want the blessing of Holy Mother Church. I have spoken to Brother Athelstan. I will take sanctuary here.'

'But you have done nothing wrong.' Robert the clerk, his moon-face all shiny with perfumed nard, scratched his thinning blonde hair, combed to cover as much of his baldness as nature would allow. The clerk then plucked at the threadbare sleeve of his master's jerkin. 'You have done nothing wrong,' Robert insisted. 'You are not a felon.'

'I must be in the eyes of God,' Peter retorted heatedly. 'I have horrid visions. They plague both my mind and my soul. I wish I was dead. I sometimes pray for that and wonder if suicide is such a horrid sin.'

'Phantasms of the mind!' Robert scoffed.

'Husband, dearest,' Amelia begged, 'come back to our house. I will cook your favourite: pheasant in broth, quail eggs in a creamy sauce, sweet manchet bread . . .'

'No, I cannot.' Peter gazed at his wife's pretty, snub-nosed face, the full-lipped mouth and arching brows above her sad grey eyes, the tendrils of auburn hair escaping from the elegant, murrey-coloured veil which matched her well-cut gown. For a moment he remembered how things used to be, recalling the good sport he and his wife had enjoyed in the great four-poster bed in their comfortable house along Dovecote Lane. He wished he could go back with her. He wished the voices in his mind urging him to destroy himself would disappear, and that those terror-drenched dreams and visions would stop plaguing his mind. 'No, what I must do . . .'

'What must you do?'

Peter and his two companions turned to face the woman who had approached them. 'I am Benedicta, widow-woman of this parish,' she introduced herself. 'Seamstress, sacristan, a member of the parish council and Brother Athelstan's housekeeper. How can I help you?'

'My name is Peter,' the miser gabbled. 'People call me Peter the Penniless but I am really very wealthy. I promised Brother Athelstan to change my ways. I . . .'

'Ah yes,' Benedicta broke in. The dark eyes in her olive-skinned face had lost their smile. 'Brother Athelstan did talk to me about you.' Benedicta studied Peter's thin, white face, the dirty stubble on chin and cheeks, the dark rings under his eyes, the black, greasy hair which hung like rats' tails begging to be washed; both his brown gown and the tunic beneath were stained with food. Peter's fingernails were bitten to the quick and large sores had appeared along his lower lip and on the corner of his mouth. 'I can see you are distressed.' she declared softly. She glanced quizzically at Amelia and Robert the clerk, who swiftly introduced themselves, rather wary of this very elegant but blunt woman dressed in her sombre widow weeds, eyes all sharp, so incisive in her speech.

'I seek the Fridstool, the peace chair, sanctuary,' Peter declared. 'I carry no weapon. I swear to observe the immunity of the church, its liberties and privileges . . .' Peter's raised voice rang through the nave and attracted the attention of other parishioners. The scrawny-headed Watkin, dung-collector and leader of the parish council, along with Pike the ditcher, sallow-featured and as slender as a rake pole, drifted across. This precious pair, as Athelstan described them, or 'cheeks of the same arse', as Cranston quietly muttered, were accompanied by their henchmen, Ranulf the rat-catcher, Hig the Pigman, Crispin the carpenter and others. 'I seek sanctuary.' Peter's voice now rose to a screech. 'I live in the adjoining parish of St Laurence but St Erconwald's holds the peace stool, the sanctuary chair . . .'

'What crime have you committed?' Mauger the bell clerk, small and rotund, face and body all bristling with importance, pushed his way through.

'I have committed no crime,' Peter confessed falteringly. He could now hear the whispers as people recognised and recalled his reputation, here and there a few sniggers. Peter the Penniless ignored these as he repeated his plea. 'I am in mortal fear of my life, I fear myself.' Peter tapped the side of his head. 'I seek sanctuary from the demons who plague me day and night . . .'

'In which case . . .' Mauger grabbed Peter's hand and escorted him up the nave to the entrance of the soaring, oaken rood screen which led into the sanctuary of St Erconwald's. Mauger almost pushed Peter through the entrance, up the steps and across to the enclave which stood to the right of the high altar. Peter went into the embrasure lit by the light of a lancet window high in the wall. The enclave contained a narrow cotbed, stool, small table and lidded jake's pot. There was a peg driven into a wall cleft on which to hang clothes. Mauger, in accordance with the canonical provisions governing sanctuary, searched Peter for weapons then gestured at him to sit on the stool, promising that victuals would be served as soon as their priest returned. Peter crouched on the Fridstool whilst Mauger went back down the steps shooing away the gaping onlookers gathered in the entrance to the rood screen.

Peter, narrow of face and weary-eyed, turned away and examined the wall fresco to his right: a most vivid depiction of divine vengeance on a fallen world, rather incongruous for someone seeking mercy. Peter had learnt that many of the paintings in St Erconwald's were the work of a rather eerie character, baptised as Giles of Sempringham but popularly known as the Hangman of Rochester, a most skilled executioner responsible for the despatch of many a felon at Smithfield, Tyburn Stream and Tower Hill. Peter studied the painting and shivered. The scenes portrayed reflected his own dire visions. He wanted to look away but he was drawn in by the eye-catching images so difficult to ignore: grey seas dark with billowing smoke; distant fires glowing behind a mountain range scorched a reddish-brown. Along this mountain ridge hordes of the dead were being driven and harassed by the invincible armies of Satan, who led his troops astride a skinny hack. He was armed with a long, cruel scythe which he used to sweep his quarry into the gaping jaws of Hell. The frescoes included a wide range of miniature yet menacing scenes: massacres; tortures; hangings; disembowelling and decapitations; cartloads of skulls; trumpet-blowing skeletons; barrow-pushing, monkey-faced demons; gibbets and gallows; earthquakes and shipwrecks, all visions from a nightmare apocalypse.

Peter muttered a prayer as he recalled his own harrowing dreams peopled by hideous spectres: the monstrous reptile with popping eyes which crawled out of his bedclothes to sit on his chest and glare balefully at him, or that ghastly throng of ancient crones with their two-horned coifs and moon-shaped mitres above gloomy, haggard faces and hollow eyes. Last night he had dreamt of a harnessed woman. She was plump, her hair as thick and yellow as wet straw. She would crawl towards him along the ground like some fat-bellied cat, her buttocks and heavy breasts glistening with sweat. On her back rode a bat-faced demon with spurs on his spindly feet, one taloned hand grasping the reins, the other carrying a whip, its thongs decorated with sharp flint. Peter the Penniless rubbed his face.

Amelia called out from where she and Robert stood, just outside the rood screen, but Peter ignored her. He was recalling the vision which had plagued his sleep and ravaged his peace of mind long before sunrise. Peter had left his bed to eat and drink something. Amelia had followed and prepared some bread smeared with honey and a tankard of light ale. Still troubled, Peter had returned to his bedchamber and the memories

50

had come flooding back as he recalled the events of his wild youth. He'd been a member of the Guild of Palmers attending night watches of the dead and trying to raise apparitions. He and others would meet the witches and warlocks during those unholy hours after midnight. He recalled one hag, Petronella, who distilled powders with spiders, black worms and scorpions. She'd mingle milfoil and other detestable herbs into her concoctions. Petronella would then give these to Peter and his companions and the visions would come sweeping in, the faces of those around him becoming bearded and horned like the heads of goats. Peter pushed the sanctuary stool deeper into the dark enclave. He was now as safe as ever he might be from such demons, but for how long? If only Athelstan would come and exorcise them . . .

Athelstan had left Cranston outside the tavern, Amongst the Tombs. He had bid farewell to the physician Limut, Beatrice and their two children. The day was drawing on and Athelstan felt he had so much to do, especially as the departure date for Canterbury was fast approaching. The friar paused on the corner of Frideswide alleyway. He felt confused and distracted, not really sure of what he should do and when. The clamour of the streets, their noise and smell, the different sights and images, all made him ill at ease and yet, behind that, there was something more sinister, like a ravenous wolf appearing out of the dark to slope along the borders of his life.

Once again murder threatened to enter his

humdrum world; that slinky, weasel-faced demon, Satan's assassin, who tempted man to kill and kill again, was making its presence felt. Simon Mephan, chief clerk of the Secret Chancery, had been the real quarry of that secret assassin. The other two were innocents who happened to be with him on that particular evening at the wrong time and in the wrong place. The deed had been done. Mephan was killed by shock, the other two had their throats twisted as tight as a farmer would a pair of chickens. Now Athelstan had to make a response. He had entered murder's tournament field and the battle would only end when all that had to be done was fully accomplished. The little friar gripped his chancery satchel even tighter. He now regretted leaving Sir John. Perhaps the coroner could have accompanied him to the bridge . . . But then Athelstan smiled, crossed himself and murmured a prayer against such selfishness. A huckster approached, offering a powder found, so he claimed, in the ruins of Troy, which had given singular beauty to Helen and Venus.

'For your doxy. For your favourite whore, friar!' the seller jibed.

'And take this for your penance!' Athelstan retorted heatedly, smacking the man in the face. The trickster fled. Athelstan hurried on through the streets. Now and again he recognised some of Cranston's 'beloved', those children of the twilight, who lived not so much beyond the law but just within its limits. Creatures like Rattle-Pate and Muckworm. The streets were clogged with such denizens of the night who, attracted by the good weather, had crawled out of their dungeons and midnight castles. Hungry-eyed and eager for mischief, these dwellers of the dark moved and twisted through the colourful, surging crowds. Athelstan pushed his way past. He did not answer their calls for he was immediately recognised as Cranston's constant companion. They would wish to draw him into conversation, beg for money or seek a favour, and it would be well after dark before he reached Southwark. Moreover, Athelstan felt uneasy. He always did on the busy London streets. Sometimes he could be swept by a panic, dark, nameless fears as if the world was pressing in close about him. At the same time, however, Athelstan remained sensitive to real danger and he felt as if he was being followed and closely observed. Now and again he would pause, turn and stare back, but he could glimpse nothing untoward and so he pressed on, hoping to ignore everything happening around him. However, as he turned a corner he passed a gaggle of mumpers preparing to mumble a sparrow, a cruel, hateful game whereby the little bird's wings were clipped and it was kept prisoner in a box whilst the mumpers tried to kill it by biting off its head. Athelstan, real- ising what was happening and full of fury, stormed in, knocking over the box. The sparrow escaped, fluttering away as Athelstan berated the gaggle of tormentors. They would have retaliated but two wardsmen who recognised Athelstan intervened and the gang fled up an alleyway.

The friar continued on, battling the crowds. Now the revolt was crushed, or ostensibly so, and high summer was making its presence felt, all of London had turned out of doors to sell, buy, barter, gawp or parade. Wealthy guildsmen and their overdressed wives moved from stall to stall, lips parted in a constant smile, eyes bright and keen for any hidden bargain. Apprentices hymned their master's goods and the prices they charged for them. Other boys darted like swallows through the crowds to pluck at sleeve or gown and so entice would-be customers to stop and buy. The real quarry of these barrow boys were the sweaty-faced burgesses and, above all, the court and city fops both male and female who had turned out to strut in all their finery. Athelstan always found their fantastical dress a matter for quiet laughter; he sometimes discussed with Sir John how such people found the time to get dressed in the morning. Occasionally Athelstan would stop and stare but he also kept an eye on anyone following him. He glimpsed a wrestling match taking place outside the Cock a Hoop tavern. Two young men, naked to the waist, were entertaining the crowd. Usually Athelstan would ignore such a contest but this time he stood fascinated. One of the competitors had managed to get behind his opponent, an arm around his throat: his victim kicked and twisted, hands grabbing as he desperately tried to free the lock around his neck.

'Surely,' Athelstan whispered to himself, 'Finchley and Felicity would have done that?' He closed his eyes. He imagined those two young people with the garrotte string tied tightly around their throats, their arms and legs flailing out. He also thought of Simon Mephan sitting at that desk in his bedchamber. The old clerk knew he was trapped. He must have also concluded that he if tried to leave any message this would be destroyed, so instead he left a cipher . . .

'Brother? Are you well?' Athelstan opened his eyes and stared at the pasty-faced tinker, pet ferret in one hand, a box of trifles in the other. 'Brother, it's Michael the Mouse, do you remember me? Are you well?' Athelstan assured him that he was, gesturing at the wrestling match which was becoming more raucous by the moment.

'I was distracted by that, Michael. But thank you.' Athelstan walked on. He was still thinking about Simon Mephan hastening up those stairs. A clever and subtle clerk, Mephan knew whatever he wrote would be seized by the assassin. The pains in his chest would have made themselves felt. It would not take Mephan long to open the Book of Gospels, score those two words, leave the quill pen there and mark it, surely?

Athelstan was now at the heart of the city, walking down Cheapside towards the bridge. A group of courtiers strode ahead in a brilliant display of ostentatious wealth: their gilt-trimmed jerkins, gleaming medallions, jewelled brooches and shimmering necklaces attracted the legion of thieves or beggars who haunted the doorways and dark entrances along the alleys and runnels. Swarming packs of cut-purses emerged, ready to strike with nimble fingers or needle-thin daggers at anything they could take; be it wallet, purse, satchel, even rings off bare fingers. These were now following the courtiers as a pack of starving dogs would their quarry. Athelstan was not troubled. A poor Dominican friar could almost be invisible both to predator and prey. Athelstan, however, loved to watch, to savour, to study and remember. He revelled in the swirl of smells coming from the bakeries and pie shops, mouth-watering and savoury; a sharp contrast to the foul miasma from the midden heaps and lay stalls reeking of human waste and the rotting corpses of rat, cat and dog. Cook boys paraded with trays offering morsels in order to entice customers into their pastry shops. A much more attractive prospect, as one pastry cook bawled, than the filth being grilled, cooked, stewed, fried or boiled over the moveable stoves of itinerant fleshers and fritterers. Both Athelstan and the cook had to step sharply aside for a number of betrothal parties all garlanded with flowers who fought their way alongside drunken pilgrims heading for this church or that with their statues, candle carriers and pattering priests.

Despite the gaiety and the busyness, Athelstan also glimpsed the effects of the Great Revolt and its sudden and brutal repression; gallows and gibbets had been set up at crossroads and small squares, all of them heavy with the corpses of the hanged; throats squeezed, faces contorted by the rictus of agonised death. Many of the dangling cadavers were naked, savagely bruised from the beatings inflicted before death. Nearby stood the executioners with knives and barrows at the ready. These killers, pardoned criminals, were prepared to cut a cadaver down and, for a price, rent out a barrow so grieving relatives could push the strangled corpse to the nearest church or death house. Close by this grim scene gathered the foreign mercenaries, members of the free companies hired by the city, the guilds and the great lords to root out rebellion. The mercenaries were the sweepings of foreign prisons, grim men, hard of face and hard of heart. Professional killers, the drinkers of other men's blood, they and their masters swallowed up other people, be it men, women or children, as if they were swilling bread. Athelstan had fulminated against both these mercenaries and those who hired them. The friar argued that such great lords were as wicked and lawless as any in London, be it the brothers of the hood, the cackling cheats, the hog-grabbers and the hen-hearted, all the denizens of the midnight mansions of the damned.

'Wickedness is wickedness.' Athelstan had informed Sir John. 'But wickedness by those in power is given the devil's baptism to appear all right, legal and moral.'

'Toad-eater!' Athelstan broke from his reverie and stared at the bearded, mad-faced beggar dressed in horse-hide, his face daubed yellow and white. 'Are we not all,' the grotesque hissed, 'toad-eaters, sin-swallowers and the gobblers of virtue?' Athelstan stepped back and stared around: he was now on the approaches to London Bridge. 'Do you have a bone-box as a heart, Brother Athelstan?' Startled, Athelstan stared at this grotesque. The thoroughfare on the bridge was always a gathering place for those who lived

57

in the twilight of London life. But how did this one know him by face and name?

'I beg your pardon?'

'And I beg yours, Brother. Be ye not afraid. I bring advice. Be prudent and on your sharpest guard in the days ahead.'

'Why is that?' the friar demanded.

'Because Peter the Penniless and all his demons shelter in your church. I heard all about it. So be on your guard.' The grotesque clapped his hands and slipped away. Athelstan continued onto the bridge, threading his way through the fortifications and the buildings ranged either side. The thoroughfare was busy as people streamed across, almost oblivious to the pounding water of the Thames crashing against the starlings which protected the massive struts underpinning the bridge. He passed the small chapel of St Thomas a Becket and, as he approached the gatehouse leading to the south side, he heard his name called. Robert Burdon, Keeper of the Gates as well as the heads impaled above them, principal member of the Fraternity of the Knife, the Guild of London's Executioners, came tripping down the steps. Athelstan forced a smile and quietly prayed for strength as this dwarf of a man dressed in the guild livery of blood-red taffeta, huffed and puffed towards him, fingers snapping the air.

'Brother Athelstan, I understand you are leaving for Canterbury?'

'Aye and not a moment too soon.'

Burdon, his smooth red face all puckered with concern, ignored Athelstan's gentle sarcasm and gestured at the iron-bound barrel standing at the foot of the steps.

'Look at that, Brother! Look at it!'

Athelstan walked gingerly across, picked up the lid then hastily dropped it back and sketched a blessing in the direction of the barrel. 'There must be at least a dozen heads?' he queried.

'Rebels,' Burdon exclaimed. 'Captured in Kent and elsewhere. Most of them around Foul Oak. The heads were severed and despatched here to be pickled, tarred and poled on London Bridge, along its gateways and turreted walls. I have to do my duty, Brother, yet I have been given no summer respite.' Athelstan tried to look as sympathetic as possible, though the sight of so many severed heads, necks all ragged, eyes empty and glassy, turned his stomach. He just wanted to flee. 'Father?' Burdon stepped closer.

'No, Robert,' Athelstan retorted, 'before you begin, your guild cannot use St Erconwald's for its masses. In God's name, man, to bring a moveable gibbet into the church followed by executioners wearing their blood-red masks – my parishioners would be terrified.'

'No, no, not that,' the little man protested.

'Then what, Master Robert?' Athelstan gestured at the far end of the bridge. 'I have a parish to attend to.'

'Canterbury.' Burdon opened his hand to show Athelstan a silver coin. 'Father, will you light three candles before the shrine? One for me, one for Isolda and one for my seven children?'

Athelstan softened and quietly regretted his lack of patience. He gently grasped Burdon's hand. 'Robert, keep your coin for your brood of children. I solemnly promise you, as a friend, I shall light four candles before the sacred bones of Becket. I shall pray most fervently for your intentions. There will be the three candles you asked for and an additional one, that you skilfully fulfil all the duties of your important office.'

With Burdon's thanks ringing in his ears, Athelstan walked on, musing that Master Robert's request was one of many such coming in. Becket's shrine was the most famous throughout Christendom. Miracles were commonplace, and the news of his parish pilgrimage was bringing in many similar requests, so what should he do? Athelstan decided that would have to wait. He left the bridge on Southwark side. The approaches to this had become a slaughter yard, the execution ground for those swept up, tried and convicted after the recent troubles. Athelstan stood, head bowed, and prayed for the victims of what was happening so close to his parish. The usual stocks, thews and pillories had been removed. The entire space was now thronged with gibbets, gallows and scaffolds, most of their branches heavy with a row of corpses dangling from every arm, a forest of the hanged with Brabantine mercenaries on guard against any of the cadavers being secretly taken down and given honourable burial by relatives. Gaunt had seized on this site, the main route from the southern shires into the city. This was now London's Golgotha; the place of the skull, of harsh and dire punishment as well as clear and terrible warning about the fate of rebels. The friar blessed this Haceldama, this field of blood, and hurried on.

Athelstan's mind teemed with the gruesome scenes he had just passed through. Vengeance was being meted out, and this was another reason why he had organised the Canterbury pilgrimage. It would be a blessed relief and great protection for his parishioners, not to mention himself, to be away from Southwark and the politics of the city. Sir John Cranston was of a similar mind. The coroner had acted decisively and courageously during the revolt. Now, however, Sir John was beginning to balk at the vengeance being inflicted and the scenes of utter degradation Athelstan had just passed through. Of course Sir John also wanted to rejoin Lady Maude and the rest of his household in Canterbury but, as he quietly confessed to Athelstan, a change was as good as a rest. Nonetheless, the coroner had warned the friar that the pilgrim route to Becket's holy and blissful bones might not be a peaceful ride through the English countryside. Men from the shire of Kent had played a crucial role in the recent revolt, and Canterbury itself had not escaped unscathed.

There were dangers, but even so, these were nothing compared to what could be found in London, where Thibault's agents were busy ferreting out the names of those who had aided and supported the rebels. Strangely enough – and Athelstan could not truly understand the reason why – Gaunt's Master of Secrets had given the pilgrimage his particular blessing and generous financial support. Athelstan had also been provided with a special licence to 'Go untroubled and be supported and protected by all royal officers and faithful servants of the Crown.' Albinus, Thibault's henchman, had delivered this special licence; the parchment all white, the script executed in the elegant calligraphy of the Royal Chancery and clearly sealed with the signet of the young king himself. Albinus had also brought a personal note from his master which politely asked Athelstan to offer a special prayer for the physical and spiritual welfare of Thibault and all his household before Becket's shrine, and to light a day-long taper. When Cranston was informed of all this, the coroner simply made a face, shrugged and said, 'There's no accounting for some people. Thibault's anxiety over his spiritual state is proof enough that the Age of Miracles is still with us.'

Athelstan startled from his daydreaming as he almost stumbled over a midden heap reeking in the summer sun. The friar blessed himself and looked around. He was now standing at the mouth of the alleyway leading down to St Erconwald's. He could see his parishioners congregating outside Merrylegs' pie shop, and at the Piebald tavern further down the street.

'If they spent as much time in church as they do in those two establishments, I'd be in charge of saints,' he murmured. 'I wonder what mischief they are plotting?' He muttered a prayer for patience and hurried down.

If he had hoped to escape the attention of his flock, he was truly mistaken. They glimpsed him immediately and surged to meet him. Merrylegs brought him a mince pie.

'And I truly mean beef.' Merrylegs winked at Athelstan to reassure him the pie did not contain cat flesh. The friar bit into the light, soft crust; the spiced mince tasted delicious, as did the frothy tankard of ale thrust into his other hand by Jocelyn, the one-armed former river pirate and now proud owner of the Piebald. Athelstan's parishioners were clearly excited about the forth-coming pilgrimage. Judith the parish mummer described how they were rehearsing their own mystery play, entitled 'Thomas a Becket meets St Erconwald'. Athelstan vainly tried to point out that Erconwald lived at least four hundred years before Becket, but this was ignored in the rush of words as everyone else joined in the conversation. Apparently the play had taken up most of the morning and everybody had been given a role. Even Godbless, the beggar who now occupied the derelict death house in the middle of God's Acre, along with his bosom companion Thaddeus, the omnivorous goat, had been assigned a part. Ursula the pig woman, with her great sow who followed her everywhere, was also involved. Athelstan quietly thanked God for small mercies. He hated that sow almost as much as Bonaventure, the one-eyed tomcat, did. Athelstan drew comfort from the fact that if the sow had been involved in the play then the beast would not have been ravaging his vegetable garden. Athelstan had carefully cultivated his different plots. He was very proud of his shallots and cabbages, as well as the different types of beans and the wide range of herbs and kitchen spices. He was equally proud of Hubert the hedgehog, who had taken up permanent residence in the Hermitage, a special nest cleverly constructed by Crispin the carpenter.

Athelstan gratefully accepted the invitation to step inside the sweet-smelling taproom of the Piebald and sit down at a table where he could finish both food and drink. His parishioners immediately crowded around him, delivering their news in noisy shouts. How the envoy of the Archdeacon of London had arrived searching for Athelstan. How Peter the Penniless, the great miser, had sought sanctuary and was now sheltering in their church. When he heard this, Athelstan got to his feet, thanked Jocelyn and Merrylegs and said he must visit St Erconwald's immediately.

He pushed his way through the throng, assuring his beloveds that he would soon return. Once outside, he grasped his leather satchel and hurried along the concourse. He passed the majestic lychgate leading into God's Acre. Athelstan paused and stared across the cemetery which sprawled to the left of the church: a sea of grass, gorse and bushes where a horde of butterflies floated and swarms of bees constantly quarried the wild flowers for their sweetness. Crickets kept up their monotonous hymn whilst the liquid call of woodpigeons echoed from the green darkness of the ancient cypress trees. Athelstan was about to move on when he heard a faint cry, followed by several more. He stood on a plinth and peered over the cemetery wall. The cries were repeated, not in pain or distress, but joyous, like a woman being pleasured. Athelstan sighed, crossed himself and murmured a prayer as he glimpsed legs, long and slender, the toes on the bare feet splayed, and the glittering bracelet around one of the rounded ankles.

Cecily the courtesan was clearly busy with a customer. In summer she spent more time in God's Acre than many a corpse did – living proof that not everybody stretched out in the cemetery was dead.

Athelstan hurried up the steps of his church, through the narrow side entrance and into the musty nave of St Erconwald's. He stared down at the towering rood screen, and above it the carved, agonised body of Christ nailed to his cross. Shafts of light pierced the windows on either side, some of which were mere lancet slits, but others were oblongs of sheer white light, covered in polished horn which greatly enhanced the sunshine. In Athelstan's eyes, however, pride of place was given to the two windows above the chantry chapel of St Erconwald's, a gift from the young king, who had sent his own craftsmen who were already busy working on the chapel of St George at Windsor. Both the windows were filled with painted glass depicting scenes from the life of the saintly bishop, and Athelstan found he could stare at them endlessly, drawn in to the fierce blaze of colour which always soothed him – but not today.

He tore his gaze away and glanced around. Everything seemed orderly. The baptismal font was locked and sealed under its thick oaken lid.

The church smelt sweetly of thyme, mint and incense; its paved floor had been carefully scrubbed, the mice- and rat-holes cleverly blocked with small sponges soaked in vinegar and a herbal poison specially distilled by Ranulf the rat-catcher. Athelstan heard a scraping of a stool from the sanctuary. Peter the Penniless was undoubtedly making himself at home. Athelstan was tempted to go down and meet the sanctuary man, but now it struck him that something was wrong. Apparently his parishioners had staged their mystery play earlier in the day, their own unique interpretation of Becket's martyrdom. Afterwards they had cleaned and tidied the area around the font, the usual place for their masques. However, the door to the tower was off the latch. Time and again, Athelstan had warned his parishioners to keep that door closed and bolted lest the children creep up the steps, which were steep, whilst the top of the tower was not the safest place for an inquisitive child.

The friar repressed a sudden shiver, a feeling of creeping danger, that all was not well. One of the Hangman of Rochester's vivid wall paintings caught his eye. The fresco depicted the fall of the rebel angels; loathsome, spindle-shanked figures with bat-like faces, eyes glowing like fiery coals. The doomed angels fell against a bloodied sky, hurtling down to be greeted by the shooting fires of Hell. Athelstan walked over to the tower door, pulled it back and froze. Pinned to the inside of the door was a dead magpie, a garrotte cord around its neck. Athelstan snatched the bird down and carefully examined the crude, stiffened parchment tag with its mocking message, 'Lord Azrael greets you', scrawled in blood-red ink.

Athelstan tried to quell his temper at this blasphemous intrusion into his life, his priesthood, his church and his community. He took the dead bird out of the church, tossed it onto the nearest midden heap and strode quickly up to the priest's house. Carefully pushing the door open, he looked around. All was quiet, clean and orderly, from his cotbed in the loft to the sturdy kitchen table which served as his dining place as well as his chancery desk. Benedicta, along with Mauger the bell clerk, had worked hard to keep his little house neat and tidy. Flowers placed in an earthenware jar in the centre of the table perfumed the air, the hearth was swept, the buttery scrubbed clean; the bread, cheese and chicken meat were fresh whilst the milk in its jug under a cloth smelt wholesome and sweet.

Satisfied, Athelstan returned to the church. He stood just within the doorway. He was distracted, his mind swerving, racing like a hare through a cornfield with different thoughts and worries: the planned pilgrimage, the safety of his parishioners, the gruesome scenes in Mephan's house and the diabolical enjoyment of the assassin in baiting Athelstan and his other intended victims. Azrael had even scurried across the Thames to issue a dire warning to him at the very heart of his community. Athelstan stared down at the rood-screen crucifix and breathed a prayer his mother had taught him, 'Turn your face to each of us as you did to Veronica . . .' The invocation and the memory of his mother soothed him. He felt himself relax and went to sit on one of the wall benches as he finished his prayer. He then wondered, once darkness fell, if he should climb the tower and study the star-strewn sky. The moon would be full and Athelstan hoped to see those shooting stars which appeared so clear on a summer's evening . . .

'Brother?' Athelstan glanced swiftly to his right. Benedicta had slipped like a shadow – and a most beautiful one, Athelstan secretly conceded – into the church. The widow-woman wore a large flesher's apron over her blue and white smock, and her night-black hair was crowned with a broad-brimmed gardening hat. In one gloved hand she carried a small trowel, a three-pronged digging fork in the other. She held these up.

'I have been tidying your vegetable patch. Why is it, Brother, that weeds grow faster than flowers or vegetables?'

'Just like sin,' he retorted, 'it grows greater and spreads more swiftly than virtue. Remember, what applies to the spiritual state is true of the physical, so the philosopher Aquinas argues – or I think he does.'

Chastened by the sinister warning pinned to the tower door, Athelstan was delighted to share the kiss of peace with this beautiful woman who, he knew, cared deeply for him and showed it in her lovable eyes and kindly ways. He embraced her warmly and let himself relax, breathing in her perfume, until he recalled the words of his ordination: 'You are a priest forever according

to the order of Melchizedek. Act like one!'
Athelstan stepped back and bowed. 'You are
lovely of face and lovely of form, Benedicta. It
is good to see you. I have, unfortunately, had a
day bubbling with evil.'

'And there's more.' Slightly taken back by the
sheer warmth of Athelstan's greeting, Benedicta
pointed up the nave. 'Peter the Penniless,' she
whispered. 'He's taken sanctuary against what
he calls a horde of demons. He believes they are
crowding in to kill him.'

Roger Empson, principal courier to Thibault,
Gaunt's Master of Secrets, also believed he was
being haunted by a demon, but one in human
flesh. The revolt was crushed but the Reapers
were posting billae, bills of indictment against
the adherents of John of Gaunt who were caught
up in the bloody aftermath. The threat of the
Reapers was dangerous enough, but Empson was
now terrified, with a deep chilling of the soul, as
he had stumbled onto a more horrid truth. The
Reapers were one thing, but treachery and treason
within Thibault's own household posed a much
more sinister threat. How else could anyone know
that he visited the Way of all Flesh? That was a
secret known only to a very few, something Roger
savoured and kept to himself, what he called 'his
little sinful secret'. Surely everyone had one of
these, a dark corner in their lives where no one
visited or even knew about? Empson loved the
soft, perfumed flesh of young men. He always
had. And that mistress of the night, the Way of
all Flesh, catered most discreetly for such tastes.

Empson had been busy about his own affairs, eager to relax and refresh himself. A few nights ago he had slipped out of his comfortable lodgings above a draper's shop in Catskin Lane. Hooded and visored, he had threaded the twisting, ancient streets of Cheapside. The houses on either side were so decadent, they leaned towards each other, held in place only by sturdy oaken struts. As usual, Empson had kept to the shadows thrown by these mouldering mansions, his destination the comfortable cellars beneath the spacious tavern of the Lute Boy. The brothel was a veritable paradise of fleshly lusts under the strict supervision of that queen of whores – be they male or female – the Way of all Flesh, as she proclaimed herself. Here Empson could broach a flask of Rhenish or a jug of Bordeaux. Above all, he could wallow in the tender ministrations of Blondell, Pierrot and other lithe young men with their satiny skin, doe-like eyes and pouting mouths. The Way of all Flesh was extremely discreet, though there again, she had to be. If the Lute Boy was betrayed and raided by city archers, Empson and others would face a grisly death at Smithfield. Others whispered that the brothel was patronised and protected by the great ones of the city. Nevertheless Empson knew how fickle fortune could be, so deeds done in the dark were best kept in the dark.

Very few knew he went there, yet, on that particular evening when he left the Lute Boy, the assassin had sprung his trap and nearly garrotted Empson. The courier, hooded and visored, had slipped out of the tavern and stupidly fallen into the ambuscade. He had reached the corner of Turnspit Street when he heard the clink of a coin. He turned and, in the light of a fiercely burning cresset torch, glimpsed the pure silver coin shimmering in the light. Without even a second thought, Empson had bent down to pick it up and, as he did so, the garrotte string went round his neck, dragging him back. The pain had been intense, his breath choked off. He began to lose consciousness, unable to move either hands or feet. Then, a miracle.

A door abruptly swung open across the street. A group of revellers burst out crying, 'Wassail to all!' The door was a concealed one, and the building it belonged to was cloaked in darkness, probably a secret drinking den, yet its customers saved Empson's life. The assassin's cord abruptly loosened. Empson fell to his knees sobbing and gasping, the burn mark around his throat causing hideous shooting pains. His assailant had disappeared like smoke in the air, and the revellers had hastened to help him. Empson had staggered into a nearby tavern where the servitors, paid generously by the courier, tended to his injuries, poured a goblet of Bordeaux down his throat and allowed him to sleep under a table in the taproom.

Since then he had not returned to his chambers or to his workplace, the royal stables at Westminster and the Tower. Empson was terrified. How many people knew he visited the Lute Boy? Its customers tended to avoid each other but, on reflection, Empson believed that Luke Gaddesden, one of the evangelists, also frequented that place. Empson had glimpsed him and Luke had done likewise. Had he betrayed Empson to the Reapers? But was it the Reapers? Why should someone want to kill him now? Yet that assassin had been waiting for him; he was no ordinary footpad or felon. Empson was as sure of that as he was that the assassin would strike again, so he must hide well away from his usual haunts. He knew the city, its twisting dark lanes, shadow-filled coffin paths, the lonely nooks and crannies, all the places where a man could hide. In the end Empson believed he had chosen wisely and carefully. He was being hunted, probably by the Reapers, who must have a spy in the chancery offices at Westminster. The courier had decided to keep away from there and Cheapside, especially the Lute Boy. Instead he would hide out in a derelict charnel house close to the ancient church of All Hallows-on-the-Wall near Hounds' Ditch, not far from the hospital of St Mary of Bethlehem.

During the time of the Great Pestilence which manifested itself in black buboes followed by an agonising death, St Mary of Bethlehem had used the much decayed building for the raddled corpses of plague victims. Since then the charnel house had stood sealed and protected in the middle of a blighted, overgrown garden. Few dared go there. People were terrified by stories of ghosts and, of course, the Plague might still lurk within, only too eager to break out again. Empson took refuge in the charnel house even though the place reeked of corruption, decay and death. The building comprised a long, dark hall, where ghosts and spectres could throng, constantly cold and shadow-filled, threatening in its silence. Empson had managed to light old lamps and these burned dimly, glimmering in corners. The floor was strewn with decaying rosemary, withered hyacinth, scraps of cypress and yew mingling with yellow, crumbling bones, ribs, whole skulls and other grisly shards of human remains. There was also a stack of forgotten corpses, some standing bolt upright in their decaying, knotted winding sheets, others mouldering in rotting coffins. Now and again some of these, disturbed by Empson moving about, would smash to the ground, spilling out more bones, dust and obnoxious odours.

At night the courier would venture out into the blighted, derelict garden but this offered little relief: a place where toads croaked around an overgrown pond and screech owls protested mournfully against the darkness. Nevertheless, the charnel house was Empson's best defence. He may slumber in corners where cobwebs stretched like nets, vermin might squeak and scurry about and bats, once darkness crept in, flit like large, black flakes through the air, yet Empson considered himself safe there. Now and again he slipped out to buy provisions and, on more than one occasion, he had been compelled to visit a goldsmith in Cheapside where he had lodged his silver. He had no choice. The courier hoped to collect all he owned and flee. He was determined to put as much distance between himself and London as possible.

Empson's thoughts returned to the question of

who was hunting him. Would the Upright Men show such vindictiveness? According to what he'd learnt in the Secret Chancery and the messages he'd taken here and there, the leaders amongst the Upright Men were now terrified out of their wits. The captains amongst the Earthworms were eager to abjure the kingdom and seek safety in foreign parts. Would these men show such dedication to this murderous task? Moreover, the Earthworms were dagger men; they would attack their enemy in the marketplace, a swift knife between the ribs or an arrow loosed in the dark.

And why should he be hunted? Of course he had played his part in the suppression of the revolt, taking messages to Gaunt, Thibault and others. Empson had committed many of these messages to memory so no written evidence remained. On reflection, he often wondered about the full truth of what was happening, how some of the messages he carried might, if proclaimed publicly, reflect poorly on Gaunt and his coven. Yet all this had taken place during the hurling time. The days of the Great Slaughter had come and gone. Empson had thought he and others would know peace now. They would return to their normal duties, follow the routine of Master Thibault's household. Empson would revert to riding here and there with messages, tending to the string of courier horses in the royal stables near Smithfield, settling with the controller of the household every quarter for robes, wages and other necessities. But not now! On that particular afternoon, the Feast of

St Mary Magdalene – the same day that Athelstan had been summoned to Milk Street – Empson sat between two coffins and reflected on the fearful news he had learnt as he slipped shadow-like through the streets. Simon Mephan and two of his household, Finchley and Felicia, had all been garrotted. The whispers and the rumours were rife and only sharpened Empson's panic. Cowled and masked, he'd hurried back to his hiding place in the charnel house where he tried to calm himself.

'This is truly perilous,' Empson whispered into the darkness, his fingers going to his lips. He could hardly believe it. Thibault's principal clerk and his two companions strangled! Empson knew little about Finchley but he'd heard rumours about Felicia, a young lady who liked to play the two-backed beast and be paid for it. Empson heard a sound and stared around the mildewed hall. The pile of coffins and funeral cloths no longer alarmed him, but he noticed the lantern-horn placed at the far end was still burning.

'I thought I'd capped that.' Empson lurched to his feet. Slipping and slithering on shards of bone, pottery and other refuse littering the floor, he carefully made his way down. The lanternhorn stood on top of a cracked, dirty barrel. Empson had bought both lantern and tallow candle in a nearby flea market where the rifflers sold stolen goods. He knelt down to open the lanternhorn, then abruptly froze. That very action sharply reminded him how on his return from the city he had knelt down to cap the candle, so . . . Empson heard a sound behind him but fear held him in thrall. He tried to move. Too late, the garrotte string swung round, snaring his throat. He was dragged back. The deadly necklace was vice-like. He could not move his hands or legs; they were trapped. He was slipping, dying, falling into the darkness . . .

Athelstan sat at his kitchen table gratefully eating the broth Benedicta had prepared. He bit into a soft piece of bread and raised his horn spoon in acknowledgement to Benedicta sitting opposite him. She smiled and watched this priest, a man she truly loved, satisfy his hunger with broth, bread, cheese and sliced apple. Athelstan ate as if he was truly famished. Benedicta was tempted to ask when he had last dined but she knew he would not tell her. Athelstan followed a secret fast: if challenged he always replied that an empty belly honed his mind and sharpened his wits.

'What will you do with Peter the Penniless?'

'Peter Sandale, actually.' Athelstan licked the horn spoon clean. 'I knew him many years ago.'

'Never!'

'I knew him many years ago,' Athelstan repeated. 'Peter entered the novitiate at Blackfriars to train as a Dominican but realised that the prospect of taking a vow of poverty, not to mention one of chastity, was too much. He left Blackfriars and drifted. He always had a curious mind and became involved in the study of black magic, the demonic rites, the midnight arts, the conjuring of spirits, the summoning of spectres and all the other nonsense. He believed he had

76

made a pact with the devil and sold his soul in order to become a prosperous merchant importing the finest leather from both Spain and North Africa.'

'Did he make a pact with the devil?'

'Of course not. Peter was just a very good merchant. The right man in the right place at the right time. Castile is now a close ally of England. John of Gaunt is married to a Castilian princess with a claim to the crown of Castile. English merchants are welcome there and the markets are many; be it fabrics, fruit or leather. God knows what truly went on in Peter's mind. He definitely changed. As a young man he was generous to a fault: from a soul who would give you the cloak off his back he became a man who would give you your cloak from your own back and make you pay for it.'

Athelstan paused as Benedicta laughed. 'All merriment aside, Peter truly changed. He became a notorious miser, niggardly, penny-pinching, avaricious. He also deepened his interest in the Black Arts and macabre midnight sacrifices. But, thanks be to God, about two months ago,' Athelstan paused and screwed up his eyes, 'yes, about two months ago, he changed again. The Great Revolt seriously affected him. Peter was truly shaken by the savagery and slaughter: it made him reflect and he reflected deeply. I like Peter, he is a man of good heart. Something happened when he was a boy, some experience warped his mind and weakened his will. Thanks be to God he decided to repent and not in the sense of crying and beating his breast but

77

practically in his day-to-day life. He visited me here at St Erconwald's. He made his confession and asked me to shrive him. I was so pleased. Peter became a new man. He gave generous bequests to the poor of this parish. He paid for certain repairs and exercised similar charity throughout Southwark.'

'And he is married, I met . . .'

'Yes, Amelia. A pretty-faced, comely woman who is desperately worried because Peter now believes he has not been forgiven. He maintains the sins of his youth have caught up with him and that he's actually possessed by demons.'

'Could he be?'

'Benedicta, what is possession? I know from others how those who dabble in the Black Arts always suffer for it. I tell you this, Benedicta.' Athelstan became animated. 'I don't believe in monkey-faced devils, but I do believe in Satan and his legion of fallen spirits, beings of pure intelligence and free will in constant opposition to God and his goodness. We are like butterflies. We rest on a flower and we conclude the only reality is that flower: what we see, hear, taste and touch. I truly believe there is another reality entwined with ours, where God's angels hover, demons lurk and evil spirits hunt for an opening. If you call into the dark, someone or something always answers, and if you look into the pit, the monsters glare back. I feel this very much. If you summon up the powers of darkness, they will not leave you alone. You may conjure up spirits but God knows what will answer. Peter too accepts this: he trained to be a Dominican priest; he studied exorcism, demonology, Satan and the fall of man.'

'And you really believe this, Brother?'

'I do. Sir John and I hunt murderers. What is an assassin but an individual who has allowed a demon into his soul? But, to go back to Peter, he really wants to be good, he does not want to be separated from Christ. I do feel his anguish. He's still mocked as a miser, hence the title "Penniless". All this has proved too much for him. Twice in the last few weeks he has attempted suicide and tried to hang himself. On the first occasion the rope snapped and he was found unconscious. On the second, an apprentice came into the shed to find Peter dangling from a beam. He promptly cut him down.' Athelstan popped the last piece of bread into his mouth. 'I met Master Giole Limut today. I would regard him as a most skilled and experienced physician. I intend to ask for his help.'

'And our pilgrimage?'

'Time is passing, Benedicta. Our good neighbour Father Wilfred from St Laurence's promises to keep matters here under close watch. He will use his own sacred vessels. We will keep ours safe in the secret arca beneath the sacristy floor. Of course, not all of our parishioners will be joining our holy yet merry journey to Canterbury. They can also help here.'

'Oh, by the way,' Benedicta announced, 'Master Tuddenham, the Archdeacon of London's clerk, visited us while you were gone.'

'What on earth did he want?'

'He said a tavern had been raided by city

bailiffs. They had received information about a priest and a whore.'

'Which priest?'

Benedicta fought to keep her face straight. 'Apparently a Spanish friar.'

'Oh no, not a Dominican?'

'No. A friar of the Sack was discovered in one of the bedchambers in flagrante delicto. The friar, whose name is Gregorio, had a choice: either to appear before the Archdeacon's court, not to mention a convention of his own order . . .'

'Or,' Athelstan interrupted, 'do public penance? And you know what that could be, Benedicta? Walking barefoot in sackcloth and ashes to some holy place and, in this case, Becket's shrine at Canterbury. Good lord, of course! The Archdeacon will want guarantees that the penance is public and properly performed. I suspect Brother Gregorio is about to join us on pilgrimage.' Whispering a prayer for help, Athelstan put his face in his hands. Benedicta leaned across and took them away.

'Athelstan, it could be worse.' She smiled. 'According to Master Tuddenham, Brother Gregorio is a most genial friar.' She grinned impishly. 'If there can be such a thing?'

Athelstan was about to reply when there was a fierce scratching at the door. 'Bonaventure,' he declared, 'it's time for his milk.'

Benedicta rose and opened the door.

'Athelstan, look!' Caught by the fear in Benedicta's voice, Athelstan turned. Bonaventure came padding across the kitchen. The great one-eyed tomcat often brought his kills to share with his friend, but this time he had been given something. A dead magpie was thrust between Bonaventure's jaws; the garrotte string, tied tightly around the bird's throat, was looped over Bonaventure's neck. The cat padded dutifully towards Athelstan and sat down, the dead magpie still held in his mouth. Athelstan gently removed this, carefully undid the garrotte and stared at the stark message scrawled on the square of parchment: 'Lord Azrael greets you . . .'

Athelstan finished his dawn mass and stared around his meagre congregation Crim the altar boy; Bonaventure, of course, keeping a sharp watch for any church mice darting across the sanctuary; Benedicta, looking particularly resplendent in her dark-green robes edged with a silvery thread and a snow-white veil and wimple.

Three days had passed since Bonaventure had brought that sinister message. Athelstan had had no choice but to explain its meaning to the widow-woman. She admitted she had heard news about the slaughter in Milk Street, since Master Tuddenham had referred to it in his brief visit to the parish. She had not seen any strangers in the parish or glimpsed anything untoward, but she agreed with Athelstan that this Azrael must have followed him across the river. Benedicta also made the sharp observation that Bonaventure, the great tomcat, was a greater recluse than Athelstan. He stayed well away from most parishioners, some of whom he seemed to positively detest, such as Ursula and her massive sow.

81

Indeed, Bonaventure would allow few men to come close, being more of a ladies' man than anything else. Athelstan agreed and wondered how Azrael the assassin, as the friar now called his murderous quarry, had got so close to this most solitary of cats.

Athelstan had since reflected on the threat, uncertain whether he was being warned off investigating the slaughter in Milk Street, or was being threatened with murder himself. In the end, the friar decided that he had better things to worry about and threw himself into preparations for the parish pilgrimage. The Archdeacon's man had not yet returned but Peter the Penniless had certainly kept Athelstan busy. The sanctuary seeker had become calmer. He had been visited by Master Giole Limut, who had listened very carefully to Peter's confession and come away shaking his head.

'I do not know,' he confessed. 'In many ways the patient is lucid and as settled as yourself, Athelstan. The blood beat in his throat and wrist is quite steady and calm. The pupils of his eyes are the normal size. He is breathing clearly and I could detect no malignancy within him. Nevertheless, the patient does believe he is being haunted by demons. However, since taking sanctuary, he claims his humours have become much calmer.' The physician had settled himself on the wall bench near the baptismal font and peered up at Athelstan. 'Will you take Peter with you to Canterbury?'

'Certainly,' Athelstan said. 'I can't leave him here, which is another reason, Master Giole, for you and your family to accompany us. For one reason or another we will certainly need your skill and expertise. Now, can I pay you?'

The physician got to his feet. 'Brother, if you even try to do that, I will join Peter in sanctuary.'

Athelstan smiled. 'Could it be something Peter eats or drinks?' he queried. 'Is he being given some noxious potion?'

'It's possible,' the physician replied. 'But this would need someone very close to him who knew different opiates, their measurement and their effect, enough to unbalance the patient's humours without causing more serious injury or even death. You have to be very skilled in managing such infusions. Indeed, it's like many a cure or remedy. I can use certain herbs and potions to good effect but, if I give too much, the cure can become the killer. I did question him closely about his domestic arrangements.' The physician's dark, sad eyes crinkled in concern. 'But what do we have there? Peter told me about them: a housewife, poor Amelia, and Robert, a simple clerk who is used to listing figures in a column. Never once has Peter seen them with any powder or herb, or indeed anything medicinal. Brother, I am sure all three know nothing about potions or powders. Oh yes,' the physician smiled ruefully, 'I also made sure that Master Peter was not poisoning himself, eating and drinking, either deliberately or by accident, what might be causing his ill humours. I could discover nothing amiss.'

Athelstan, leaning against the altar, broke from

83

his reverie. He stared over his shoulder at Peter sitting in the enclave, hands joined together in prayer, ave beads lacing his bony fingers. Athelstan forced a smile and turned back as Benedicta coughed, as she always did, to startle him from his constant habit of daydreaming. The friar joined his hands together and bowed towards his little congregation.

'*Ite, missa est finis* – Go, the mass has ended.'

'*Deo gratias* – thanks be to God,' Benedicta sang back.

Athelstan had no sooner disrobed in the sacristy than he was joined by a breathless Tiptoft, Cranston's eerie-looking messenger. A tall, lanky man; Tiptoft's narrow, snow-white face was crowned by fiery-red hair heavy with a greasy nard so it stood up like Hubert the hedgehog's quills.

'You must come, Brother,' Tiptoft blurted out. 'You must come now! I realised you were saying mass so I kept to the shadows, but Sir John, at the behest of my Lord of Gaunt and Master Thibault, requires you at the Tower.'

'For what reason?'

'The usual, Brother Athelstan. Gruesome murder.'

Part Three
The Sooty Stink of Satan

Athelstan arrived at the Tower just as trumpets and horns brayed the message that the dawn watch was over. The great fortress was busy, bristling with armaments and ready for war. As Tiptoft led Athelstan along Red Gulley, the friar stared around. The crenellated walls and turrets of the different towers were manned by Cheshire archers and Hainault men-at-arms. Knights, dressed in half-armour, clustered at entrances, their warhorses in the Tower stables all harnessed and ready for their riders. The royal standard was planted along the walls overlooking the river, whilst off the water-gate, through which traitors were brought, war barges crammed with bowmen displaying the King's personal emblem, the White Hart, kept constant watch.

Tiptoft had to use his warrant to force his way through the press of soldiers, not to mention the men, women and children of the Tower garrison. The narrow passageways which snaked around the different towers were busy as any Cheapside street. At last they entered Tower Green, the great, grassy bailey dominated by the White Tower, resplendent after its recent fresh coat of paint. The young king himself had ordered this following the suppression of the revolt. During the great tumult, the peasant armies had stormed and taken the Tower. They had seized and barbarously executed leading officials of both Crown and Church, including Sudbury the Archbishop of Canterbury and Hailes the Treasurer who, many of the rebels believed, were responsible for the hated poll tax. Now that peace had been restored, young Richard had immediately ordered that his fortress be purged, purified and cleansed. He had also issued a proclamation saying that the royal standard would be kept unfurled at the Tower whether he was in residence or not: a stark warning that any violence in the Tower would subsequently be construed as treason.

Tiptoft explained all this as he led Athelstan down the outside steps of the White Tower into one of its cavernous cellars: a grim, forbidding chamber ill lit by tallow candles flaring in wall crevices and lanterns placed around the corpse table. On the latter stretched a cadaver beneath a stained canvas sheet which covered most of the corpse except for the hands and booted feet. Tiptoft begged Athelstan to wait in the dark whilst he hurried off and returned with a solemn-looking Cranston. The coroner threw both cloak and miraculous wineskin at Tiptoft to hold and instructed his messenger to wait outside. He then gave the friar a fierce hug before leading him over to the corpse table and pulling back the makeshift shroud.

'I wish you Christ's peace, Athelstan, but this, I am afraid, must be the first business of our day.'

'Who is he?'

'Roger Empson, former courier and messenger for Gaunt and Thibault. Azrael's most recent victim.'

Athelstan murmured a requiem, nostrils pinched against the sickening smell, as he scrutinised Empson's mortal remains.

'A fine horseman, Roger,' Cranston added. 'He did good service with Sir Walter Manny . . .'

'So a soldier,' Athelstan murmured, 'but a former one.'

'Very much so, Brother.'

Athelstan inspected the corpse. Empson was a balding, lean-faced man, though his stomach was now bulging and swollen from the corruption within. The dead man's face was loathsome, hideously discoloured and twisted, his blackening tongue pushed through purplish lips. Empson's eyes, still popping with death-fright, were beginning to sink into their darkened hollows. Athelstan asked Cranston for his dagger and used this to cut the garrotte string tied tightly around the dead man's throat. He read the usual macabre warning, 'Lord Azrael greets you', and threw it on the floor.

'Strange.' He touched the corpse's throat. 'Yes, that's what I thought I saw.'

'Brother?'

'Empson's throat is marked with a deep, blue-red laceration, this is his death wound. But look, Sir John, a little further up.'

'I see it, Brother, another wound, similar but not so deep. This was beginning to heal when the second laceration was inflicted.' The coroner straightened up. 'Empson's corpse was found yesterday evening in a charnel house near All Hallows-on-the-Wall. The place is a real abomination, disused and derelict for decades. They say ghosts, ghouls and spectres constantly haunt both the house and the surrounding garden. I have ordered the entire place to be torched. I've also made some enquiries. Apparently Empson disappeared a few days ago, before Mephan was murdered. The courier was glimpsed in the city markets. Hooded and visored, he tried to disguise himself, but there is very little which escapes the hawk eyes of my street spies led by Master Muckworm, whom I believe you have met?' Cranston did not wait for an answer. 'He glimpsed Empson not far from the charnel house buying up supplies. So how did this all happen?'

'Two wounds, Sir John. One much lighter and half healed. I believe Azrael attacked Empson some time ago but the courier managed to escape. Terrified out of his wits, Empson fled the Chancery and his own lodgings for what he thought was a safe refuge: a disused, decayed and abandoned charnel house. After the first attack failed, the cunning killer followed his prey and took careful note. He would wait. Then at an hour chosen by him, he attacked and finished what he'd begun. But why was Empson's death so necessary? We have no evidence that he received Azrael's usual warning, because it would have meant very little to him.'

Athelstan covered the corpse and went to sit down on a stool. He looked up at Sir John, who looked all trim in his nut-brown cote-hardie, dun-coloured hose and low-heeled walking boots. Athelstan went on reflectively, 'We know that Gaunt and Thibault sit in their chambers plotting – it's all about power and Gaunt's grasp of it. The chain between this precious pair is not only comradeship and a common goal but five other people: Simon Mephan, the Evangelists and Roger Empson. Two links in this chain have now been broken, whilst the other three links are threatened, as am I for being involved. Immediately I ask who is responsible, and why? It could be the Reapers, but that seems unlikely. Yes, we may have disaffected rebels thirsty for revenge, but this is too skilled, too well plotted for the Upright Men: they are now more concerned about saving their own skins rather than wringing the necks of their enemies. And why me and not you, most powerful colleague? More importantly, why not the Reapers' true opponents, Gaunt and Master Thibault?'

'You will have your chance to ask them both,' Cranston broke in. 'They want to meet us in the council chamber, just close to the chapel of St John the Evangelist.'

'My happiness is complete,' Athelstan whispered. 'Truly, I am not looking forward to that. Oh, by the way . . .'

He told Cranston all that had happened since they'd last met. Cranston heard him out and whistled under his breath.

'So Azrael, the wicked bastard, followed you to Southwark?'

'On his certain journey to Hell,' Athelstan retorted. He still felt angry at how the assassin had used his good comrade Bonaventure to issue his blood-chilling threats.

'And no one saw him?'

'Nobody, Sir John. But there again, people can move about disguised. My concern is why Bonaventure let Azrael draw so close.'

Cranston continued: 'And then there's your good friend Master Tuddenham from the Archdeacon's court, leaving word of Brother Gregorio, our disgraced Friar of the Sack, and the prospect of this Hispanic sinner joining us on our pilgrimage to Canterbury. Brother Gregorio is another reason for your summons here. The Archdeacon has also been in contact with me: they need my help. To cut to the quick, Master Tuddenham is bringing Brother Gregorio to the Tower. I have summoned him to appear here.'

'I thought Gregorio would be imprisoned?'

'You know the way of the world, Brother. If Gregorio does not wish to face up to his sin and flees then he is just another fugitive, one more defrocked priest who can join the rest of his kind begging for a living. However, if Gregorio does penance for his sins then his order will welcome him back with open arms. From what I gather this is the bond Gregorio has entered into. He is to stay in a certain place and, when summoned, he must be there on time. Now Athelstan, believe it or not, there is a connection between Gregorio's sin and the fiend Azrael. But first, let's leave Master Empson to the cold darkness and, while we wait, enjoy a moment in the sunshine.'

'A moment, Sir John.' Athelstan rose, pulling

his hood up over his head, and took a stole from his chancery satchel, along with a small leather case which held three phials for the oil, water and chrism taken from the stock sanctified the previous Holy Saturday, Easter Eve. He pulled back the filthy shroud sheet and deftly conducted the last rites, Cranston murmuring the responses. Once Athelstan had finished, Cranston assured the friar that a similar anointing had been done by the priest at St Mary le Bow for the three corpses taken from Milk Street. Athelstan placed the phials back in his chancery satchel and followed Cranston out into the sunlight.

They sat on a bench watching children play around the great engines of war: the monstrous mangonels, catapults and trebuchets which rejoiced in names such as 'Flesh-Shatterer', 'Bone-Breaker' and 'Skull-Crusher'. The Tower was certainly busy, its community immersed in myriad tasks like any village or town. There were a number of markets, each containing a range of stalls selling goods, from local merchandise such as flour from the mills near the Tower, to oranges, dates and other fruit brought in by the cogs berthed along the Thames. A fleshing yard was busy slaughtering pigs, chickens and other livestock. The air was thick with the stench of blood and riven by the strident calls of the animals being herded to the slaughter sheds. Archers, soldiers and servants mingled with the washerwomen pushing barrows and handcarts piled high with dirty linen, eager to reach the wells and water outlets. Wandering troubadours, minstrels and mummers had been allowed in along with chanteurs, storytellers, relic-sellers and other tinkers and traders. A tall, garishly dressed fire-eater proclaimed himself the Salamander King: this mountebank included everyone in his constant patter, as he claimed to hold the sandal that had slipped off Jesus' feet as the Lord was arrested, and described a building in Jerusalem called the House of Evil Council, where the chief priests and others had plotted against Christ.

Athelstan turned to his companion. 'Now, my Lord Coroner, please tell me everything you have discovered about Empson. You have been busy, I can see that.'

'Empson was Thibault's special courier. Remember, Athelstan, not all messages are written, but often they are committed to memory. Envoys, ambassadors and others in that walk of life must not only be physically able and good horsemen but have an excellent memory for what cannot be put in writing. Remember what Scripture says, Brother? "Put not your trust in princes nor your confidence in the war chariots of Egypt or the swift horses of Syria."'

'I certainly do,' Athelstan retorted, 'and I never forget that other verse by the disillusioned psalmist: "I said in my excess all men are liars."'

'Very true,' Cranston agreed. 'Men like Gaunt and Thibault do not like to render themselves vulnerable to the truth. Remember, treason is only treason if it fails. Gaunt's abiding desire, his great dream, is the Crown of England, but he must never betray this. Now Empson, whether he realised it or not, carried messages which, if written down and seized by the young king's advisors, would send Gaunt and his coven to the scaffold on Tower Hill. Empson therefore was an important person in Thibault's household. He would be hated by the Upright Men and a quarry for the Reapers, though I am beginning to suspect that the Reapers have nothing to do with our fiend Azrael.'

'I would agree, Sir John, but do continue.'

'Now what I have learnt, Brother, comes from rumour and tavern gossip, but, more importantly, from the sightings of my street spies, the likes of Leif, Rawbum, Muckworm and the Sanctus Man. From what these tell me . . .' Cranston paused at the shrill screams from the slaughter shed where the hogs were having their throats cut. Athelstan stared across the grassy bailey. The Salamander King had been joined by others of his troupe allowed into the Tower to entertain the garrison: the horde of mercenaries lodged there as well as the wives and children of officers and clerks.

'You've learnt what, Sir John?'

'Empson was a bachelor with lodgings in Cheapside. According to rumour, he liked young boys, so he frequented a tavern known as the Lute Boy – a clean swept, grandiose, even majestic hostelry with one difference. The tavern is simply a veil for what happens in its warren of spacious cellars, underground chambers built God knows when or why. The owner is a Mistress Alianora Devereux, more publicly known as the Way of all Flesh. Brother, I leave it to your imagination why she is called that. Anyway, Mistress Alianora caters for every possible lustful appetite you have listened to in confession and a few more you certainly haven't. She has male and female whores, and a few in between. She feeds human depravity until it's gorged. I shudder to think what goes on in those underground chambers.'

'And she is allowed to do this?'

'You can imagine the reason why, Athelstan. She has powerful friends in the Guildhall, on the King's council and even more so at court. Anyway, Empson was one of her customers, assaulted close to the Lute Boy. According to a group of revellers who came out of a secret drinking den, they emerged just as Empson was being attacked. They are certain it was he. The assassin had vanished, Empson was on his hands and knees gasping and sobbing. They helped him to a nearby tavern. Once he'd recovered, Empson fled his usual haunts and went into hiding.'

'In other words,' Athelstan declared, 'Empson believed Azrael was hunting him. But how did Azrael know Empson frequented such a hostelry? Though, there again,' he conceded, 'the assassin could have been keeping Empson under close watch and followed him there that night. Such careful planning would frighten a man like Empson. He would realise this was not just some street affray, but that he'd been marked down for assassination. He fled to that charnel house near the London Wall but our black-winged angel, the Lord Azrael, caught up with him and finished what he had begun.'

Cranston leaned closer. 'However, there is more, Brother Athelstan – a link with the slaughter in Milk Street. You recall the house-maid at Mephan's lodgings, the young Felicia? Well, before Azrael caught up with her, Felicia was a lithe, toothsome wench who was not above earning extra coin at the Lute Boy under the strict supervision of the Way of all Flesh. Now our Brother Gregorio, whom you are going to meet very soon, the Spanish friar of the Order of the Sack, was residing at a tavern in Farringdon, close to Milk Street and not all that far from the Lute Boy.

'Sir John, what on earth was Gregorio doing there or, indeed, in London in the first place?'

'Well, you can ask him that yourself, but from what I gather, something about the Minister General of his order, who apparently resides in Castile, being deeply concerned about the fate of his brothers in London because of the troubles here.' Cranston spread his hands, lowering his voice: 'You recognise that is a legitimate concern, Athelstan. The rebels were not amicable to foreigners, as the Flemings found to their cost. Now Gregorio is a linguist, much travelled and, I understand, extremely charming. Young Felicia apparently thought so too. Gregorio, desirous of a little human company, met Felicia in the cellars of the Lute Boy by courtesy of the Way of all Flesh. Apparently, they were much taken with each other and, as often happens in such brothels, arranged a second assignation at another tavern, the Mitre in Nutkin Lane, Cheapside.'

'Where Brother Gregorio had taken lodgings?'

95

'Precisely, little friar. I think Gregorio takes to fornication as a bird does to flying.' Cranston picked up his miraculous wineskin which Tiptoft had left close to the bench. The coroner took a generous mouthful and persuaded Athelstan to do the same.

'So Gregorio was betrayed?'

'Yes, I believe he was. Gregorio didn't reside at any of the friaries of his order and those he was visiting must have become suspicious.' Cranston waved a hand. 'You know how the story goes. They knew where he lodged, they could watch who came and went, and they notified the city bailiffs, that's what I have learnt from Flaxwith and his lovely lads. Brother, we have walked the streets of London. How many times have we seen a priest caught in fornication, seated on a horse facing its tail, being taken down to the public pillory to the raucous shrilling of bagpipes and the catcalls of onlookers? The city bailiffs just love to catch a priest fishing where he shouldn't. The Mitre was raided, and Gregorio acted all courteous. He protected Felicia and she escaped, but he was taken up and handed over to the Archdeacon's court. The bailiffs suspected it was Felicia, but of course they had no proof, as she had fled.'

'And I know the rest.' Athelstan laughed quietly. 'Gregorio is to join us on our pilgrimage . . .'

He broke off at the shrill call of trumpets. People were now streaming up from the Lion Gate, running before the outriders, all garbed in the gorgeous livery of the self-proclaimed regent, John of Gaunt. Banners, standards and pennants floated in the breeze, an array of brilliant colours from azure to vert with a host of heraldic insignia and devices proclaiming Gaunt's status as a prince, a great duke, the heir to the English throne as well as a claimant to the ancient crown of Castile. The horsemen cantered onto the great, grassy bailey which stretched around the formidable White Tower. A mounted cohort of Sherwood archers in their Lincoln green jackets and earth-coloured hose followed next, deadly warbows slung across their backs, quivers of goose-feathered arrows slapping against their rough leather saddles. These cleared the way for Gaunt's personal party, his household knights dressed in half-armour and their master's livery.

The horsemen debouched onto the great bailey followed by Gaunt's chamber priests and his principal henchmen. Thibault was prince amongst these and the Master of Secrets looked resplendent in his blue and gold surcoat, blonde hair fashionably crimped, his innocent, choirboy face fixed into that gracious smile which had duped even the most cunning of observers. Gaunt came last, alone, very much the great prince in his cloth-of-gold cotehardie and silver hose. The regent's wrists gleamed with precious bracelets, a magnificent silver Lancastrian 'SS' gorget circled his throat, and a chapelet of gold adorned his corn-coloured hair, which he grew long so it fell to rest on his shoulders. Gaunt exuded arrogance, one gauntleted hand holding the reins of his magnificent destrier, lavishly caparisoned in the Plantagenet colours of blue, scarlet and gold, and the other hand bearing the royal standard with its three crouching, snarling leopards. The banner openly proclaimed that the boy king Richard was not the only royal Plantagenet in the kingdom.

Athelstan watched Gaunt's party spread out across the bailey. Ostlers and grooms from the regent's household hurried to help their masters dismount. Others prepared to lead the horses away. Orders were shouted, people milled about. Gaunt waited for a dismounting block. He then handed the standard to a squire and effortlessly slid from the high, horned, gilt-edged saddle. Athelstan, sitting not far from where the regent stood, studied Gaunt closely. Weeks had passed since the revolt had been crushed and the regent had kept to the shadows. Now he was displaying himself in the full glory of a summer's day. Athelstan wouldn't trust Gaunt as far as he could spit; indeed, in the friar's mind, Gaunt was the most accurate likeness of Lucifer before the fall. The regent was tall, slender, golden-haired, his skin a lovely olive sheen. He had the eerie light-blue eyes of the Plantagenets, a full, sensuous mouth, the lips ready to part in a smile which never actually happened. Athelstan was fascinated by him. Physically very handsome, on a spiritual level Athelstan regarded Gaunt as one of the most dangerous men he'd ever met; an exquisitely beautiful snake who would lunge and kill on a mere whim.

Gaunt stood slapping his gauntlets against his thigh as he looked around the Tower bailey, very much the powerful prince, the master of the house. Athelstan also noticed how the regent's party were beginning to break up. Six months earlier guards would have locked shields around him. Now confident in victory, fresh from his forays along the Scottish March and secure in the kingdom's principal fortress, Gaunt had decided to lower his guard. He was presenting himself as the benevolent prince, confident that he would face no danger here in the Tower where his soldiers gathered and the walls bristled with armaments. Cranston, however, was not so confident. He abruptly seized Athelstan's arm and pointed.

'Brother,' he rasped, 'the Salamander King, the fire-eater, look at him and his coven.'

The Salamander King was demonstrating his skill, offering to eat from the fiery torch he carried. He was now moving amongst Gaunt's escort, teasing and laughing, disarming any fear as he continued to blow fire from his mouth. Others accompanied him, a small troupe of five or six, huddled around their wheelbarrow heaped high with the Salamander's tools of trade: cresset torches, tallow candles and a small, moveable stove packed with glowing charcoal. Alarmed, Cranston pulled at Athelstan's sleeve then hurried towards the regent, shouting his warning.

The Salamander King was now very close to Gaunt. He stopped abruptly and threw the flaming torch he carried at a group of soldiers. He then fumbled beneath his garish robes for the sword and dagger hidden away. At the same time his comrades around the wheelbarrow also cleared the top of their cart to snatch up the weapons concealed there. The Salamander King had not moved as swiftly as Cranston. The would-be assassin had sword and dagger out, hovering close to the regent, who could only draw a dress knife to defend himself. Cranston crashed into the Salamander King and the fire-eater staggered back, then lunged forward screaming one of the battle cries of the Upright Men:

'For the Commons! For God's true Commons!'

He then closed with Cranston who, sword and dagger drawn, stood between the assassin and his intended victim. The Salamander King's accomplices were also armed and eager to strike at the regent, but Gaunt's escort were now alerted. Two household knights successfully blocked the assassins' first charge, which gave other bodyguards time to throw a veritable ring of steel around Gaunt. The attack was now common knowledge. Mothers screamed in fear, snatching their children up, fleeing from the bloody affray spreading across Tower Green. Warhorses whinnied, and squires hastened to quieten them and lead the destriers away as their sharp, flailing hooves could be as dangerous as any warrior's whirling sword. More soldiers were hurrying onto the green. Gaunt remounted his warhorse, his henchmen gathering about him, weapons at the ready, but the melee was nearly over.

Cranston, despite his bulk, was agile as any street fighter, and his opponent, now cornered, was fearful, clumsy and slow. The coroner, sword and dagger twisting, was successfully driving the assassin away from the regent. Cranston then abruptly stooped and delivered a shattering blow to his opponent's right ankle, and the Salamander King collapsed screaming to the ground. The attack was over. Two of the assassins were killed outright; the rest, grievously wounded, were being disarmed and forced to their knees.

Athelstan found himself rooted to the spot. He could never really comprehend the swiftness of such violence. One moment a glorious pageant on Tower Green; the next violence and bloodshed erupting with the song of the sword and all the horror of bloody battle. Now a chilling silence descended, that brief aftermath of any murderous melee when men realise what they have done and stare at the wounds inflicted. Somewhere a horn wailed. Two of the glossy-feathered war ravens which by tradition protected the Tower, floated over the place of slaughter as if attracted by the blood now snaking in thin, red lines across the closely cropped grass. Horses whinnied, still restless at the violence and the pervasive stench of blood. Leather harnesses creaked. Swords and daggers rasped as they were re-sheathed. A child cried. Gaunt moved his horse forward, urging the great destrier so he was almost on top of the huddled prisoners now moaning at their wounds. Gaunt drew his sword, holding it up by the crosspiece as he proclaimed sentence.

'I, John of Gaunt, Duke of Lancaster . . .'

The magnificent titles rolled out. Gaunt then moved his sword, grasping the handle and turning the point of its blade towards the prisoners. He condemned them as traitors, taken in arms whilst the banner of the King was unfurled and the royal arms publicly displayed. Accordingly, all were guilty of treason, sentence to be carried out immediately. Gaunt, nimble and adroit, slipped from the saddle. He balanced himself with a slight stoop, sword grasped between his gauntleted hands. Groaning and protesting, the prisoners were dragged in front of him. Arms bound behind their backs, they were made to kneel, heads forced down. Gaunt, sure as any plunging hawk, swung his great two-edged sword back and sheared off the head of each prisoner. One head was bouncing, one torso gushing blood like a fountain as the next victim was dragged forward to be as quickly despatched. Athelstan closed his eyes. Gaunt would brook no interference so the friar whispered the words of absolution and the requiem for these hapless souls being despatched to judgement. He watched five heads bounce away, five blood-spouting trunks collapse to the ground. The executions were carried out in a deathly silence. Gaunt lifted his sword, his blade gleaming like a fiery light in the sunshine.

'So die all traitors!' he bellowed. 'Take their heads and pole them on the top of the White Tower. Their corpses are to be tarred, quartered and displayed above the Lion Gate and at each end of Tower Bridge.' He paused. 'Let the grass be cleaned of their filthy blood. Let no memory of them remain. We shall celebrate. Let the wine tuns be opened, the ale casks broached, the kitchens fire their ovens and stoves. Let us rejoice and thank God that the wickedness of these demons has been brought to nothing. Let us cry Alleluia!' Gaunt's proclamation was

102

greeted with roars of approval. The mangled remains of the assassins were heaped together, a gruesome mound of flesh, bone and blood. Huge water carts were trundled across to clean the gore whilst the prospect of free food and drink for the garrison and all in the Tower swiftly changed the mood. The regent watched his orders being carried out before striding across to Cranston. He said nothing at first but touched the coroner on the shoulder then gently caressed Cranston's face between his hands. Only a trickle of sweat down the regent's face betrayed his agitation.

'God bless you, Sir John, and my thanks,' he murmured. 'Once matters are settled, we shall meet in council.' His hands fell away and he stood back. Thibault, standing behind his master, smiled beatifically: he raised his hand as if blessing both the coroner and friar, then they swept away. Gaunt's escort broke up as courtiers, chamber priests, household officials and body-guard went their different ways. The bloody affray on Tower Green now seemed like a nightmare, the assassins dead, their hacked remains piled into a cart. These would be taken down to Master Burdon's workshop on London Bridge to be quartered, pickled and tarred. Albinus, Thibault's silent shadow, drifted over, his voice scarcely above a whisper. He gave his master's apologies, explaining that the convening of the council might take some time. So would my Lord Coroner and Brother Athelstan accept the deepest regrets at such a delay from both his master and His Grace, my Lord of Gaunt?

'Do we have a choice?' Athelstan asked.

Albinus' snow-white face, with its singular blue-white eyes, broke into a lopsided smile. He shrugged and sauntered off. Athelstan watched him go then turned back to stare over Tower Green. The friar was bemused, still chilled by the speed and ferocity of the assault, its bloody aftermath and the now almost frantic work to remove all traces of the slaughter yard. The ale and wine casks were being rolled out to be fixed on stands ready to be broached. A huge turnspit had been set up on the stone paving and a log fire, a virtual pyre, was being prepared just beneath. Gaunt was desperately trying to restore everything to normal. Nevertheless, at the same time, Athelstan glimpsed Thibault's minions moving amongst the crowd, questioning various individuals, some of whom were seized by the accompanying guards and hustled away.

'*Hic est terribilis locus,*' he murmured, '*porta ipsa inferna* – this is a terrible place, the very gate to Hell, Sir John.' He sketched a blessing towards the coroner. 'And you, Sir, are a veritable Hector!'

'Who is he?' Cranston demanded. 'I have heard the name.'

'Hector of Troy,' Athelstan informed him. 'Gaunt must be furious to be attacked here at the very heart of the crown's great fortress. How could the Salamander King and the others get in so easily? To all intents the Great Revolt is over, yet that attack recalls the old days.'

'I think the opposite.' Cranston came and sat down next to Athelstan, cradling the miraculous wineskin in his lap. 'Trust me, Brother, when Gaunt and Thibault calm down, they will agree with my judgement. The attack was a very desperate throw by very desperate men and probably the last of its kind. They thought very carefully and planned most assiduously. You see, the Salamander King was what he claimed to be, a fire-eater, a travelling mummer probably well known in the Tower and elsewhere. However, he was also a leading adherent of the Upright Men – not a street warrior or a leader of a cohort, but probably their principal courier and messenger. It must have been so easy for the likes of the Salamander King to travel across this city and into the surrounding shires with all his tricks and marvels. People would accept him for what he is, a crowd pleaser, a minstrel, a troubadour. Secretly he was part of the great conspiracy, and now the Salamander King represents its remnants, the Reapers. As for being in the Tower, I suspect he and his coven were admitted because they were habitual visitors who paraded across Tower Green on numerous occasions. Today the Salamander King seized his chance. He threw the dice, he lost and paid for it with his life, his accomplices likewise. Oh, there will be others of his coven but they will flee, taking their stories with them.

'At this moment Gaunt will be indulging in a royal rage. He will berate the constable and other officers of the Tower as well as anyone else he wishes to point the finger of blame at. He'll kick over furniture, tear tapestries from the wall, draw his sword and hack at chests and coffers. He will shout and scream. Afterwards he will calm down. He may even begin to wonder, and I would not reject this out of hand, if his attackers were really Upright Men or just a coven of assassins despatched by one of his many enemies. The Lord knows, Gaunt's got many, nobles such as FitzAlan of Arundel.' Cranston paused as a voice shouted their names, and the three evangelists, garbed in the livery of the Chancery, strolled across to meet them. All three brothers carried goblets of wine. They stood toasting both the coroner and the friar with their cups, then laughed as Cranston lifted his miraculous wineskin in reply.

'You are here to do business?' Athelstan asked, peering up at the three clerks who looked as if they'd drunk quite deeply.

Matthew replied: 'We do have work here, but the attack on my Lord Gaunt has certainly shattered the harmony of the day. So, as St Paul says, we take a little wine for our stomach's sake.' He raised his goblet.

'Aye,' Cranston retorted, 'and as the psalmist preaches, "wine gladdens the heart of men whilst *in vino veritas*".'

'Oh yes, wine will bring the truth out,' Luke Gaddesden replied, leaning down to stare into Athelstan's face. The friar tried not to flinch at the clerk's breath, richly spiced from the wine he'd drunk. He also caught the fear in the man's eyes.

'Is all well?' Athelstan murmured.

'We've heard about poor Empson found garrotted in that charnel house,' Matthew said. 'Another victim of Azrael, eh?'

'Did you know Empson well?' Cranston asked.

Matthew looked at his brothers, who pulled faces or shrugged. 'We knew him in the Chancery. We would exchange pleasantries, but all he took from us were letters and other documents to be despatched or carried here and there. Sometimes he would commit messages to memory, but then he would be alone with Master Thibault or Albinus.'

'But all is now well with you?'

'We are not too sure, are we, brothers?' Matthew turned and glanced at his siblings. Now they had drawn close, Athelstan could almost smell their fear, and he noticed that Matthew in particular was unshaven and red-eyed, the hand grasping his wine cup trembling continuously.

'You've heard the news?' Luke slurped. 'Master Thibault and our good selves . . .' He knocked away his brother Matthew's restraining hand.

'You are not . . .'

'Matthew, I will have my say. Brother Athelstan, Sir John, we are joining you on your pilgrimage to Canterbury. Master Thibault wishes to give personal thanks for his safe deliverance. In addition Master Thibault will accompany us: he hopes to meet with certain envoys from Castile and treat with them. I believe,' Luke stammered, 'that's the reason for your summons here.' His voice faltered and he fell silent.

Athelstan could only stare in surprise. Cranston cursed beneath his breath, whilst the other evangelists, openly embarrassed at their brother's abrupt proclamation, made their farewells. Luke shouted that they should while away their time with a little fishing or bird-snaring amongst the reed banks along the river.

'Satan's tits!' Cranston breathed, watching them go. 'Brother Athelstan, should we go to Canterbury or flee and seek sanctuary somewhere else? In God's name!'

'In God's name it will be, Sir John.' Athelstan took out his ave beads, threading them through his fingers. 'There's a real mystery here, Lord Coroner, and, like a mist above a marsh, it's beginning to gather and thicken.' He pointed across to where the Tower ravens, glossy black feathers gleaming, were now clustering over the place of blood, digging with their cruel dagger beaks at the gore-sodden earth. 'There will be more blood by and by. But whose, where and when?'

Athelstan paused as he heard his name called, and he glimpsed pale-faced Master Tuddenham, the Archdeacon's man, his black robe flapping, striding across the bailey, sending the ravens whirling up around him. Tuddenham appeared extremely agitated. He stopped in front of Cranston and Athelstan, taking deep breaths to calm himself.

'I am sorry,' he gasped. 'I was delayed. I heard about the attack, the executions, the bloodshed.' He abruptly looked over his shoulder at Tower Green before lifting his feet to inspect his sandals.

'You will find no blood there, Master Tuddenham,' Athelstan soothed. 'The wetness comes from the water poured out to clean the ground, although some mystics say, "Blood spilt in anger will not truly disappear until the day of vengeance."'

'We live in the time of vengeance,' Tuddenham retorted. 'Anyway, God's work goes on. Our guest has arrived. I have lodged Brother Gregorio in St Peter ad Vincula.'

'Master Tuddenham, why exactly is Brother Gregorio joining our pilgrimage, and not somebody else's?'

'Think, Brother.' Tuddenham forced a glacial smile. 'You, my Lord Coroner and possibly others, or so the rumour says, will be witnesses enough that Brother Gregorio's penance has been completed in accordance with the norms of canon law. The Bishop of London has ordered this and, I believe, he has the support of Prior Anselm at Blackfriars.'

'May God and his saints bless them both. Master Tuddenham, lead us on, Brother Gregorio awaits.'

'One moment,' Cranston ordered.

'Yes, Sir John?'

'Tell me, did Brother Gregorio arrive in London by himself?' The Archdeacon's man looked up and, just for a second, Athelstan saw him swallow hard, lick his lips and glance away. The usual gesture, Athelstan had learnt, from someone about to tell a lie or at least not the full truth.

'Of course. Why do you ask?'

The coroner sketched a mocking bow. 'Master Tuddenham, lead on.'

They crossed the bailey and entered the grim, dusty nave of St Peter's ad Vincula. Athelstan recalled the legends about this chapel: at certain times of the year, particularly the eve of All Hallows and other days of solemn mourning, the spirits of those who had met violent deaths in this formidable fortress, gathered in ghostly chapter to sing their own funeral vespers, and their chanting could be heard all over the Tower.

'Well, after today,' Athelstan whispered to himself, 'more souls will join that ghostly choir.'

'What was that?' A figure strode out of the gloom to the right of the doorway. Athelstan started and stepped back, almost colliding with Master Tuddenham.

'I am sorry.' The stranger walked into the light thrown by one of the high lancet windows. Apparently full of confidence, he gestured at Athelstan to join him further up the nave, close to the sombre, rough-hewn rood screen where the light was better. 'Such a gloomy place,' he called over his shoulder. 'I would say you English love such haunted corners. But, unfortunately, churches like this are common enough, even in Castile.' The stranger turned before the rood screen and, one hand on his chest, bowed elegantly. 'I am Brother Gregorio, a humble Friar of the Sack, envoy of our Minister General in Castile, a servant of the servants of God . . .'

'And now a public sinner in the King's own city of London,' Master Tuddenham broke in harshly. He thrust a slip of parchment into Cranston's hands. 'Brother Gregorio is now in your care, my Lord Coroner, Brother Athelstan. He and . . .' Tuddenham gestured at the saddle bags and panniers, neatly secured with fine twine,

110

stacked near the entrance to the rood screen, '. . . all his worldly possessions.' Tuddenham bowed curtly in mocking imitation of Brother Gregorio, then the Archdeacon's man was gone, slamming the door behind him.

Brother Gregorio shook his head and stared up at the agonised, crucified face of the carved figure of Christ on his cross. He muttered something quickly in Spanish and then translated it, as if for himself. 'Thank God he has gone!'

'Have you had much dealings with him?' Athelstan asked.

'As little as possible. But thanks be to God, he has gone! Brother Athelstan, Sir John Cranston, my Lord High Coroner.' Gregorio clasped hands and exchanged the kiss of peace with his two new keepers, then stood back smiling at both of them. Athelstan studied the Spaniard closely even as he tried to conceal his amusement. Brother Gregorio exuded good humour. The Spanish friar was slender, of medium height, and his dark, reddish hair had been neatly cut but not in the clerical style, shaven to reveal the tonsure; his moustache and beard were closely trimmed and, when he smiled, his teeth were white and even. A most attractive man, Gregorio's large, dark eyes danced with impish merriment. Clearly a ladies' gallant, Athelstan concluded, one of this world's troubadours who drank deep and often of the wine of life: his priesthood and his vows were irrelevant to what he enjoyed and what he experienced.

'Do I pass scrutiny, Brother Athelstan?'

'You certainly do.' Cranston came to stand

111

beside Athelstan and gestured down the church. 'Why were you hiding in the shadows?'

'I wasn't hiding!' Gregorio stepped forward. Athelstan noticed how Gregorio's robe was of pure wool and spotlessly clean, the cord around his waist snow-white, the sandals on his bare feet, thick-soled with good leather uppers and thongs. He had delicate hands, long-fingered, and clean, pared nails. He lifted one hand rather elegantly as if taking an oath.

'I wasn't hiding.' Gregorio repeated. 'I was drawing. I etch my memories, my dreams, my thoughts, anything which catches my attention. You must look at what I have done.'

'I would be honoured,' Athelstan replied. 'But first, Brother, let us learn a little about you as you will undoubtedly learn a little about us.' He waved towards the wall benches. Cranston and Athelstan rearranged these so that they both sat opposite their enforced guest. Gregorio, at Athelstan's invitation, told them about his early life. He was born into a wealthy merchant's family in Castile. In the cathedral school of Toledo he had shown himself to be a talented scholar with a gift for languages. He was now fluent in the tongues of Spain, the Latin and Greek of Scriptures, Norman French, English, the Lingua Franca of the Middle Seas as well as a working knowledge of Flemish. Gregorio had also studied philosophy, theology and logic at Salamanca and, for a time, the art of physic for which that university was famous.

Athelstan listened intently. He had no means to verify what the Spanish friar was saying but, as Sir John often said, the proof of the pudding was in the eating, and Athelstan was determined to learn more about this enigmatic character over the next few days. Undoubtedly Gregorio was a highly intelligent man with a gift for languages. He could slip easily between English and Norman French with only a slight tinge of an accent. Indeed, the Spanish friar's career was a story that Athelstan had heard before: the highly talented son of a mercantile family, the offspring of parents who doted on their only son whilst he responded by entering the church. Apparently Gregorio's talents had soon been recognised by his superiors, being despatched as an envoy across Europe.

'And so you came here?'

'Not for the first time,' Gregorio retorted. 'I know London very well. Sometimes I come in disguise.'

'Why?'

'I work for my order but, there again . . .'

'Others would hire you, I assume?' Cranston asked. 'This count? That duke? This archbishop? That abbot?'

'Exactly, Sir John.'

'People might claim you are a spy.'

'People,' Gregorio laughed, his face full of humour, 'can go hang. I am a journeyer. Last time I was in London I was a relic seller. I could offer you the arm of St George,' he pulled a face, 'shrunken as it was when I took it down from an execution spike. I could sell you one of the water pots from Cana, an ear from St Dismas well, at least five of them. Scraps of roasted flesh

113

from St Lawrence. Three of the stones hurled at St Stephen and two of the molars of the giant Goliath, being six inches long and weighing twelve pounds . . .'

He paused as Athelstan laughed.

'And this time,' Cranston intervened, 'your superiors sent you to ensure that all was well with your brothers in England?'

'Yes, and I like coming here. I enjoy your bizarre ways.'

'Such as?'

'Well, before I was seized, I visited a rat-drowning in a tavern close to Newgate. Have you ever been to one?'

'No, never!' Athelstan exclaimed. 'I hate rats.'

'Likewise.' Gregorio rubbed his hands together. 'A legacy from my youth, of being locked in filthy cellars. Anyway, there is nothing like watching a rat-catcher drown his quarry – it's better than plucking plums from a branch.'

Athelstan stared at this fellow friar. Gregorio was courteous, witty, charming with a fine sense of humour. Yet there was something wrong. For a few moments when Gregorio was talking about being imprisoned in filthy cellars, the bonhomie had slipped like a loose mask betraying a hardness of soul, a man with a great deal to resolve. Athelstan could never explain how he reached such conclusions. He believed it was the fruit of questioning people closely either in the pursuit of some assassin or under the seal of confession when shriving a soul burdened with sin. In such cases Athelstan recalled the Confessions of St Augustine. That great sinner turned saint had described humans as beings full of every kind of emotion: fear, fantasy, dream and experience. Nevertheless there was an underlying basic trait each person had, what the Greeks called 'Karpos', the very essence of their being, whether as a sinner or a saint, and this *karpos* would bear fruit for good or bad. This seemed to be true of Brother Gregorio, so much so, Athelstan wondered if this Friar of the Sack was really what he claimed to be and if, despite all his worldly charm, he was in fact something else.

'So you arrived in London?' Cranston continued the questioning, now fully aware that Athelstan was in one of his reveries. 'And all was well?' Cranston grinned. 'I mean, until you discovered the delights of Mistress Felicia and the forbidden pleasures of the Way of all Flesh? Brother Gregorio laughed, shifting to sit slightly sideways as he flicked dust from his robe. Once again Athelstan caught it, a sense that this man was acting as if he wore a mask in a mummer's play. Every gesture, expression and movement had been rehearsed time and again until the actor and the role he adopted became one. Athelstan could almost sense what Gregorio was going to say.

'Sir John, Brother Athelstan,' Gregorio beat his breast in mock sorrow, 'as the psalmist says, "my sin is always before me".' I love a pretty face, a well-turned ankle, dancing eyes and a merry mouth.'

'And Felicia?'

'Oh, I know all about the secrets of the Lute Boy and the lustful services offered by the Way of all Flesh. I have supped at that chalice on other visits to London.' Gregorio grinned and spread his hands. 'But, of course, I denied that before Master Tuddenham.'

'Felicia?' Athelstan insisted, ignoring Gregorio's good humour.

'Felicia.' The Spanish friar's smile was now forced like that of a master in the schools dealing with some dumb ox of a scholar.

'Yes, Felicia.'

'I met her at the Lute Boy. I was very pleased with her ministrations. I asked her to visit me at the Mitre. I offered to make it worth her while. Of course she came. Somebody, however, had kept me under close watch.' He held a hand up. 'And no, I don't know who. Probably some Brothers of the Sack who wondered where I lodged and were jealous of my freedom. Anyway, my chamber at the Mitre was raided by city bailiffs. I managed to protect Felicia and arrange her escape. However, it was obvious I was a priest, a friar and, as one of the bailiffs put it, that I'd been playing the two-backed beast with the young lady whom I had helped through the window and who had been glimpsed fleeing from the tavern. I was taken up, proclaimed as a public sinner, and so here I am. Brother Athelstan, I am now in your care. I will return with you to Southwark?'

'Yes, you can lodge at the the Piebald Tavern,' Athelstan retorted. 'It's not of the same luxury as the Lute Boy, nor does it offer such services. However, it's merry enough. Of course, you cannot celebrate mass or exercise

116

any of your priestly powers until your penance is complete.'

'I agree.'

Athelstan gestured at the saddle bags and panniers close to the entrance of the rood screen. 'And you have everything you need – money, clothing?'

'I am as richly endowed as you are, Brother Athelstan. You know that I must walk to Canterbury in sackcloth and ashes with nothing on my feet.'

'We will see about that,' Athelstan declared. 'Once we are on the Canterbury road, who cares? Is it not so, Sir John?' The coroner, sleepy-eyed, clambered to his feet and nodded. Brother Gregorio and Athelstan also rose. The Spaniard went to sift amongst his possessions and brought back a thick, square folio, its richly decorated calf-skin covers holding scrubbed parchment sheets between them, at least a hundred in all. Gregorio thrust the folio into Athelstan's hand.

'My drawings,' he declared proudly. 'The sum of all my dreams, what my mind perceives and my soul is drawn to. Brother, look at these whilst I, with your permission, will wander this great fortress of which I have heard so much. I understand a fight has been arranged between two old crones. The winner will be the first to draw blood.' Gregorio shook his head. He lifted his hand in mock blessing and quietly left the chapel.

'In heaven's name,' Athelstan declared, 'we do meet some strange souls, do we not, Sir John?'

'Interesting,' Cranston agreed. 'You have reservations, Brother?'

117

'Aye, enough to make me think.'

'About what?'

'Is Gregorio what he claims to be?'

'If he isn't,' Cranston countered, 'you, my little ferret of a friar, will establish the truth. But now I must go. I have friends here, old comrades . . .'

Athelstan half listened as Cranston gathered himself and left. The friar heard the door thud closed and stared down at the parchment folio Gregorio had entrusted to him. Intrigued, he took it over to a high stool beneath one of the more spacious windows and the generous shaft of light pouring through it. Athelstan opened the folio onto a graphic scene, 'The Tavern of Damned Souls', illustrating a popular legend about the damned on their journey to Hell being allowed one last moment of drinking, lovemaking and human companionship before the eternity of Hell shut them off forever. The tavern was portrayed as a huge, cracked egg on struts. Climbing a ladder up to it, his back turned, was a sinister figure, an arrow embedded deep in his anus. He was naked except for a cowl. In one hand, this infernal figure grasped a set of barrel-red bagpipes, and in the other, a morning star, an ugly battle mace. This figure, probably a demon, was climbing to meet the damned souls to herd them on to punishment. The background to the drawing was most forbidding: flames clawed a winter's night; demons leapt and cavorted above the tongues of fire . . .

Athelstan turned the page. The next drawing was different. It depicted the fox of legend, Master Reynard, a cross between his paws, a mitre on his head, preaching to a congregation of ducks and geese in a poultry yard. They all thronged about, fascinated by the preacher, depicted so sanctimoniously. Yet Reynard's eye, shaded by russet fur, betrayed a cruel gleam: the mitre was about to slip and those jaws, open in sermonising, were fiercely sharp . . .

'A man who believes in the topsy-turvy world,' Athelstan whispered to himself. Similar drawings in the folio emphasised this anarchistic view of the world, and the friar once again wondered who Gregorio really was. Lost in such thoughts, he made himself as comfortable as he could on a bench and dozed for a while. He had no idea how much time had passed when he was roughly shaken awake by an anxious Cranston.

'Brother Athelstan, please, I am sorry. Azrael is here. He has struck again. Luke Gaddesden took a Tower boat and went out onto the river. The bargeman saw him. He rowed out, then the Fisher of Men, on his usual patrol . . . Well, never mind.' Cranston steadied the little friar who, roused from his sleep, swayed precariously on his feet.

Athelstan collected himself. 'And you, Sir John, weren't just visiting old friends and comrades?'

'Very interesting, Athelstan, but that must wait.'

The friar tightened his sandals, made sure that he was presentable and followed Cranston out of St Peter's across the grassy bailey towards the water-gate. A crowd had assembled there, gathered around a two-wheeled sloping handcart.

Athelstan glimpsed the top of the head and the boots of the corpse that was covered by a canvas shroud. Albinus was directing matters as Thibault conferred with the two evangelists who, deep in their cups, were grief-stricken at the sudden and tragic death of their brother. Matthew, the eldest, looked as if he would collapse and, at Thibault's urging, both evangelists returned to their chamber in King's Lodgings, a spacious mansion of wood and plaster on a stone base which served as a hostelry for guests visiting the Tower.

Cranston waited until they had gone before shouldering his way through. Thibault raised a hand in greeting, snapping his fingers at Albinus to accompany him over to King's Lodgings. The crowd began to thin. Cranston declared who he was and sketched a bow towards the eerie, sombre-clad figure of the Fisher of Men and the Fisher's principal retainer Ichthus, garbed as usual in a black tunic gathered tightly at his neck and falling to just above his well-sandalled feet. Cranston issued his orders, telling onlookers and bystanders to move away and adding that the nave of St Peter's would be the best resting place for the corpse until it was moved to the death house at St Mary le Bow.

As Cranston busied himself, Athelstan studied the Fisher and his companion. Both of these singular individuals had gone very quiet during the revolt. They and their retinue of gargoyles had simply vanished from their eerie church and mortuary, the Chapel of the Drowned Men on its deserted quayside past La Reole. Apparently they had gone into hiding deep in the wastelands

120

along the estuary. On reflection, this was a prudent move. The Fisher and his household, led by Icthus, and including a cohort of rejects and grotesques, such as Brick-Face, Maggot, Hackum and Sham-Soul, were still city officials. They harvested the Thames on behalf of the council, gathering corpses, the victims of suicide, accident and, of course, murder. They were feared by the commons, who envied them for the revenues they collected from both the city and those who came to their macabre mortuary to claim the corpses of relatives drowned in the Thames. Rumour had it that the Fisher was a man of great wealth, his coffers bulging with silver and gold coin, a great attraction to the wolfsheads and outlaws of the city.

The appearance of both men invariably provoked unease and disquiet. The Fisher of Men was tall, his head completely shaven, and his eye-catching, skeletal face was shrouded by a fur-lined black leather hood which only emphasised his snow-white skin. Ichthus looked like his Greek name proclaimed, a fish. Ichthus was youngish, of medium height and very thin. He had no hair, not even on his eyelids. The similarity to a fish was enhanced by his oval-shaped face and jutting cod-mouth, whilst his fingers and toes were webbed. Little wonder he could swim like a porpoise, swift and slippery as an eel.

Cranston now had the measure of what was happening. Gregorio also joined them, volunteering to help push the corpse cart across into St Peter's. Cranston shooed away the curious, saying that only those involved in the '*Qaestio Mortis* – the Question of Death' would be admitted to the chapel besides himself and Athelstan. This included Gregorio, who declared he had seen Luke Gaddesden down near the water-gate earlier in the day. The Tower bargeman was also summoned along with the Fisher of Men and Ichthus, who'd actually found the murdered clerk slumped in his boat out on the river.

Once Cranston had closed the chapel door on the curious throng, Athelstan pulled back the corpse cloth. Luke Gaddesden lay sprawled, his face nightmarish in both colour and expression, a lurid blueish-red with tongue thrust out and eyes popping, the agonised death throes caused by the garrotte string tied so tightly around his throat. Athelstan insisted that he first administer the last rites though he found anointing Luke's twisted face chilled his heart and belly. Once finished, he grasped the dagger that Sir John had handed over. He slit the garrotte string, then held it up to read the same murderous message as before on the square of stiffened parchment: 'Lord Azrael greets you'. Athelstan handed this to Cranston then scrutinised the corpse from head to toe. Luke Gaddesden was dressed as Athelstan had last seen him, garbed in the livery of the Chancery. The friar turned the corpse over, searching for any other injury, but he could find none. He felt the dead man's clothing; there was some heavy dampness on the left knee but nothing really significant. Athelstan murmured a prayer, crossed himself and glanced

122

quickly around. Gregorio stood in the shadows thrown by two of the drum-like pillars which ranged either side of St Peter's.

'Brother?' Athelstan called out. 'You claim to have seen Luke Gaddesden down near the water-gate?'

'I certainly did. Not many people wear the livery of the English Royal Chancery.'

'Have you seen him before?' Cranston demanded.

'Perhaps.' Gregorio half smiled.

'Please don't fence and parry with us!' Cranston snapped. He pointed at the corpse. 'Have you seen this man before?'

'Perhaps, I may have glimpsed him at the Lute Boy, but more than that I cannot say. When I saw him near the water-gate, I think he was probably looking for you.' He gestured at the bargeman. 'I mean, he wanted a boat.'

'Did you notice anything untoward?' Cranston demanded.

'Well, the water-gate and the mooring place are fairly deserted, aren't they?' Gregorio replied. 'There's a horrid stench. A Tower archer told me that the river sweeps in rubbish which is trapped there. He also said that's the way traitors are brought here.'

'That's correct,' Cranston agreed.

'Anyway, on my journey around the Tower I went down there. I am sure I glimpsed Gaddesden, very much the worse for drink.'

Athelstan went back to stare down at the corpse. The friar murmured a prayer and crossed himself. The mystery was gathering! How could a fairly young, vigorous man in a small, narrow boat on the Thames be strangled so expertly yet with little or no sign of resistance or struggle? Gaddesden had been savagely attacked, he must have died thrashing in agony. Even if he was drugged or drunk, surely there would be some evidence of a violent confrontation between assailant and victim?

'I need to see the boat,' Athelstan stated, 'now, before . . .'

Cranston agreed, virtually forcing the Tower bargeman through the door and across the bailey to the water-gate. The crowd had now dispersed. Only one archer stood on guard. The bargeman recognised the skiff as the one in which the corpse had been found. The Fisher of Men and Ichthus, who had also followed them out, agreed.

'Let us have a look.' Athelstan crouched down. He pinched his nose at the disgusting stench from the filthy moat water which slapped against the iron-grilled water-gate before flowing back towards the narrow quayside. The boat bobbing on the swirl looked forlorn; really nothing more than a narrow punt with three crude plank seats at prow, stern and middle, with two short oars fixed on iron rings on either side. The ugly grey boat betrayed nothing about the heinous act committed on it.

'No blood, no sign of violence,' Athelstan murmured. 'No evidence of any resistance.' He leaned down closer. 'The inside of the boat is almost bone-dry. Yet if someone climbed in to strangle Gaddesden sitting on the middle bench it would be obvious, surely? This boat would have twisted and rolled from side to side, taking on water. Yet there is nothing.' Athelstan straightened up and turned to the bargeman. 'Would you agree?' The man nodded.

'What you say is true, Brother,' the Fisher of Men called out. 'These boats are not the safest at the best of times. When the river becomes choppy, they take on water.'

'And where did you see him?' Athelstan asked the bargeman: the fellow refused to meet the friar's gaze. Instead, mumbling beneath his breath, he took Athelstan around through the water-gate and onto the narrow quayside which ran along the base of the Tower wall.

'Lonely and bleak!' Athelstan observed. The friar also noticed the deep enclaves in the Tower wall all caked with the dirt swept in by both wind and water: places where people could huddle waiting for boats – now moored halfway down the quayside attached to ropes lashed around iron poles.

'Few people use these boats now,' the bargeman murmured. 'They are not very safe and, above all, you have to row yourself, which is not recommended on this river.' Athelstan agreed: he would never dream of oaring a boat along the Thames. Moleskin the boatman had begged him never to do this.

'But you saw Master Gaddesden come out here and take a boat?'

'Yes, I did.'

Shaking his head in disbelief, Athelstan returned to the chapel. He moved a bench and set it before the rood screen then stared at the others gathering around. The friar wondered about the ghosts lurking in the encircling shadows of the church and shivered as his gaze caught a row of ugly gargoyle faces clustered at the top of one of the pillars. He glanced up at the lancet window. The light pouring through it illuminated the various carvings but it also showed that the day was beginning to die. It must now be late afternoon and Athelstan wondered how much longer they would have to stay here. He needed to return to Southwark. He had pressing business in his parish. There were panniers to be packed, matters to be settled, letters and instructions to be drawn up – yet, Athelstan conceded to himself, the mysteries now confronting him here held their own macabre attraction . . .

'Brother?' Cranston called out.

'Yes, yes. My apologies.' The friar beckoned the bargeman who stood nearby. 'What did you see?'

'That dead clerk in his livery. Well, he was very much alive then. He had his hood pulled up but that's usual on the river where a strong breeze carries a spray. People often protect their hair and face. Anyway, he clambered into the boat and pushed off, rowing out towards midstream.'

'This man here?' Athelstan pointed at the corpse.

'The same. I am sure of it.'

Athelstan stared hard at the bargeman, who seemed agitated and frightened.

'What is the matter?' Athelstan got to his feet and walked over. 'What's your name?' he demanded.

'Maulkin.'

'Maulkin, are you frightened?'

'No. Yes. Well . . .' The boatman fingered his lips. 'I mean, I saw the clerk, the one who lies murdered here. I followed him onto the quayside. I saw him get in and row away. At the time there was nothing out of the ordinary. However, who or what followed him out onto the river and cut off his breath, I don't know. I mean, is it a devil?'

Athelstan could see the man was truly frightened, so he dismissed him, though he felt Maulkin had not told him the truth. The friar had no evidence for that, nothing but a nagging suspicion. Once he was gone, Athelstan turned to the Fisher and Ichthus sitting close together on one of the wall benches. He then stared quickly around. Gregorio, still and silent as a shadow, sat on the steps leading up into the sanctuary. Cranston leaned against a pillar staring into the darkness. Athelstan walked over to the corpse. Once again he scrutinised it from head to toe and, just for a brief moment, Athelstan felt a profound chill, a nameless fear, a spasm of sudden terror as if his own soul was brushing real evil. Was the assassin here in the chapel hovering close by? Or was it the realisation that once again the Angel of Death, the Lord Azrael, a true demon in human flesh, had struck, guttering out a life as you would a candle flame? Athelstan took a deep breath and walked over to the Fisher.

'Tell me, what did you actually see?'

'We were busy on the river.' The Fisher's voice was clipped with tension. 'There are those who

127

say we kill people to increase our revenue. Down near the water-gate I heard whispers that we'd done the same to this poor soul . . .'

'Nonsense!' Cranston barked. 'A farrago of lies!'

'I would agree with my learned coroner,' Athelstan murmured, 'so do continue.'

'Brother, we are very busy. We are still finding corpses of those killed during the Great Revolt, river-soaked and heavy. Some of these were drowned with weights in their clothing, but as the cadavers begin to rot the weights slide away . . .'

'Yes, yes.' Athelstan soothed.

'We were in our own barge. Ichthus kept a sharp eye for anything untoward then we saw this little boat, the narrow skiff you inspected. It was just bobbing on the water with a man squatting, bending over slightly. He was seated on the middle plank. He was kept upright by the seat in the stern which basically trapped his legs. The boat seemed to be drifting, the oars, locked in their clasps, trailing the water either side. Now the river was very calm. Perfect weather for a crossing, Brother. The man was leaning against the oars but he never moved. Curious, I hailed him, but there was no reply. We approached and hailed him again; obviously something was very wrong. We rowed alongside, knocking the oars away, drawing in as close as we could. I pulled back the hood, it was ghastly, that garrotte string tight around his throat! Now, from the very start there was a mystery. I have heard of people dying quietly, the heart failing, even the effects

128

of apoplexy. But how could anyone have strangled a man on a boat like that? Sir John, Brother Athelstan, have you seen it? If two people just sat in that boat it would be quite dangerous. If someone got in and began a violent struggle with its occupant, trying to strangle him, the boat would capsize and hurl both of them into the water.'

'That's the mystery,' Athelstan murmured. He crouched down again and stared at the victim. 'Luke was a fairly vigorous young man who knew he faced danger.' He tapped the dead man's belt. 'He carried a dagger still in its sheath. He was probably used to the river with a liking to fish or snare birds. I recall him saying that he would do that today to while away the time. So he takes one of the small rowing boats or skiffs kept tied to the Tower mooring and off he goes. The bargeman saw him leave and no one has offered any evidence to the contrary. Sometime later the boat is found floating, Luke Gaddesden sitting there slightly stooped. There is no other sign or mark of violence except that this clerk has been silently garrotted to death in a narrow, shallow boat on a busy, swift-running river.' Athelstan got to his feet, wiping his hands on his robes. 'Azrael the assassin acts and strikes as if he has no body. He can kill, strangle, but leave no trace except that garrotte string around his victim's throat. Now I recognise Azrael to be a man of sharp mind and wicked soul, but this?'

'Brother Athelstan,' Cranston stepped out of the shadows, 'I would like urgent words with you and our good friend the Fisher of Men.'

Athelstan, accompanied by the Fisher and Ichthus, followed the coroner out. Cranston gave instructions to the archer on guard regarding Gaddesden's corpse. Athelstan glanced up at the sky: it was now late afternoon and he wondered how long he would be delayed here. He breathed a prayer for patience and followed Cranston through the main door of King's Lodgings. Cranston had a word with the porter, who ushered them into a small antechamber furnished with tables, chairs and a poorly painted triptych celebrating the life and martyrdom of Thomas a Becket.

'Most appropriate,' Cranston murmured, pointing to the painting. He closed the door and indicated that his three companions should sit on the stools placed around the table. Cranston made himself comfortable, offering the miraculous wineskin to his guests. Athelstan refused but the Fisher and Ichthus took generous slurps; the latter went to take some more. Cranston snatched the wineskin from his bony fingers, growling that it wasn't so miraculous and he needed what was left to ease the labours of the day.

Athelstan tried to hide his exasperation. 'Sir John, we are waiting.'

'I received a message from our good friends here,' Cranston replied, pushing the wine stopper back into place. 'Then matters were overtaken by the corpse they found in that rowing boat on the Thames. Isn't that correct, my friends?'

'We'd heard about the slayings in Milk Street,' the Fisher intoned. 'After all, it's in our interest to keep a sharp eye and ear on what is happening in the city and the surrounding shires. We sent a message to our noble coroner and, God be our witness, we then encountered the corpse of that strangled clerk.' The Fisher leaned across the table, his skeletal face all taut. 'You see, Brother, that's not the first time we have come across such a murder victim. About eight days ago Ichthus found a corpse, all swollen and dirty with river water, floating in the reeds between Timberhithe and St Paul's wharf. A fairly young man, an Iberian, I believe, with his face badly marked and pecked.'

'Was he Spanish?'

'Castilian, Aragonese, Portuguese,' the Fisher shrugged, 'whatever, his skin was dark brown. A man raised under the hot sun of the south. He was naked except for a very thin linen undershirt which was tightly hemmed at the bottom. Despite being soaked I felt a weight. I undid the hem and found two newly minted coins bearing the royal insignia of Castile.'

'So he was Spanish?'

'Brother, I like to be precise. I would say Iberian. Whatever he was, he was definitely carrying Spanish coins. These had been sewn into the hem of that linen undergarment as some form of reserve if he ever lost the rest of his possessions.'

'Yes, yes,' Athelstan retorted. 'It's a common enough practice.' He tapped his own robe. 'I do it myself, a few coins hidden away to use if I have nothing else. But this man . . .?'

'Murdered, Brother Athelstan. Garrotted,

though there was no string around his neck like the one we found today. Ichthus believed the corpse was in the water probably a day and a night. In the end no one claimed the poor man's mortal remains so we handed them over to St Peter's the Less, which is the nearest church to where the corpse was found.'

'So,' Athelstan rose and walked slowly up and down the chamber, 'we have an Iberian, probably Castilian, garrotted, stripped and thrown into the Thames. Mere chance or coincidence? Did he – and this is confidential – have anything to do with our other Spaniard, Brother Gregorio?'

Cranston rapped the table. 'What is equally interesting, is that we have had no enquiry either at Westminster or the Tower about a subject of a Spanish prince, whoever that maybe, as missing in London. The victim certainly was a man of means – he wore a linen undergarment and he had two pure silver coins hidden away. Now if he was a merchant or the member of a visiting envoy's household, you would agree, Brother, enquiries would have been made? Our sheriffs would have been instructed to search for a missing person, but in this case, I wonder . . .'

A knock on the door made him pause. Albinus sauntered into the room. 'Sir John, Brother Athelstan, my Lord of Gaunt demands your presence in the Council Chamber.'

Part Four
Venenum: a Hideous Poison

As the bells of the Tower begun tolling in common with those in the hundreds of steeples throughout the city, Ralph Chobham, mine host and owner of the Sign of Hope, a magnificent tavern, the first on the pilgrim route from Southwark to Canterbury, was in a most jovial mood. Chobham lay back against the bolster in his own bedchamber on the first gallery of his splendid hostelry. Chobham's heart sang with contentment. The Sign of Hope, despite all the recent troubles, was prospering. The marching of troops here and there, the thundering hooves of mail-clad knights, the surging hordes of rebel peasant armies; the great clouds of dust thrown up by this cavalcade or that, the raucous noise of battle chants and songs of protest were now relics of the past. The Upright Men had marched on London under their great, swirling black and blood-red banners. Wat Tyler, Jack Straw and Simon Grindcobbe had led their unruly hordes out of Kent up into Southwark. Eventually they had crossed the great bridge intent on victory only to meet fierce resistance, bloody defeat and vengeful pursuit. The Great Community of the Realm had collapsed and the rebels had fled like pigeons before marauding hawks. Ah well, it was all over.

Chobham swung his fat legs off the broad four-poster bed, truly a place of pleasure with its oaken columns and cream and rose counterpane with matching tester and curtains. He picked up the pure woollen robe from the chest at the foot of the bed and wrapped it around his plump, pink body. Chobham stared down at the bed, still creased from where young but nubile Marisa had given him such splendid sport. After a great deal of furtive pursuit and a hunt which had lasted for weeks, Chobham had at last brought the young chambermaid to bed. Oh, she had teased him till his mind was plagued and his dreams troubled, though she had done so carefully. Marisa only indulged in such games when Chobham's sharp-eyed wife Margaret, who was even fatter than her husband, was not circling and watching as a buzzard would a cornfield. However, when she could, Marisa had acted all enticing, with her tightly fitting smock and bodice, or her hips swaying so provocatively as she climbed the stairs before the landlord. Or when she sat on a stool and leaned forward to display even more of her splendid breasts. Ah well, Margaret had insisted on visiting her brother, owner of the Mitre tavern in Farringdon ward, so Chobham had seized his opportunity. Marisa had brought him up a goblet of the finest Rhineland wine. She had closed the door and the merriment had begun. Marisa had acted all coy and reluctant, but the implicit threat of dismissal, along with the prospect of future enhancement – not to mention a silver coin and a few mouthfuls of cold, white wine – had won the day. Marisa had proved to be adept, skilled and enthusiastic in their games on the bed. Chobham certainly looked forward to future assignations.

The taverner moved over to the oriel window, pulling back the shutters and staring down at the front of his tavern. The great rutted yard lay quiet. Chobham peered through the glass up towards the ancient road which ran past the curtain wall and majestic lychgate of the Sign of Hope. Chobham was very proud of the entrance to his tavern. He remembered standing there cheering the rebels as they streamed towards Southwark; ferocious Earthworms in their garish dress, faces painted, jostled with yeoman archers, veterans from the French wars and all the outlaws of Kent and Essex: the wolfsheads, peace-breakers, rapists, arsonists, fire-drakes and all the merry crew. Chobham had watched them go with their stupid dreams of establishing a new Eden along the banks of the Thames and a heavenly Jerusalem arising from the ashes of Cheapside and Farringdon. He congratulated himself on his cunning. Secretly he had assisted the rebels with money, provender and other purveyance. Of course, as he often now proclaimed in the tavern taproom, the revolt had been doomed from the start.

Chobham had stood under that fortified gateway and watched those same rebels, beaten and fearful, flee out of London back into the shires. He had closed both his soul and his door to their plight. No mercy, no compassion. Instead he openly supported the city council, the sheriff's men and the great lords of the shire whose troops poured in and out of London to inflict cruel and vindictive punishment on all suspects. Chobham himself had witnessed many hangings on the great gallows at the crossroads further down the pilgrim path. Anyway, the revolt was over. Kent had been brutally pacified. The pilgrim path was now open for all and the faithful came flocking, eager to pray before Becket's blissful bones, one large party after another. He was particularly pleased at the group coming out of St Erconwald's in Southwark.

Chobham jumped and almost screamed as he felt the garrotte cord slip around his throat and begin to tighten.

'Do not move,' the voice hissed. 'Do not turn.' The garrotte string tightened slightly. 'Do you understand? Nod if you do!' The taverner hurried to obey. 'Now listen, Master Chobham, and listen well. You are safe, you will not be hurt as long as you do exactly what I tell you to. Lift your right hand in agreement. Good! If you disobey me, I will personally ensure that your good wife Margaret knows all about your bed sports with young Marisa and others.' Chobham swallowed hard. He had not even heard the bedroom door open, not a sound. The tavern was full of guests. One of these must have been watching him. Chobham, terrified but his mind now whirling, recalled one individual sitting hooded and visored close to the inglenook. 'Don't worry about who I am, Master Chobham. I am the Lord Azrael, the Angel of Death who comes swooping and swift, eager to envelop you in his cold embrace.

136

I know of your wicked ways, not only your dalliance with the doxy Marisa but the sustenance you supplied to the rebels. A bill of complaint could be submitted to the sheriff in Colchester or even my Lord of Gaunt's minions at Westminster. You could still hang or, even worse, suffer the full rigour of the penalties for treason. Now,' the cord tightened then relaxed, 'all should be well, Master Chobham. Do as I say. Listen very carefully about those pilgrims coming from St Erconwald's and what is to be done . . .'

Athelstan stared down the long oval table. At the far end Gaunt slouched in his throne-like chair. To the regent's right sat Thibault, and Albinus on his left; both henchmen looked noticeably ill at ease. Gaunt had loosened the Lancastrian SS collar around his throat and sat playing with it, moving the gorget around his fingers. He looked as if he had drunk swiftly and deeply. He had staggered to his feet when Albinus had ushered them in and, swaying backwards and forwards, forcefully thanked the coroner for his help during the recent treasonable affray on Tower Green. He toasted Cranston with his goblet before wearily waving both of them to their chairs. The evangelists were already there, each with a brimming goblet before them, their faces stricken with grief. For a while, there was silence. Athelstan could even hear the soft strings of a harp and the melodies of other musical instruments as Gaunt's household prepared to entertain the regent at supper immediately after sunset.

'My Lord,' Thibault shifted the writing tray placed in front of him, 'we thank God for our own safe deliverance today. The attack on you,' Thibault raised his hand delicately, 'heinous though it be, was really nothing more than sparks from dying embers: the last desperate acts of a few desperate men. God, however, has vindicated our prince, but we must now confront a much more deadly foe, this Azrael.' Thibault paused as Gaunt tapped the table, nodding vigorously in agreement. 'Azrael,' Thibault continued, 'is now guilty of the murder of Master Mephan, Luke Gaddesden,' he paused at a groan from one of the brothers, 'not to mention our most trusted courier Empson, nor must we forget those two unfortunates who lived with Mephan. Brother Athelstan, have you made any progress?'

Beneath the table Athelstan gently touched Cranston's arm as a sign to remain silent. 'Master Thibault,' he replied, 'we have scarcely begun. This Azrael literally flies from one place to the other. Each of the murders you mention is shrouded in deep, cloying mystery. I cannot make any sense of the reason behind these gruesome slayings.' Athelstan was determined to be as forthright as he could. 'The root question is not so much how but why this assassin Azrael should be murdering members of your Secret Chancery.'

'The Secret Chancery is not mine,' Gaunt said. 'It's the King's, the Crown's.'

'But in truth and in practice, those clerks answer to you, Master Thibault,' Athelstan snapped. 'Do they know something they shouldn't? Are they being silenced, punished, or both?'

Thibault forced a smile. 'Brother Athelstan, of course these clerks know matters of great confidence. They work at the heart of the Secret Chancery. The same is true of myself, Albinus and, of course, His Grace. Even you, Athelstan, together with Sir John, have seen, heard and learnt things others certainly have not. I understand you also have been threatened, Brother? The Dominican priest of a poor parish in Southwark . . .'

'The answer to that is quite obvious,' Cranston broke in. 'Our little friar here is not a member of your household, Master Thibault. But you know, I know and God knows that this Dominican friar will do his very best to trap Azrael and bring him to judgement; that's why he's been threatened.'

Thibault ignored Sir John's outburst. 'There could be other reasons why these clerks have been slain, Brother Athelstan.'

'Such as?'

'His Grace and I are being weakened. We are losing loyal and skilled retainers, men who serve us body and soul, day and night against all enemies both within and without. Some dark soul has laid siege and broken through to inflict terrible injury deep in our household against our most loyal and trusted henchmen.'

'I would like to speak.' Matthew Gaddesden brought his hand down hard against the table. 'Your Grace, Master Thibault, God knows you have had no better servants than myself and my brothers.' Matthew paused in tearful and mournful silence, then continued: 'We truly believe that both Simon and Luke were murdered because of our fidelity and loyalty to the House of Lancaster. We played a crucial part in the suppression of the late Great Revolt. We now pay the price.'

'As do we all.' Albinus spoke up, his voice surprisingly strong. He opened his jerkin and took out a bulging pouch which he handed to Thibault, who shook out the contents: three garrotte strings, each with its own macabre message attached to it.

'They were found,' Thibault declared, 'looped over the door handle to this chamber. One for Albinus, one for myself and the third, undoubtedly for His Grace.' Thibault slid the three strings down the surface of the gleaming table for Athelstan to catch.

'When were they found?' he asked.

'I found them,' Albinus replied, 'just over an hour ago as the first curfew bell tolled.'

Athelstan glanced at Cranston. Apart from his short outburst, the coroner had remained silent throughout, though that was nothing new. Cranston detested the regent; he often proclaimed he did not trust him as far as he could spit, and he preferred to keep silent in his presence. The coroner studied the garrotte strings then pushed them away and wiped his fingers on his jerkin.

'So, Your Grace,' Cranston said slowly, 'what is to be done?'

'My Lord Coroner, what you do so well. You have already referred to it. Let your little friar trap this assassin then you can hang him from the highest gallows in London.'

'Easier said than done, I agree,' Thibault intervened tactfully, 'but at least we will escape the danger in the city. You leave for Canterbury on Monday morning?'

'Just after dawn,' Athelstan confirmed.

'Good.' Thibault rubbed his hands together. 'We will join you – Albinus, myself and our two clerks. The summer heat means poor Master Luke must be buried tomorrow morning after the churching of his corpse and the requiem has been sung.'

'We agree. We believe it will be safer,' Matthew broke in, his face all worried, 'to be out of London, and indeed to be closer to you, Brother Athelstan.'

'It would be safer.' Gaunt leaned forward. He no longer looked or acted as if befuddled from drink. 'Equally important is what will happen in Canterbury. As you know, Sir John, Brother Athelstan, I have, through my marriage to the beloved Spanish Infanta Constanza, a claim to the crown of Castile.' Gaunt's voice rose as if he was about to proclaim his titles and rights. Athelstan just nodded, even as he recalled that Constanza may be 'beloved' but Gaunt was also deeply smitten by the charms of his mistress and the mother of a brood of illegitimate children, Katherine Swynford. 'Envoys from Castile,' Gaunt continued, 'will very soon land at Dover. They are deeply desirous of visiting Becket's shrine. Master Thibault, together with our beloved clerks here, will meet and treat with the Castilians in Canterbury. They can negotiate with the Spanish envoys in a much safer, more

141

protected place. And I agree: it would be more prudent for them to be out of London away from the malign doings of Azrael.' He straightened in his chair. 'Is there any other business? No, I don't think so. Athelstan, I wish you well.'

Athelstan held up a hand. 'Your Grace, before we leave! We, who have all been threatened by Azrael – is there anything at all that Sir John and I should be told which might assist us to discover the truth?'

Silence greeted his question and Gaunt glanced away. Albinus tapped the table.

'Brother Athelstan, before I forget, you had a visitor, a physician from Farringdon, Master Giole Limut. He approached the guards at the Lion Gate and left a message for you. He regretted not meeting you, but unless he hears to the contrary, he will be with you tomorrow morning at the Jesus mass . . .'

Athelstan stared round at his small congregation who stood, sat or squatted within the rood screen of St Erconwald's. A lovely day, Athelstan mused; even at this early hour the sunlight was pouring through the windows. The friar turned and blessed Peter the Penniless who was kneeling, hands devoutly clasped, before turning back to the altar. He winked at Benedicta and Crim, both of whom looked fresh-faced, whilst the rest were more sleepy-eyed. Physician Giole was there openly admiring Benedicta, as was Brother Gregorio, who had been waiting for Athelstan as he left the council chamber late yesterday afternoon. Eager with speculation, Gregorio had

142

questioned Athelstan closely about Gaunt and Master Thibault, heatedly discussing their determination to join Athelstan's pilgrimage to Canterbury.

The Spanish friar had talked unceasingly till they reached Southwark. Athelstan, who'd hired a porter to carry Gregorio's baggage, breathed a prayer of thanksgiving when they reached the Piebald. He paid off the porter and lodged his garrulous companion with a whole host of his parishioners in the sprawling tavern. From what Benedicta had told him, Gregorio had taken to Athelstan's flock and they to him, like long-lost, beloved siblings. Apparently Gregorio had performed a Spanish dance, told some very amusing tales about the sexual exploits of a Spanish Dominican, sung a haunting love song and finished the evening by leading them in a wild, whirling dance around the taproom. They had drunk and drunk again and certainly heard the chimes of midnight. Gregorio, now flanked by an adoring Cecily and her sister Clarissa, reminded Athelstan of Bonaventure after he had feasted deeply on a bowl of cream. Indeed, even that great, solitary tomcat seemed fascinated by the new arrival and now squatted close to Gregorio's feet.

'Judas-cat!' Athelstan whispered to himself. He looked to his left where Amelia and Robert the clerk stood, the latter scratching his face with stubby fingers stained with ink. Athelstan recalled Master Giole's belief that Peter the Penniless could only be fed some noxious potion to disturb the humours of his mind by a very skilled

143

apothecary or herbalist. Athelstan had scrutinised Robert very carefully and concluded he was a minor chancery clerk who might even have difficulty counting a column of figures or writing out a proper bill of sale, let alone concoct some subtle potion.

Benedicta coughed loudly, followed by Crim. Athelstan smiled, blessed them all and announced mass was ended. He did not return to the sacristy but walked out of the sanctuary and across to the small chantry chapel of St Erconwald's. The cloistered warmth and fragrance of that serene place always soothed him: the stained-glass window bright with light, the thick turkey carpets on the floor, the cushioned seat and prie-dieu before the altar, the air sweetened with incense and crushed herbs. Athelstan swiftly divested, and sat down on a chair to stare at the crucifix. He thought back to a peculiar incident which had occurred after the council meeting in the Tower the previous evening. He and Cranston had gone downstairs out into the bailey when he realised he had left his ave beads behind. He made his excuses and hastened back up the twisting spiral staircase into the council chamber, where he found his rosary. He was halfway down again, passing one of the stairwells, when he heard voices from a nearby chamber where the door had been left half-open. Athelstan imme-diately recognised Gaunt's rich voice, now clear and precise, not marred or slurred by drink. He was speaking in Spanish to a man who boldly replied: Athelstan was sure it was Albinus – was he educated in the Spanish tongue? Why should

Gaunt and his henchman talk so swiftly in a different language unless they were discussing business of a highly confidential and secretive nature?

Athelstan's thoughts drifted to Cranston, and he idly wondered what his friend was doing – probably preparing for Canterbury. The coroner had certainly planned their pilgrimage to the last detail. Sir John believed they could travel fifteen miles on a good summer's day. They would spend their first evening out of Southwark at the Sign of Hope tavern where chambers had been hired and arrangements made with mine host Master Chobham about food and sleeping places. There was a gentle knocking on the chantry chapel door, then Gregorio's smiling face appeared through the open door.

'Brother, may I have a word about these mysteries?'

Athelstan shrugged and gestured at Gregorio to enter and sit on the wall bench.

'I have heard about your present troubles.'

'Which ones?' Athelstan laughed. 'Brother, I feel like someone in sanctuary surrounded by a sea of troubles. By the way, I gather you have become firm friends with Cecily and Clarissa. Let us pray that Master Tuddenham does not return.'

'My thanks to the two ladies.' Gregorio grinned. Once again Athelstan secretly wondered who this smiling Spanish friar truly was, even though Gregorio had come into the sacristy before mass to show him letters written in Latin, signed and sealed by the Minister General of the Order of the Friars of the Sack, introducing Gregorio and describing his mission.

'Now, you wish to discuss my present troubles?' Athelstan asked abruptly.

'Brother Athelstan, I have remembered something from my conversations with the lovely Felicia who has now gone to God.'

'Oh aye?'

'Oh aye, Brother,' Gregorio echoed. 'We were in the Mitre, having great sport in my chamber. Afterwards,' he continued blithely, 'we talked about her life. I asked about the future. Now Felicia could chatter like a spring sparrow. I asked how long she would stay with the Way of all Flesh and act as a maid for Master Mephan. She replied that she expected great things and changes for the better in the months ahead.'

'Did you ask what she meant?'

'Of course, but it was only bedchamber chatter. She said she would stay in Master Mephan's household because now the revolt was crushed, he especially would greatly prosper, and she with him. One day he would be rich and live in great splendour. A strange remark, Athelstan, from an ageing clerk, even one who works in the Royal Chancery.'

'Strange indeed,' Athelstan agreed, watching the Spaniard curiously. 'There is something else?'

'Yes, there is.' Gregorio took out a freshly minted silver piece from his belt wallet and offered it to Athelstan, who examined it carefully. He realised it was an accurate replica of what the Fisher of Men had found on that corpse,

146

found floating near St Paul's Wharf: a newly fashioned coin bearing the arms and insignia of Castile. 'It's a mass offering,' Gregorio explained. 'I would like you to say a requiem as soon as possible for Bernadine.'

'Bernadine?'

'My brother,' Gregorio explained. 'It will soon be the anniversary of his death. A mass has to be said, a requiem sung.'

'Tomorrow,' Athelstan declared, getting to his feet. He walked over and thrust the coin back into Gregorio's hand. '*Pax et Bonum*, Brother,' he whispered. 'I shall celebrate the mass for charity's sake and pray for the repose of your brother's soul.' Gregorio's smile faded, replaced, for the briefest of moments, by a look of profound sadness.

'Thank you,' he murmured. He opened the door and slipped out of the chapel. Athelstan intended to follow when Amelia and Robert came bustling in.

'Father, Peter seems more composed,' Amelia began. She was dressed quite sprucely in a white veil and spring-green gown with a heavy gold brooch at her throat and jewelled bracelets around her wrists.

'Yes, he does,' Athelstan agreed.

She grasped Athelstan's fingers. 'Father, we would like to stay here for the day. Peter says you are going on pilgrimage to Canterbury and that he will accompany you. If he does, we must go as well.'

'Oh, you would be most welcome.' Athelstan concealed his deepening disquiet. As he had

147

remarked to Sir John, the way matters were proceeding, half of London would accompany them!

'In the meantime, Father, is there anything we can do to help – I mean around the church?'

Athelstan glimpsed the empty vase before the statue of St Erconwald's and remembered others had not been filled. 'You could pick some flowers in God's Acre – God knows we have a magnificent array – and fill the empty vases around this church. Peter would be most comforted by your presence . . .'

Both Amelia and Robert were enthusiastic in their reply and set off straight away to do so. Athelstan watched them go and then walked down to meet Physician Giole, who was waiting close by the St Christopher pillar near the entrance to the church. He and Athelstan exchanged the kiss of peace.

'Matters Spanish,' Athelstan murmured, stepping back.

'Pardon?'

'Oh, I don't know. Perhaps it's John of Gaunt's claim to Castile, his wife being the Infanta Constanza, the presence of Brother Gregorio and, of course, your good self. I feel something of Spain has entered my life. What is your story, Giole? Come.' Athelstan gestured. 'It's a beautiful day to sit in the sun and talk.' They walked outside and made themselves comfortable on the bench Crispin the carpenter had built into a recess to the left of the main door of the church.

'I came to the Tower yesterday afternoon.' Giole turned his face to catch the sun. 'No, that's not true, I came here first and that beautiful widow-woman told me where you were, so I hurried back over the bridge. I fear water and I hate crossing that river by barge. I just dread it. Anyway, I reached the Tower, but this was after the attack. Archers guarded every entrance to the fortress and I didn't have a pass, so I left a message. I wanted to tell you about the warning as well as assure you that I will be here before dawn on Monday next.' The physician tapped his foot noisily. 'More importantly, Beatrice and I wanted to invite you to supper last night in our banqueting chamber, but . . .' he waved his hands. Athelstan patted the physician on the shoulder.

'My friend, I shall certainly take up that invitation on our return from Canterbury.'

Giole shifted on the bench to face Athelstan. 'Meals, food – that's where it all began, Brother. Beatrice and myself are the children of cooks. I mean, real cooks as skilled as any craftsmen. In Toledo our parents hired their service out to what you call tavern masters. The philosopher Galen says, "Good food and good health have always been the closest of allies." I was raised to make spiced chestnut cream, dates mixed with egg and cheese, the sharpest of brie tart and figs stuffed with cinnamon eggs.'

'Stop!' Athelstan laughed. 'You are making me hungry. Thank God Sir John is not here.'

'Good food led me to the study of herbs, potions and how they affect the humours of the body, Giole continued. 'I studied at the cathedral schools before going on to the universities of

149

Salamanca, Paris and finely Salerno in Southern Italy. The Arabs have a great deal to teach us; they, rather than us, are the guardians of the ancients. Anyway, I came back to Toledo. I have known and loved Beatrice since I was a boy. We married and decided to combine our skills and talents. Time passed. Your Lord of Gaunt and other English lords came to Castile forming allegiances, alliances and treaties on both military and matrimonial matters. Ties between our two kingdoms have always been very close. The present king's great grandfather was the son of a Castilian princess. As you know, our Princess Constanza married my Lord of Gaunt and came to England accompanied by a large Castilian retinue.' Giole placed his hand on his chest and bowed mockingly. 'Myself, Beatrice and our two children are part of that retinue. England is good for us despite the recent troubles. They passed over us without harm or hurt, which is why we are so pleased to join your pilgrimage to give thanks to God and all his great saints.

'One other thing,' Giole lowered his voice, 'I spent yesterday playing the assassin.' He gestured back at the church. 'I remembered our discussion about Peter the Penniless, the poor man in sanctuary. I opened my books and manuscripts to study deadly potions. I was correct: there are certain powders and juices distilled from this herb or that plant which, if administered in small doses, will cause dire dreams and hideous illusions as the humours of the mind crack and mix.' Giole rubbed his hands. Athelstan hid his smile: the physician reminded him of his good friend

Brother Philippe at St Bartholomew's who had the same constant, deep curiosity with anything to do with physic or medicine, be it for the body or the mind. 'Athelstan, you must have heard about the witches and warlocks who claim that they can fly through the midnight sky to join the festival of fiends and dance with demons in some moonlight glade? They really believe this because they have experienced it, and they have done so because they imbibe noxious potions which create a world of eerie dreams, erotic fantasies and hideous nightmares.'

'And the source of these noxious potions?'

'You would be surprised, Athelstan. Go into any good, common garden and you will find enough poison to annihilate a small village. The glistening skin of a toad and the juices they secrete; certain wild mushrooms; herbs known as belladonna, banewort, deadly nightshade, lily of the valley. All of these are killers, but in minute – and I mean very minute – doses, certain alarming symptoms can be provoked which eventually pass. We considered the possibility that Peter's wife Amelia and Robert the clerk could be feeding him some tainted substance but they are not apothecaries, herbalists or leeches. Moreover, I do constant business with the guilds in the city. I assure you, Athelstan, the purchase of certain powders would be noted and remembered and sooner or later discussed . . .'

'Good morrow, Father.'

Athelstan turned, shading his eyes, and peered up at the Hangman of Rochester. He introduced both men, explaining that the hangman's real

151

name was Giles of Sempringham. As the hangman gave the reason for his two names, Athelstan studied his parishioner very closely. This eerie individual supervised the gallows and gibbets at Tyburn and Smithfield, but he was also a highly skilled artist who spent every available hour either dreaming about some wall painting or preparing to create it in St Erconwald's or elsewhere. The hangman seemed much more composed recently: he'd lost that agitation caused by his involvement in the Great Revolt. Even the hangman's straw-coloured hair was beginning to grow again after he had shaved it all off when he was forced to go into hiding during the recent troubles. The hangman always proclaimed he was an Upright Man, although once the revolt had broken out, a number of the Earthworms wanted to settle grievances with him over the execution of some of their comrades.

'You are busy today?'

'No, Father.' The hangman brushed his dirty smock all stained with streaks of paint, 'If you are agreeable, there is a small painting I would like to begin: a wall fresco close to the leper squint about sinners coming to judgement, and I will have these arraigned before Christ's High Court: the fornicators, the gamblers, the gluttons and the panders.'

'Yes,' Athelstan laughed, 'we have discussed this before, but remember we leave for Canterbury on Monday.'

'How could I forget?' The hangman nodded at the physician. He was about to leave when Athelstan grasped him by the arm.

'My good friend, a favour.' Athelstan got to his feet, and extended his other hand to the physician, who clasped it. 'Master Giole, if you have no other business with me, I would like to invite the hangman here into the sacristy to garrotte me, or at least try to, and you to witness it.' Athelstan laughed at the shocked surprise on both men's faces. 'Come.'

They entered the church. Athelstan led them up the nave under the rood screen, stopping only to genuflect before the pyx, and to greet Peter the Penniless. Once they were in the sacristy, Athelstan closed the door firmly behind them.

'Now, my friend, the garrotte.' Athelstan blessed himself swiftly. 'You have strangled many a criminal on the public gallows, have you not?' Athelstan opened his purse and drew out the garrotte string, then handed it to the hangman, who examined it curiously. 'Oh Giles?' The hangman glanced up. 'Not a word of this to my parishioners, you swear?'

'Father, I swear. I've heard about the killings in Milk Street. Some of the sheriff's posse were gossiping about it.' The hangman held the cord up. 'Fine twine, Father, much tougher than it looks.'

'An assassin, a true child of Hell, uses that, Giles. He strangles his victims but there is no trace of any struggle or resistance. For heaven's sake, yesterday this assassin was in the Tower. He left deadly warnings for others and, at the same time, strangled a clerk in a boat on the Thames, yet no one saw or heard anything untoward. Not a shred of evidence indicating resistance or the slightest

153

disturbance.' Athelstan shook his head in wonderment. 'It's almost as if the victims simply gave up their throats to be throttled.' He turned his back on the hangman. 'Well, Giles, use it now.'

Athelstan braced himself. Almost before he knew it, the cord was around his throat, tightening slightly. His hands were free and he could till lurch forwards and backwards. The hangman, fearful of hurting his priest, slipped the cord loose. Athelstan turned, rubbing his throat. 'If you were the killer and I was your victim,' he declared, 'this sacristy would be wrecked as I lurched backwards and forwards.'

'And if you had a dagger or were able to grasp a weapon or anything to use as one, you could do me grievous damage.' The hangman stepped closer, his lined white face all anxious. 'Father, are you sure you are unhurt?'

'Unhurt, my friend, but the mystery remains. Why didn't Azrael's victims fight back?'

'There are hand clasps, manacles or gyves,' the hangman offered. 'I have seen them used by the sheriff's men – wooden or metal braces which can be clasped on each wrist, held together by a tight chain. They use similar restraints on the ankles, though putting them on would be very clumsy. I cannot see any of the victims offering their arms and legs to be pinioned in such a way.'

'Especially a vigorous, young clerk on a narrow, small boat on the Thames, or indeed any of the victims in Milk Street.' Physician Giole spoke up. 'Do you remember, Athelstan, we saw no evidence of the victims being pinioned?'

'One thing you could look for,' the hangman

declared. 'Master Giole, open your hands.' The physician did so. 'Look . . .' The Hangman of Rochester traced the soft, unmarked palms of the physician's hands. 'However,' the hangman continued, 'if you use the garrotte, it would leave deep streaks, if not cuts, on your hands and fingers. I have to be very careful about the ropes I use to hang wolfsheads. The hempen is rough, coarse, it can easily burn your hands.'

'What about gloves, gauntlets?'

'On the scaffold I use heavy gauntlets, but that garrotte string requires skill and very nimble fingers clear of any obstacle. Gloves would be too thick: they might protect your skin but they would be an impediment as well. So, when you hunt your assassin, look for the burn marks on the palms of his hands. Now, Father, if you don't mind, there is a church wall I would like to examine.'

The hangman made his farewells and left. The physician followed soon afterwards, saying he would walk Athelstan's parish then go back into the city. He asked if his family could bring baggage over to be stored in readiness at St Erconwald's, and Athelstan said he could use the sacristy. Physician Giole murmured his thanks and left.

Athelstan walked back into the church. Peter the Penniless was now dozing in the enclave. Athelstan glanced up and marvelled at the sun piercing the lancet windows like rays of light from heaven. He walked down the nave and decided he would climb the church tower and recite Francis of Assisi's 'Canticle of the Sun'

155

in praise and thanksgiving for such a beautiful day. Ave beads wrapped around his hand, he slowly climbed to the top of the tower. He pushed back the trap door and pulled himself up, enjoying the feel of the summer breeze, then went and leaned against the crenellations. The friar stared up at the beautiful blue sky and began to intone verses from the canticle.

'Praise be to thee, oh Lord, for Mother Earth who nourishes and sustains us all with different flowers, fruits and herbs. Praise be to thee, oh Lord, for Brother Fire who illuminates the night for us as he is fair and merry, boisterous and strong . . .'

Once he had finished, Athelstan looked to the north where he could make out the spires and steeples of the city. Usually the friar only came up here at night to marvel at the stars, what the ancients called the 'Blossoms of the Night'. The distant sound of laughter made him look down where all of God's Acre, the great cemetery of St Erconwald's, stretched before him. He smiled as he recognised some of his parishioners. Godbless and Thaddeus were wandering back and forth, Godbless, as usual, talking incessantly to the goat, who trotted beside his master as if hanging on every word. Brother Gregorio was now being escorted by Cecily and Clarissa deeper into the cemetery. Athelstan wondered what mischief that unholy trinity would get up to amongst the thick shrubbery on the far side of God's Acre. Amelia and Robert the clerk were busy plucking wild flowers. Intrigued, Athelstan began to study both of them closely as they wandered through the spacious cemetery with its sea of bushes, wild flowers and other plants and herbs. Athelstan continued to watch until he was convinced about what he had seen.

He sat down, resting against the wall, as he plotted what to do next. Once he had decided, he went back down into the church, summoned the hangman and told him to go as fast as a lurcher through God's Acre: he was to carefully note what Amelia and Master Robert wore on their hands. He must do so secretly and tell no one except Athelstan. Intrigued, the hangman asked why. The friar said he would tell him later, but it was essential that he do exactly as he asked. The hangman hurried away and Athelstan strode up and down the nave, trying to impose order on his jumbled thoughts. He heard a sound, glanced up and smiled as Master Giole walked out of the shadows.

'Brother Athelstan, I have come to say farewell until Monday.'

'Beloved physician,' Athelstan replied, 'I have two great favours to ask of you. First, would you stay a little longer? Secondly, carefully examine what is about to be brought into this church and then,' Athelstan added as an after-thought to himself, 'I will send the hangman to my good friend Sir John Cranston . . .'

Athelstan's good friend the coroner was not in the best of moods. As Sir John informed his clerk Osbert and his scrivener Simon, the sooner he was off on his blissful pilgrimage to even more bliss with the Lady Maude, the better for all.

Cranston had risen very early, and shaved and trimmed his luxurious white beard and moustache. He'd rubbed perfumed oil into his hands and face, then donned his finest raiment: a linen shirt especially made in Cambrai, dark red woollen hose and a long but light murrey-coloured cotehardie with a dark blue mantle. Using a polished piece of steel, Cranston made sure the chain of office around his neck could be clearly seen. He then pulled on his favourite Cordovan boots and clasped his broad leather warbelt firmly around his waist, ensuring that both sword and dagger slipped easily in and out of their sheaths. Cranston felt as if he was at war with banners unfurled.

The previous evening, he had sat and watched that henchman of Satan, John of Gaunt. Cranston had stayed silent for most of the time, keen-eyed and sharp-eared. Whatever Gaunt and Thibault said, Cranston truly believed that somewhere, somehow, a great lie was being told, a tapestry of falsehoods cleverly spun by a weaver steeped in deceit. Something was very wrong, and Cranston was determined to discover what, as well as assist 'that little ferret of a friar'. The coroner had already established that, apart from Mark Gaddesden, the other evangelists had not been in the city during the Great Revolt. These three, together with Mephan, had accompanied Gaunt north to the Scottish March. Empson had been Gaunt's envoy, his link with Thibault, who had remained in the south to keep a sharp eye on what happened in London and the surrounding shires. Mark Gaddesden had also been active in London on Gaunt's affairs, but he had been trapped and executed. Only when the revolt collapsed and Gaunt decided that the Scots were no longer a threat did the regent, Mephan and the other evangelists return to Westminster. Gaunt had entered the city like a conquering hero, as if he was emulating his famous, war-like father and had won a great victory. The regent had paraded through Cheapside with banners unfurled, even though he had spent most of his time marching up and down the Scottish March and being drawn into furious arguments with the powerful Percys of Northumberland.

Cranston wondered about the real reason behind the deaths of Gaunt's clerks. The coroner was also deeply suspicious about Brother Gregorio. Was that Friar of the Sack one of Gaunt's entourage – some subtle spy, perhaps, a cunning plotter the regent had hired through his close ties with the Crown of Castile? Cranston had been busy long before dawn despatching Muckworm here and there whilst Tiptoft his courier had been equally busy collecting information. Cranston had also taken certain matters into his own hands, closely questioning Flaxwith and other city bailiffs about the habits of Simon Mephan and the evangelists, the doings of sweet Felicia at the Lute Boy and the arrest and seizure of Brother Gregorio at the Mitre.

Cranston now sat enthroned in the spacious window seat reserved especially for him in his 'favourite parish church', the magnificent Lamb of God hostelry which overlooked the broad sweep of Cheapside. Cranston had left his court chamber at the Guildhall, taking his two helpers with him – Osbert the fat-faced clerk and the more scrawny Simon the scrivener. Both men had feasted most royally on pheasant pastry and the tavern's home-brewed ale. Now, bellies full and hearts gladdened, they sat, quill-pens poised, ready to take down Sir John's conclusions.

'Item: I have,' Cranston began, 'visited the Royal Chancery at Westminster and the Tower only to establish the obvious. Mephan and the evangelists were indeed industrious, highly skilled and very loyal. I understand they were pleased to be back in London from the Scottish March. They deeply grieved the murder of their brother Mark, hearts bent on vengeance because of it. They frequented different hostelries in Cheapside. Luke Gaddesden was a little more adventurous. He was also a visitor to the Lute Boy, on more than nodding terms with the Way of all Flesh. There is, however, nothing of note here.

'Item,' Cranston took a deep drink from the frothing blackjack mine hostess had placed before him, 'Brother Gregorio is a true trouba-dour, a merry minstrel sent by his Minister General in Castile to make sure that the English friars of the Order of the Sack are safe. Apparently Gregorio knows London well. He does not consort with his community; he lodges at the Mitre and visits Felicia at the Lute Boy. They are definitely attracted to each other. This latter-day Héloïse and Abelard plan to meet at the Mitre, which is raided by city bailiffs, who know there is a fornicating friar having a merry time there. Now, the arrest of a priest given over to lust is certainly common enough in this city. We have stories by the sackful, whilst every painting I have seen on Hell or Purgatory always has a lecherous priest and his concubine as constant inhabitants in those fiery places of the afterlife.'

Cranston picked up his blackjack. 'And here's the rub, my beloved clerk and scrivener. Oh yes, here's the mystery.' Both of Cranston's colleagues looked up expectantly. They were fascinated by the story of the fornicating friar and would have loved to hear more spicy details. Indeed Simon the scrivener had already secretly promised himself a visit to the cellars of the Lute Boy, eager to meet that voluptuary, the Way of all Flesh.

'Sir John?'

'Yes, yes. Item: the Mitre was raided. Brother Gregorio was caught in flagrante delicto, though he acted the perfect gentleman and made sure the frisky Felicia escaped through a window and was gone like a thief in the night. And here's another mystery. The bailiffs at the Guildhall were informed not by any known individual, lay or clerical, but anonymously through a memorandum left in the hands of a bailiff guarding the Guildhall gates. Matters become more curious still. The memorandum is now lost, thrown away, but, from what I have recently learnt, it gave precise details about Gregorio's assignation with Felicia: the day, the time, the very hour,

161

the actual chamber and its place in the Mitre, with a very close description of Brother Gregorio and his concubine.' Cranston supped hastily at his blackjack. 'Now, you don't have to be a master of logic to conclude that the only people who would have known such details were the two lovers themselves.'

'You mean one of them informed the Guildhall?' Osbert exclaimed.

'So it would appear, as extraordinary as it may seem.'

'But why?'

'God knows.' Cranston thrust forward a stubby thumb. 'Item: the Mitre holds another mystery. Brother Gregorio certainly lodged there, a Spanish Friar of the Sack, but the landlord and his minions also recall a frequent visitor to their taproom, another Spaniard, a soldier by the look of him. He carried impedimenta, panniers and warbelt. But then he abruptly disappeared. I do wonder if his corpse was the one found almost naked floating in the reeds near St Paul's wharf.'

'Do you think that stranger had anything to do with Gregorio?'

'According to mine host and his household, they saw no tie or relationship between this mysterious Spaniard and Brother Gregorio. The stranger, who remained nameless, would drift into the taproom or the eating hall. Apparently, he met no one else and did not talk to any of the other customers at the Mitre.' Cranston thumbed his lower lip. 'I appreciate the number of Spaniards in London has increased considerably due to Gaunt's marriage to a Castilian princess, but I do find it a coincidence that these two Spaniards, both of whom are men of mystery, lodge at the same tavern. I truly wonder.'

'If they know each other, they must have met somewhere else,' Osbert declared. 'Why not the Lute Boy?'

'Good man!' Cranston breathed, smiling at Osbert. 'Of course! Anyway, gentlemen, I have now given vent to my suspicions. It's a beautiful day. Make sure everything is locked away in my chamber at the Guildhall then go and enjoy this lovely weather with your families.'

Both clerk and scrivener needed no further encouragement. They packed up their writing equipment, made their farewells and left. Cranston sat for a while brooding to himself. He wondered what Athelstan was doing then reflected on all the preparations for the pilgrimage. Cranston was looking forward to this. Indeed, he had ridden the entire pilgrim route and prepared the way at different hostelries and places, hiring chambers for himself and others whilst arranging warm, dry stables to house the rest. On hearing this, Athelstan had insisted that he too would sleep in an outhouse: 'It will take me back to my days as a soldier and scholar.'

Sir John glanced up as mine hostess, pink-cheeked and all a-fluster, hurried over and asked if he wanted more? Cranston just stared at her, his mind still distracted by the pilgrimage. He wished Thibault and his coven were not joining them. Yet he'd been informed, just recently, that they too had arranged lodgings along the way. Just why were they coming? The coroner recalled the recent attack on Gaunt in the Tower, Luke Gaddesden's strangled corpse . . .

'Sir John?' mine hostess repeated. 'Do you want more ale?'

'Monkshood!' Cranston exclaimed. 'I want to speak to Monkshood, and the sooner the better as, according to the bill given to me, he is to hang at Tyburn.'

'Sir John?'

'Monkshood, my dear. A leading Upright Man, a prisoner Gaunt is determined to hang.' Cranston sprang to his feet, strapping on his broad leather warbelt. 'Mine hostess, if anyone comes in enquiring, tell them Sir John is visiting that very pit of despair, Newgate prison.' He scooped the tavern mistress up in his arms and kissed her roundly on both cheeks. Still murmuring 'Monkshood' in reply to mine hostess's good wishes, Cranston swept out of the Lamb of God, up Cheapside, past St Michael's Church and into the Shambles, London's great fleshing market.

Here the butchers, flayers, skinners and slaughterers prepared their stock for sale. The chopping and cutting of cows, calves, sheep, ducks, geese and hens was so constant that the very air was sprayed with blood which stained all passers-by and formed thick, dark puddles across the cobbles. The summer breezes reeked of a variety of foul odours as entrails cascaded out of slit bellies, slopping into the waiting buckets and tubs. Around this reeking mess crouched the apprentices, saturated in gore, who had to fight

164

to keep the offal for themselves, driving away the hordes of beggars, itinerant cooks and traders who viewed such bloody portions as their legitimate booty.

The great fleshing market and its myriad customers attracted every kind of miscreant under the sun. They swarmed out of their dungeons of perpetual night near Whitefriars, along the River Fleet and elsewhere, creeping out, eyes keen for a mistake by anyone who left their property, be it a purse or a stall, vulnerable to being filched. The salamander men, the pimping princes and their gaggle of garishly painted whores, charlatans, conjurors and counterfeits, all set up camp along that broad thoroughfare. The unexpected appearance of Cranston, however, sent them scampering back into the shadows of runnels and alleyways, hiding under stalls, carts and wheelbarrows. Cranston strode through this mayhem, dodging the dung- and refuse-collectors, shouting warnings when some emboldened rogue hurled abuse or cat-called him. At every step Cranston kept his hands close to the dagger and sword on his warbelt. The coroner was tolerated and respected but, there again, he had to be wary of the madcap, the toper or the man with a grievance who might think they could strike at London's coroner and escape.

At last Cranston reached the sprawling concourse which stretched in front of the towering, sombre mass of Newgate prison built into the old city wall. Newgate's appearance justified the gaol's description as 'the Devil's

Domain', 'the Mansions of Midnight', 'the Halls of Hell' and other such bleak judgements. Every window overlooking the concourse was heavily barred both within and without. Each door, no bigger or narrower than a serving hatch, was reinforced with iron bars and heavy metal studs. Sheriff's men, really no better than the rogues they guarded, milled about in their dirt-stained livery, cracking their whips or slashing their canes against those who swarmed around, desperate to get messages or sustenance to friends and relatives within.

Cranston was swiftly admitted through a postern door and entered what he considered to be the very antechamber of Hell. Newgate was a living nightmare; the stench alone made people grievously ill. The stygian darkness, hot and fetid, closed about the coroner like the breath of some unseen, foul-mouthed monster. Cries, groans, screams and curses echoed along the narrow corridors, the walls glistening with a perpetual fetid damp, whilst the ground under-foot was thickly carpeted with cockroaches and a legion of fat-bellied fleas and lice. Every foot-step crunched these down, leaving them as fodder for the rats which swarmed through the gloomy bowels of the sombre prison. These rodents grew long and powerful, ravenous and aggressive enough to attack prisoners too weak to defend themselves.

Cranston murmured a prayer as he followed the balding, waddling, grossly overweight keeper across the press yard, where one prisoner who had refused to plead was being crushed under

166

a heavy iron door with spikes on one side and heavy weights on the other. The man's screams of agony were piteous in the extreme. They entered what was popularly called 'the portals of purgatory' where the 'pits of despair', small, narrow cells, housed the felons who were condemned to the gallows. No daylight here, not a chink of a sunbeam, nothing but perpetual dark and eternal night if it were not for the fiercely burning cresset torches and glowing lanternhorns flaring through the gloom.

The keeper opened a cell door and Cranston entered to stand over the prisoner who sat manacled to the wall on a bed of slimy, black, wet straw. Cranston, aware of the open door behind him and the keeper guarding the gallery outside, crouched down and stared into the face of Monkshood, one of London's leading rifflers. Few people knew his real name but Monkshood was regarded by the authorities as a leading captain of the dreaded Earthworms. He had been betrayed, tried and found guilty of being involved in the storming of Gaunt's residence, the Savoy Palace, plundering it and reducing that magnificent mansion to a heap of blackened timber.

Monkshood, who, according to the bills posted across the city, was to hang the following morning on the Smithfield gibbet, gazed coolly back at the coroner. Now and again he would move his hair, long and greasy, off his face and scratch at the tangled moustache and beard all caked in dirt and riddled with fleas and lice. Cranston recalled scraps of information about the prisoner. Monkshood had a reputation for

167

being quick-witted, of good family, a former scholar of St Paul's cathedral school. He had obviously decided to take another path through life and was about to suffer the consequences. Cranston pinched his nostrils at the foul stench.

'Not to your liking, Sir John?' Monkshood grinned.

'Nor to yours either, by the look of it, but you'll soon be gone, strolling through heaven's gardens.'

'I am not too sure about that, Sir John. I will certainly die tomorrow. One of the parishioners of your friend Athelstan, the Hangman of Rochester, will bid me adieu. Thank God. I understand he is expert and sober. You have heard what the Carnifex here at Newgate did? He was so drunk he almost hanged one of the guards. Now, Sir John . . .' Monkshood scratched his beard and gestured around. 'Welcome to my solar, my banqueting hall, my chancery chamber. You want something – you must do, otherwise you wouldn't be here.'

'Tell me about the Upright Men.'

'Broken like a potter's vase. No form, no substance, only fragments, shards of former glory.'

'And the Earthworms?'

Monkshood spread his hands. 'Sir John, look at me. As I am, so are most of the rest.'

'Gaunt was attacked yesterday at the very heart of the Tower,' Cranston said, then graphically described the assault on Tower Green, and how the Salamander King had infiltrated himself between Gaunt and his bodyguard.

'I know him,' Monkshood confessed. 'The Salamander King was certainly one of ours. A true zealot but, in the end, his assault was only the last desperate fling of the dice.' He took a deep breath. 'And believe me, Sir John, the dice are now cogged, loaded heavily against us.'

'And the murders amongst Gaunt's clerks, his minions in the Secret Chancery? Oh, you haven't heard of them?' Monkshood looked perplexed so Cranston described the slaughter in Milk Street and the mysterious, sudden murders of Empson and Luke Gaddesden. Monkshood listened intently then whistled under his breath.

'The work of the Upright Men, you think? No, not this. The attack on Gaunt at the Tower, yes, I would accept that. But Mephan and the others? That's the work of a very skilled professional assassin. The Upright Men would have nothing to do with such a killer: they wouldn't even know how to hire him.'

'And how do you hire a professional of that sort?'

'I don't know, Sir John. Such people do exist, they sell their services like any mercenary. Each has their own speciality – one is skilled in poisons, another the garrotte, the third a dagger. They reach an understanding with their employer. They make a contract. They seal an indenture with one great difference. There is no document, no parchment, nothing in writing. It is, as we used to say in the schools, *'per verbum'*, by word of mouth, nothing more and nothing less.' Monkshood turned away to sneeze and sneeze again in a rattle of chains. He wiped his face

on the back of his manacled hands. 'Sir John, in my youth I was a roaring boy. I hunted with the cruellest in the pack. You know what they say? If you lie down with wolves, when you wake up, if you wake up, you will do so howling. I remember one such assassin. He was called Ragusa, a Sicilian, skilled in the garrotte and the stiletto. But it's some years since he was in London. I never met him. Just chatter and gossip amongst the rifflers and roaring boys of the city.'

'How do I hire such a professional?' Cranston asked.

'You don't. They approach you and ask if you need their help. Oh, it's all done in parables, masked and hooded at the dead of night in a place of shifting shadows. So, Sir John, if you were my Lord Arundel who, as we all know, hates Gaunt to the very heart of his being, such a lord might be approached and asked if there is anything that can be done.' Monkshood laughed drily. 'Like any tinker or trader, they display their wares, yet their business is human life. They offer murder; the sale is arranged and carried through for gold and silver deposited at a certain time in a certain place.'

'Of course.' Cranston edged a little closer, keeping his voice down. 'And once the sale has begun and the deed is done, both the hirer and the hired are sealed in a murderous compact.'

'Or they'd be joining me on the scaffold.' Monkshood shuffled closer in a rattle of chains. 'Sir John,' he begged in a whisper, 'is there any chance . . .'

The coroner leaned over, grabbed Monkshood by the front of his filthy gown and pulled him close so their faces were almost touching. 'Do you think,' the coroner roared, 'I am here to save your filthy arse and unwashed neck? You are going to hang tomorrow.' He shook the prisoner. 'Do you understand?' Monkshood swallowed nervously, then relaxed as Cranston winked and pulled him even closer so the prisoner's flea-bitten ear was almost touching the coroner's lips. 'Tomorrow,' Cranston breathed, 'be ready, be vigilant and be swift. You will be given one opportunity, seize it.' He shook the prisoner again and pushed him away.

'Go rot!' he bawled. 'Make your peace with God before you meet him personally, just after the Angelus bell tomorrow.'

Sir John left Newgate in finer fettle than when he entered. His good humour deepened a little further when he found Flaxwith and a cohort of bailiffs waiting for him on the great concourse in front of the prison. The coroner even toler-ated Samson sniffing at his boots, desperately trying to climb Cranston's thick, muscular leg.

'We have been to the keeper of corpses,' Flaxwith declared. 'Neither he nor his retainers have found the corpse of any man who might be considered Iberian or, indeed, from foreign parts. So, Sir John, the Spaniard found floating off St Paul's must be the one who visited the Mitre. It explains his total disappearance.'

'Very well,' Cranston replied. 'Now to a task you will surely enjoy. Off to the Lute Boy fast as you can. Tell the Way of all Flesh that I want

171

to meet her now in my confessional,' Cranston grinned, 'at the Lamb of God.'

'Why not go yourself, Sir John? They say those cellars are fascinating with their mirrors and manacles – the sights you'd see and the sounds you'd hear . . .'

'I do not wish even to be seen going in there,' Cranston replied, all prim and proper, trying to kick Samson off his leg. 'The Lady Maude will soon be back in London: she will certainly make enquiries about the company I have kept.'

'And if the Way of all Flesh refuses to come, Sir John? She rarely leaves the Lute Boy.'

'If she refuses,' Cranston snapped, 'if she keeps me waiting, if I am not helped with my legitimate enquiries into the murder of my Lord of Gaunt's servants, then, rest assured, I shall personally visit the Lute Boy. I shall be accompanied by you, Master Flaxwith, with every bully boy you can whistle up, along with forty Cheshire archers from the Tower. And, as you know, Flaxwith, those who sport the White Hart, the King's personal livery, are not known for their gentleness or their love of whores . . .'

Cranston was halfway through his blackjack of ale, lounging in the window seat and staring out over the Lamb of God's exquisitely arranged herb garden, when Flaxwith ushered the Way of all Flesh, together with two of her burly body-guards, into the tavern solar. Cranston flicked Flaxwith a coin and told him to take the two oafs to the taproom whilst he entertained their mistress. He then waved the Way of all Flesh to

172

the comfortable quilted seat opposite him. Once settled and sitting ever so elegantly, a silver goblet brimming with the best chilled wine of the Rhineland in her right hand, the Way of all Flesh simpered at Cranston, toasting him with her cup. The coroner stared back, carefully scrutinising his guest. She was dressed as simply as a Franciscan nun: a brown woollen habit with an ermine-trimmed hood pulled up over an old-fashioned white starched veil and wimple. These framed a face which could only be described as bland: doe-eyes under arching brows, cream-coloured skin with a sharp, thin nose, slightly bloodless lips and dimpled chin. The Way of all Flesh looked as fresh-faced and innocent as any novice, but Cranston knew this woman to be the most successful whore-mistress in London.

'Alianora Devereux.' Cranston toasted her with his blackjack. 'Alianora Devereux,' he repeated, 'once a novice, a Benedictine who fled her convent at the dead of night . . .'

'Before I took solemn vows.'

'Before taking solemn vows,' Cranston agreed. 'You left your order and fled the nunnery to marry one Reginald Tacaster, owner of the Lute Boy, built over the cellars of a once great mansion. Tacaster was at least thirty years older than you. Some say he died out of sheer pleasure. Now a widow, you have established beneath the Lute Boy a warren of passageways and a range of comfortable chambers which cater for every lust known under the sun and a few which might be viewed as fairly original. You have, before you threaten me with them, very powerful friends

173

both in the Church and at court.' Cranston leaned across the table. 'If I know you, Alianora Devereux, you must surely know me. I couldn't give a fig if you drink beer with the Holy Father in Rome. I am here to ask questions. You are here to answer them truthfully or else. To me you are not the Way of all Flesh but Mistress Devereux, that is your proper title. So, Mistress Devereux, tell me about Brother Gregorio, the Spanish friar.'

'Like so many of his kind,' Devereux smirked, 'frisky as a March hare. He liked Felicia, and she liked him so much the little whore decided to sell her favours to him at a different time and in another place. I was not pleased but,' again the smirk, 'who am I to lecture anybody?'

'Who indeed,' Cranston answered. 'What else do you know about Gregorio?'

'Nothing, he was very secretive.' She shrugged. 'In the circumstances, that is understandable.'

'Was there another visitor, also Iberian, possibly Castilian, youngish in bearing, who looked like a former soldier?'

'Yes, there was. He arrived a few weeks ago.' She smiled. 'He paid good Spanish silver but never gave a name. He was also keen on Felicia. He must have come two or three times, and on each occasion asked for her. I tried to discover his personal preferences but I was unable to.'

'Did Felicia ever talk about Gregorio or this other mysterious Spanish stranger?'

'Never. You see, Sir John, that's part of the code. Even whores have honour. You never discuss a customer with someone else.'

174

'And Luke Gaddesden?'

'He was harmless enough. He never went with any of, how can I put it, my household. Luke liked to peer through squint-holes and watch others at play. But more than that, I cannot say. Oh, and of course, Empson the courier. He was very fond of young men.'

'And Felicia and Luke Gaddesden were both cruelly strangled. Do you know any reason why?'

'Should I?' she retorted. 'No, I do not.' She caught Sir John's glint of anger and continued placatingly, 'I am a whore mistress, nothing more. The murders of Luke Gaddesden, Roger Empson or those hideous slayings in Milk Street mean little to me.

Cranston tapped the table. 'Empson and Gaddesden, did they give any hint that something was wrong? Did Felicia intimate anything about Master Mephan?'

'She once let slip that they might be travelling, that Simon Mephan was being offered great advancement by the regent, and he and his clerks might be sent on a diplomatic mission to Castile. Apparently Gaunt had promised to lavish them with money and honours, but more than that,' she pulled a face, 'just tittle-tattle, gossip.'

Cranston studied Devereux carefully. He sensed she was telling the truth, as much as she could, and there was probably little more he could learn from her. He thanked her and waved her towards the door.

The coroner returned to his brooding until he felt a hand on his shoulder and looked up to see the Hangman of Rochester smiling down at him.

'Sir John, Brother Athelstan desires your company at St Erconwald's.'

'And I,' Cranston heaved himself to his feet and clasped the hangman's arm, 'need to have urgent words with you about a gentleman called Monkshood.'

Part Five
The Matins of Midnight

Peter the Penniless did not know whether he was dreaming, dying or truly under diabolical attack from the Gates of Hell and all their power. Crouching in the sanctuary enclave at St Erconwald's, he could only stare in dread at the crone who, spider-like, was now crawling towards him. He had heard her coming, dragging herself like some loathsome snail up the nave, leaving a glistening slime behind her which filled the church with the foulest stench. Petrified, Peter watched the old hag with her white face, her eyes small and black like currants, all shiny and brimming with hatred.

'I know you,' he whispered to himself. 'You remind me of a witch I consorted with many, many years ago.'

Peter lifted his head. Someone was playing the bagpipes. A shadow crossed the sanctuary like a column of black smoke. He watched it. The shadow crouched and hopped as if resting on a crutch. Peter heard a groan and stared at the naked man hanging on the rood screen where the crucifix should be. The man's belly was being slit by a demon. Next to this, a devil queen all shrouded in black reared up, in one hand a repulsive toad, in the other a rotten egg. A sound made him jump. He glanced at the church walls;

the paintings there had assumed a life of their own. A cohort of the damned was being savaged by Hell hounds. A fish-devil was swallowing a glutton up to his belly whilst another demon gnawed at the man's genitals. Against another wall, imps of Satan spurred on a legion of lost souls with red-hot goads; they were herding them towards baths of hot, pitch-reeking sulphur around which other demons offered a diet of toads, snakes and reptiles. Some of the hellish apparitions were turning towards Peter, as if growing aware of his presence.

He could take no more. He took off his belt and picked up his cloak. He would end these hideous visions and stop the heinous sounds, the abominable stench, yet he seemed to have left it too late. The demons were gathering around him. They were led by the old crone and assisted by two hooded devils, whilst a third forced a foul drink between his lips. Peter screamed. The sanctuary was moving, demons held him fast. He could not end it and Peter the Penniless fell into a dead faint. The people around him, who had been attracted by Peter's screams and yells as well as Athelstan's calls for help, lowered the unconscious man to the sanctuary floor.

'I came in to do work in the sacristy,' the friar explained. 'The screaming began. He was having a frenzied fit.' Athelstan paused, shaking his head. 'The poor, poor man.' He asked Benedicta to bring some blankets as the unconscious man was now beginning to shiver. Physician Giole, who'd stayed at Athelstan's request, assisted by

Gregorio and Benedicta, made Peter as comfortable as possible. Athelstan noticed with amusement that Gregorio, although first attracted by the charms of Cecily and Clarissa, now seemed intent on paying court to Benedicta.

'What caused this?' Gregorio asked.

Athelstan decided for the moment to keep his opinions to himself.

'He will be well enough,' the physician offered. 'I've given him a light sleeping draught.'

'But what caused it?' Benedicta insisted, crouching down beside Peter. 'I brought him food and ale which I can vouch for.'

'I know, I know,' Athelstan murmured reassuringly. 'Anyway, I have sent our hangman to fetch Sir John, I need his authority.' He turned as the corpse door crashed open. Amelia and Robert the clerk burst into the church and hurried up the nave through the rood screen. Robert paused just within the entrance but Amelia hastened forward and sank to her knees, hands fluttering.

'My poor, hapless husband!' Amelia lifted her tear-stained face, glaring wildly about. 'What has happened?'

'Robert,' Athelstan called, 'follow Benedicta. She will take you to the priest's house, and you can stay there for a while.' Athelstan put a hand over Amelia's clenched fist. 'Your husband is in good care, in fact the best.' Athelstan gestured at Master Giole. 'My friend here is an excellent physician. Peter suffered a frenzied fit. Now he is sleeping. God knows what is happening,' Athelstan hurried on, 'but we will wait to see. Oh, Benedicta . . .' The widow-woman, who was

179

about to leave the sanctuary, turned back. 'On second thoughts, take Robert to the Piebald, and ask Jocelyn to take good care of him.' Benedicta caught the warning look in Athelstan's eyes and nodded.

'Why can't I stay with Amelia?' Robert protested.

'Because,' Athelstan retorted, 'when Peter awakes I do not want too many people around him. Now go.'

Reluctantly, Robert followed Benedicta out even as Peter began to stir. Athelstan rose and walked around the sanctuary enclave then across to the entrance through the rood screen. He started when the devil's door down near the baptismal font crashed open.

'Sir John, you have arrived!' Athelstan exclaimed.

Cranston, the hangman hastening beside him, strode towards the friar. 'Athelstan, good to see you. Who is that with the fair Benedicta?'

'Robert the clerk. Giles,' Athelstan nodded at the hangman, 'I am in your debt. Sir John, a few words with you in private.'

Athelstan led the coroner across to the sanctuary enclave where Peter, now awake, sat with his back to the wall. His face had a deathly pallor, his eyes startled and shadow-ringed, his mouth half-open, dribbling like a babe, whilst his lips twitched as if he wanted to speak but couldn't form the words.

'He will soon regain all his humours,' Giole declared. 'He is weak, thirsty and hungry but he is in no great danger.'

180

Ignoring Cranston's questions, Athelstan led the coroner across into the sacristy and closed the door behind them. In hoarse whispers, he explained what was happening, his suspicions, how he planned to deal with them and what the coroner must do. Cranston heard him out then laughed, shaking his head in mock disbelief.

'Only you, Athelstan, could climb to the top of a church tower on a summer's day and, keen-eyed, discover assassins plotting murder and the evidence to be used against them, their very own actions.' He pointed at the door. 'So, let the trial begin.'

Athelstan and Cranston returned to the sanctuary enclave. Peter was now much recovered. Benedicta had returned saying Robert was ensconced at the Piebald and seemed very uncomfortable. Athelstan merely shrugged and arranged for a bench and some stools to be brought, placing Amelia between her husband and Benedicta whilst insisting that physician Giole and Brother Gregorio, who hardly seemed to acknowledge each other, remain close.

'Brother Athelstan,' Amelia pleaded, 'what is this?'

'Murder, Mistress Amelia, or at least attempted murder.' Amelia gaped. Peter seemed to be shocked out of his dullness, and both of them protested heatedly. Amelia made to rise but Benedicta, sitting next to her on the bench, gripped her arm and forced her to stay still.

'Attempted murder. The plot to slay another innocent human being. Isn't that a hanging offence, Sir John?'

181

'Undoubtedly, Brother.'

'Especially as we have witnesses.'

'Especially so,' Cranston agreed. 'In fact,' the coroner continued, 'wives who kill their husbands are not hanged, they are burned alive at Smithfield and they are not shown the mercy of the hangman strangling them first. A hideous death, Brother Athelstan, especially if their executioners decide to use fresh wood wet with sap and not dry kindling.'

'Brother Athelstan, Sir John,' Amelia gasped, 'what is this?'

'An opportunity to confess,' Athelstan retorted. The friar glanced at Peter the Penniless. The sanctuary man did not seem so surprised now, but was rather close-faced, more like a juror waiting to hear the evidence. 'Primo,' Athelstan began, pointing at Peter, 'your husband is a man I know well. I have some inkling about the humours of his soul. He did something very strange, out of the ordinary. He is not an outlaw, a wolfshead, yet he takes refuge here. He seeks sanctuary against the demons he believes are polluting his soul. I do wonder if, deep in the depths of that soul, he truly feared you and Robert the clerk. In fact, he wished to flee your company and that of your malignant paramour because he believed you meant him ill. This was a half-formed suspicion, an allegation or accusation Peter could not bring himself to form against you, but instead it lay like some unknown sickness deep within him.

'Secundo.' Athelstan held up a hand. 'No, no, Mistress, you will hear me out. So secundo. What

182

could be the source of the frenzied attack Peter suffered? Satan and all his cohort? Let me assure you, Mistress, in my view, the Lord Satan keeps himself well hidden lest people really begin to question the reality around them. Moreover, why should he show his hand so publicly when malevolent souls like you and Master Robert do his will so faithfully? Tertio. Mistress, I shall now move to specific evidence. You and your paramour Master Robert asked if you could perform some service for our church whilst Peter stayed in sanctuary. I invited you to collect flowers and herbs in God's Acre. You did so. I watched you from the top of the church tower. I wasn't spying on you, just admiring the sky on a beautiful summer's day. Now you and Robert thought you were hidden by the long grass, the headstones and memorial crosses. I watched you and Robert touch each other tenderly. Now God knows there's no sin in that. Then I noticed that both of you were wearing gloves on a warm summer's day . . .'

'There are nettles, brambles, briars and other sharp plants . . .'

'Of course there are. However, when I asked one of my parishioners, the hangman, to go and look more closely, he discovered the gloves you wore were not the gauntlets or thick canvas cloths we sometimes use when we weed our plots and herbs. No, your gloves were more fashionable, like doeskin, to protect your fingers from something much more malign. Moreover, when you brought the basket in, you were no longer wearing those gloves.' Athelstan stretched out a

183

hand. 'Your gloves, Mistress – hand them over or I will have you searched.'

Amelia pulled the gloves from a pocket in her gown and gave them to Athelstan, a small ball of very soft but protective calfskin. Athelstan shook them out. 'Yes, these would shield your fingers should you by mistake pluck at the berries or the highly poisonous flowers of herbs such as belladonna which, physician Giole assures me, certainly thrive in our cemetery outside. This brings me to my fourth point. I noticed the tenderness between you and your paramour but there was something more. Robert was guiding you away from plucking certain plants whilst indicating what you should gather. Now my good friend Philippe, physician in chief at St Bartholomew's hospital, once walked our cemetery here. He found it rich in all kinds of plants, some most beneficial to us humans, others of a much more malignant nature. Philippe believed that the cemetery once housed flower gardens and herb plots as it was so rich in what it contained. Physician Giole, who also knows a great deal about such flora, would agree with Philippe's conclusion.'

'Yes, I certainly would.'

Giole had sat silent throughout. Athelstan noticed once more how he and Brother Gregorio seemed to have little in common apart from the usual greetings and pleasantries. Gregorio now sat deep in the shadows thrown by the high altar while Giole was leaning forward, a slight smile on his saturnine face.

'Yes, I would agree,' he repeated.

'So to my fifth argument,' Athelstan continued. 'You brought a basket of flowers and plants into St Erconwald's, a large basket?' Amelia did not answer. She sat round-eyed and pale-faced, lower lip quivering with fright, and Athelstan believed he was telling the truth. He was pleased that he had separated her from Robert, who was undoubtedly the stronger of the two. Peter sat head down, glaring at Amelia from under bushy eyebrows, and Athelstan wondered if the poor man had always suspected the truth but had refused to admit or confront it.

'I showed that basket of cuttings to physician Giole. He assured me that neither you nor Robert, despite plucking and gathering for a considerable period of time, had collected one single noxious plant. Strange? No! I suspect Robert is a trained leech and apothecary who knows only too well what plants should be avoided. We shall confront him soon enough, though your full confession might mean no hideous punishment under the law.'

'We are finished.' Peter the Penniless lurched forward but Athelstan pushed him back. 'We are finished,' Peter repeated, spitting out the words. He turned pleadingly to Athelstan. 'But what about these visions?'

'They are nothing,' Giole replied quickly. 'Nothing but illusion. Think, my friend, of when you drink too deeply on strong red wine and the fanciful notions which appear. Certain foods also encourage nightmares where all forms of dreadful shapes lurk and prowl. The potions and powders that you were fed simply unlocked memories

185

and fears hidden away as you would lock something in a deep cellar and forget it.'

'But how was this done?' Gregorio demanded.

'We ate today.' Peter pointed accusingly at Amelia. 'We shared a scone cut into three portions wrapped in a linen cloth. I remember it tasting very nice and Robert gave me a drink from a small wineskin he carried.'

'I am sure whatever you drank or ate was carefully coated with some infernal powder or juice.' Athelstan put his hand gently on Peter's arm then pointed at Amelia. 'In truth you were plotting the most devious murder – not death by poison but, as you have tried before, and indeed almost succeeded, driving Peter to suicide, to hang himself, the only possible escape from his nightmares. He had told you about his past, his hidden fears. You met the murderous Robert, if that's his true name, a skilled herbalist, an apothecary. He assumed the disguise of a common clerk desperate for employment, even for a pittance, which made him all the more suitable to Peter. You played the two-backed beast with Robert. You were also growing alarmed at Peter's change of heart since the revolt, as he had renounced his miserly ways. Peter was beginning to share his wealth with others, to take from you what one day you'd seize as your own. You fiercely resented his almsgiving, and so this murderous masque began. You act so loving but in fact you are like the apples of Sodom, all fresh without, all corrupt within.' Athelstan studied her. 'So, Mistress, how do you plead?'

'Brother Athelstan . . .' Peter rubbed his face

between his hands then sighed noisily. 'I do not want to see her or her paramour tried, convicted and punished. I just want them to go. I do not wish,' he stumbled on his words, 'to be publicly depicted as a cuckold, deceived so cruelly in so many ways.'

Athelstan glanced at Cranston who nodded imperceptibly. Sir John leaned over roughly and grasped Amelia's arm.

'On one condition.' The coroner's voice rang through the church, 'You make full and frank confession.' Amelia stared around, her face all fearful, eyes blinking furiously, mouth gaping. She went to talk but the words were mumbled. Cranston made her take a generous swig from the miraculous wineskin; it was obvious she was going to confess. Athelstan relaxed and glanced around. Physician Giole sat fascinated, so too Benedicta, whilst Brother Gregorio continued to stay deep in the shadows of the sanctuary.

'It is as you say.' Amelia's voice was shrill, almost gabbled. Again Cranston seized her arm and warned her to be clear and honest. 'I met Robert. I was concerned about Peter's humours, his disordered mind.' She paused as her husband scoffed mockingly. 'I did love you,' she continued wearily. 'But I became so tired, Peter, tired of your dreams, your fears, your constant harping on the past. I searched for powders and philtres to help you. I visited Robert. He has an apothecary's trade in Broad Street near the Austin Friars.' She swallowed nervously. 'We became friends then lovers. You needed a clerk. Robert came to see you. He did not bargain and you,

187

who at the time wanted everything as cheaply as possible, hired him. Let us be honest, Peter, you could not believe your good fortune. And so our relationship deepened.' Amelia lifted her hands as if in prayer. 'You seemed not to love or like me, not even life itself. I accepted what Robert offered and so we began as it happened today. We shared a scone: the portion we offered you was heavily brushed with a noxious powder which creates dangerous dreams and noisome nightmares. I am sorry, I am sorry . . .'

Her voice faltered as the corpse door was flung open. Loud voices echoed through the silence and Robert the clerk, brushing off attempts by the Hangman of Rochester to restrain him, came up into the sanctuary: he stopped abruptly at the faces staring accusingly at him.

'Time for a hanging, my friend.' Cranston walked over and clapped the hangman on the shoulder. He then grasped a startled Robert by his jerkin and pulled him close.

'Your doxy, your leman, your accomplice,' Cranston grated, 'has confessed all. Look on that and see for yourself.' He pushed Robert across the sanctuary. The clerk staggered but then drew himself up, hand going to the dagger in his belt. Brother Gregorio, surprisingly swift, lurched out of the shadows and drew his own knife. Amelia sprang to her feet, knocking over the stool.

'They know, Robert,' she said flatly.

'I know, you know, we all know,' Peter called out. 'Judas! Traitor! Brother Athelstan, please get them out, both of them. Sir John, please! I do not want them arraigned, just to go.' Athelstan rose and, clutching Amelia by the arm, led her across to Robert, who now stood flanked by the hangman and Brother Gregorio. The clerk stood, chest heaving, face all furious, eyes full of venom as he stared around and realised that his most subtle of plots had been uncovered and laid bare. Athelstan caught and held his gaze. Over the years the Dominican had confronted many a murderer, a veritable horde of assassins, men and women who had deviously plotted the death of another. Athelstan had trapped them and, at the moment of truth, stared into their souls. This was singularly different, a very rare occasion. Robert showed no remorse, no sorrow, but neither did he show any fear at the prospect of being hanged, of public disgrace. Nothing but a raging anger at being exposed and trapped. He hardly bothered to glance at Amelia, but instead kept staring at Athelstan. Robert the clerk had been on the verge of seizing and enjoying a very wealthy widow and all she possessed. He was not even concerned about how he had been exposed, only that he had been. He glared at Athelstan, lifting a hand, fingers curling.

'Be careful,' Cranston warned.

'Be careful too,' Robert spat back. 'Prosecute me before the justices, and what real proof will you offer? No poisons, no noxious potions or powders have been found on me or her.' He flung a hand out at his accomplice. 'No one can testify that I gave him anything particular.'

'You hid your true self, your calling as an apothecary.'

'I never hid it. When did I ever deny being

189

who I am? I am at liberty to do as I think fit. After all, you are a friar yet you act like an officer of the law.'

'Banish them,' Peter the Penniless groaned. 'Banish them from my life – who cares? I will be rid of them and the nightmares.'

Athelstan held Cranston's gaze. They had quickly discussed this in the sacristy and the friar accepted deep in his heart that Robert had spoken the truth. Amelia's testimony might convict her but Robert would deny being involved. True, there was a case to answer, but it was doubtful that there was enough evidence to convince a jury to send a man to the gallows and a pretty young woman to a cruel death at Smithfield.

'Let them go,' Athelstan murmured.

'Leave.' Cranston gestured at the rood screen. 'Both of you go. You are banished from this city and from Southwark. You must be gone by sunset tomorrow. If not, I will hang you myself.'

'What about our property, and possessions?' Amelia wailed.

'By sunset tomorrow.' Cranston lifted his hands as if he was taking an oath. 'Be gone or I will hang you on the gallows near London Bridge.'

Athelstan had rarely seen the concourse in front of St Erconwald's so busy or so noisy. The great pilgrimage was about to depart and all the faithful had assembled. Watkin sat enthroned in his great dung cart, now clean and scrubbed and well furnished to take his brood, as well as the families of Pike the ditcher and Crispin the carpenter. Watkin was eager to leave and blew lustfully on his bagpipes to proclaim this. Ranulf the rat-catcher beat on his drum, whilst Herne the huntsman, Mauger the bell clerk and Moleskin the boatman wailed on their horns. Crim the altar boy, along with Judith the mummer, Beadle Bladdersmith and Benedicta, had ceremoniously taken the parish banners from their sacred place behind the high altar. Athelstan had solemnly unfurled these: three brilliantly hued standards of billowing cloth bearing the image of St Erconwald's, a blood-red cross and a picture of the Virgin. The different colours – green and gold, scarlet, blue and silver – caught the early morning sun and shimmered in its light. The banners rippled and fluttered as Athelstan, armed with a holy water stoup and thurible, solemnly blessed them.

The parish church had been locked and sealed, its keys entrusted to Father Wilfred, who now stood in the shadow of the main porch along with those parishioners who had elected to stay, watching the proceedings with deepening astonishment. Athelstan sat on the battered but comfortable saddle thrown over the back of his old warhorse Philomel who, now he had finished his morning feed, seemed as eager as anyone to be off.

Athelstan gathered the reins in his hands and stared across God's Acre, recalling the confrontation with Robert the clerk and Amelia. Both miscreants had fled the church with Peter the Penniless' imprecations against them ringing out,

191

underscored by Cranston's powerful voice, threatening all kinds of punishment if they were not gone by the following evening. According to all the evidence they had. Nevertheless, Athelstan could not forget the look of seething hatred in the clerk's eyes. Gregorio had watched Robert storm off, almost dragging Amelia with him, then had gripped Athelstan's arm and pulled him close. 'Be careful, Brother,' he whispered, 'for there stalks murder incarnate.'

Athelstan had tried to forget the chilling confrontation; he did not wish this great occasion to be blighted. Everyone was gathering. Horses and sumpter ponies had been hired, arrangements made along the pilgrim way for replacements. Most of the parishioners had hitched horses to their great carts, which were nothing more than massive boxes made of planks borne on two or four great wheels. A few had more comfortable carriages fashioned out of slats with a lattice covering and a window trellis, their hard, hewn wheels protected by huge nails with prominent heads.

Athelstan glanced across at Master Thibault, Albinus and the evangelists, the latter still red-eyed from mourning after attending the funeral rites for their brother and comrades. Despite the tragedy which had engulfed them, Athelstan found it hard to hide his smile at Thibault's luxurious travelling arrangements. The Master of Secrets and his henchmen were all dressed in dark-coloured cotehardies which stretched down beneath the knee, almost covering the green leggings pushed into their shiny leather riding boots, all buckled and spurred. They had hoods against the rain and straw hats to protect them from the sun. Their horses were magnificent, specially selected from the royal stables at the Tower, their harness and metal pieces polished and gleaming.

However, what had really provoked the envy of the parishioners was the carriage Thibault had hired so that, when tired of riding, he and his companions could relax in the most comfortable surroundings. This carriage had six wheels and was pulled by massive dray horses, their thick manes hogged and tied with red ribbon. The carter and his assistant, armed with whips and canes, sat on the postilion seat ready to go. Athelstan studied the carriage: its thick beams rested cleverly above the axles whilst the cart itself was a canvas archway rounded like a tunnel. Both the beams of the carriage and its covering were brightly painted and edged with shiny gilt. Athelstan had been allowed inside to marvel at the dazzling tapestries hanging there; its seats were covered with plump, embroidered cushions, whilst the windows were screened with thick blue taffeta stiffened with weights. He had complimented Thibault on the carriage whilst secretly vowing that if any of his parishioners, particularly the women or children, needed rest or good solace, he would demand that they too journey in such comfortable and soothing luxury.

Cranston had also been deeply impressed by the sheer opulence of Thibault's preparations. 'No hardship or penance there,' the coroner had whispered. The friar stared across to where the coroner, resplendent in his long, deep-blue cote-hardie trimmed with silver gilt, sat in solitary majesty on his destrier, Cranston's favourite warhorse, Black Bayard. The coroner rose from the great high-horned saddle; his booted feet, spurs jingling, thrust firmly into the stirrups. Sir John was issuing instructions as if he was deploying a cohort of archers in battle array.

Physician Giole had also arrived. He had hired a comfortable canopied cart which he insisted on managing personally, guiding the two horses with long reins and a good-natured sumpter pony tied to the rear. Giole now sat perched on the postilion seat talking volubly to Beatrice, Felipe and Maria. All were studying the makeshift chart Cranston had drawn up to plot their way to Canterbury. Brother Gregorio had offered to don sackcloth and ashes and walk barefoot out of Southwark, but both Cranston and Athelstan had totally rejected such humiliation. Sprightly as a sparrow, Gregorio had fully agreed and, with an impish smile, elected to join Benedicta on her cart. Athelstan recalled Peter the Penniless' desire to continue with the pilgrimage. Physician Giole, however, had declared Peter far too weak, a verdict Cranston and the others had concurred with. In the end, Athelstan had written a letter to the Custos of St Bartholomew's hospital, recommending Peter as a patient who needed to purify his humours with clean water, sleep, nutritious food and the care of a good physician.

'Because the daughters of Zion are haughty and have strutted with outstretched necks and wanton glances, the Lord will make their heads bald and take away their ornaments. Instead of a sweet smell there will be a foul stench . . .'

Athelstan gazed in astonishment at the itinerant preacher, head and face shaved to gleaming, who strolled onto the enclosure like the Prophet Jeremiah. The new arrival was garbed in the earth-coloured robe of a Franciscan with a girdle around his waist, a stout walking stick in one hand and a set of battered panniers in the other. The parishioners parted as Cranston pushed Black Bayard forward to greet this stranger. Athelstan followed suit, reining in beside the coroner. Both stared down at the round, friendly, merry-mouthed face smiling up at them.

'Satan's hairy tits, Brother!' Cranston gestured at the friar. 'Summon the Hangman of Rochester quickly.'

Athelstan did so. Giles of Sempringham hurried across.

'Not so loud, Sir John.' The new arrival looked nervously to the left and right, then he squeezed himself between Black Bayard and Philomel so the Hangman had to do the same.

'Monkshood!' The Hangman clasped the Upright Man on the shoulder. 'So you escaped safe? Sir John.' Shading his eyes, the Hangman of Rochester looked up at the coroner. 'I did what you asked. Monkshood here climbed the gibbet ladder, and its scaffold arm jutted out overlooking the crowd. Monkshood's comrades had gathered there. I turned him off and, as planned, the rope snapped with a crack. Down plunged Monkshood to be ringed by his comrades. The cords around his wrists were sliced and they

195

fled like hares through the mob, who shouted their approval and did everything to impede the sheriff's men.'

'I went to the stews,' Monkshood declared, 'and hired a barber who shaved me completely while I soaked in a tub of hot water. My comrades gave me help and behold I am now Brother Giles, a lay brother of the Franciscan Order taking messages from Greyfriars in London to our good brothers in their house at Canterbury.'

Cranston leaned down. 'Of course, you will smuggle yourself out of London, along the pilgrim road through Kent into Canterbury. I gather the sheriff's men are very busy along that same road, keen-eyed and vigilant for fleeing rebels. You will reach Rochester and the Medway and, with a bit of luck, take ship to foreign parts. You will remain there a year and a day before creeping back to England under a different name and calling.'

'You could say that, Sir John, but,' Monkshood lowered his voice, 'I also wish to earn my passage with you. I give you good warning. The Reapers, those Upright Men who still cling to their dreams, know all about this pilgrimage. Their spies will see Master Thibault in all his finery and they may well attack you, seizing the golden opportunity to inflict great damage on Gaunt's principal henchman. Sir John and Brother Athelstan,' Monkshood's voice faltered, 'I only bring you warning. I am nothing but the messenger, not the message.'

Athelstan glanced at Cranston, who'd voiced the same fear as soon as he heard Thibault was joining them.

'*Alea iacta*,' Athelstan whispered, 'the dice is thrown. Sir John, we should go, and you, Brother Giles, had best follow for we cannot drive you away.' Athelstan decided to ignore the suspicions which pricked his mind about Monkshood. He would reflect on them and, at the appropriate time, take counsel with Sir John, Watkin and Pike the ditcher. The friar glanced up at the sky. 'It is time we left.'

Cranston stood high in Black Bayard's stirrups and shouted for silence. Once this had been achieved, Athelstan bestowed his most solemn benediction and finished with the declaration, '*In nomine Christi procedamus* – let us go forward in the name of Christ.'

'Saint George!' Sir John bellowed.

'Pray for us!' the rest thundered back.

'Saint Erconwald!'

'Pray for us!'

'Saint Thomas a Becket!'

'Pray for us!'

The loud and joyous response sent the birds whirling up into the air. Carts creaked and rattled. Carriages clattered. Horses and donkeys whinnied, their hooves scraping the cobbles. Bonaventure leapt onto Benedicta's cart from where he kept a wary eye on Godbless and Thaddeus as well as Ursula the pig woman and her enormous sow. Everyone was excited. Prayers were recited. Snatches of hymns mingled with more raucous tavern songs. Bagpipes wailed, horns blew and trumpets brayed. Banners, standards and pennants snapped in the breeze. Voices shouted. Children laughed. Women called out to each other as their

197

menfolk managed the carts, carriages and barrows. The great pilgrimage of St Erconwald's parish had begun.

Peter the Penniless sat on the high-backed chair in his spacious flagstoned kitchen. He stared into the hearth, all clean and readied by the maids who had now left. He then glanced at the lantern-horn burning fiercely on the table. Peter had insisted it be lit. At this juncture he did not want to be in the dark, he could not face that. He would rest here for the day. First thing tomorrow morning he and the maids would lock the house up and, once everything was settled, he would take Athelstan's letter to the Custos at St Bartholomew's. He could stay there a month, perhaps remain in the hospital until after Michaelmas. He would eat well, sleep soundly and recover in both body and soul. He heard a sound, glanced up and stared in horror at Amelia standing in the doorway. Peter cursed; he'd meant to lock the door behind the maids, but he had forgotten! He stared at his former wife, who looked like a ghost, a dreadful pallor on her face framed by the hood of the green gown which covered her from neck to toe.

'You are to be gone!' he shouted. 'You should not be here!' Peter quietly cursed his own slowness. He had not considered this; he was still not thinking clearly. He should have kept his servants here until he left.

Amelia hastened forward and, before he could prevent her, she fell to her knees. 'Peter,' Amelia begged, her red-rimmed eyes full of fear, 'I would do anything for you to take me back.'

198

She paused and tensed, as he did, at a sound further down the passageway, the footfall of someone creeping towards them. Amelia turned and made to rise as Robert the clerk, his hood pulled back, slipped like the shadow of death into the kitchen.

'Peter, I did not . . .' But then Amelia reeled away as the bolt from Robert's handheld arbalest shattered her face. Peter lurched to his feet but a second bolt caught him full in the throat. Gagging on his own blood, Peter collapsed to his knees then crashed to the floor. Robert the assassin searched both corpses and swiftly ransacked the house, taking any small precious objects and coins he could find. He placed his plunder in a sack tied to his belt and returned to the kitchen.

'I followed you,' he murmured, staring down at Amelia's corpse. 'I knew you would come back here like a dog to its vomit. As for your stupid husband,' he kicked Peter's corpse, 'I was so near, so very close, but . . .'

Robert seized the oilskins he'd glimpsed earlier, slit them and, plucking up the lantern-horn, threw it on the spilt oil. He watched the flames erupt into a furious fire, then, satisfied, he left the house, his mind milling with the prospect of more murderous mischief.

Athelstan revelled in the journey. They had now left Southwark, following the ancient road allegedly built by the Romans which stretched through the Kentish countryside, down past St Thomas's watering place, where they planned to spend two nights so they could take full stock of everything. Once they were satisfied that all was well, they would travel on to Rochester, then a further eighteen miles to Offspring, and finally another nine into Canterbury.

Athelstan was pleased with the organisation and the harmony of the pilgrimage. Since leaving Southwark he'd had a most interesting and secret conversation, more of a muttering really, between himself, Watkin and Pike. Athelstan had promised both these former Upright Men that he would resolve their anxieties together with his as soon as possible. He had then conferred with Sir John, who agreed with Athelstan's conclusions, though the coroner advised the friar to wait for the right opportunity. Until then, Sir John promised, he would keep close watch and even closer guard on Master Thibault. Sir John had been true to his word and, with his sword slapping against his thigh, now rode alongside Gaunt's henchman deep in conversation about future changes in the government of London.

Athelstan glanced away. He gathered the reins in his hands, closed his eyes and breathed in the different smells: wood smoke from distant cottages and the strong reek of horse flesh, mingling with the sweetness of the wild flowers growing in profusion along both sides of the trackway. Athelstan felt a deep, creeping sadness as he recalled making a similar journey along this road when he had brought his brother's corpse back from France. He recalled staying at a local farm and the kindness of its owners, Marc and Christine Freeman. He wondered what had happened to them.

Athelstan opened his eyes. He did not wish to become upset. He would deal with such memories at the appropriate time and in their proper place. The friar stared round. All seemed well: carts rattled along, the clip-clop of horse's hooves echoed dully, and the pilgrims' cortege threw up a screen of dust, but a refreshing westerly breeze wafted this on. The highway was certainly busy. Time and again Athelstan and his fellow pilgrims had to pull aside as couriers, envoys and sheriff's men galloped backwards and forwards on this errand or that. Vestiges of the Great Rebellion were also plain to see. Blackened manor houses, roofs and walls scorched with fire. Fences overthrown, paddocks, gateways, walls and outhouses ruined and in need of repair. Occasionally they would pass a crossroads gallows, its four or six branches heavy with corpses rotting and putrefying in their chains: a cruel, stark reminder that not everything was merry and green in this garden of England.

On one occasion they passed a derelict manor house declared accursed and polluted after the ravaging of the Great Pestilence some thirty years before. The once stately mansion stood on the lea of a hill just past Welling. One of the pilgrims asked Physician Giole if he had ever treated victims of the plague. The physician, tongue firmly in his cheek, described the morbid symptoms: the chilling stiffness which preceded three savage blows to the flesh, the hard lump which boiled up in the armpit or in the groin

201

close to the scrotum. This lump provoked a putrid, burning fever and severe headaches. These were always followed by the vomiting of blood as the corruption of the bodily humours intensified and erupted in a foul stench. Physician Giole enjoyed shocking his fellow pilgrims, who responded with groans, cries and exclamations, as well as demands for more lurid descriptions, in which the physician blithely obliged. He described how he had heard, when he lived in Albi in the south of France, of serpents and toads falling in a thick rain: these had ravaged the countryside and killed and devoured a number of people. Benedicta cried that that was nonsense, but Physician Giole, the laughter bubbling within him, turned to his family for support, and they confirmed that they had lived in Albi for a number of years and witnessed such horrid manifestations.

The repartee between the physician and the pilgrims continued, provoking more merriment as well as teasing about the medical profession. Once the laughter had subsided, the different pilgrim groups settled down to gossiping amongst themselves. Athelstan drew alongside Physician Giole's cart. For a while the friar exchanged pleasantries with Mistress Beatrice about the pilgrimage as well as their life in London. Beatrice declared that their tavern Amongst the Tombs had been left in very capable hands, adding that she and her children were very excited at the prospect of praying before Becket's gorgeously splendid tomb. Benedicta particularly looked forward to seeing the famous jewel left

202

by a visiting king of France which glowed as if it had a flame inside it. Athelstan described the other attractions of both Canterbury Cathedral and the city itself. As he chatted the friar kept a sharp eye on Monkshood as well as the two evangelists. The friar noticed that Brother Gregorio, despite being distracted by the charms of Benedicta, was also keeping Thibault and his household under close scrutiny.

'So much, so much,' Athelstan whispered to himself.

'What was that, Brother?' Athelstan turned back to Giole, who slouched on the cart seat flicking the reins above the sweaty rumps of the two dray horses.

'So much is here,' Athelstan declared. 'So many different lives with a host of secrets, regrets, memories: it's like watching a river all placid on the surface but turbulent beneath.'

'Do you think Azrael is here hiding amongst us?' Giole asked. 'Is it possible, whoever he is?'

'Very much so,' Athelstan replied quickly without thinking. 'Indeed, it is very probable. Why, what do you think?'

'Well, if he is, that means he will strike again,' the physician whispered, leaning slightly forward so that Athelstan could hear him. 'We were not in the Tower when Luke Gaddesden was murdered and my Lord of Gaunt and his henchmen threatened. However, if Azrael could strike there at the very heart of the English court . . .' Giole's voice trailed off. 'I have learnt some of the details. I mean, to garrotte a man on such a narrow skiff on the Thames and leave no trace.

Tell me,' Giole indicated with his head, 'Brother Gregorio – are you sure about him, Athelstan?'

'Why?'

'Nothing,' the physician replied, 'except the man is a veritable grasshopper, all smiling and pleasant even when those close to him . . .' The physician flicked the reins. 'It is as you say, Brother, we all have our secrets. God save us all and bring us safely to Canterbury.'

'Amen!' the friar retorted and he pulled back on the reins, gently stroking Philomel's neck. He then turned to ride alongside Benedicta, Crim and Brother Gregorio, the latter sitting on the tail of the cart, smiling as if he hadn't a care in the world. He greeted Athelstan and beckoned him close.

'Are you happy with the salvation of Peter the Penniless?' he asked.

Athelstan pulled a face. 'I have deep fears about Master Robert. There was something about him, something destructive. A man who couldn't care about himself, never mind anyone else.'

'I would agree,' Gregorio concurred.

Athelstan nodded and stared around. It was a brilliant summer's day, and fields stretched out to the right and left, meadow and ploughland dotted with small copses of trees and clusters of bushes. A spring-like freshness hung over everything despite the dust, the clash and the clatter of the cavalcade. The air grew rich with a variety of odours both sweet and sweaty. Voices chatted, sang or chanted. Children laughed or screamed whilst their parents exchanged morsels of gossip. Cranston was still guarding Thibault whilst the two evangelists clustered close in deep conversation. The parish banners, still unfurled, floated like war standards in the carts where they had been placed. Athelstan quietly rejoiced in the warmth of the deep relationships which permeated his parish yet he also felt a creeping chill of apprehension. He recalled his conversation with Giole. There was a very strong possibility, indeed a logical probability, that Azrael, the dark demon of horrid murder, also swirled in their midst like Herod dancing amongst the innocents.

'Brother Athelstan?'

He glanced to his right. Matthew and John Gaddesden now rode alongside him.

'A time for confession?' Athelstan teased.

'Sorry, Brother?'

'We are free of London. We travel to seek the help of the blessed Becket and must do so with quiet conscience. You have something to say?'

'We certainly wish to tell you something, Brother,' Matthew conceded. 'First, my Lord of Gaunt was thinking of sending us on a delegation to Castile, which he said would be of great profit to both himself and to us . . .'

'Would it have been?' Athelstan queried.

'Oh yes. My Lord of Gaunt, now the revolt is over, wishes to pursue his claims in Castile. He has friends and allies there who would favour him and us. But there is something else. We have talked to Master Thibault and he suggests we tell you.' Matthew paused, collecting his thoughts. 'Master Simon Mephan was a clever, subtle clerk, Brother Athelstan. We work in the Chancery from dawn to dusk. Sometimes, when we have to wait for a certain task, some clerks sleep, others go for a walk. Simon was fascinated by puzzles and words.'

'And?' Athelstan asked.

'We understand,' Matthew continued hurriedly, 'that when Master Mephan was found dead in his chamber above Milk Street, he had copy of the Book of Saint Luke's Gospel close by.'

'That is correct.'

'Well, Brother Athelstan, in the last days before his death Simon seemed fascinated by that passage, the story of the Gesarene demoniac. On a number of occasions he wrote it out on a scrap of parchment and then started playing with the words as if they contained some secret message. The scraps of parchment are now long gone . . .' His voice faded away. 'We just thought we should tell you.'

'And you could tell me more,' Athelstan retorted, 'but you won't.' Both brothers refused to meet his gaze. 'Not now, but circumstances may force you.' Athelstan sensed he was right. These two clerks could tell him more, but the friar decided the time was not opportune. However, once they reached the Sign of Hope perhaps he and Sir John could question them more rigorously. He watched them move back close to Thibault's carriage. Athelstan drew a set of ave beads out of his belt wallet and closed his eyes, mind and ears to the sights and sounds around him. He wanted to concentrate on the mysteries which fogged his mind. He must impose order on his turbulent thoughts. He needed to fillet the problem as a flesher would a piece of meat, taking each morsel and examining it carefully. He murmured a prayer for wisdom and began.

Item: the slayings in Milk Street. Athelstan threaded his ave beads. According to all the evidence, the assassin had been invited into Mephan's house. True, the murderer could have slipped in, yet three people lived there. If an intruder appeared he would be seen and the alarm quickly raised. One of those three could have run into the streets and shouted 'Harrow! Harrow!', a call which would have brought neighbours to their aid. Nevertheless, there was not a shred of evidence that anything like this had happened. And the same macabre, silent mystery shrouded the three murders in that narrow house in Milk Street. Finchley and Felicity were apparently garrotted downstairs but there was no sign of resistance or disturbance, not even a shred of evidence that they had tried to escape. To all intents and purposes Finchley and Felicia went freely to their deaths like innocent lambs to the slaughter knife.

Simon Mephan, however, was different. According to the evidence he had fled upstairs. Why didn't he try to escape into the street? Athelstan shook his head, going deeper into his studious speculation. No, he reasoned to himself, Simon Mephan must have seen the two corpses then fled upstairs. He was given a short respite; the deep fear for his life, the hasty flight and a weakened heart combined to achieve Mephan's death. The elderly clerk had opened the Gospel of St Luke and underscored those two words 'legion' and 'many,' or at least the Latin version, and had then collapsed, dying immediately. The assassin would have made sure of this then left as silently as he had arrived.

Item. Roger Empson the courier was Azrael's next victim: it had proved easy to trap, corner and kill the terrified fugitive. Nevertheless, once again neither Cranston nor Athelstan himself had detected any sign of violence or resistance. The same was true of Luke Gaddesden, savagely garrotted on a narrow, shallow skiff. Surely the boat would have capsized? Any struggle aboard such a craft would make it roll over, hurling both assailant and victim into the water. Or was Luke first garrotted then placed in the boat? But how was all this done without mark or sign?

Item, why were these high-ranking clerks, members of the Secret Chancery, being murdered in such a way? Reference had been made to their being sent to Castile on a diplomatic mission. Was that what Felicia had meant about Mephan and his colleagues receiving some sort of advancement? Item, Mephan's conduct just before he died was strange. Athelstan was convinced that the remaining evangelists had not yet told him the full truth but already they had conceded that Mephan seemed to know something. He was a senior clerk used to ciphers and secret writing, to codes and hidden messages, the use of strange alphabets and symbols. Mephan had underscored two words in that Book of Luke's Gospel. He'd done this just before he collapsed and died, yet there was evidence that he was fascinated by these phrases in the days leading up to his death. Athelstan quietly promised to study those verses for himself.

Item, why were Thibault and the rest really coming on the pilgrimage to Canterbury? He had noticed that the Master of Secrets was very subdued, almost withdrawn. Was he frightened? Were Thibault and the rest being kept out of harm's way, or was there some other more nefarious reason?

Item, who was Azrael? Why did the assassin take such a name – the title given to one of Satan's henchmen, the fallen angel? Before he had left London, Athelstan had sent urgent enquiries to Brother Norbert, librarian and archivist at Blackfriars: he just hoped such information would be with him soon. Athelstan returned to his speculation. Was Azrael with them now? Who could it be?

Gregorio was a strange man. On the one hand jovial and merry, yet he seemed little affected by the death of Felicia – or was that just the Spaniard's soul, a man totally absorbed with himself and his own pleasures? And that other Spaniard whose corpse the Fisher of Men had taken from the reeds near St Paul's wharf – was he another of Azrael's victims? Yet no written warning had been left, and why had the stranger been murdered in such a barbarous way? Who was this stranger and what was the connection between him, Gregorio and Felicia? Their paths seemed to have crossed at both the Mitre and the Lute Boy. Athelstan was certainly intrigued by Gregorio. Who had informed the Guildhall that a visiting Spanish friar was breaking his vow of chastity with his lady love? Such incidents were a daily occurrence; why was Gregorio singled out and every detail supplied so the friar could be seized?

Item, Azrael, again. 'I always come back to you,' Athelstan murmured, staring up at the sky. 'You have spread your dark wings over my life and placed me in the land of deep shadow.' He sighed deeply. 'If I walk in the Valley of Death . . .' he murmured. Yes, that was it. He had entered the Valley of Death, going along its snaking pathways while those deep shadows lurked on either side. Athelstan was convinced that Azrael had nothing to do with the Upright Men, the Reapers or the events of the recent revolt. Azrael was a professional assassin and more. He seemed to relish killing, to enjoy it, to bait and taunt his victims. Why did he appear so abruptly in Mephan's garden to threaten and frighten Athelstan? Why use the grisly emblem of a dead magpie throttled to death and then repeat that warning using Bonaventure?

'I suppose I have never met you,' Athelstan murmured, 'yet you regard me as your heart's own enemy.' He accepted there was a certain logic in threatening Gaunt, Thibault and the evangelists, although he could not understand why. Cranston and Athelstan had been brought in to investigate the murders and immediately Azrael had turned on him. Why? Because he was investigating these slayings – but then so was Cranston. And why make such mockery of the colours of a Dominican being like those

210

of a magpie? Athelstan accepted that his order was hated by some factions of society, and he had to concede that might be the case here.

Item, the kingdom of Castile – this also seemed to figure in the mystery. Physician Giole and his family were Castilian, and the same was true of Gregorio and perhaps the mysterious stranger found drowned off St Paul's wharf. Mephan and the evangelists had been informed that they could be sent to Castile. Finally, and Athelstan vowed not to forget this, Thibault and the others were to meet Castilian envoys at Canterbury. The friar remembered the conversation he had overheard in the Tower – Gaunt talking in Spanish, possibly to Albinus . . .

Philomel snorted, and Athelstan gathered his reins and stared around. They had passed St Thomas's watering place and were on the narrow road leading to the Sign of Hope. Benedicta came up to him, smiling, and offered a pannikin of wine, which he gratefully accepted and returned to his brooding. Azrael had on three occasions used the corpse of a magpie to taunt him. Could this also be a connection to Castile and Spain? Such mockery of his order was commonplace in other kingdoms where the Dominicans acted as inquisitors, being particularly hated in southern France, northern Spain and parts of Lombardy where the Cathar, Albigensian and Free Spirit heretics still had a firm grasp on the loyalties and beliefs of the laity. The King of France and his barons had swept south with fire and sword to root out such sects but the Inquisition, and by implication the

211

Dominican order, still believed that many of these heretics simply concealed their beliefs . . .

'Brother Athelstan, are you asleep?'

Athelstan turned to see Gregorio smiling up at him. 'No, I am not.' Athelstan leaned down. 'But tell me, my friend, do you not mourn Felicia? Did you not want to attend her funeral obsequies?'

Athelstan was surprised at the change in Gregorio: his perpetual smile and good humour promptly disappeared.

'Brother Athelstan,' Gregorio almost hissed, 'when you have lost what I have lost you cannot grieve. Anyway, as you know, of all waters, tears dry the fastest.' He tapped his chest. 'I grieve here for Felicia in my own way.' Gregorio raised his hand in mock benediction and walked off to rejoin Benedicta.

Athelstan watched him go and looked around. Cranston still rode close to Thibault. Monkshood, continuing to act as a Franciscan preacher, trailed behind. 'I don't believe you, Monkshood,' Athelstan murmured. The Dominican looked to the fields on his right and left: they were now moving through open countryside. Everything was peaceful and Athelstan was confident it would remain so. St Erconwald's pilgrims might be involved in prayer, hymns and doing good works, but they were also very well armed and would resist any attack, from Upright Men or from anyone else. Moreover, time and again Athelstan had seen the sheriff's men pass, and none of these had reported any outlaws or wolf-sheads being active along the route. Athelstan patted Philomel's sweat-soaked neck. 'If you could understand, my old friend,' Athelstan whispered, 'I would repeat the same time and time again: this is one pilgrimage I shall not forget. Mark my words . . .'

'Let us pray and thank God, Saint George, Saint Erconwald and Saint Thomas a Becket for a safe journey on this first day of our pilgrimage.' Athelstan stood on a stool in the splendid taproom of the Sign of Hope and beamed at his fellow pilgrims. Everyone was here, according to Mauger the bell clerk, who kept a strict register, except for Maria, physician Giole's daughter, who was suffering from stomach cramps, whilst the elusive Monkshood had simply disappeared from sight. They had all assembled here. Mine host had promised Cranston and Athelstan they could use the taproom for meetings as well as to celebrate mass.

'It's a long time since I have had such a large congregation,' Athelstan announced to laughter and good-natured repartee from all those gathered around. He smiled at them even as he felt his heart sink at the thought that Azrael the demon could well be there, hiding behind one of these smiling faces. A killer with a clever mask who would drop that mask whenever it so suited him. Cranston coughed noisily, a sign that his 'little friar' was sinking into one of his reveries.

'Very well. Take out your hand crosses or your ave beads,' Athelstan declared, 'and let us recite one decade of the Rosary, Saint Dominic's favourite prayer. Sir John, you will lead off and we shall deliver the refrain.'

'Hail Mary, full of grace . . .' Cranston's powerful voice boomed across the taproom. Athelstan got down from the stool and walked around, noticing how many of the pilgrims had crucifixes, paternosters and finger chaplets at the ready. Ranulf the rat-catcher was kneeling beside the cage which housed his two favourite ferrets, Audax and Ferox. Watkin even believed the ferrets slept in bed next to Ranulf. Ursula the pig woman rested against the heaving flank of her huge sow which, despite its bulk, had waddled behind a cart. However, according to Benedicta, the sow had also been allowed onto the cart to sit there like the Queen of Sheba riding in splendour.

Athelstan was pleased to see his old friend Bonaventure crouching beside Benedicta. Apparently the great tomcat had a most comfortable journey sprawled out on soft bedding in the widow-woman's cart. Well rested and refreshed, Bonaventure was now very alert and inquisitive about what might lurk in the corners of this strange room. Athelstan continued his walk and mentally beat his breast. He'd forgotten about the two other parishioners who were absent. Godbless and Thaddeus had arrived and been registered, but only for a short while. The fey-witted beggar man had loudly proclaimed to the squeak of bagpipes from Watkin, that Thaddeus' insides were irregular and sickly so it would be safer and cleaner if he and his goat stood outside until the problem was resolved. All the other

214

parishioners had heartily agreed and were now gathered in their family groups thundering their response to Sir John's prayer:

'Holy Mary, Mother of God . . .'

Athelstan continued to gaze around the taproom, pleased at what he saw: like the rest of the tavern, this was most comfortable, clean and resplendently furnished. The hostelry was a four-storied building ranged along three sides of a great cobbled bailey with stables and outhouses. Beyond these stretched spacious, well-filled herber, kitchen and flower gardens. The tavern also had its own livestock; chickens were plentiful, pecking at the seeds in the yard, whilst in the fields which flanked the approach to the tavern, cattle and sheep browsed. There was also a large piggery situated, because of its stench, at the far end of a meadow and, closer to the main house, a well-stocked duck and carp pond.

The kitchens were richly provisioned and furnished: two great chambers built of stone which housed their own bakery with a range of ovens either side of two huge fireplaces. Here scullions and turnspits cooked, grilled, fried or boiled, in a constant mist of savoury smells, a wide range of meats to the constant clatter of platters, pots and pans. The taproom itself was most comfortable with proper benches, stools, chairs and tables. The floor was clear of any rushes. The well-scrubbed paving stone was covered with cord matting, dyed a deep blood-red.

The tavern offered a wide choice of chambers and rooms, from narrow garrets just beneath the roof tiles to spacious chambers as luxurious as those in any palace or royal manor. These rooms had wide, glass-filled windows and thick turkey rugs on the floor. The ceiling beams were gilded and decorated, the walls painted or panelled: such chambers were richly furnished with chests, aumbries, a chancery desk and scribe's chair. Each boasted a most comfortable four-poster bed all hung with heavy linen curtains, whilst crisp white sheets, coloured counterpanes, feather-filled mattresses and bolsters guaranteed a restful night's sleep. In Cranston's chamber, there was even a design showing Venus, the Goddess of Love, casting Ovid's 'Remedies for Love' into a fire as well as intricately woven tapestries describing the Battle of Hastings and the slaying of England's last Saxon king.

Despite Cranston's protests, Athelstan had asked for a common chamber, saying that he'd only feel uncomfortable in anything more luxurious. Master Chobham had promised that the other chambers would be allocated later in the evening after the supper Cranston and Athelstan had ordered for Thibault and his henchmen. Lost in own thoughts, Athelstan continued to walk around the taproom. He paused next to physician Giole and his family and noticed they had no ave beads, so he lent them his, smiled and walked on.

Thibault and his party sat away from the rest. Gaunt's Master of Secrets looked deeply pensive, Albinus likewise, and the two evangelists appeared highly anxious. Quietly reciting the refrain to the 'Ave', Athelstan walked past

216

the great board with its casks, barrels, tuns and pipes of wine. Above these, hanging from the cherry painted rafters, were cheeses, hams, filches of bacon and other meats being cured in their herb-soaked sacks and white nets. The sight of these made Athelstan recall Mephan's kitchen – what had he seen there? Something he had at first taken for granted but now it nagged at his memory, items he'd glimpsed when he had passed through that house. Athelstan walked back to his own place.

Among the pilgrims' faces, there were some that he did not recognise, but then he recalled that a number of travelling chapmen, tinkers and traders, had joined the rear of their cavalcade. It was a common enough occurrence for solitary travellers to seek the comfort and protection of a large, well-armed group. Athelstan had accepted these for what they were, though, on one occasion, he had noticed Gregorio confer with two of these late arrivals. Athelstan frowned at the Hangman of Rochester, who was knotting his ave beads into a noose; the hangman hurriedly unravelled his rosary beads and swiftly crossed himself.

'Gloria Patri . . .' Cranston intoned, bringing the rosary prayer to an end, after which the pilgrims began to separate. Some would eat in the tavern, while others would go out to cook food they had brought over makeshift fires. Athelstan followed Cranston and physician Giole into the kitchen, which billowed with a misty steam full of the most delicious odours. Giole and his family had persuaded the portly, fleshy-faced Chobham, tavern master and vintner, to let them participate in the supper being boiled, broiled, roasted and grilled in different parts of the hostelry. Chobham, a thick apron covering his bulk from neck to toe, a large cream napkin over each shoulder, welcomed Giole into his kitchen. Chobham was very flattering, hospitable and gracious, but Athelstan did not like or trust the taverner. There was something unpleasant and shallow about the man, a sly cunning which portrayed itself in a too ready smile and constantly shifting eyes. Nevertheless, Chobham acted the part, calling the physician and Beatrice 'the Master and Mistress of haute cuisine'. Thibault and the evangelists, hungry after their long journey, also wandered in to watch proceedings and encourage Giole.

'Simon Mephan believed you to be the finest cook in London,' Thibault declared. 'A true master of the kitchen.' The evangelists heartily agreed.

Giole sketched a bow. 'I always advised Simon that good food and good health are close bedfellows. Didn't I, Beatrice, Felipe?' Both wife and son agreed.

'Where is Maria?' Athelstan asked.

'She is not well,' Beatrice explained. 'The journey was long. I am glad to be here, so let's celebrate.'

'Let us celebrate indeed.' Giole had already donned a cook's apron, Felipe and Beatrice likewise. 'Our meal,' the physician announced, 'or rather yours,' he grinned, 'will begin with charette together with beef broth and a parsley omelette dusted with onion. This will be followed by chicken with cumin and cream and partridge in a nutted wine sauce, not forgetting the dilled veal.'

'Enough, enough!' Cranston cried. 'Mistress Beatrice, I am so hungry I could eat you now.'

Cranston and Athelstan left the kitchen and returned to the taproom. The friar grabbed Sir John by the arm and led him across to where Gregorio sat deep in conversation with one of the chapmen who had joined them along the road. The tinker, a black-haired, swarthy individual, saw Athelstan approach and immediately excused himself: the fellow rose and rejoined his companions at another table. Athelstan sat down on a chair, the coroner beside him.

'You have made friends?' Athelstan indicated with his head to where the chapman sat drinking quietly with the others.

'I am a travelling troubadour, a minstrel of mirth, God's own herald. I meet and greet whomever I encounter and wherever that may be.'

'And God's own herald is doing his penance?'

'Sitting next to the beautiful Benedicta on my journey here proved to be most pleasurable, not painful.' Gregorio shrugged. 'What does it matter? Master Tuddenham and the Archdeacon of London do not give a fig. Poor Felicia is dead, and who else cares? So, my friends, what do you want with me?'

'The Franciscan Brother Giles,' Athelstan stated. 'Keep a close watch on him both before and after supper. Make sure he does not approach Master Thibault or his henchmen.'

'You fear mischief?'

'I fear worse. Promise me?'

Gregorio pulled a face and spread his hands, murmuring it was no problem for him and he would do as Athelstan asked.

Part Six

If Only We Could Trap Him: Death is Dead

A short while later Cranston and Athelstan sat in the supper chamber which lay at the heart of the tavern, an exclusively sophisticated room, its walls covered in hangings with embroidered scenes from the Bible. On one wall, the tapestry described the Creation of Paradise, the Fall of Man and the saga of Noah's Ark. Similar scenes from the Old Testament covered the other walls whilst the ceiling was painted and emblazoned with the signs of the Zodiac. The floor, laid with painted tiles, presented an ingenious map depicting the kingdoms of the earth as well as the different seas, rivers and mountains.

The food served was a series of delicious concoctions whilst the wine, both the red and white, came from the tavern's special cellar. Athelstan began the meal with a blessing as well as fulsome thanks to Thibault and His Grace the regent for donating to the parish such a generous amount to finance this pilgrimage. Thibault returned the toast of thanks, saying that his master's munificence simply reflected the excellent service both Athelstan and Sir John had performed for the Crown during the recent

221

troubles. The servants had hardly left, closing the door behind them, when Thibault broached the reason for this meeting.

'You did ask for it?' he demanded.

'Of course we did,' Athelstan snapped. 'We are all in danger of death, Master Thibault. You know full well that almost everyone around this table,' Athelstan's gesture took in Albinus and the two evangelists, 'has been threatened by Azrael. This killer is responsible for the murder of at least three of your household, leading henchmen such as Master Mephan and Luke Gaddesden. I believe it is only a matter of time before he strikes again.'

'Even here, now, on pilgrimage?' Matthew Gaddesden exclaimed.

'Never! Impossible!' his brother expostulated.

'No, I speak the truth,' Athelstan insisted. 'I believe Azrael will strike again, and Sir John does likewise. In a word, I believe Azrael is a member of our community. He skulks low and deep. But he's here and he's murderous.'

'Who is he?' John Gaddesden demanded.

'For heaven's sake!' Cranston exclaimed. 'If we knew that . . .'

'How can we help?' Thibault asked.

The Master of Secrets seemed as perplexed as anyone about the swirling mist of murderous mayhem and sudden slaughter which now confronted them – but was this the truth? Was this beloved henchman of Gaunt innocent of any involvement in these hideous murders? The Master of Secrets had his head down: abruptly he looked up, his smooth face pale and drawn.

'Brother Athelstan,' Thibault repeated, 'how can we help?'

He was sinister and treacherous, the most cunning of connivers, a man of blood seeped in all forms of trickery. Nevertheless, the simplicity and directness of Thibault's question, his eyes as well as the tone of his voice, finally and firmly convinced Athelstan that this serpent in human flesh was not only innocent of any involvement in these hideous murders but as fearful as anyone of what might possibly happen next. Athelstan understood why the Master of Secrets had been so subdued and withdrawn. Thibault was used to controlling events but now, to the greater extent, they controlled him.

'Why are you on this pilgrimage?' Athelstan asked.

'We must meet Castilian envoys at Canterbury. What we will discuss with them is covered by the Secret Seal.' Thibault sighed heavily. 'I also think my Lord of Gaunt is relieved we are out of London, out of harm's way, even though, as you say, Azrael may be amongst us. Surely we will be safer together. It will be easier to detect an enemy,' Thibault smiled thinly, 'or so it could be argued.'

'I do not wish to pry,' Athelstan said, choosing his words carefully. 'I understand this is secret business, but your meeting with the Castilian envoys . . .'

'Is very important,' Thibault cut in. 'We meet nobles who favour my master's claims to the throne of that kingdom.'

Athelstan turned to Albinus. 'And what role

do you play?' Albinus merely smiled with his eerie-looking eyes.

'Albinus has Spanish blood,' Thibault retorted, lifting a hand as a sign for his henchman to remain silent.

'Castilian?' Athelstan queried.

'My mother was of Basque origin.' Albinus chose to ignore his master. 'She fled the persecutions which constantly rage in that province. My father was English, a priest in fact, a Benedictine monk. A long story, Brother Athelstan, and one I shall share with you at the appropriate time.'

'Yes, you must.'

'Albinus is most skilled in the Spanish tongue,' Thibault interrupted, 'very adept with the different dialects. He will sit with us.'

'Of course!' Athelstan smiled. 'The Castilians will not know that, so, when they revert to their own tongue in heated discussions between themselves, you will know exactly what they are saying.'

'Precisely,' Thibault said. 'However, let us return to the depredations of this fiend Azrael.'

The friar glanced quickly at Cranston, who nodded.

'Look, Master Thibault . . .' Athelstan paused; he wanted to be prudent and not give offence. 'After Simon Mephan was murdered, you sent Albinus here to ensure that any documents from the Secret Chancery that were still intact should be removed from his house?'

'Yes, I did.' Thibault agreed. 'But that's only logical and proper.'

'And, was there anything missing?'

'No,' Albinus replied, just above a whisper. 'I could detect nothing wrong.'

'Except that Mephan's money coffer had been broken into and emptied.'

'It wasn't a money coffer,' Matthew Gaddesden declared.

'So what was it?'

'A receipt box where Simon kept a tally of what he spent.'

'So why should that be broken into and the receipts taken?'

'Brother, I don't know.'

Athelstan fell silent, letting the others chat to each other as they dined on the different courses being brought in by the servants and scullions. He also watched them drink. Thibault and Albinus were abstemious, but the two evangelists matched Sir John goblet for goblet, stimulated by their fear of what the future might hold. Athelstan waited until the end of the meal before returning to his questioning, this time addressing the Evangelists.

'On the journey here,' he began, 'I said that you have not told me everything. I believe that is still the truth. Now I demand that you reveal what you have so far kept secret.' Athelstan noticed how fearful both brothers had become. He glanced at Thibault and concluded that the clerks were more frightened of him than anything else.

'Speak,' Thibault murmured, running a finger around the rim of his goblet. 'In God's name, our lives – your lives – could depend on it.'

'Simon Mephan was a most able and skilled clerk,' Matthew Gaddesden paused at Thibault's murmur of agreement, 'but he was greedy for money to the point of being avaricious. He was also inquisitive, and very proud of his sharp mind and keen wits.' This time his brother murmured his agreement. 'He immersed himself in the world of the Secret Chancery with its hidden ciphers and different alphabets. Simon loved words as he did creating patterns out of them.'

'What else did he do,' Cranston intervened, 'once he left the Chancery? Some clerks play bowls, while others practise archery, fish, snare birds, or,' Cranston waved a hand, 'eat and drink.'

'Simon certainly loved his food,' John Gaddesden declared. 'He was a regular visitor to various taverns and pastry shops.'

'Any in particular?'

'The Mitre and the Lute Boy, whilst he had the greatest admiration and respect for Giole Limut and his family's culinary arts. You must remember that Giole was both the ward physician and Simon's personal doctor.'

'There is more?' Athelstan demanded.

'Yes, there is.' Matthew looked at the friar from beneath his eyebrows. 'Simon mentioned the possibility of my Lord of Gaunt sending us on a mission to Castile.'

'Would you have liked that?'

Matthew made to reply but paused at the roars of laughter coming from the taproom. Athelstan had observed earlier that Cecily and Clarissa, acting all offended by Gregorio's open admiration for Benedicta, had attached themselves to

Monkshood. Both sisters had demanded that on their first night out of Southwark, they should hear the chimes of midnight and make the rafters ring with merriment.

'Well?' Athelstan insisted.

'Of course the opportunity to visit Spain would be most welcome. But there too, there is a problem,' Matthew continued in a rush. 'I do not know what Simon meant, but one day, working in the Chancery office, not long before he was murdered, he became excited as if secretly relishing something. He declared he could earn great treasure, but more than that he wouldn't say. He also claimed he was being followed, in fact he was sure of it.'

'Was he?'

'Brother Athelstan, on two occasions when we left the Chancery chambers in Parchment Lane and were making our way to King's Steps, Simon gripped my arm and made me look back. On both occasions I did glimpse someone, a black-haired man, dark-skinned.'

'Hispanic, Iberian?'

'Possibly, but I never saw him again. This was shortly before Simon was murdered.' Matthew fell silent, playing with the crumbs on the platter before him.

Athelstan glanced round. Matthew and John had drunk deeply, as had Cranston, but it was Thibault who intrigued Athelstan. The Master of Secrets was usually sly, swift and devious in his conversation but he still remained strangely silent, lost in his own thoughts, more like a spectator than an actor in the murderous masque

227

being played out around him. Athelstan stared at one of the slender candles guttering out. Azrael was here in the Sign of Hope. Athelstan truly believed that, but when would he strike next, and against whom?

He tapped the table, then did so again, arousing both Sir John and the two clerks. 'Tell me this: Simon Mephan, Empson and your beloved Brother Luke were killed by Azrael. Was Mephan's murder the first time you encountered that assassin?'

'No,' Thibault intervened, leaning against the table. 'Sir John, you told me that certain murders are reported to you in the sheriff's returns every quarter.'

'And the Exchequer makes a copy for you,' Cranston assented.

'Yes, we know what goes on. We did come across some similar murders, powerful merchants. They had been garrotted in the same way as these other victims, with dire warnings left on their corpses.'

'Well, there was actually more than that,' Cranston stated. The coroner half closed his eyes. 'If I remember correctly, the warnings left read: "Lord Azrael greets you. Fear us because our name is legion for we are many."'

'Yes,' Thibault agreed, 'such information came to the Secret Chancery. Simon Mephan would have seen it.'

Athelstan sat back in his chair. 'Our name is legion,' he whispered to himself, 'for we are many. That crucial verse from Luke's Gospel is the key to unlock this mystery . . .' He stared down at the tablecloth. 'Whoever you are,' Athelstan whispered to himself, 'you are most cunning.' He glanced up, tempted to declare that Thibault and his henchmen could tell him more, but the day was done, 'And we are for the dark,' Athelstan whispered.

'Brother?'

'Master Thibault – we should retire, I understand Master Chobham will now allocate the rest of the chambers.'

Monkshood crouched in the lonely outhouse in the darkest corner of the stableyard at the Sign of Hope. Night had fallen. The sun had set in a fiery glow. Monkshood had watched this and recalled what his old teacher had said: 'The setting sun is red because it approaches Hell.' Tonight, once the darkness had settled, with the tavern in its sleepy embrace, Monkshood was prepared to despatch Master Thibault in hot pursuit of that Hell-bound sun.

Monkshood recalled his miraculous escape from the gallows at Tyburn, that frenetic, frantic race through the crowd along the warren of alleyways and runnels into Whitefriars. Here sheltered the last remaining coven of Earthworms in the city. At first they had welcomed Monkshood with open arms. However, after explaining his escape, Monkshood had sensed his comrades' deepening suspicion at such occurrence, which verged on the miraculous. He had caught the whispers, the sly-eyed, sideways glances and the murmur of debate. Had he truly escaped or had he been allowed to? Monkshood would not be the first cat's-paw used by Master Thibault. Time and again the Upright Men and the Earthworms had to mete out harsh justice to traitors and informers. Was this another ploy by Gaunt's Master of Secrets to seek out and destroy the Reapers, the last remnants of the Great Revolt?

Within hours of Monkshood's arrival, the suspicions had hardened into allegation and then outright accusation. Monkshood had furiously defended himself, pointing out how he had been captured, cruelly imprisoned and sentenced to hang, and yet there was the rub. He could not confess to being allowed to escape because he was assisting the Lord High Coroner of London on a totally different matter. The Earthworms would find it almost impossible to accept that either Cranston or the hangman would allow a captain amongst the Earthworms to escape, especially one with Monkshood's reputation.

The situation became extremely perilous and Monkshood feared that the Earthworms might take the law into their own hands and hang him from a tavern sign with a notice pinned to his corpse proclaiming him to be a traitor. In the end, Monkshood had sworn an oath. He would demonstrate his loyalty to the Great Community of the Realm by joining Athelstan's pilgrimage, which was now common news, as was Thibault's participation in it. Gaunt was beyond their reach, Monkshood had argued – the failed attempt on the regent's life by the Salamander King at the Tower had proven that. Thibault was more vulnerable. Monkshood would demonstrate his fealty to the great cause by sacrificing Thibault on its altar. His comrades had agreed. They reasoned that if Monkshood was a traitor he would just flee and they would be free of him forever. However, if he was a member of the true and loyal Commons, Thibault would die.

Monkshood had dug up the few coins he had buried to buy a new robe, fresh linen and stout sandals. He had visited a barber in the Stews, emerging back on the streets as Brother Giles of the Franciscan Order. He had been accepted by both Cranston and Athelstan, though Monkshood was astute enough to realise that the Dominican had his reservations, which would explain why Monkshood felt he had been kept under close watch since he had joined this merry pilgrimage.

Now he drew the long dagger from its scabbard then pushed it back. He was ready. The Upright Man moved from the outhouse. Earlier in the day, while the rest of the pilgrims were assembled in the taproom for communal prayers, he had, like any skilled assassin, searched out chambers, stairways and passageways. He'd moved silently as a shadow. He had glimpsed that woman flitting from one room to another but he ignored her. Monkshood had learnt from servants and scullions that Thibault was lodged in the first gallery – ensconcing himself, of course, in the most comfortable chamber.

Monkshood looked up at the star-filled sky, stifling his doubts about the wisdom of what he was planning. He gripped his dagger, raced across the cobbled yard and slipped through the postern door he had secretly wedged open earlier. The tavern was settling for the night. Monkshood crept down the passageway leading to the main stairway. He was about to steal up it when he heard a sound behind him and felt the sharp nick of a steel point against the side of his neck.

'Good evening, Monkshood.' Athelstan stepped out of the shadows, accompanied by Watkin and Pike. Monkshood's dagger was abruptly seized. He swung round and stared into Cranston's smiling face.

'Let us go ever so gently up to my chamber,' Cranston murmured, 'not far, along the first gallery as befits the Lord High Coroner of London.' He sheathed his sword and mockingly gestured at Monkshood. 'Let us not waste any more time, my friend.'

A short while later, Cranston locked the door to his chamber and brought down the latch, a small, square piece of wood which swung on its screw into the waiting clasp. The coroner settled himself behind his chancery desk and stared at Monkshood squatting on a stool before him. Athelstan and his two parishioners made themselves comfortable along the edge of the great four-poster bed.

'You were suspicious of me, weren't you?' Monkshood blurted out. 'You realised . . .'

Athelstan interrupted him: 'I didn't believe that the Upright Men would attack our pilgrimage in the vain hope of assassinating Thibault. Look at us, we are many and we are well armed. Both Sir John and I watched you keep Thibault and his coven under close scrutiny, and my good friends here,' Athelstan gestured at Watkin and Pike, 'agreed with my suspicions about you.'

'We are not traitors,' Pike declared.

'Nor Judas men,' Watkin rasped. 'Monkshood, we recognise you as a comrade. We did not want to see you die. You would be cut down or captured before you ever reached Thibault. If you survived, they'd hang you out of hand. You know that.' Watkin leaned forward, rubbing great, dirt-engrained hands together. 'Monkshood, the Great Cause is finished. When Adam delved and Eve spun, is a fast-fading song. One day it will be lustily sung again in this kingdom, but I suspect by the time that happens we will all be floating on the winds of heaven.'

Monkshood sat all composed and quiet, listening intently. Athelstan suspected that this former captain of the Earthworms was deeply relieved by the decision being made for him.

'We noticed you were missing from our prayers in the taproom,' Watkin continued. 'I guessed you were spying out the lie of the land. Pike and I knew you would strike either tonight or tomorrow . . .'

Athelstan got to his feet, drew out his ave beads and dangled the cross in front of Monkshood. 'Now, Monkshood, swear an oath here on this cross that you will offer no injury to Thibault or his henchmen then you are free to go. Tomorrow you can decide whether you wish to stay with us or seek your salvation elsewhere.'

Monkshood sighed heavily and sat staring at the floor. Eventually he raised his right hand and cupped the small crucifix between his fingers.

'I swear. I will offer no injury to Thibault or

233

any of his coven. As for the rest,' Monkshood shrugged, 'it's best if I continued with you, at least until we reach Rochester and the Medway. Once there, I can search for a ship to take me to foreign parts.'

Athelstan patted Monkshood on the shoulder. 'Rest assured, we will make certain that you take food, good clothing and,' he glanced at Cranston, who nodded, 'some coins to help you on your way.'

Monkshood rose and clasped the hands of each of them. 'In which case, I will continue with this strange pilgrimage where young ladies make themselves so available, going from one chamber to another.'

'Cecily and Clarissa,' Watkin murmured, 'those two ladies are . . .'

Monkshood however was no longer listening. He left the room and paused for a while. He thought of staying and having a word with Watkin and Pike, but that could wait. Now he needed to think, to plot his way forward. He reached the outhouse and crept inside. As the darkness gathered about him, he felt something slip about his throat and then tighten brutally. Terrified, Monkshood tried to resist, but he was held fast for those last few heartbeats of life.

Athelstan stared down at Monkshood's corpse, fighting back tears. He tried to master his shock at seeing this vigorous young man garrotted so swiftly, his life light snuffed out like a candle flame. Only a few hours ago Monkshood was full of life and mischief; a good-looking, handsome man, but now his face was grotesquely twisted by the horror of his savage death.

'A garrotte cord,' Athelstan murmured, crouching down to peer a little closer. 'But I can see no greeting from Azrael.' The friar straightened up and looked at mine host, who stood quivering like one of his jellies, his fat face all pasty and sweat-soaked.

'This is not good for business,' he muttered. 'This is not acceptable.'

'I suspect Monkshood would agree with you,' Cranston retorted, 'if he could. For heaven's sake, man, this poor soul was murdered, and cruelly so.' He entered the outhouse and tapped his boot on the dirt-encrusted floor. 'Monkshood was found here?'

'Yes. One of the stable boys came across to collect a bag of feed.' Chobham pointed to a row of sacks along a shelf.

Cranston looked around intently, then patted Chobham on the shoulder and told to go back to his other guests.

The coroner gestured at Athelstan to draw close. 'Once again,' he murmured, 'there is no disturbance, no resistance, just a man violently strangled.'

'And why?' Athelstan asked. 'Why murder Monkshood? We talked to him, what, about an hour before midnight?' He pressed a hand against the dead man's tortured face. 'His corpse is now fairly cold. I suspect he was murdered soon after he left us, almost immediately, in fact. But why, why, why? Did he see or hear something untoward? But what? And why kill him so speedily?

235

This time there is no mocking greeting, but Azrael must have regarded Monkshood as a real danger to him. So, did Monkshood have more secrets than we realised?' He glanced at Cranston who simply shook his head.

'As far as I know,' the coroner murmured, 'Monkshood had little if anything in common with Thibault and the evangelists, but is it possible that he was their spy amongst the Upright Men?' Cranston broke off at the sound of raised voices and a violent, crashing echo across the yard. Master Chobham reappeared all a-quiver, exclaiming loudly that confusion and chaos had engulfed his tavern, and that now Master Thibault and his clerks could not rouse John Gaddesden, whose chamber remained locked and clasped. Cranston bellowed at the taverner to stay calm. Once he'd ceased his moaning, Athelstan asked about the chamber window.

'It is a large window,' Chobham declared. 'It has a casement door, but it's shuttered firmly with clasps both within and without.' The taverner wiped the sweat from his face on a napkin. 'I believe something terrible has happened.'

The coroner and the friar joined the hubbub on the gallery, its polished floorboards glistening in the morning light which pierced the oriel window at the far end. Thibault and Albinus were there, cloaks thrown over their nightshirts. Matthew Gaddesden had also been roused by the same servant who, instructed by his brother John the night before, had brought up a blackjack of light ale and some toasted cheese to break his fast. The servant had tried to rouse John and, when he failed, raised the alarm.

'Sir John,' Athelstan hissed, 'impose some order, and get that door broken down.'

Using all the authority of his office, Cranston cleared the gallery except for Thibault, Albinus and Matthew Gaddesden. Servants were summoned, an ancient yule log found. Cranston believed the chamber door was firmly locked, the clasps brought down, and it would have to be forced. The battering began, as hard and as ruthless as any ram used against a castle gate. The pounding became incessant. Scraps of plaster fell from the surrounding wall as the door began to buckle then snap free on both sides. The locks, clasps and leather hinges ruptured and the door fell like a bridge into the room. Cranston, who'd listened intently to Athelstan's whispering, ordered everyone, even Matthew Gaddesden, to stand back.

'Please,' Athelstan begged, 'I ask you to stay outside. Let me first inspect the chamber.'

'But I need to see my brother,' Matthew pleaded.

'Please,' Athelstan repeated. Cranston drew his sword and mounted guard as Athelstan stepped over the door and entered the shadow-filled chamber. He immediately noticed that the candles on their spigots had guttered out, as had the small lantern placed on top of a chest. The friar warily crossed to the window, lifted the bar and pulled back the shutters, then he opened the casement window and pushed open the outside slats so the light poured in. He had already glimpsed a shadow-like bundle lying on the four-poster bed, its curtains slightly pulled open. For the moment, Athelstan ignored this, as well as the pleas from those standing outside on the gallery.

The friar gazed around the chamber, trying memorise what he saw, then, finally, he moved towards the bed. He pulled back the curtains and stared down at the frightful-looking corpse lying there: a mocking imitation of a man put lovingly to bed. John Gaddesden was still fully clothed, he was even wearing his boots: his body had been laid out in repose, legs together, arms crossed over his chest like a penitent prepared to receive the Sacrament. All this was in cruel contrast to his face, agonised in death, the garrotte cord still tight around his throat. Athelstan stretched over and twisted the small parchment square: despite the poor light he read the same taunting message, 'Lord Azrael greets you'. Athelstan felt physically sick. He turned and walked back to the centre of the room and stood there for a while, taking deep breaths, before beckoning the others in. The dead man's brother hurried past him, took one look at the corpse and burst into loud sobbing. Athelstan steadied himself and stared around. He must note and recall everything as it was.

'And that's the mystery,' Athelstan murmured to himself. 'So deathly peaceful, yet murder has been committed.' Still feeling ill, he excused himself. He hurried out along the gallery and downstairs, pushing aside parishioners and others till he reached the garden, which was thankfully deserted. The friar slumped down on a turf seat

238

and breathed in the early morning fragrance of the flowers. He then closed his eyes and prayed fervently for help.

'Come, you Father of the Poor,
Light Immortal, Light Divine . . .'

The words poured out of him, cleansing the clinging filth of what he had seen and felt in that room. Athelstan took some more deep breaths, then he rose and returned to the death chamber, excusing himself for his abrupt departure. Matthew Gaddesden had been taken away by Thibault and Albinus, whilst Cranston was busy organising the removal of the corpse. This was only completed when Athelstan summarily performed the last rites, both anointing and blessing the remains, after which he again inspected the dead man and the murder chamber. Once the cadaver had been removed, Athelstan demanded the door be turned over so he could inspect the wooden clasps at top and bottom. It was a simple but very effective mechanism: both latches had been brought down to rest in their clasps so the door would be secure. Now they were nothing but shattered shards. The lock had also buckled as it had been turned by Gaddesden when he retired the night before. Cranston handed Athelstan the key from where it had been left on the bedside table and gestured at the fallen door.

'For what it's worth, that's the key to that lock.'

Athelstan inspected it and handed it back. 'So difficult to believe!' he exclaimed, sitting down on a stool. 'Correct me if I am wrong, Sir John, but this is the mystery which confronts us.

239

John Gaddesden, a fairly young, vigorous man, retires yesterday evening. He comes into this chamber, he locks the door, takes the key out and places it on the table next to his bed. He also brings down the latches on the door, one at the top and the other at the bottom, to make the chamber even more secure. The room's one and only window is firmly locked and shuttered. Not even a flea could squeeze through that, yet we are to believe that during the night Azrael the murderous demon swept in here, God knows how, and garrotted John Gaddesden without leaving any trace of violence or resistance. Look around, Sir John! Absolutely nothing is disturbed in this room, whilst the victim is laid out as if ready for bed except for that gruesome garrotte cord fastened around his throat and the hideous expression on his face. Azrael is a killer, a true son of Cain, a slayer to the very marrow of his heart, but he is also a mocker. He ridicules us, Sir John, he sneeringly taunts us.' Athelstan clasped his hands together and stared down at the floor, his mind teeming with all the possibilities. Cranston coughed noisily. Athelstan glanced up and smiled. 'Sir John, go and see Master Thibault. Tell him to use all his power and authority to requisition this tavern. I know it can be done under the royal ordinances on purveyance.'

'Why must he do that?'

'We are not leaving here,' Athelstan declared, 'until this mystery is solved and Azrael hanged on the nearest scaffold. Thibault, Gaunt, the King's Council, yea, even the King himself, all owe you and me a great deal. The cost of all this can be borne by the Royal Exchequer. Seek out Thibault now. Once he agrees, and I am sure he will, we need to meet all the pilgrims in the taproom to explain as well as to question. But first, Sir John, fetch up mine host and the hangman.'

A short while later both men followed the coroner into the bedchamber, Master Chobham wringing his hands, his face twisted into a doleful grimace.

Athelstan pressed the chamber key into Chobham's hand. 'Look at the door, mine host. Is this the appropriate key?' He pointed to the thick bunch of keys hanging from a hook on the broad black belt around the taverner's very generous waist. 'And do you have a master?'

'There is no master key,' Chobham mumbled, 'only a duplicate, and that is here.'

The taverner fumbled with his belt and undid the keyring, then inspected it closely and pulled one key out. 'You see . . .' He held up the key Athelstan had given him alongside the one on the ring. Athelstan peered at both and could see they were identical. Each bore the same symbol on the grip. 'This keyring never leaves me,' Chobham declared.

'So, last night John Gaddesden had a key to this room and so did you?'

'Of course,' Chobham replied testily.

Athelstan turned to the coroner. 'Sir John, the lock to this room has been forced; however, please make sure that both keys do fit that lock whilst I and my friend Giles here have a brief discussion.'

The coroner and mine host became busy around the fallen door, Chobham summoning servants to assist. Athelstan plucked at the hangman's sleeve and led him to the far corner of the chamber.

'Another strangling, Brother?'

'Another strangling,' Athelstan agreed. 'Tell me, Giles, could you garrotte a man like John Gaddesden in a place like this and leave no damage?'

'Impossible,' the hangman replied. 'Father, I have already advised you of that.'

'And remind me, how long would it take for the assassin to choke his victim?'

'A truly trained one . . .' The hangman pulled a face. 'It's just like hanging, you have a choice: to snap the neck or choke your victim.' The hangman's strange face broke into a grin. 'You could say, how long is a piece of string, if you pardon the joke.' Athelstan didn't smile.

'Well,' the hangman continued hurriedly, 'no longer than it would take you to recite an ave. In Spain, where they garrotte criminals publicly, it's simply a matter of turning a handle, a few heartbeats. As for the lack of disturbance,' he blew his cheeks out, 'I would ask myself, were all the victims drugged with some potion? But I can see no cup or goblet, can you, Father? Or, as I mentioned before, were all the victims clasped in some trap, hands and feet held fast by an accomplice? It's all possible.'

Athelstan thanked him. The hangman left, promising he would assemble everyone in the taproom below. Cranston and Chobham had finished examining the door and Athelstan walked over to join them. Cranston pointed out that both latches had been clasped shut, which was why they were now shattered, whilst the lock had also been snapped. Nevertheless the portly, perspiring taverner assured Cranston and Athelstan that the key left on the bedside table was the correct one, whilst the duplicate had never left his keyring. He also pointed out that the window had been securely shuttered and, of course, there was no secret entrance or passageway into this chamber or to any in his tavern.

'I must go back to my kitchen,' he pleaded. 'You have to eat, I have to cook.'

Athelstan agreed and watched him go. 'Curious,' he murmured, 'and curiouser still.'

'What is it, little monk?'

'Little friar! Nothing really, Sir John, just a feeling that all is not well with mine host.'

'Well, his tavern has been turned into a slaughter house.'

'Oh, I think it's more than that . . .' Athelstan broke off as Thibault and Albinus, accompanied by Matthew Gaddesden, who now had some control over his grief, walked into the chamber. There were not enough seats, so Athelstan declared they would deal with matters quickly. Thibault readily agreed to pay for the pilgrims to remain longer at the Sign of Hope until the mystery was resolved.

'I am of the same mind as you both, Brother Athelstan and Sir John. It is foolish to continue as if there's nothing wrong. Azrael has followed us here! He is a member of our company and he has to be rooted out. The Exchequer will certainly pay all bills whilst I will use a royal writ of purveyance to ensure mine host complies.'

'So we are in agreement,' Athelstan insisted, 'the pilgrimage stops here? We rest at the Sign of Hope until Azrael is caught, unmasked and hanged. I will tell my parishioners the same.'

'And if the matter is not resolved?' Matthew asked.

'I am not too sure,' Athelstan admitted. 'You have the Castilian envoys waiting for you at Canterbury. I don't know what I would advise about that. Sir John and I would probably stay here. Perhaps Watkin and Pike could take the rest of our parishioners back and, if all goes well, later in the autumn, we might consider another pilgrimage. However,' Athelstan forced a smile, 'let us pray for the best and plan for the worst. Gentlemen . . .' Athelstan then delivered his formal condolences on the death of John Gaddesden, adding that they should all gather for a short funeral service as soon as he had finished meeting with his parishioners. Until then . . .

A few hours later in the early afternoon, Athelstan sat in his scribe's chair, head in his hands. He stared disconsolately down at the fine grain wood of the chancery desk, wishing fancifully that he could become tangled in its skein of colour. He let his hands fall away and smiled as he recalled how he used to do the same as a child. He would stare at a piece of wood and become lost in its circles and wild patterns of grain as if they housed some secret world.

Athelstan crossed himself. He sincerely wished he could escape his own world, as he found it impossible to fathom the mysteries bubbling around him. He had blessed John Gaddesden's corpse for a second time and then Thibault had hired two of the tavern servants to take both corpses back to the death house at St Mary le Bow in London. Apparently the Gaddesdens owned a family plot there, close to the Jericho Gate. Monkshood, on the other hand, would be buried in Haceldama, the Field of Blood, that area of God's Acre reserved for strangers or those with no kin.

Physician Giole, who'd spent the evening cooking and cleaning, carefully scrutinised both corpses as Cranston asked. The physician agreed with Athelstan's conclusions. He could find no other sign of violence or resistance. In addition, he had scrutinised the inside of the mouth of both cadavers. Giole admitted he might be wrong, but he could not establish that either man had been given any potion or powder.

'I can smell wine,' he conceded, 'but the strange thing about sudden death is that the vapours of the stomach and throat are very clear. Many sleeping potions have a definite smell or tang, as do most poisons.'

Athelstan had thanked him and then questioned Matthew Gaddesden, insisting that he and Cranston be allowed to meet him without Thibault or Albinus being present. The Master of Secrets had turned surly but admitted that he had no challenge to that. In the end, the clerk could tell Athelstan very little. He and his brother had arrived in good spirits at the Sign of Hope. They had been with the others in the taproom when Sir John led the rosary. Afterwards, as Athelstan knew, they had dined in the supper room. John, like themselves, had eaten well and drunk deeply. They had both been allocated their chambers. Once the supper was over, John declared he was tired and retired for the night, and that was the last time Matthew had seen him alive. The clerk was grief-stricken, finding it increasingly difficult to talk to Athelstan, who eventually thanked him and let him go.

He and Sir John then met all the pilgrims in the taproom. Athelstan had explained the problem, giving as few details as possible about the murder of Monkshood and John Gaddesden. The friar informed his parishioners that the two killings were connected to something he and Sir John had been investigating before they left Southwark and the assassin could well be amongst them. This caused, as Cranston remarked, some fluttering in the hen coop. However, Athelstan reassured his congregation that it was nothing involving the parish, although they should remain keen-eyed and sharp-witted and report anything suspicious. In the meantime, Athelstan continued, they would stay at the Sign of Hope. Master Thibault had assured Sir John that the Exchequer would pay all costs and Master Thibault would settle with mine host before they left. This provoked a great cheer because the parishioners of St Erconwald's were much taken with the tavern: they certainly did not view an extended stay as a hardship but revelled at the opportunity.

Finally Athelstan made an appeal, if anyone had glimpsed anything suspicious the previous evening . . . However, apart from some jokes at Watkin's expense, nobody could help. Once the meeting finished Athelstan took the hangman aside and asked him to keep a close eye on everyone's hands and look for the burn marks which the garrotte strings must have left on the assassin's fingers. The Hangman of Rochester replied he'd already begun such a search but without any success.

Full of frustration, the friar had decided to withdraw to his own chamber and brood. Athelstan murmured a prayer for help and pulled across the piece of parchment on which he had scribbled his thoughts so far. Yet reading this, he could make little sense or progress. The most recent murders were particularly baffling. Monkshood, a born street fighter, had been seized and swiftly garrotted in that outhouse, but why? The only logical explanation was that the former Earthworm had seen or learnt something highly injurious to Azrael, but what?

Athelstan heard the clatter of hooves from the courtyard below. The friar rose and walked to the window, then opened it and peered down. Tiptoft, Cranston's messenger, had arrived in great haste from London bringing despatches for the coroner and, Athelstan hoped, some specific information he needed about Azrael. Athelstan had encountered this angel's name in his own studies, but he had to make sure of his facts. He also hoped Tiptoft had brought the information he wanted about the Marcher lands between

France and Spain. He was tempted to go down and join Sir John but decided not to. Instead, he returned to the death chamber.

The corpse and all of John Gaddesden's possessions had been removed, the broken door pushed to one side. Athelstan went in and stared around, trying to recall his memories of the place. He was certain something had been moved, not maliciously, probably when the corpse and other items had been collected. Yes! The scribe's chair now squarely faced the small chancery desk, but when Athelstan had first entered the room after the door had been forced, the chair was facing the other way. It would seem that the previous evening John Gaddesden had moved the chair around from the desk so as to greet someone else, but who?

Athelstan glanced across to the stool resting against the far wall. Had Gaddesden's nocturnal visitor pulled it across and sat down? Athelstan pictured him first facing Gaddesden, then rising, slipping behind the clerk and swiftly garrotting him. Afterwards the assassin would have moved the stool back but perhaps mistakenly left the chair as it was. If this was true, then Azrael first appeared as a friend, somebody Gaddesden relaxed with. Indeed, that would fit with Athelstan's suspicion, indeed certainty, that Azrael was a member of their community, somebody Gaddesden accepted as amicable. Could it be his own brother? Or Master Thibault, Albinus? Of course, how Azrael struck so swiftly and silently then disappeared from a heavily locked room where both window and door were tightly secured, was still the deepest of mysteries.

Athelstan crouched down and pulled back the cord matting. He noticed recent scuff marks on the floor and felt a tingle of excitement. Could it be Gaddesden's boots? Or the leg of the chair he was sitting in as the garrotte string tightened around his throat? In which case, Gaddesden should have sprung to his feet, even if he only had a few heartbeats of life remaining. Apparently he didn't, so he must have been held fast, but how? Athelstan glanced over at the bed. A most mocking, macabre murder! Choking a man to death here in a chair before moving his corpse and arranging it so it seemed he was ready for a good night's rest. Athelstan heard a sound on the stairs. He made to rise when he glimpsed something gleaming: a small shard of wire caught in the rough cord matting. Athelstan plucked this free and held it up. A piece of wire mesh, but from what?

'Brother?'

Athelstan rose as Cranston swept into the death chamber. The friar explained his conclusions, which the coroner agreed with before scrutinising the thin piece of wire.

'I could be mistaken,' Cranston twirled the piece of metal between his fingers, 'but it reminds me very much of Toledo steel – have you seen any of that, Brother?'

'I've come across it in swords and daggers. I know it has a reputation for lightness, but it is also extremely strong.'

'True,' Cranston murmured, peering at the

249

shard. 'Toledo steel, the best of its kind, is like silk. It is very pliable but surprisingly strong. You suspect this may have been Azrael's, a fragment from his weaponry, his dagger, perhaps even the garrotte cord?' Cranston sighed, handed it back and brought a stool to sit by Athelstan.

'Brother,' he began sadly. 'I have dire news about Peter the Penniless. He was burnt to death in his house. Amelia also, she was with him. Both were murdered.'

'Murdered?'

'Murdered, Brother. The house was reduced to blackened timber. The fire was fed with oil, the ruins reeked of it. They also discovered two skeletons who must have been at the heart of the blaze . . .'

'And they are sure?'

Athelstan tried to keep calm and ignore the pang of deep regret at the thought that Peter perhaps should have come with them.

'Don't feel guilty, Athelstan. Peter was in no humour to travel. He was weak, his wits still frail. We would only have had to send him back.'

Athelstan crossed himself. He stared down at the floor, closed his eyes and murmured the requiem for Peter. For a brief while Athelstan recalled happier days. He opened his eyes and lifted his head. 'What happened, John?'

'From what the sheriff's men told Tiptoft, the burning was definitely arson. The wolfshead responsible, and it must have been Robert the clerk, killed Peter and Amelia with crossbow bolts loosed very close in the same chamber. Money boxes and coffers, or what remained of them, were emptied of all coin. The sheriff believes Amelia visited her husband to seek a reconciliation. Robert must have followed her in. He murdered both husband and wife, plundered the house then burnt it. A vindictive, evil man. We should be careful. Tiptoft also brought some gossip,' Cranston continued. The coroner narrowed his eyes, rocking backwards and forwards on the stool. 'A sign of the times, Brother.'

'What is?'

'Do you remember me saying that there had been similar murders with the garrotte? In fact there have been three, powerful merchants with one thing in common: they were all fervent supporters of Gaunt, and they subsidised him in all his forays both foreign and domestic.'

'So if that is true, Azrael could have been hired by Gaunt's enemies to kill the regent's allies as well as his trusted clerks?'

'Oh, it's more than that, Brother.' Cranston laced his fingers together. 'I said the world was changing. The Upright Men are broken. The Great Community of the Realm no longer exists. In the eyes of the great lords, the common threat has dissipated. Our king is a boy. Some of our lords nourish the most murderous designs and they engage in treasonable activities. They are like a wolf pack, Athelstan. If one moves to seize a prey, the rest will join in. They will kill each other. It's not a matter of sharing power but owning it: power over the young king, power over the royal council. The great lords are not ready for war, not yet, but they have always been ready for murder. Tiptoft has heard that professional assassins have entered the kingdom, ready to offer their services to whoever needs them. Now whether these are just moon-spun legends is a matter for debate.'

'But it's not just gossip, Sir John. Azrael is very real and deadly. God knows what other demons are mustering in the city or elsewhere, but we have to deal with him.'

'And that reminds me, Brother . . .' Cranston dug into the inside of his jerkin and drew out a small, thin scroll. 'Tiptoft, as directed, also visited Blackfriars. Prior Anselm and the rest of the brothers send their warmest regards to you, Athelstan, along with this, a response to your query from the librarian at Blackfriars.'

Athelstan broke the small, reddish seal and unrolled the scroll, holding it up to take full advantage of the light pouring through the window. He read it quickly, quietly translating the Norman French. Brother Norbert the librarian had been most thorough and given a full explanation.

Athelstan glanced up. 'Amongst other things, I asked our librarian to do a detailed study of the name Azrael. Brother Norbert has not disappointed me.'

'And?'

'Azrael is definitely a great angel. In many of his forms he is depicted as having four faces and four wings. According to the Jewish tradition, he is a leading baron of heaven, a celestial earl commanding the angels of God. Very little is written about him in Christian theology. However, in Islamic writings Azrael truly is the Angel of Death who separates the dead body from the soul.' Athelstan tapped the scroll. 'I just wonder why this cruel assassin assumed such a title.'

He paused as Cranston took a leather collar from inside his jerkin and handed it to him. The collar was about two inches deep, of the finest leather with a soft, woollen skin on the inside, and fitted with a clasp and buckle.

'Here.' Cranston rose and went behind Athelstan. He looped the collar strap around the friar's throat and secured the clasp on the side, then pulled up the edge of Athelstan's robe to hide it. Athelstan swallowed hard, moving his head and stretching his neck.

'It's certainly comfortable enough, Sir John, and I can guess what it is – protection against the garrotte cord.'

'The leather is stiffened yet light,' Cranston explained. 'It will not save you but it will delay the assassin and confuse him.' Cranston chewed the corner of his lip. 'I know you discussed the garrotte with the hangman. Well, before I left London, I visited some old rogues who are quite skilled with what they call "the strangle string". One of them gave me the collar. Athelstan, that evil soul Azrael has brushed you with his dark wings. Wear the collar, hide it beneath the edge of your robe, and, if you can, carry a dagger with you. Finally, my little friend, try not to be alone.'

Athelstan stared into Cranston's blue eyes, no longer bright with merry mischief but sad and anxious. Deeply touched by his friend's care,

Athelstan leaned across and gently stroked him on the side of his face. 'My friend,' he murmured. 'For your sake, I shall wear it. God forbid I ever have to depend on it. Now, what are your thoughts about Castile? Why is Thibault journeying to meet Castilian envoys at Canterbury?'

'I believe it is to do with Gaunt's ambitions in that direction,' Cranston replied. 'A few years ago, King Henry of Castile died. There was no clear heir to the crown. Gaunt, through his marriage to the Infanta Constanza, acquired a claim to the Castilian throne. Some there oppose him as a usurper, while others point out that Gaunt is not only married to a Castilian princess but is the great-grandson of the saintly Eleanor of Castile, wife of Edward I. Thibault, I suspect, is set to meet the Castilian envoys who favour John of Gaunt's claim. If he can get their full support, Gaunt will then go to the Commons and ask for an army to support his bid for the Castilian crown.'

'And will he get it?'

'There are those in England who would pay a king's fortune to see the back of Gaunt.' Cranston rose. 'But, little friar, that's for the future. Now I will leave you to your thoughts. I shall meet you below, yes?'

Distracted, Athelstan nodded absent-mindedly.

Cranston left and Athelstan returned to his own chamber. For a while he just sat listening to the noises of the tavern. He thought of Gaddesden stretched out on the bed, Monkshood all twisted in that outhouse. Azrael had certainly struck, but Athelstan was determined to see if the assassin had made a mistake. He recalled the ancient description of Azrael, four-faced, four-winged and devious. 'But you do not have the wisdom of the Holy Spirit,' Athelstan murmured. He returned to reflecting on Simon Mephan, and that dark shape in the garden, sinister and threatening, disappearing when Cranston and Giole appeared. And, of course, Mephan himself, slouched dead over his desk, and the riddle he had left. Intrigued, Athelstan rose and took the Book of Luke's Gospel from his chancery satchel. He found the page describing the Gesarene demoniac and ran his fingers across the two underscored words, 'legion' and 'many'.

'Our name is legion for we are many,' Athelstan whispered. He suddenly stopped, and smiled at his own foolishness. 'I've concentrated on the translation,' he whispered to himself, 'but Mephan underscored the Latin text.' Hastily, he laid out his writing tray and, taking a scrap of parchment, inked a quill pen and wrote out time and time again the relevant passage. He tried to imitate Mephan's absorption with words and letters, in particular these two, the ones Mephan had especially emphasised just before he died.

Athelstan was barely aware of the knock on the door, which abruptly opened without him answering. A shadowy servant brought in a tray and Athelstan returned to his study, but he raised his head when his hooded, visored visitor turned the key in the lock.

'What in God's name!' Athelstan exclaimed.

'Stay where you are, Brother Athelstan.'

The friar sat rigid, watching the dark figure

255

place a goblet of wine on the nearby table. He then stepped back and brought up the arbalest, all primed, the ugly, jagged bolt ready to be loosed. The figure, one hand holding the arbalest, pulled back his hood and unloosened the visor covering the bottom half of his face.

'Robert the clerk!' Athelstan exclaimed. He sat back in the chair, his mind teeming, wits all sharp. 'You are a wolfshead, wanted for the hideous murders of Peter and Amelia. You will hang from the nearest scaffold.' Athelstan leaned forward, determined not to show fear. 'If you want, I can shrive you, hear your confession and deliver absolution for your many terrible sins. You truly are a son of Cain. In the end, when you meet just punishment, I could have a word with our hangman so your end is swift, a broken neck rather than a long, choking death. You hunted those two, poor people. You blighted their lives. You have foully murdered them and sent their souls unprepared into the light.' Athelstan paused, searching his adversary's face, but he knew his words had little effect. Nevertheless, he was determined to keep talking, hoping against hope that Cranston or one of his parish-ioners would come up or, even better, have glimpsed Robert lurking below or slipping up the stairs like the dark, evil wolf he was. The clerk seemed unperturbed.

'Well, well, well.' Robert made himself comfortable on a stool. 'You will not be hearing my confession, priest. I am not frightened by your stories or pretended powers; I just thought we'd have a little chat before I gave you a choice and sent you to join that stupid couple, Peter and his wife Amelia.' Athelstan noticed that the arbalest was held firm; Robert's hand was steady. The friar had no illusions about his opponent. Robert was a killer to his very marrow but, like all his tribe, he loved to talk, to boast, to demonstrate how clever and subtle he truly was.

'Why?' Athelstan asked. 'Why did you kill those two people?'

'Listen, you little, interfering friar. You prattling, inquisitive priest.' Robert held up his left hand, forefinger and thumb slightly parted. 'So close,' he murmured, 'so very, very close. I have worked, laboured and slaved for years. Then Amelia comes tripping into my dirty little shop. You wouldn't understand, friar. You have nothing of the stallion in you. No hot blood, no rampaging lusts,' Robert shrugged, 'except for gazing moon-eyed at that widow-woman.'

'I do know what it is to love,' Athelstan retorted. 'I also know what is right and acceptable to God.'

'Well, you can discuss all that with him when you meet within the hour. As I said, friar, you don't understand. Amelia was plump, loving and better than a Cheapside whore when it came to tumbling on a bed. Believe me, priest, she knew so many tricks, lovely!' Robert licked his lips. 'And it was all wasted on that moonstruck idiot, Peter the bloody Penniless! Oh, I wined and dined Amelia and she told me all about her life. I led her as gently as any lapdog down the pathway of removing him forever. The plan was very simple. Peter was a miser. He needed a

257

clerk, he could hire me cheap and you know how it is.'

'I certainly do,' Athelstan replied. 'The fox stole into the hen coop to help himself to whatever he wanted.'

'True, true.' Robert grinned. 'It was only a matter of time before Peter's mind was turned, his humours upset and his wits collapsed; when that happened, a truly amorous, very rich widow was my prize. Oh, it was so simple, so easy. A drop of juice here, a smear of paste there and Peter the Penniless was despatched into the world of goblins, monsters and demons.' Robert blew his cheeks out. 'Until you appeared with your nose twitching like some lurcher on the hunt.'

Athelstan stared into Robert's red-rimmed eyes. He recalled Prior Anselm's homily on demonic possession: how an evil spirit can take up residence in human flesh and wax strong, growing in power and ruthless dedication to its own evil will. Robert the clerk was one of these. He had been frustrated and foiled. Many another soul would accept the loss, but not him. He was committed to a fight to the death, bent on vengeance and punishing all those who had frustrated him. Amelia and Peter had paid the price and Robert was now determined to exact the same of Athelstan.

'Friar, you should keep your twitching nose out of other people's business, but you don't. You think yourself so subtle and wise, yet you are stupid.' Robert swayed slightly on the stool. Athelstan wondered if his opponent had drunk a little too deeply on ale, wine or both.

He would remember that. Robert thought he would frighten him but Athelstan was determined to resist and to seize any opportunity he could.

'Stupid?' Athelstan turned his head slightly. 'You call me stupid?'

'Do you know what is going on here during your pilgrimage?' Robert sneered. 'Most of your companions are as fit for Hell as I am. You hunt the strangler, or so I hear?'

'I am also hunting you.'

'Not for long,' Robert jibed. 'I have studied your little flock, Athelstan.' He preened himself, and the friar secretly marvelled at why murderous souls such as Robert always seemed crammed with their own importance: they exuded an unbelievable arrogance at how superior they were to the rest of humanity.

'What are you implying?' Athelstan asked, listening keenly to the sounds from the taproom below. Cranston must be becoming curious as to why Athelstan had not joined him and the rest.

'I'm talking about Gregorio,' Robert replied. 'He was out last night in the fields across the road, he and his confederates.'

'Confederates?'

'Yes, those chapmen who have joined your company. I just tell you that because you will never have the chance of finding out the truth behind it all. Look,' Robert scratched the side of his unshaven face, 'time is passing, friar. A swift death,' he lifted the arbalest, 'or . . .' He gestured at the goblet. 'Mingled it myself, I did. Good Bordeaux with a strong infusion of what you call banewort, Devil's herb, witch berry or, even more memorable, belladonna.' Robert sniffed. 'I picked it myself from the cemetery at St Erconwald's – most fitting, wouldn't you say? I wandered there once you had left. Goodness, you could poison a cathedral full of people, must be something in the soil. The belladonna grows two to five feet high with spreading branches: its leaves always grow in pairs, one being longer than the other. The flowers, and you must have noticed these, are dark violet, rather attractive; the fruits are a shiny black plum with purple juice.' Robert smacked his lips. 'Very nice, the first sip. Every part of that plant is highly poisonous.'

'Will you go first?' Athelstan taunted. 'Will you join me in my cups?'

'No, friar. You have a choice: drink the wine or I will kill you with a crossbow bolt which will shatter your head. Perhaps I could do both. I mean, once you have drunk, the symptoms are fairly obvious and repulsive: raging fever, dry mouth, frenzied thoughts. You feel as if you are slowly choking. You'll probably put your hand out, eyes popping, to beg me to release the bolt . . .' Robert paused at a knock at the door. The handle was tried but it was locked.

'Father, Father?' Crim's voice echoed. 'Are you awake?'

'Answer it,' Robert hissed. 'No, on second thoughts . . .' He brought the arbalest up. 'Answer it from where you sit.'

'I am awake,' Athelstan called out. 'I have bolted the door because I am thinking . . .'

260

'Sir John wonders if you would like something to eat and drink?'

'Not here,' Robert whispered hoarsely and grinned. 'You can order the meal you'll never eat.'

'Tell Sir John I will be down shortly. I would like a large cup of Rhenish and lampreys grilled and mixed with shallots. Tell him now.'

Athelstan caught Robert's quizzical look. 'My favourite meal,' he whispered. Athelstan heard Crim clatter away down the gallery.

'Well friar, cup or bolt?' He leaned forward. 'Or both.'

Athelstan picked up the pewter goblet and weighed it in his hand. He glanced across at Robert. 'I wish to say a prayer.'

'A short one . . .'

'Oh yes.' Athelstan, still holding the goblet, bowed his head. He began to recite the 'Confiteor' but pretended to stumble over the words so he began again. His heart was beating vigorously and sweat sheened his skin. He almost sighed as the door rattled.

'Father?' Benedicta called. 'You must come. Something has happened. Father?' The door now shook.

'Let her in,' Robert grated. 'She can drink as well. Yes,' he nodded, 'you can die with your whore in this tavern bedchamber.'

Still carrying the goblet, Athelstan crossed to the door, shouting that he would open it. He turned the lock and pulled it open, even as he hurled the goblet with all his might at his opponent. Robert moved to avoid the cup. He slipped and steadied himself.

Cranston burst through the door, his great, two-edged sword already swinging back. The razor-sharp blade scythed the air and bit deep into Robert's neck, almost severing his head. The muscle and the flesh of the neck were completely sheared, the head tipped eerily to one side as spumes of blood sprayed the chamber . . .

Part Seven

For the Love of Gold is the Root of all Evil

Hours later, Athelstan sat with Cranston at a table in a window embrasure of the tavern's taproom.

'A time of blood!' Judith the mummer had proclaimed.

The sudden and violent death of Robert the clerk in such gruesome circumstances had swept the tavern, followed by the heinous news that Robert had tried to murder their beloved parish priest. Athelstan was greeted with shouts and acclamations whilst Cranston was hailed as God's own warrior. Mine host Chobham had been frightened out of his wits by what he described as 'the bloody carnage of the battlefield'. Thibault and his henchmen had been more reserved but shocked and surprised at Robert daring to pursue his blood feud along the Pilgrim Way.

In the end, all the pilgrims had gathered in the taproom. Athelstan, still fairly weak after his deadly confrontation, had to explain exactly what had happened. If Cranston had not stopped them, Watkin, Pike and other parishioners would have seized Robert's blood-soaked, battered corpse, impaled it close to the tavern piggery and left it there to rot. Instead Cranston had persuaded them

263

to help clean the chamber, take Athelstan's belongings to another and remove Robert's corpse so it now lay sheeted and coffined, ready to be carted to the nearest cemetery for swift, summary burial. At last some order was imposed. Mine host Chobham was promised compensation whilst the mess of 'the great carnage' was soon cleared up. Athelstan stared down at the bowl of vegetable pottage Giole and Beatrice had insisted on serving him, 'according to a rare and special Castilian recipe', or so they said. Athelstan found it delicious.

'Not lampreys grilled with shallots,' Cranston teased, 'or a large cup of Rhenish? I always remember you telling me how you intensely hate the sight, smell and taste of lampreys. Shallots are also despised, whilst you hold Rhenish in the same low regard.'

'The fruits of a misspent youth,' Athelstan confessed. 'I spent some time at our house in Oxford. God bless him and give him rest, Brother Eudo the cook loved lampreys and shallots and thought everybody else should. We had lampreys in shallot sauce from Prime to Compline. I prayed that you would remember that.' Athelstan sighed deeply. 'Robert was a killer.'

'Yes, he certainly was,' Cranston agreed. 'Tiptoft brought me some gossip about him – how he sold powders to women who wanted to get rid of a child, and there were some very unsavoury tales about some of the potions and powders he sold and what they were intended for. A nasty, twisted soul. Anyway, why don't you like Rhenish?'

'I was drinking Rhenish when they brought my brother's corpse back into camp. The very taste of it takes me back and, indeed, it is my late brother who now concerns me.'

'You wish to visit his grave?'

'Yes, as I mentioned to you before. Four miles from the Sign of Hope stands Saint Grace's Priory, a Carthusian house, isolated, rather desolate. I regard it as a place of profound holiness. When Stephen-Francis was killed I had his body cleaned and ready for transport back to England. I have also told you this, Sir John, the news of his death . . .' Athelstan fought to keep the tremor out of his voice, '. . . killed my parents. I could not take my brother's corpse back to the West Country, I just couldn't. In the end the captain of the cog I secured passage on berthed at Tilbury. I journeyed inland along with my travelling companion, Ralph Sherwin, a Carthusian monk coming from the mother house La Grande Chartreuse in France. During the voyage he and I had become great friends. He heard my confession and shrived me after I'd told him about my earlier life, the death of my brother and the tragedy which befell my parents. He described Saint Grace's to me; I thought it would be ideal. I had some money, some treasure and, in the end, Ralph interceded with the prior and so my brother now lies buried under the flagstones of a chantry chapel in the main church of Saint Grace's Priory.' Athelstan took a deep breath. 'I intend to journey there tomorrow morning by myself.'

'Brother, you must be careful. I am sure you will not forget Robert the clerk.'

265

'Sir John, I thank you for my rescue.' Athelstan patted Cranston's sword arm. 'God bring Robert the clerk to judgement, a true sinner. He lived a bad life and died a worse death.'

'I suspected he would come,' Cranston admitted. 'The little I learnt of him was highly unpleasant. A truly vindictive man. He decided on vengeance, we are not difficult to follow, and it's easy for a stranger to mingle amongst us.'

'Which reminds me.' Athelstan informed the coroner about Robert the clerk's comments on Gregorio and the Spanish friar's strange meetings in the fields outside the tavern during the dead of night.

'There is something else.' Cranston looked quickly around. 'Last Thursday, Margaret Chobham, wife of mine host here, went into the city to visit her brother, who happens to be the owner of the Mitre in Farringdon ward. You see how all these vintners are related. Mistress Margaret even knows my golden girl at the Lamb of God in Cheapside.' Cranston smacked his lips. 'God bring me safely back there. I would love one of her pies.'

'Sir John!'

'Ah yes, Brother. Anyway, Mistress Margaret heard about Mephan's death during her visit to the city. Now, whilst you were involved with the murderous Robert, I was chatting to Mistress Margaret who, by the way, keeps a very sharp eye on her husband and the games he plays with the serving maids.'

'Sir John!'

'Ah yes. Mistress Margaret said it was good

riddance to Mephan. He was a bully who used his power, status and knowledge, particularly what he learnt about individual taverners, and he would use this to his own advantage.'

'Meaning?'

'Athelstan, the recent troubles are now over. However, in the months and years preceding them, many taverners, and I suspect this includes Master Chobham, had to serve two masters: the Crown and the Upright Men. They were frightened of the Earthworms, who, of course, used taverns and alehouses for their own secret purposes, such as the storing of arms and provisions, or meetings long after midnight. We both know that. We have come across it time and again. Now Mephan was a senior clerk in the Secret Chancery close to the workings of both Crown and Church. He would acquire a great deal of information about taverns and alehouses in the city and the surrounding shires, and he could use that. If Master Mephan decided to threaten a taverner, it would be a serious matter . . .'

'But why should he threaten them?'

Cranston tapped his own belly. 'Taverns such as the Mitre buy very good food; their purveyance is of the highest order. Mine hostess at the Lamb of God constantly complains about the price butchers demand for good fresh meat. If Master Mephan had all his meals paid for, that would amount to a tidy sum: fresh food, good wine, strong ale, free use of chambers, the best of this and the best of that, both in a particular tavern or to be delivered to his house. Athelstan, if the Lady Maude and I no longer needed to pay for food or drink, we'd become very wealthy.'

'So, Mephan was corrupt. He would be in very good company in that.'

'Undoubtedly, Brother, but I recall my training as a lawyer and I remember that axiom, *'Falsus in parvis, falsus in magnis, falsus in uno, falsus in omnibus.'*

'False in small things,' Athelstan translated, 'false in great things. False in one, false in all. How does that apply to Mephan?'

'What if Mephan was of the *mens rea,* the criminal mind? The Great Revolt is over. We suspect – even know – that Gaunt's meddling and his treacherous intrigues against his nephew the young king, and his double-dealing with everyone else, could weigh heavily against him. Just take one fact: when the Great Revolt was about to break, where was Gaunt? He takes the Crown's only army north to the Scottish March. The Scots did not pose a threat, and even if they did, Percy of Northumberland would act as a stone wall against them. Now that's only one item amongst many. What if Mephan used such information to blackmail his former master and, by implication, his Master of Secrets, the ever smiling Thibault?'

'That would be a very dangerous game,' Athelstan declared, 'to blackmail Gaunt and Thibault.'

'But it might explain the murders of Mephan and two of the evangelists.'

'I don't think so,' Athelstan disagreed. 'Let us say for the sake of argument that the evangelists were persuaded to participate in Mephan's blackmail of their master, they would now realise he is striking back and flee. They certainly wouldn't go on pilgrimage to Canterbury with Gaunt's principal henchmen.'

Cranston scratched his head. 'Yes, I can see there are gaps in my argument, but my main point is that Mephan was a blackmailer. Did he turn on his masters? Perhaps only some of the evangelists are involved. Perhaps Mephan insinuated that they were all involved when in fact they are totally innocent and ignorant of any such blackmail.'

Athelstan toasted Cranston with his tankard. 'Your main hypothesis, Sir John, that Mephan was a blackmailer, is certainly a strong possibility. Let's turn your argument around. In the end, Gaunt and Thibault must be deeply concerned about what Mephan and the evangelists know. There doesn't have to be blackmail. Gaunt and Thibault could decide that now the revolt is over, their role in it could lead to all sorts of trouble; Mephan and the evangelists know too much and so have to be silenced. Gaunt and Thibault could be directly responsible for the murders. We know that Albinus is a veteran killer, or they might be using someone else such as the mysterious Gregorio. Are the evangelists united, or is one of them prepared to kill his brothers? It would not be the first time in history. Of course, we know Azrael has levelled threats against Gaunt and his henchmen, but that could only be a pretence, an attempt to divert suspicion. So yes, all in all,' Athelstan supped from his blackjack, 'it's a strong possibility. In which case there will be more murders.'

He took another sip, half listening to the sounds of the tavern: the laughter of his parishioners, the neighing of horses and the clip-clop of hooves from the stables outside. 'It's interesting, Sir John, what you say about taverners being blackmailed. Yes, very interesting. I will return to all this once I have paid my respects to my brother, God rest him.'

'I will go with you,' Cranston offered. 'All is well here: your parishioners are behaving themselves. Bonaventure believes he is in heaven, sprawled in Benedicta's lap or that of Mistress Beatrice.'

'No, Sir John. I am grateful for the offer, but this is one journey I want to make alone.' Athelstan leaned over and squeezed the coroner's wrist. 'But I do ask you one favour, my Lord High Coroner: when I leave, make sure no one follows!'

Athelstan left the Sign of Hope early the following morning. A thick, heavy mist had swirled in from the sea, blanketing the Kentish countryside and gathering everything into its thick embrace, deadening sound and covering the land like a cold, clinging shroud. Athelstan crossed himself, murmured the early morning offering and made himself as comfortable as possible in the high-horned saddle. He was glad of the thick woollen robe with its deep capuchon. The sun would eventually rise and the summer heat return, but until then he would keep warm.

He slouched on his horse, the reins loosely held, gently directing Philomel along the trackway. The clip-clop of the old destrier's hooves was the only sound to break the eerie silence. The ancient hedgerows either side lay strangely silent. The birds would only sing their morning office once the mist had lifted.

Athelstan became lost in his own thoughts. He was determined to use the silent loneliness of his journey to probe the mysteries which swirled around him like an invisible mist. Once again he took his ave beads out, sifting each one through his fingers as he listed what he knew. First, he reflected, there was the Gospel passage about the Gesarene demoniac and those two words, 'legion' and 'many'. Athelstan had been deeply surprised by the possibilities these words, at least in Latin, offered to a man like Mephan. According to all the evidence, Mephan loved resolving problems, but he also had a rather nasty trait of using secret information to extract favours, even if it was just free victuals at this tavern or that.

Secondly, Mephan's murder. Athelstan could not make sense of it. He wondered about that mysterious figure who had appeared in Mephan's garden to threaten him. Who was free that morning to do so, and who had the ability and strength to climb a garden wall? Albinus? Gregorio? One of the evangelists?

Thirdly, Roger Empson the courier. He had fled into hiding, scuttling in and out to make the necessary purchases. Who had the means to keep this fugitive under constant scrutiny so that

Azrael could enter the death house and kill the courier? Fourthly, who had been at the Tower that day to lure a fairly young and healthy man to some desolate place, strangle him, place his corpse in a skiff and push it out onto the Thames? Fifthly, John Gaddesden – killed so brutally yet so mysteriously here in his bedchamber at the Sign of Hope tavern. Athelstan had stayed up into the night pondering on this problem. He believed he knew how the murder had been committed, though that would take time to prove.

Sixthly, undoubtedly Azrael was a professional assassin. Had Gaunt and his party hired him to wreak such damage, but if so, why? Did Azrael consider Athelstan to be part of some coven, and was that why he had been threatened? Seventhly, these murders might be resolved by establishing the location of the various possible suspects at the time that the different killings had taken place. In which case, there were other mysteries Athelstan had not addressed. Did Azrael follow him back to Southwark to leave those grisly mementoes, the strangled magpies in his parish church and looped around Bonaventure's neck?

'One thing I do know,' Athelstan murmured to himself, 'is that Azrael loves what he does. He truly revels in it. He almost regards murder as something slightly humorous, but of course the laughter is always at his victim's expense.'

Athelstan tightened the reins and coaxed Philomel down the trackway. The friar glanced up. At least the sky was brightening – it might turn into a fine day once the mist lifted, but for the moment, the sombreness seemed to reflect his own mood. The rich green countryside remained hidden, and no flash of colour or bustle of activity burst through the misty dullness, as if all of nature was waiting for a certain sign. Athelstan recalled making the same journey with his beloved brother's corpse. He wondered if the dead were gathering to greet him, all his family and kin hovering along this misty path stretching out before him. Suddenly a bell tolled, clear and carrying. Athelstan sat up in the saddle, crossed himself and sighed with relief as the mist parted and the main gate of St Grace's Priory came into view.

Once there, Athelstan stood in the porch-way of the main priory church. The bare, undecorated nave stretched before him down to the rood screen, a simple wooden partition with a stark crucifix above the narrow entrance to the sanctuary. Athelstan was always fascinated by the austerity of the Carthusian Order, its constant insistence that its monks live alone in their self-contained cells, which included a study room, bedloft, dining chamber and small garden, all grouped round the great cloisters. Ralph Sherwin, now prior, had greeted him and they had briefly discussed what had happened to each other over the intervening years. The prior had ended by offering refreshment which Athelstan courteously refused.

'I can see you wish to be on your own, Athelstan.' The prior blessed him. 'And so you shall be. Rest assured, you are always welcome here, whatever the season, whatever the time.' The prior had then brought Athelstan across to the church and immediately left, closing the door behind him. Athelstan continued to stare into the darkness, summoning up the courage to confront the guilt which always shrouded him in a deep, heartfelt sorrow whenever he thought about this part of his life. Stephen-Francis, his beloved brother now gone to God, lay buried beneath the flagstones of this church in the small chantry chapel dedicated to St Stephen the Martyr. The chantry stood partitioned off behind trellised black oaken screens to the left of the rood screen and just before the lady altar.

Athelstan breathed in the incensed air, the faint fragrance from the herb pots and flower vases. He crossed himself, then slowly walked down to the chantry chapel and stepped inside. He was surprised at how dark it was. He glanced up; the narrow window was shuttered and no candle-flame fluttered against the gloom. Athelstan could smell candle smoke and glimpsed the pole which would be used to open the shutters. He dug into his own chancery satchel and drew out the small leather sack containing a tinder. He used this to light the two candles on the small altar, then lifted these to place them on the flag-stones before the dais. The sight that met him made him stop and stare in horror: the corpse of a magpie, its throat all twisted, had been placed on the flagstone over his brother's tomb.

A surge of rage swept through him. Athelstan knelt to place the candles down when he heard a sound behind him. He half rose and dropped one of the candlesticks as the garrotte cord whipped round his throat. Athelstan fought back even as a hood was swiftly pulled over his head, blinding his sight. His wrists and ankles seemed to be held by a fine mesh of chain; he could feel the links on his bare flesh. The collar around his throat afforded some protection, and he struggled violently. Athelstan shook himself, and the attacker gasped and staggered back. Athelstan's right hand broke free; he was still holding the candlestick. He lashed out with this, using it as a war club before, beside and behind him. He heard a scream of pain, muffled as if his assailant was thickly masked. The garrotte cord loosened and slipped. Athelstan's left hand also broke free and he used both hands to wield the heavy, ornamented candlestick. Athelstan could feel the battle fury rage within him. He went to lift the mask but was violently pushed and sent staggering against the chapel wall. He crashed into it, the blow winding him, and he slid down, gasping for breath . . .

'Shall I call the physician?'

'No, Sir John.' Athelstan touched the collar on the table before him. He scrutinised it carefully as he half listened to the bellows of laughter from the taproom where Brother Gregorio was regaling the pilgrims with a story about a fat bishop, a young maid and a lusty clerk. Athelstan had arrived back at the Sign of Hope and immediately went up to his chamber. Locking and bolting the door behind him, he'd stretched out on the bed, staring up at the ceiling and trying to pray, to master the different emotions which had swept through him since he'd left the

Carthusian Priory: a deep sadness at how both a holy place and a most sacred occasion had been blasphemously violated. This sadness was coupled with a seething rage at Azrael daring to mock his brother's memory and use his tomb as a murder place for Athelstan. Yet, strangely enough, Athelstan also felt relieved. Azrael had struck once again and failed, and in doing so he had revealed more about himself than Athelstan had ever suspected.

'Brother, are you well? Tell me what happened.'

Athelstan tapped the collar. 'You were correct, Sir John. This saved me. The garrotte string slipped, Azrael could not secure a killing grip.' He smiled thinly. 'I am also sure I wreaked great damage with that candlestick. I have tried to recall details accurately, but the attack was so sudden and brutal . . .' He rolled the goblet between his hands. 'Apart from you, nobody else knows.'

'Brother, you slipped back like a ghost. Try and recall exactly what happened.'

'I saw the corpse of that bird,' Athelstan murmured, closing his eyes, desperate to remember everything. 'The garrotte string went around my throat, a hood over my head, my wrists and ankles were seized and held fast. I felt a mesh of chain mail. I was definitely marked down for death but that collar protected me. Azrael was unable to get a secure hold. I broke free, lashing out with that candlestick.' Athelstan opened his eyes. 'As I said, I did damage with my war club and it will take some time to heal. I struggled violently. I was pushed, crashing against the wall; it fair knocked the breath out of me. I sank down. Of course I recovered, but by the time I was free of the hood, Azrael and all sign of him had vanished. I tidied up the chantry chapel and left. Prior Sherwin and the good brothers sensed something was wrong but I was hasty in my departure. I said I would return soon, and I shall.' Athelstan took a generous sip from the goblet of rich Bordeaux Cranston had placed in front of him. Again he felt that cold ruthlessness smother the agitation in his heart and steel his nerve. He half suspected who Azrael was but he needed to prepare his indictment. He peered up at the coroner. 'Who left after I did?'

'No one. I watched you go. In fact,' Cranston sat down on the high stool next to Athelstan's chair, 'I followed you for a while. I saw nothing. Nobody followed you.'

'And who left the tavern this morning?'

Cranston shrugged. 'People were coming and going. It's almost impossible to say. I am sure Gregorio left. I glimpsed him crossing the stable yard. Didn't the brothers at St Grace's notice any strangers?'

'Indeed, they did not. Azrael probably scaled a wall and escaped the same way. I suspect he takes great pride in his silent, subtle ways. I asked the wrong question, didn't I, Sir John? You say no one followed me. Well, that's logical, because what truly concerns me is that Azrael went before me. He was lurking in that chantry chapel ready to kill me. Nobody, Sir John, apart from you, was informed about my visit to Saint Grace's, but now I find that Azrael knew exactly where I was going, the reason why and what I intended to do.'

'Of course!' Cranston breathed. 'Azrael must have left here before you. But how did he know which day?'

'He learnt from my preparations.' Athelstan made a face. 'I told the stable boys to feed Philomel early and to saddle my old friend just before dawn. I also made it clear, didn't I, that I would be absent from the Sign of Hope. Moreover there is still the possibility that Azrael waited until I left and simply travelled more swiftly than me to Saint Grace's. Once there, he would find it very easy to enter those hallowed precincts. The Carthusians live an extremely solitary life. They meet in their church for prayer but their rule is very clear; they spend most of their time locked in their own cells. Azrael is a born hunter, skilful, silent and subtle. He would ride out there, hobble his horse, scale the wall and enter the church. After that, it was just a matter of waiting.'

'Let me see.' Cranston rose. 'Let me just find out if anyone did leave around the same hour you did. But you are correct, Athelstan, Philomel is not noted for his speed. How long did it take you, an hour?' Athelstan nodded. 'Someone could walk faster to the priory, especially on a morning like this with the mist concealing everything. Anyway, stay here.'

Cranston left the chamber. Athelstan ran his finger around the rim of his goblet, his mind teeming with all the scraps of information he had garnered and sifted like winnowing chaff.

278

Above all, there was that text from St Luke's Gospel, Chapter 8: Christ's confrontation with the Gesarene demoniac. Mephan had analysed those verses, scrutinising two words in particular, not in the translation but according to the Latin text. Secondly, there was this, a fresh, violent assault on himself. Azrael must have left the Sign of Hope at some early hour. In the end, the assassin may not have taken a horse – that would have attracted attention – unless, of course, he collected a mount somewhere along the trackway. 'That's possible,' Athelstan murmured to himself, 'but I strongly suspect Azrael went on foot to the priory and returned the same way.' After the assault Athelstan had spent at least an hour at St Grace's tending to his brother's tomb, recovering from the attack and talking to Prior Sherwin before collecting Philomel from the priory's stables.

Thirdly, there was Master Chobham to deal with. On his return from St Grace's, sitting slouched in the saddle as Philomel plodded along, Athelstan had carefully reflected on all the logical possibilities behind John Gaddesden's murder here at the Sign of Hope. There was one that he was determined to pursue. Cranston returned, shaking his head.

'As far as I can learn, Brother,' he declared, 'nobody took a horse this morning.'

'It's only four miles to Saint Grace's Priory,' Athelstan replied, 'nothing more than a swift walk, and the same for the return journey. Moreover, I would wager that the trackway I rode along was not the shortest route.' He

279

tapped the table top with his fingers. 'It's very clever, Sir John. Saint Grace's was ideal for an ambush. Nothing is more desolate or lonely than a Carthusian house: it's part of the rule for the good brothers to avoid each other. Even if a stranger was glimpsed it would not necessarily provoke interest. And there is something else . . .'

'Brother?'

'This business of Castile, Sir John, I think it's more important than we realise. I am trying to create a picture, resolve a puzzle. Now, correct me if I am wrong: there's a king of Castile on the one hand and the claims of John of Gaunt on the other, and these claims are taken very seriously.'

'Of course, Brother. You must remember who Gaunt is: the son of the famous Edward III, younger brother to the ruthless Black Prince. Both these princes took armies to France. The prospect of an English army landing in Castile or crossing the border from Southern France is not too fanciful. Naturally they claim it is secret business, but it's not hard to guess that Thibault is meeting the envoys in Canterbury to discuss the possibility of an English army entering Castile and what support it will receive. Why do you ask now, Brother?'

'We are making progress, Sir John, but it's like going through a castle where all the doors are locked and we have to open them.' Athelstan got to his feet. 'Let us close with our enemy. Time is passing. I have a deep suspicion that Azrael may be preparing to flee and do his best to evade

280

capture. Bring Master Chobham here. Oh, and whatever I say, agree with.'

'Brother, what are you playing at?'

'I am playing at nothing. I am pursuing the truth. We are on the verge of unravelling this great mystery. But come, hurry, we have waited long enough.'

Cranston left and returned with a sweaty-faced Chobham. The taverner was swathed in a great bloodstained apron. He began to apologise for his appearance.

'Oh shut up!' Athelstan tried to curb the rage still seething within him. 'Just shut up!' The friar pointed at the chair. 'Sit down and tell me the truth or else.'

Chobham hurried to obey. 'Brother Athelstan,' he flustered, 'what is this? What do you mean, the truth?'

'John Gaddesden. He invited his killer, the assassin known as Azrael, into his chamber, but Gaddesden was dead when Azrael left. How he died or who was there is not your business. Nevertheless, let me assure you, the only way the murderer could have escaped that chamber was through the door. So he must have had the duplicate key which, as you informed me and the King's officer here, never left the keyring you hug so close to your fat belly. Now that's a lie, you know it is, and so do I. I suggest you were ordered, forced, coerced or black-mailed to leave the key out to be collected and told it would be returned on the morning after the murder. I suspect you found it where you left it.'

'But the latches on the door?' Chobham gasped, mopping his brow.

'Never mind those, master taverner. I will, in God's own time, resolve that mystery as well. I wish to deal with you. So, Sir John?' Athelstan glanced at the coroner. 'What is the punishment for being the accomplice in the murder of a royal clerk?'

'Hanging.' Cranston had caught Athelstan's mood and tenor. The coroner moved to tower over a now quivering taverner. 'Of course, the Crown's lawyers could argue it was misprision of treason or even high treason itself, bearing in mind who Master Gaddesden was. That's not all,' Cranston leaned down to glare at Chobham, 'there's your deceit, your pretence. Oh yes, mine host, it could be the filthiest pit in Newgate for you followed by a brutal journey on a sledge to Tyburn to be hanged until you are half dead, then your body opened. Who knows, Brother, the Crown lawyers may even argue that Master Chobham who, by his own admission, controlled the second key, was the murderer. Now that could entail a very, very nasty end.' Chobham put his face in his hands and began to sob.

'Or,' Athelstan intervened, 'you could tell us the truth and we would leave you alone. I have a feeling, Sir, that you were forced. I truly believe you did not realise the game you had been drawn into. So come,' Athelstan snapped his fingers, 'what do you choose, life or death?'

Chobham needed no further encouragement. In short, sharp sentences he blurted out how he had been attacked here in his own chamber at the Sign of Hope. How he had been threatened and told to wait for a message which would instruct him to allocate a certain room to one of the guests and to hand over the duplicate key to that chamber.

'I was told that it was in connection with your pilgrimage. Once you'd arrived here, the message would be sent.'

'And it was?'

'Late on Monday evening after you arrived here,' Chobham confessed, 'a scrap of paper was pushed under my door. It could have been written by anyone. I burnt it when I found out what had happened. The message was simple enough: I was told to give John Gaddesden a certain chamber and to leave the duplicate key in the lock to the washtub.' Chobham shrugged. 'That's an old laundry room, an outhouse overlooking the stable yard, which has a door with a huge, disused lock. You can easily fit a key in there and no one would notice it. I left it as I was ordered to. I never imagined what would happen.'

'But you must have heard about the murders in the city?' Cranston demanded. Chobham just shook his head.

'I never, I never . . .' His voice faltered.

'You didn't think to keep the washtub door under close watch?'

'Go out yourself, Brother, and see. The old wash house stands between stables. People constantly pass it tending to their horses or moving from one part of the tavern to another. Moreover it was after dark. The door is ancient, the lock deep. Nobody would notice a key

283

inserted there. I left it and found it returned the following morning.' He paused at a knock at the door. Athelstan rose and answered it, listening carefully to what Crispin the carpenter told him before thanking his parishioner and closing the door.

'So,' Athelstan sat down, pulling the chair closer to Chobham, 'you have no idea who threatened you?'

'No!'

'So why did you obey?'

Chobham wiped his greasy face with a rag. 'I had no choice,' he mumbled. 'He knew things about me. I didn't realise what he was plotting.'

'Do you know anything about him?'

'Just a mocking voice, rather young, and a garrotte string around my throat. Nasty threats to reveal my secret sins. As I said,' Chobham gasped, 'I never imagined it would lead to two men being cruelly murdered in my tavern. Yet even if I handed over the key,' Chobham's face abruptly changed, the tears drying up, replaced by a knowing, cunning look, 'the latches,' he continued, 'they were brought down. I mean . . .'

'I have also considered that,' Athelstan retorted, 'and I know the answer, as you do, master taverner.' Athelstan rose and crossed to the door of his own chamber. He opened it and pushed it sideways, the door moved going back on its three supple, well-oiled leather hinges. Athelstan closed the door and pushed again. 'You see,' he declared. 'If I push this door to the side, back on its hinges, a gap is created on the other side.

The hinges are not metal but supple enough to move. Now, on some of your chamber doors, master taverner, the gap is quite narrow, but it is much broader on others. Anyway, it's quite easy to push the door back on its hinges, create a gap wide enough to insert a dagger and prise the latchet down at both top and bottom. Once I have, I lock the door with the duplicate key as the assassin did, and walk away.'

Athelstan paused. 'And, of course, there is another way, isn't there?' He returned to his door and pulled up the latches. 'It's quite possible to lift the latch so it hangs over the clasp. But when I slam the door shut the latch falls down. It may drop into its clasp or drop beside it. But that doesn't really matter, does it? The door is locked and will have to be forced. Both lock and latch will be damaged.'

Athelstan stood for a while staring at Chobham busy dabbing his eyes or scratching his unshaven cheeks. 'I asked a member of my parish, Crispin the carpenter, to go along the galleries of your tavern, Master Chobham. He found the latches well-greased. More importantly, some chamber doors, if pushed back on their leather hinges, create a gap wide enough for a dagger and, in some cases, even your fingers, to pull the latch down. But,' Athelstan stood over the taverner and stared coldly down to him, 'you know that, don't you? There have been occasions here when some traveller becomes very sick or even dies and the door has to be forced, the latches pulled free, the lock turned with the duplicate key. Anyway,' Athelstan paused, 'tell me, Master

Chobham, how did Azrael threaten you? Your love of soft, perfumed flesh? Of romping on your bed with some pretty maid, your wife being absent in the city visiting her brother at the Mitre?' The taverner just stared back. 'And, when were you actually threatened, the day and the time?'

'Thursday last in the afternoon.'

'Impossible!'

'Brother Athelstan, I assure you it was then. My wife,' the taverner gulped, 'as you say, being absent.'

'Why is this significant?' Cranston demanded.

'Sir John, Thursday was the time when Azrael was busy in the Tower killing and threatening, some twenty miles away on the other side of the Thames.'

'He could not be in two places at the same time.'

'Sir John, I wonder, I truly do,' Athelstan murmured. 'After all, Azrael has four faces and four wings.'

'What do you mean?' Chobham gabbled.

'That does not concern you.' Athelstan clapped Chobham so firmly on the shoulder the taverner startled. 'Go away,' Athelstan whispered, 'and wait until I am truly finished here.'

Chobham scuttled out of the door. Athelstan and Cranston waited until his footsteps faded along the gallery outside.

'What are you going to do now, Brother?'

'I am going to hunt a demon, Sir John, trap him and, hopefully, despatch him to judgement, although it could be difficult and arduous. I need

286

to study and reflect, so I am going to become a hermit. I do not wish to see anybody, I have nothing to say to anybody. Sir John, I want my parishioners to take turns guarding this chamber. I would also be very grateful if you would personally supervise both them and whatever food is brought up for me to eat.'

'And then what?'

'Sir John, trust me. Let the day go, the night come, the moon set and the sun rise. In the end, God's justice will be done and seen to be done.'

True to his word, Athelstan became a hermit. He set out his writing tray, lit candles to create a constant pool of light and prepared to list everything he had learnt. Most of the time he sat staring into the middle distance as he recreated everything that had happened since he had walked into Mephan's house in Milk Street. Time and again he reviewed the sequence of events and began to list what he called 'milestones to murder', significant details which might lead to a solution. How this solution would be worked out, Athelstan had yet to plot. Nevertheless, as he conceded to Sir John, time was of the essence and might be running out. He recalled that violent affray in the chantry chapel at St Grace's: his assailant had been injured and would need some form of physic and medical care. Occasionally Cranston came up to sit beside him. Athelstan would ask after everyone then insist on returning to his task.

'I am revising time and again,' he assured Cranston, 'and when I am finished, then we shall move. In the meantime, have you noticed anything untoward about any of our fellow pilgrims?'

Cranston shook his head and informed Athelstan that many of them were keeping to their own chambers or bedlofts. Athelstan worked on. Eventually he had the list he wanted, a possible path through the tangled thicket of murderous mystery. First, the description of the Gesarene demoniac in Chapter 8 of St Luke's Gospel: the way '*legio*' and '*multi*' had been picked out and why Mephan would be fascinated by the verses as well as the secret contained in those two words. Secondly, he now understood the ease with which Felicia and Finchley had been so swiftly murdered and why no one had fled into the street. Thirdly, he believed the ransacked receipt coffer was worthy of note and was linked to what he had glimpsed in Mephan's kitchen. Fourthly, the timing of Azrael's sinister appearance in Mephan's garden; the taunting of Athelstan with a corpse of a magpie, its neck all twisted, the reference to its plumage being the same as Athelstan's robes, were all items of great importance. Fifthly, Mephan's greed, and his boasting to young Felicia about the profits to be made played a decisive part in the clerk's murder and that of his household.

Sixthly, the garrotting of the courier Empson. Athelstan now understood how this elusive messenger was discovered, trapped and murdered. Seventhly, the warnings delivered to Athelstan in Southwark. On reflection, Athelstan realised it would have been easy for Azrael to steal across the river, entice Bonaventure and loop the corpse of that magpie around the cat's neck. Eighthly, the incidents in the Tower. The warnings delivered to Gaunt and his henchmen, was Azrael just demonstrating his power? Athelstan also concluded how Luke Gaddesden had been trapped and so easily murdered. The mystery around his death had been created by the bargeman Maulkin, who had been forced, bribed or possibly both, to lie about what he had seen. On that particular Thursday afternoon, Azrael had been busy murdering in London as well as blackmailing Chobham so as to prepare for another murder here at the Sign of Hope. Athelstan now understood how it all had been carried out.

Ninthly, Athelstan was now certain about how John Gaddesden was so mysteriously killed here in his chamber at the Sign of Hope. He also understood why poor Monkshood had paid a terrible price for not attending that communal prayer meeting in the taproom below, just after the pilgrims arrived at the tavern. Finally, the violent assault on himself at St Grace's. The friar also realised how and when Azrael had learnt about his brother's tomb as well as the friar's determination to visit St Grace's.

At last Athelstan was finished. On the evening of the third day after his return from the Carthusian house, Cranston asked Athelstan if he would like to join the rest in the taproom below. Physician Giole and his family had announced that they could not delay any further; they intended to return to London and make the

289

pilgrimage on another occasion. As a fond fare-well, physician Giole had promised to cook a splendid evening supper to which all were invited. Athelstan excused himself but advised Cranston to be ready and armed early the next morning. The friar then invited Pike, Watkin and the hangman to his chamber. He begged them not to drink too deeply and to have their weapons ready. More than that, he would not say, except that he pleaded with all three parishioners to keep silent on what he had asked.

A servant, as arranged, woke Athelstan just before dawn the following morning. The friar had sat and listened to all the revelry the previous evening. He had reviewed and revised his indictment then prayed fervently for divine guidance by reciting both Vespers and Compline. Afterwards he had slept for a few hours and was now refreshed, ready for the fray. He hurriedly dressed and sent the same servant to rouse Sir John and his three parishioners, who had decided to sleep in a warm, comfortable hay loft above the stables. Athelstan decided not to wait for anyone but went down into the great taproom where, as he suspected, physician Giole and his family were seated around a table close to the great window overlooking the tavern gardens. The shutters had been pulled back, the early morning light bathing the table and those grouped around it. Athelstan felt a tingle of fear. In the half-light Giole and his coven looked truly dangerous; cloaked, cowled and booted, baggage and weaponry heaped on the floor beside them. A scullion had served them ale, bread and cheese to break their fast. They had eaten and now seemed ready to leave. Four dark, sinister figures against the light, assassins, Athelstan thought, murderous members of the tribe of Cain.

'We have to leave, Athelstan.' Giole didn't even bother to rise. The way he spoke, fingers tapping the dagger in his belt, as if he'd already realised Athelstan had deduced the truth about them. 'We have to leave,' Giole repeated.

'Of course you do.' Athelstan picked up a stool and sat down facing them. 'You must return to London. I wonder, I truly do, which one of you I injured at Saint Grace's? I delivered a powerful, bone-crushing blow. You, Giole, could attend to it, but I suspect real physic is needed and you can hardly let the injured person hobble around for me to see.' Giole mockingly clapped his hands.

'You accuse us of what, friar?'

'Let me see . . .' Athelstan quietly prayed that the servant had roused Cranston and the others. The friar felt genuinely afraid sitting in this deserted taproom confronting these four killers who crouched like wolves ready to attack.

'What do you want with us, friar?' Giole's voice was low and threatening.

'You call me friar and not Athelstan, and that's a good place to start. You truly hate me, don't you? Not just because I investigate your bloody, nefarious handiwork but because I am a priest and, above all, a Dominican.'

'*Canes Domini*,' Felipe called out.

Athelstan noticed that the young Spaniard sat rather awkwardly and wondered if he was the one he had injured during the affray at St Grace's.

'Yes,' Athelstan replied, '*Canes Domini* – the hounds of the Lord. You've had dealings with my order before, I am certain of that.' He paused and glanced swiftly to his left. He was sure he had heard a sound and glimpsed a shadow flit behind the board where the drink and food were served: the great barrels, tuns and vats stood in a long line behind the boarded trestle table. Athelstan suspected someone was lurking there.

'We really should be going.' Beatrice rose, flouncing out her skirts.

Athelstan made to rise when he heard footfall behind him and the click of a crossbow as the twine was winched back and held in place. Athelstan glanced round and sighed with relief. Cranston, flanked by Watkin, Pike and the hangman, emerged out of the shadows around the door. Beatrice retook her seat.

'You will not be going,' Cranston declared flatly.

'Well, not for the moment,' Giole cheerily called back. 'We will listen to what the friar has to say but then be gone.'

'Be that as it may,' Athelstan declared, 'our librarian at Blackfriars, or rather our archivist, is Brother Norbert, a most learned Dominican, a man well versed in the history of our order and its work in different countries throughout Europe. I asked him to send me information on two particular matters: the Angel of Death, known as Azrael, and a commentary on the Basque country, that stretch of land in Northern

Spain and the tribes which inhabit both sides of the great mountain chain separating Spain from France. Now these tribes are truly ferocious and warlike. They have never been properly conquered and have proved to be a great obstacle to armies who try to pass between the two countries, as the paladins Roland and Oliver found to their cost. The mountains are in some places impenetrable. The passes are needle-thin trackways. In winter, a whole army can be lost, whilst during the summer, a scorching heat dries up the pools and springs. The Romans tried to pacify this mountainous area. The great seigneurs of France and Castile have attempted the same, with little effect.' Athelstan paused. 'Holy Mother Church has also launched crusading missions which, to a certain extent, were successful but did not eradicate the pagan beliefs and practices amongst the tribes. The Holy Inquisition, or not so Holy as many would say, played a prominent part in this. The Inquisition is led by the Dominican Order which works on behalf of the Pope in Rome.'

'And the relevance of all this to us?' Giole snapped.

'Now these tribes,' Athelstan continued unruffled, 'have ancient rites. One of these is human or animal sacrifice where blood is not shed. In their belief, bloodshed diminishes the efficacy and power of their offering. Consequently, those who follow such pagan rituals become very adept and skilled with the garrotte and the strangulation of their victims.' Athelstan pointed at Giole and his companions. 'I truly believe you belong

293

to such a sect. I also suspect that you and yours have been hunted, yes, even persecuted by the Inquisition. Its investigators show little mercy or compassion; they condemn people such as you to the horrifying death of being burnt at the stake.'

Athelstan paused. Simply by their expressions he could see that Giole and his coven had kinsmen and loved ones who had experienced all the terrors the Inquisition could inflict: the constant hunt, capture, brutal interrogation and ferocious torture followed by the cruellest of deaths. 'The best place to hide,' Athelstan continued, 'is as deep as possible amongst your enemy, to become like them in every way.' He waved a hand. 'I am not too sure whether you four are a family or just a coven of murderers, of skilled assassins who do not accept for a moment anything I or Sir John believe in. To be sure, that doesn't really matter now. Giole, you told me your life story; whether it's the truth or not is irrelevant, you are what you pretend to be. You did inform us on our way here that you'd lived in Albi, a city notorious for its opposition to Rome. Anyway, you came out of the mountains, you mingle and merge into Castilian society, becoming both a physician and a very good one,' Giole spread his hands and bowed mockingly, 'as well as a tavern master, a cook par excellence.' Again the mocking bow.

'But you are all Azrael.' Athelstan held up his hand, fingers splayed. 'Azrael is supposed to be four-faced with four wings, which means you, Giole, and your three companions. One coven or family, one demon but four murderous souls. You pretend to be Castilian and Catholic, in truth you are pagan. Your only allegiance is to your own ancient culture, religion and rituals. For all I know, Azrael could be one of your demon gods. You must have rejoiced to take such a title. Giole, you are extremely arrogant yet you also have the darkest sense of humour.'

'Friar, all these compliments! I thought you were going to accuse us.' Giole turned and spoke swiftly in Spanish to his companions. Maria laughed mockingly, fingers covering her mouth. Athelstan flinched at the hateful look the young woman threw him, lips moving silently as if whispering some curse. He also sensed an assurance, a certain confidence, as if this murderous coven owned a secret, something which they could use as both protection and a safe conduct.

'I strongly suspect,' he continued, 'you mingled deep in Castilian society. By day a physician, a bon viveur, a master cook, a loving, charming family. Once darkness fell however, away from the light, you were assassins, very skilled and gifted ones, employed only by the powerful and rich. A great source of profit. I confess, I do not know how you hawk your murderous services, but I suspect you were probably chosen by the present monarch of Castile for a most important task here in this kingdom.'

'You have proof of this?' Beatrice challenged. 'You keep us here when we should be gone.' She threw an anxious glance at Felipe. Athelstan sensed that they were a family group, killers to the bone but very close. The friar also believed that his earlier suspicion was correct. Felipe had been injured at St Grace's, and Beatrice wanted her son out of here.

'Evidence and proof,' Athelstan countered. 'You are assassins despatched into England some years ago after John of Gaunt proclaimed his right to the throne of Castile. Following the regent's marriage to the Infanta Constanza, many Castilians flocked to this kingdom, you four amongst them. Once again you mingled with the crowd, you used your wealth to buy and develop that spacious tavern, Amongst the Tombs. An excellent disguise. You became a respected family in Farringdon. You, Giole, were appointed ward physician. You acted your part and waited for your secret orders.' Athelstan wetted his lips. 'You are a consummate mummer, Giole. You have a charm and tact to inveigle others to accept you. I found you of great assistance in the trapping and unmasking of Robert the clerk.'

'A garrulous, inept moon-man,' Giole scoffed.

'Not like you, eh? The silent, deadly assassin. In the main you kept hidden. Occasionally you struck, garrotting certain individuals who might finance Gaunt in his ambitions for the crown of Castile.' Athelstan smiled thinly. 'You ask for evidence, but of course you supplied it yourself.'

'What do you mean?' Giole snapped.

'Your dark sense of humour, physician, your desire to ridicule our scriptures, your love of puzzles and mysteries. You do seem particularly fascinated by those verses from Chapter Eight of Saint Luke's Gospel which describe Christ's

296

confrontation with the Gasarene demoniac. I now understand why. The possessed man claims that his name is legion because he shelters many devils. The Latin word for legion, *'legio'* can also be formed into your name Giole, whilst *'multi* – many' also contains every letter of your family name Limut. So we have Giole Limut. Correct?'

The physician simply smiled, gesturing with his hands that his companions should also remain silent. 'You're fascinated with that account of the Gasarene demoniac, aren't you? It suits both your mood and the way you have forged four souls into one. You even took another phrase from the same account, for Luke's Gospel describes how the demoniac lived 'amongst the tombs'. You borrowed that phrase 'amongst the tombs' for the name of your tavern, claiming quite wrongly that it was built over ancient sepulchres.' Athelstan rose, pulling the stool beneath him closer to his adversaries, who were half hidden in the shifting grey light of dawn. Behind him he heard Cranston growl at Master Chobham, informing the taverner that he and others should stay out of the taproom until told otherwise.

'You love playing with fire,' Athelstan continued, 'baiting and taunting a society you deeply despise and reject. Nevertheless such secret jibing carries its own dangers.'

'Meaning?'

'You murdered one of Gaunt's supporters, a wealthy merchant, and left your mocking message, "Lord Azrael greets you. Fear us because our name is legion for we are many." Of course this cryptic, mysterious message passed through the Secret Chancery at Westminster and into the hands of a very experienced and skilled cipher clerk, Simon Mephan. Now Mephan loved word puzzles and began to study this enigmatic message. He already knew you as a taverner, Giole, and as the ward physician who became his personal doctor. Mephan studied those phrases. God knows how, but I suspect he first stumbled on the similarity, as I did, between 'Giole' and '*legio*'. Once he'd achieved this, Mephan would move to Limut and realise that it shared the same letters as the Latin word for many – '*multi.*'

'Mephan was an old fool,' Giole spat out to murmurs of approval from his companions. Athelstan sensed their deep hostility to that ageing clerk who had stumbled on their secret and threatened to reveal it.

'I did wonder,' Athelstan continued, 'why you didn't silence Mephan through poison or arrange some accident in the street. However, as Robert the clerk discovered, poisoning can be as dangerous for the perpetrator as it is for his victims, whilst an arranged accident can provoke suspicion. And there were two further factors. As I have said, for you garrotting is part of some ritual or rite. Secondly, it wasn't just Mephan you had to take care of, there were the evange-lists, Mephan's comrades in the Secret Chancery, as well as their courier Roger Empson. I am correct?'

Giole made a face. 'I told you, friar, state your

298

case.' The physician patted his doublet, 'and I shall state mine. Oh, by the way,' Giole pointed to Cranston and the three parishioners, 'I would ask you to be most careful with your weapons. We are what we are, as we shall prove, so be most prudent.'

Athelstan hid his surprise. He was disconcerted by Giole's calm statement as well as by the cool assurance of the physician and his fellow murderers.

He continued: 'Mephan was also fascinated by the Gesarene demoniac who lived, so the verse says, amongst the tombs – the name of your tavern. This would not have escaped Mephan's attention. True to his blackmailing nature, Mephan began to hint, didn't he, at your great secret? You see,' Athelstan sighed, 'Mephan had grown accustomed to bullying, hectoring and blackmailing people to fill his belly. Now,' Athelstan spread his hands, 'you might dismiss all these allegations as sheer nonsense. After all, you could take any group of words or letters and fashion a litany of interesting theories. Mephan, however, stumbled on something much more sinister. He was being followed by a lone Spaniard. This individual was glimpsed in the street as well as in the taverns Mephan frequented, including yours. God knows who this Spaniard was, but you would be alarmed: he was certainly not of your coven, and I suppose those who are not with you are against you. Mephan complained to you, didn't he, about this mysterious individual? You realised he was correct and, for your own secret, devious purposes, murdered that

299

Spaniard and sent his corpse floating in the Thames.'

Athelstan paused as Giole languidly got to his feet. Cranston stepped forward but Athelstan held up a warning hand. Giole strolled arrogantly across to the great board. He picked up one of the jugs of ale, filled it and then brought it back. He replenished his own blackjack and those of his three companions, put it on the table and sat down whispering to his companions.

'You are correct,' Athelstan declared. 'Mephan was a truly stupid man, highly intelligent, a very skilled, even gifted cipher clerk, but he knew little about human nature. He totally under-estimated you. He thought he could blackmail you, wipe his lips and walk away.'

'If he suspected us to be assassins,' Felipe scoffed, 'he would never have dared . . .'

'Mephan did dare and he thought, with no risk to himself, and so he made his second grievous mistake. Mephan intimated he had shared his secrets with the evangelists and the Secret Chancery courier Empson. He did this to protect himself, or so he thought. I actually don't think he did inform his colleagues, indeed, I am sure of it, but he certainly insinuated to Felicia that good profit would come his way. In the end you made the judgement that Mephan and all his associates should be marked down for death.'

Athelstan paused at a sound from behind the great board. Ignoring Cranston's murmur that it was probably some tavern cat or slithering rat, Athelstan went across and around the great serving table. He walked past the huge vats and barrels on their heavy, oaken struts. He could see nothing untoward but felt a cold draught of air and glimpsed a large horn-filled window creaking back and forth in the early morning breeze. He secured it and returned to his stool.

Giole and his confederates were deep in hushed conversation. The friar turned and glanced at Sir John, who stood with the crossbow he had primed. Watkin, Pike and the hangman, fascinated by what they were hearing and seeing, whispered amongst themselves, their weapons also primed and ready.

Athelstan tapped his sandalled foot noisily on the floorboards and spoke again: 'Master Mephan had already started to profit, or so he thought, from you. I noticed in his kitchen the Spanish wine and the gammon cured and cooked in mustard. I saw a similar wine and ham in your tavern when Sir John and I were your guests – a most singular visit which I will return to. Anyway, you would not let Mephan run for long. Your truly resented, even hated him and his arrogant, smug belief that he'd discovered who you were and could use this to his advantage. Nobody baits you. Nobody like Mephan dares meddle in your affairs. You sent your accursed warning to Mephan, the evangelists and Empson the courier, "Lord Azrael greets you". Mephan may have been mystified but you soon demonstrated what this message meant. On that particular evening, Physician Giole, you and your coven of assassins arrived at Mephan's house in Milk Street. He might have been surprised yet he had no choice but to smilingly admit this leading physician and

301

his kin into his home. I doubt if Mephan ever realised that all four of you were assassins.'

'Why didn't Mephan go to the authorities?' Felipe called out. 'Why not share his suspicions with my Lord of Gaunt or Master Thibault?'

'Oh, in time he might have done,' Athelstan replied. 'But events were moving swiftly, weren't they? Moreover, Mephan had really very little proof and he was extremely greedy. He looked forward to milking you of money. He was used to blackmailing taverners and escaping unscathed. He thought the same would happen with you, but it didn't. On that particular evening, once you were inside, the door was bolted. I am not too sure when and how you killed Finchley and Felicia, but I suspect you sent Mephan up to his bedchamber on some spurious excuse. Finchley and Felicia were separated and dealt with. A few breaths, their lives choked off and their corpses placed next to each other. Mephan came down. He realised what was happening. The door to the street was locked and guarded so he hastily fled back to his bedchamber but the shock, the fear and the panic are too much. Mephan feels an intense pain grip his chest. He sits down at his chancery desk and opens the book of Luke's Gospel. He takes a quill pen and underscores those two words '*legio*' and '*multi*'. He may have also searched for the phrase 'amongst the tombs' but it's all too much. The pain in his chest is now intense. Mephan closes the book. He pushes it away, collapses and dies and that's how you found him. You are a physician. You realise he's dead, whilst a swift examination of the desk reveals nothing untoward.' Athelstan cocked his head to one side and smiled. 'You overlooked that book of the gospels, didn't you, Azrael? Your first great mistake. Mephan may have been foolish but in his death he helped us trap you.'

'I was with you,' Giole taunted, 'that morning in Mephan's house when Azrael appeared.'

'Nonsense! All four of you carried out that murder in Milk Street, Azrael the demon with four faces. I wondered why your hands were not scored. You wear gauntlets of Toledo steel; they fit more like a mesh of the finest silk which allows you to grip and to twist without marking the palms of your hands. Toledo steel is the best, the finest and the costliest: one of the great products of Castile. I found a link from one of these special gloves in John Gaddesden's chamber. You, Giole, do the garrotting. The others, be it all three or just two, seize the victim's wrists and legs, not for long, just a few heartbeats, as when it is needed, the mask is pulled down and the garrotte string whipped around the victim's throat.' Athelstan glanced over his shoulder at the hangman. 'How long would you say, Giles?'

'As you remarked, Father, a few heartbeats. The shock alone would petrify victims: the hood, the seizure of their arms and ankles. They would be like a rabbit turned to stone by a stoat. The garrotte would be easy for someone so skilled.'

'I agree. Let us imagine one such death. Young Felicia separated from Finchley and Mephan.' Athelstan spread his hands. 'Let us say she is in the kitchen with all four of you. Giole slips

303

behind her, the garrotte whips around her throat and is pulled. She is literally petrified. Beatrice pulls over the hood if you needed one. Giole's garrotte is already tightening. Felicia's hands and ankles are seized. So swift, so deadly!' Athelstan took out his ave beads. 'You regard such killings as part of some ancient religion, you certainly reject ours. I noticed when we gathered here for common prayer, just after we arrived at the Sign of Hope, that none of you had prayer beads, rosaries, Ave Maria cords, a crucifix or a Paternoster ring. In fact, I had to lend you mine, do you remember? Moreover, none of you supposedly devout Castilian Catholics wear any crosses or religious artefacts.'

'Superstition,' Maria blurted out before Giole could stop her.

'And you, of course, regard such things as meaningless?' Athelstan pointed at Felipe. 'As for Giole being with us when Azrael appeared in Mephan's garden, that was to deliberately mislead, to create an illusion. Felipe appeared there, hooded and masked. He was waiting for you, Giole, to take us out there, and you did, remember? I also recall how you first arrived at Mephan's house, accompanied by your son Felipe. You met Sir John, who explained he was waiting for someone to come from Southwark to assist him: Athelstan, the Dominican priest. You fervently hate both me and my order. You told Felipe what to do before you parted. Felipe, one of the four faces of Azrael, was waiting in the shadows of that dark garden not only to mislead but, above all, to throw down the gauntlet, the gage of battle, the corpse of a magpie symbolising the colours of the Dominican Order, its throat cruelly twisted as you planned to do to mine.'

Athelstan crossed himself. 'God rest him, but Mephan was truly stupid. As I've said, when he hinted at blackmailing you, he also insinuated that his comrades in the Secret Chancery were party to the secret, but that was a lie. Mephan truly believed that such bluffing would be a strong shield against you.' Athelstan shook his head in disbelief. 'Master Giole, I openly concede I would never play such a game with you.'

'Dangerous in the extreme,' Beatrice murmured, 'if it was the truth.'

'You *are* highly dangerous,' Athelstan retorted. 'You are not only killers, you hate your victims for what they are: Catholics, servants of the Crown, royal clerks, Dominican priests. You have the arrogance of Lucifer. No one ever threatens you and walks away scot free. Mephan was dead and you turned on me. You had learnt a great deal about Sir John's Dominican priest. It would be easy for you to slip across to Southwark. I suspect it was one of the ladies, yes, Beatrice? Anyway,' Athelstan continued, 'my great friend and colleague, the tomcat Bonaventure, haunts St Erconwald's and that Judas cat can easily be suborned by a pot of cream or some other delicacy. The corpse of one magpie is nailed to the tower door; another, its throat all twisted, is tied around Bonaventure's neck for him to bring home to me, an expression of your deep hostility for what I am and for what I do.'

'People were coming and going in the days before the pilgrimage,' Watkin burst out, 'strangers arriving and making enquiries about the pilgrimage.'

'True.' Athelstan held a hand up for Watkin to remain silent. 'Apart from myself and Sir John, Bonaventure avoids men. He is a chevalier, a knight who likes the ladies.' Athelstan half turned. 'Sir John, didn't you tell me on at least one occasion that here at this tavern, you had seen Bonaventure on Beatrice's lap?' Athelstan half smiled. 'That cat never forgets a kindness. I understand he shelters most of the time with Benedicta, but naturally, he is ever hopeful. Perhaps the lady who fed him so generously in Southwark might repeat the kind gesture here in this tavern.'

'Animals like me, friar.'

'I am glad someone does,' Cranston growled.

'Animals like me,' Beatrice repeated, preening herself.

Once again Athelstan wondered if Giole and his companions were just waiting to see how much he and Cranston had discovered, and then what? Did they have some form of royal protection?

'Let me arrest them.' Cranston was following the same line of thought as Athelstan. The coroner stepped forward. 'They sit there like innocents all ready to go.'

'No, let me finish my indictment. That's what you are waiting for, isn't it, Giole?' The physician,

306

his face half-hidden behind one beringed hand, just shrugged. 'Once you had committed those murders in Milk Street, you ransacked Mephan's tally casket where the clerk kept his receipts. Being Mephan's personal physician you would know a great deal about his house.'

'Why should I ransack a tally casket?'

'Don't bait me, Giole. I suspect the coffer contained receipts, tallies, bills. All of course issued from your tavern, Amongst the Tombs. You certainly didn't want someone discovering just how often Mephan visited your hostelry for free food and wine, such as the ham and wine I glimpsed in his kitchen.' Athelstan put his rosary beads away. 'Empson, the Secret Chancery's courier, was your next victim. You probably knew . . .'

'Probably, probably, probably!' Giole mimicked. 'Friar, I thought you dealt in certainties?'

'Not for the time being, but let me hurry on. You probably learnt that Empson visited the Lute Boy. He too liked the services offered by the Way of all Flesh. You attacked him leaving that pleasure house, but you were interrupted. Empson broke free and fled. He thought he'd be safe in that ancient death house but you'd followed him there. Four of you could keep such a terrified fugitive under close watch and, when ready, you garrotted him.' Athelstan paused at the hammering on the taproom door. He rose, and both he and the coroner opened the door. Thibault stood there, cloaked and armed, and Albinus likewise.

'I understand from Chobham,' the Master of

Secrets hissed, stepping forward, 'that you are involved in a most serious confrontation with physician Giole and his family. Allegations and accusations have been levelled.' Thibault drew himself up. 'This is very serious. I, we should have been informed.'

Athelstan shifted his gaze to Matthew Gaddesden, standing in the shadows behind his master. The clerk looked grief-stricken and terrified, his face white as snow, his eyes red-rimmed from lack of sleep and crying, dirty fingers constantly going to an unshaven cheek.

'I should have been informed,' Thibault repeated.

'Why?' Athelstan closed the door behind him and stepped closer. 'You may be my Lord of Gaunt's man, but remember, I have the King's own word that I can approach him directly on any matter. So, Master Thibault, on your most solemn oath of allegiance to the King, do you, my Lord of Gaunt or Albinus have anything, and I mean anything, to do with physician Giole, his family or his tavern?'

Thibault raised a hand as if taking an oath. 'I swear neither I, Albinus nor my Lord of Gaunt have anything to do with him or his kin. Naturally, we are curious, even more so as we are about to meet Castilian envoys at Canterbury. Because of that, it's appropriate for me to be present, to establish if your confrontation has any bearing on that meeting, and I suspect it does.'

Athelstan hid his surprise. There was one part of his indictment which depended more on supposition and conjecture than anything else.

He'd always wondered if Thibault was involved somehow with Azrael but he now believed the Master of Secrets had told him the truth.

'Brother Athelstan, I must insist we join you.'

The friar stepped aside and gestured at the door. 'Do so, but I beg you, do not interfere with what I say or do . . .'

Part Eight

A Hymn to the Night and the Gathering Dark

Athelstan ushered Thibault and Albinus into the taproom. The Master of Secrets turned quickly and told Matthew Gaddesden to go back to his chamber. Once the door was closed, Giole immediately broke free from his hushed conversation with his family. He stood up full of righteous anger, snapping his fingers loudly.

'Master Thibault,' he almost shouted.

'Sir?'

'We have been detained by this . . .' Giole gestured at Athelstan. 'And when he has finished his prattling preaching I want words with you.'

'And so you shall, Sir.' Thibault glanced quizzically at Athelstan's three parishioners who stood, crossbows primed. He shrugged and gestured at Albinus to join him on the wall bench just inside the door. Athelstan retook his seat.

'Luke Gaddesden,' he declared, 'cruelly murdered in the Tower.'

'We weren't there that day, I told you, we had no pass.'

'Oh, you were there. How you gained admission is a matter for debate. On that particular day events in the Tower were deeply disturbed by the attempted assassination of my Lord of Gaunt. No,' Athelstan held his hand up, 'I believe Azrael was there, or at least two to three of you. One of you, I suspect Felipe, had been despatched here to arrange another murder, that of Luke Gaddesden, a fifteen-mile journey from Southwark, eh Felipe? You came secretly in disguise to observe Master Chobham, and he is so easy to judge and weigh in the balance. A taverner who likes the maids. A man with a rather murky past, as many taverners have, especially one who owns an establishment on the road leading from Kent to Southwark, the route so often used by the Upright Men. Master Chobham had a past and even the vaguest threat of revealing previous sins, would render him all a-tremble.'

Athelstan shrugged. 'I will come to that by and by, but first the Tower. There were three of you there. If you had been noticed, you would have cheerfully agreed that you had been allowed in. Moreover you could have been there in disguise. However, by claiming you were absent you deepen the mystery of who Azrael might be.' Athelstan paused. 'You hunt like wolves, don't you? Luke Gaddesden was the chosen prey because he made himself vulnerable like a deer that strays too far from the herd. He went out onto the water-gate quayside, a dank, lonely place. Few people go there because of the stench, and the only reason, perhaps, is to take one of the battered skiffs moored close by. You followed and you struck. Luke was garrotted. We noticed his left knee was wet, his hose soaked – that's because Luke was kneeling to unloosen the

312

mooring rope. You, Giole, and your accomplices crept silently up behind him. You were confident no witness was present. The garrotte cord whips around Luke's throat and he is dragged into one of those darkened enclaves overlooking the narrow quayside. In that gloomy, murky corner there would be no need for the hood. Your two accomplices gripped his arms and ankles and death followed swiftly. Afterwards the corpse was placed in the skiff. The mooring rope was freed, the boat pushed out and the powerful current swept it away out onto the river.' The friar glanced swiftly at the window: the light was strengthening.

'You forget what Maulkin the bargeman told you,' Maria shouted before Giole could intervene.

'Who told you about Maulkin?' Athelstan shot back. 'You maintain you were never in the Tower. How would you know about Maulkin, let alone what he told me?' Athelstan could see Maria's outburst had angered the rest.

'Stupid girl,' he taunted. 'Everything Maulkin told us is a lie. You know it was. You threatened and bribed him to tell his tale to deepen the mystery. A poor Tower boatman threatened in some lonely place by three sinister figures, all hooded and visored. I believe Maulkin saw or heard nothing connected with Luke's death. On his return to London my Lord Coroner will confront the bargeman with his deception.'

Athelstan stared down at the floor. He secretly accepted that there were pieces missing from his argument. There was something that gnawed at his mind; he had his suspicions but he could not articulate them. His hand went to the pocket of his robe. He touched his ave beads as he silently prayed for God's help. He felt he was blundering towards the light but he was fearful of what the outcome might be.

'Friar, we are waiting.'

'Aye and God waits for you killers!' Athelstan retorted heatedly. 'So we come to this pilgrimage. You knew all about Master Chobham, mine host here and his tavern the Sign of Hope.

'How?' Felipe demanded.

'Oh, I've said Chobham is an easy book to read. You visited this tavern, but, more importantly, Giole Limut is a vintner, the owner of a grand hostelry in Farringdon ward. Sir John has told me that the world of vintners is a small one. Giole would know a great deal about the Sign of Hope: details about its chambers, galleries and doors, not to mention its owner.' Athelstan paused to clear his throat. 'You were also appraised about the itinerary of our pilgrimage. You decided to accompany us, to continue your pursuit of Mephan's circle, and I expect you wanted, for your own secret purposes, to be close to the Castilian envoys when Master Thibault meets them in Canterbury.'

'Why?'

'I do not know. It does not concern me. Suffice to say you are here, and you intended to finish the pilgrimage, until that unpleasant affray at Saint Grace's which led to your son's injuries. Now you and your pack are obliged to return to your lair in Farringdon to lick your wounds and

314

prepare for another time.' Athelstan glanced across at Thibault, who sat chewing the corner of his lip. He wondered if the Master of Secrets had any suspicions about what was now unfolding.

'Friar?' Giole demanded. 'Time is passing!'

Athelstan continued: 'On Thursday last Felipe came here and threatened Chobham. You know what happened then. On the evening of the day we arrived here, the taverner was forced to give John Gaddesden a certain room and later to hand over the duplicate key to that chamber. Why should we waste time telling you what you already know? You can rest assured, Chobham was obliged to confess everything to Sir John and myself. Of course nothing, not even murder, runs smoothly.' Athelstan rubbed his hands together.

'You remember Monkshood, a former captain of the Earthworms, an Upright Man who masqueraded as Brother Giles?' He paused at the sharp intake of breath from Thibault, but the friar had already decided to shield Sir John and the hangman from what had actually happened and take full responsibility. 'Monkshood, the former rebel, had performed the most singular service for me. He escaped the gallows, so I agreed to him accompanying us as Brother Giles. Monkshood hoped to reach the Medway and seek passage abroad whilst I pleaded for a pardon from His Grace the King.' Athelstan turned and glared knowingly at his three parishioners but they remained impassive, eager not to provoke Thibault's suspicions.

'Of course,' Athelstan went on, 'Monkshood was mischief incarnate. We all decided to

315

assemble here for communal prayer but Monkshood, true to his nature, slipped round this tavern seeking some profit.' Athelstan closed his eyes for a moment; it was a necessary lie, he reflected. He opened his eyes and pointed at Maria. 'Monkshood was not the only one creeping along the galleries of this tavern, was he? Servants clatter up and down but Monkshood flittered like a moonbeam up the stairs and past the chambers. He met someone equally stealthy. You, Maria, searching for which chamber would be most suitable for your next victim, John Gaddesden. A room where the door could be pushed back on its hinges, where the gap on the other side allowed someone to bring down the latches at top and bottom, to check that they moved easily on their screw. Maria would hear any servant coming and going, but not Monkshood, he was as stealthy as her. Anyway, they glimpsed each other. Our former Upright Man simply thought it was rather strange and said as much. He talked of young women flitting from one chamber to another. Maria, however, realised the danger of being seen doing such a thing. She reported as much to Giole and Azrael swooped. The hapless Monkshood was strangled. You could not have him alive the next morning when John Gaddesden's corpse was discovered. Monkshood was quick of wit and sharp of mind. He would soon realise the significance of what he had seen.'

Athelstan started coughing: his throat was dry and he gratefully accepted the blackjack of ale Albinus brought across. The friar sipped thirstily.

316

'And so,' Athelstan put the blackjack down on the floor beside him, 'we come to your last murder: John Gaddesden. You had prepared well. You made sure he was lodged in a certain chamber and that Chobham had handed over the duplicate key. Late that evening you left the kitchens and made your way up onto the gallery. Skilled assassins, you moved silently and knocked on the door of John's room. He would admit you. After all, he hardly suspected. You would act all friendly – perhaps you'd brought some wine or a delicacy from the kitchens. Once inside that chamber John's fate was sealed. He sits in his chair facing his guests, Giole glides behind him, he pulls the garrotte string out and the pack closes in. John is murdered. One of you slipped out of the chamber to keep watch. He or she would alert you to any danger. Of course, there is none. The other guests are tired, sleepy. They have travelled all day, eaten and drunk heavily. You leave the chamber, pressing back the door to create that gap, then you prise the latches down and lock the room with the duplicate key; the other is left in the chamber. You have deliberately created a perfect mystery to block and frustrate any investigation. Such obfuscation is essential. You are not only removing any threat to yourselves but also thwarting the hunt for the truth as well as mocking our attempts to discover it.'

Athelstan took a sip from his tankard and gestured at Felipe. 'Would you like to stand, walk and demonstrate that you are not injured?'

'My son is no tinker's monkey,' Giole snarled, 'to dance to your tune or anyone else's.'

317

'He is a filthy assassin, as you are,' Athelstan countered. 'You tried to murder me above my brother's tomb at Saint Grace's.' Athelstan gripped the tankard tightly as the rage surfaced within him.

'How would we know where he was buried or where you were going?'

'Don't play games with my beloved brother's memory. You know full well . . .' Athelstan leaned forward. Giole and the others were truly enjoying seeing his rage, but Athelstan could not help it even as he realised how swiftly it gave way to hate – and Athelstan truly hated this coven. He drew a deep breath and tried to remember some prayer which would soothe him. 'I talked about going to Saint Grace's when I visited your tavern.' Athelstan fought to stay calm. 'I was in a chamber there, alone with Sir John, when I informed him of what I would do and where I would go. You eavesdropped. You planned and plotted. The priory is only four miles away; it was easy enough to slip stealthily out early on that mist-strewn morning and then return. A walk of four miles would not be arduous and you knew the Carthusian priory would be desolate. You would scale its walls and wait, slipping like shadows into that church. I thank God and Sir John that I escaped. As it was, you blasphemously desecrated my brother's tomb. You shattered what was supposedly a hallowed, sacred occasion.'

Wearily, Athelstan got to his feet. 'You joined our pilgrimage to commit murder, to silence any who might threaten you, as well as to be in

318

Canterbury when Master Thibault meets the Castilian envoys – but that is politic and does not concern me. What does concern me, is that you be arrested, confined and committed for trial before the King's justices of Oyer and Terminer at Westminster. I am sure you will be condemned to be hanged at Smithfield or Tyburn and, God forgive me, I would like to see that happen sooner rather than later. Sir John,' Athelstan waved a hand, 'arrest them.'

'Master Thibault.' Giole sprang to his feet along with the other three. Athelstan noticed that both men had strapped on their warbelts, whilst Beatrice and Maria grasped small arbalests. 'Master Thibault, you must read this.' Giole dug into a pocket in his robe and drew out a copper scroll holder. He unstoppered this, shook out the creamy-coloured parchment and handed it to Thibault. The Master of Secrets unrolled and read it. He stood staring at the manuscript, sighed heavily then closed his eyes, shoulders sagging. Athelstan's heart sank. His suspicions were well founded: Giole and his fellow demons were protected.

'Brother Athelstan, Sir John,' Thibault gestured at the door, 'a word with you.'

'We will stay for a short while,' Giole sang out, 'but then we really must be gone. So much to do . . .'

Athelstan followed Cranston, Thibault and Albinus out into the hallway. Thibault beckoned them to gather close. He held up the scroll so Athelstan could inspect the cursive Latin script written in the most clerkly hand and sealed with blood-red wax. He glimpsed the opening lines: 'Juan, by the grace of God, King of Castile, to all . . .' and groaned loudly.

'The King of Castile's own hand,' Thibault confirmed, 'verified by his personal seal.' He handed the parchment to Athelstan. 'Look, Brother. King Juan bestows on Giole Limut, his family and entourage all the rights, dignity and appurtenances of accredited envoys, royal envoys. They are to be allowed safe passage and conduct, to be untroubled by any foreign prince or his agents.'

'And so on, and so on,' Athelstan agreed, quickly reading the parchment before handing it back. 'They used this to gain entrance to the Tower.'

'Brother Athelstan, they have the full protection of Castilian law, the rights accredited to diplomatic envoys, and therefore the full protection of our own king.'

'But they have committed dreadful murders here, in the city and elsewhere!'

'Brother,' Thibault shook his head sadly, 'Sir John will confirm what I say. True, they are murderers. They deserve to hang, but they enjoy diplomatic status. It would take months, if not years, to resolve and then nothing would really happen. If we lay a finger on them, every single Englishman who happens to be in Castile will suffer. Merchants would be seized, their goods confiscated, envoys imprisoned. English officials would be hampered and hindered.' Thibault grasped Athelstan's hand, squeezed it, then let it go. 'We are on pilgrimage, Brother. Think of the stream of people from this kingdom who visit the great shrines of Santiago di Compostela, Oviedo and other such places. It also means that our own king's envoys to Castile, not to mention my Lord of Gaunt's, could be refused permission to enter all Castilian territories.'

Thibault shook his head. 'I am sure King Juan would pretend to be deeply shocked at what Giole and his coven have perpetrated, but there will be many on his council who would be only too pleased to use their arrest as a pretext to strike back . . .' Thibault broke off as the door to the taproom crashed open.

Felipe, hobbling slightly but still full of arrogance, carried out his baggage, his sword hilt within easy reach. He was followed by the two women, who smirked at Athelstan, Maria giving him an exaggerated wink. Giole swaggered out, one hand holding a pannier, the other resting on the hilt of the long dagger in its sheath on the front of his warbelt. He bowed mockingly as he passed but then sauntered back, his face only a few inches from Athelstan's.

'Be careful, friar,' he hissed, 'especially at night when the terrors gather.'

Then he was gone, joining the rest out in the stable yard, calling for their horses. Athelstan turned away so the others could not see the tears of rage well in his eyes. Cranston put a hand on his shoulder then stepped back. Athelstan stood listening to the laughter and shouts, the clatter of hooves on the cobbles, the cries of ostlers as saddles were thrown over the backs of horses, harness and reins being tightly secured. Athelstan was about to walk back into the taproom when the stable yard fell ominously silent. There was a cry, then voices shouted loudly in Spanish, followed by hideous screams, the neigh of rearing horses, hooves clattering frantically, the yells of stable boys and the groans of souls in mortal agony.

Athelstan and the rest hurried out. The early morning light had strengthened. Sconce torches flared fiercely in the buffeting breeze. At first Athelstan could not comprehend what had happened. Horses skittered about; stable servants cowered in doorways; other men wearing warbelts with arbalests slung across their backs were trying to quieten the four horses and the heavily laden sumpter pony. Athelstan walked forward and stared down at the corpses, four in all, sprawled in thick puddles of blood and filthy water. Giole, a crossbow bolt to his throat and chest. Beatrice with similar wounds. Maria's face had been shattered to a bloody pulp, whilst Felipe had received a quarrel to the chest and another in the back of his head.

'They were all mounted. The foreigners were all mounted.' A stable boy crept out of the shadows to explain. 'They were laughing and chattering in Spanish. A voice rang out telling them to desist. They ignored it. The voice shouted again in Spanish and crossbow bolts whirled through the air, emptying the saddles as quickly as snuffing out a candle-flame.'

'Who gave the order?' Athelstan demanded.

'I did.' Brother Gregorio, no longer dressed as a Friar of the Sack but garbed in dark fustian, high-heeled riding boots, one warbelt across his chest and another buckled around his slim waist, emerged out of the shadows cradling a large crossbow. He strolled towards Athelstan and stopped, sketching a bow. Others gathered behind him, similarly dressed and armed. Athelstan peered close and recognised the chapmen and itinerant tinkers who had attached themselves to the pilgrims, and who had been sheltering nearby. He recalled what Monkshood had said: that he had glimpsed Gregorio talking to the men in the fields close by the tavern at some ungodly hour of the night.

'Who are you, Sir?' Cranston came and stood beside Athelstan. 'I am minded that you surrender your weapons.'

'My name is Enrico Ayela Guerrero and I will not be surrendering my weapons. I am a *Miles Christi*, a soldier of Christ, a captain in the secular arm of the Holy Inquisition. I carry papers for myself and my men.' He undid his wallet.

'No, no.' Thibault now joined them. 'Not here but in the tavern.'

The coroner instructed Enrico's men to lay out the corpses in the yard together with all their possessions and to mount close guard over them until he ordered otherwise. The Spanish captain's companions appeared not to understand English. Enrico offered to translate, then spoke quickly and decisively, confirming Cranston's orders but enforcing his own authority on the situation.

Once back in the taproom, Cranston and Athelstan sat in one of the large window seats with Thibault, Albinus and Enrico on stools on the other side of the long trancher table. A very nervous Chobham served them ale, cheese, strips of fresh bread and a dish of spiced plums. Whilst they waited to be served, Athelstan studied Master Enrico. No longer the frolicking friar, the jolly companion and jovial comrade, the Spaniard was now hard of face, his voice harsh and clipped. He deftly laid out his papers on the table. Athelstan and the rest scrutinised the heavy parchments and their clerkly script.

They were licences issued under the direct authority of the Pope, the cardinal responsible for the Holy Office and the Inquisitor General. They declared Magister 'Enrico Ayela Guerrero, *Legatus a latere*' – the personal envoy of both the papacy and the Holy Inquisition. Enrico was described as '*Miles Christi* – a Soldier of Christ', commissioned to hunt down and extirpate – Athelstan noticed that word – heresy and schism both within and without. All loyal Catholics, members of the Universal Church, were under the gravest moral obligation to cherish, encourage and support him, be they lay or clerical, prince or pauper, king or peasant. There were no exceptions. Opposition of any sort would be met with the sanction of excommunication, cutting the offender off from God and the Church both in this life and the life to come. The principal letter developed all these themes. Athelstan read quickly, noticing that the documents bore the personal seals of the Pope and the Inquisitor General. His own order played a prominent role in the Inquisition, and he had heard of these

'*Miles Christi*', the secular arm of the Inquisition, soldiers of Christ, warriors of God totally dedicated to their vision.

'You come armed with all the power and anger of heaven,' Athelstan declared. 'Quite a change from the fornicating friar with a liking for the ladies! Did you know from the start that Giole and his family were the four-faced demon Azrael?'

'I have been hunting Azrael for years,' Enrico replied slowly. 'Azrael is responsible for many deaths, including members of the Inquisition, brothers of our order murdered at Burgos, Oviedo, Leon and elsewhere. The Inquisition has also received reports of similar garrottings at Bayonne in Gascony and Pamplona in Navarre. Yes, I began to suspect Giole and his coven but I had little proof. In addition I could not decide if he was the sole assassin or if he had the support of one or more of his family. Moreover, my suspicions ebbed and flowed. I often wondered if someone else was Azrael.'

Enrico paused as Athelstan filled his tankard. The Spaniard smiled his thanks and lifted his drink to toast Athelstan and the rest who sat listening. 'We recognised that Azrael was a skilled, professional assassin who had no fear of God and certainly no love of our church. He seemed to delight in murdering, in the most macabre and mysterious fashion, any member of our church and, in particular, the Holy Inquisition. He would often bait his victims before he struck and leave taunting messages on their corpses. He was so skilled and successful, he was only hired by the great ones, those high on the councils of the mighty. Consequently, Azrael was both well protected and well hidden.

'I admit he was a Castilian problem until King Henry died and my Lord of Gaunt married Infanta Constanza and, through her, gained a claim to that kingdom. One effective way for Gaunt's enemies in Castile to oppose his claims was assassination. Now Azrael had gone very quiet. We thought he'd returned to the great pit. He had been hunted and wanted for many crimes but then, to our surprise, we heard that he had emerged in England, and that a few of Gaunt's supporters had been garrotted, sacrificed on Azrael's altar. So the demon had fled to England. We also thought it was no coincidence that Giole Limut and his family had also joined that stream of Castilians who thought they'd try their fortunes here. The Inquisition organised a cohort to go in pursuit. We entered England at different times, in different places and in different disguises. I arrived last, posing as a Friar of the Sack. The Minister General of that order was only too pleased to be of assistance.'

'And you gathered in London?' Cranston asked.

'Of course, we believed Azrael would draw as close to Gaunt as possible. Now your regent is well protected, but others are more vulnerable, members of his household. One of my henchmen, Bernadine of Segovia . . .' Enrico looked sadly at Athelstan. 'I called him my brother, and so he was in spirit if not in the flesh. It was he whom you sang that requiem

326

mass for.' Enrico stared down the table top, collecting his thoughts.

'My entire cohort was spread out across London watching different people. Bernadine decided to scrutinise Gaunt's Secret Chancery.' The Spaniard glanced apologetically at Thibault. 'We did not wish to interfere in your affairs but simply watch to see if Azrael came out of the dark to hunt. Bernadine believed Simon Mephan was the most vulnerable to corruption. He was correct. Bernadine told me how Mephan would swagger into this tavern or that to eat and drink free of charge. He seemed to have an increasing preference for Amongst the Tombs, where he seemed to act very much the lord of the manor. Bernadine followed others of the Secret Chancery. He found out about the Mitre, the Lute Boy and the attractions of the Way of all Flesh. He noticed the doings of Luke Gaddesden, Empson and young Felicia. He reported what he knew to me then abruptly disappeared. We suspected he had been murdered. He had crossed swords with Azrael and lost, but we concluded the demon was very close. We were confused about what to do. I decided to act the jolly friar visiting the Mitre and the Lute Boy as well as savouring the pleasures of the Way of all Flesh. I deliberately cultivated young Felicia, who mentioned on two occasions that her master Simon Mephan was looking forward to making great profit.'

'And you heard about this pilgrimage?'

'Oh yes! This pilgrimage and Master Thibault's desire to join it.'

'True enough.' Albinus spoke up. 'We had

mooted such an enterprise some time ago.' He waved a hand. 'Pardon my interruption . . .'

'I understand all this,' Athelstan countered, 'but Master Enrico, why did you get yourself arrested? I mean, it was you who left the anonymous information at the Guildhall about a visiting friar fornicating with his lady friend at the Mitre, wasn't it? It had to be.' Athelstan ignored Cranston's bark of laughter. 'You gave the bailiffs the precise time and the exact place.'

'You above all should know why.' Enrico pointed at Athelstan. 'I needed to protect my own disguise. Azrael hated the Church, the Inquisition and anything to do with Rome. He has garrotted at least nine brothers of mine, men like Bernadine. If anyone went hunting Azrael, Azrael went hunting them. I was deeply concerned that somehow Azrael may have seen me speaking to Bernadine or realised we shared the same doxy.' Gregorio shrugged. 'Before you ask, we never used Felicia to communicate, it was just that she could help us both with information. I was very wary. I met Bernadine in secret but Azrael was cunning and astute. I needed to demonstrate that I was just another lecherous friar with an eye for a pretty face.'

Enrico paused to take a sip from his tankard. 'Of course, Azrael was hunting others, and events moved swiftly. I had heard about your pilgrimage and learnt from Felicia that Master Thibault and others were joining you, blending devotion with politics, praying before Becket's shrine and meeting the Castilian envoys. Giole and his family also wanted to accompany you

328

and my suspicions began to harden.' He took a deep breath. 'I approached Master Tuddenham. I pointed out that I could do penance on the pilgrimage, and of course, he was delighted to get rid of me, and so I came along.'

'And what of your suspicions about Giole?' Athelstan asked.

'As I said, they were beginning to harden into a certainty after Luke Gaddesden was killed. I knew that you would discover the truth. You see, I couldn't intervene. I had no evidence, and, let me be blunt, you don't take people like Azrael prisoner, you kill them. I have done the same to others of his kind and, God willing, I will do the same again.'

'You were in the taproom, weren't you,' Athelstan asked, 'behind the great board?'

'I was there at the beginning and I heard enough to convince me. You see, Athelstan, I knew the outcome.' He grinned. 'I have heard of your reputation, I have seen your skill. I could not allow Giole and his coven to wipe their lips and ride away, savouring their evil and relishing what to do next. I had to prepare their execution.'

'And you will take full responsibility, not the English Crown?' Thibault asked.

Enrico turned to him. 'You have seen my warrants and my licences, Sir. What I have done, I have done.' He lifted his tankard in silent toast. '*Roma locuta est.*' He whispered, '*Causa perfecta est*: Rome has spoken. The matter is finished. In a hundred years' time, who will be king of Castile, England or France?' He smiled thinly.

'Who cares? But the Universal Church will still be here, growing like the mustard seed, protected by the Holy Inquisition. The kings of this earth and its princes must always subject their selfish whims to the vision of my masters.'

He cleared his throat. 'Athelstan, you have seen my drawings. We live in a topsy-turvy world. The Universal Church, protected by the Holy Inquisition, is the one constant. I will go to Canterbury and inform the envoys there. I shall send urgent despatches to Toledo. The Holy Inquisition will take full responsibility for what occurred outside. Rest assured, no one will raise any objection with your king, your council or your church.'

'Tell me,' Athelstan asked, 'you suspected Giole – did he suspect you?'

'We were very wary of each other,' Enrico conceded. 'I think he was growing suspicious, perhaps wondering if Bernadine was alone. However, like all skilled hunters, Giole would deal with the quarry he was stalking before he turned on fresh prey.'

'And the men who helped you?' Cranston asked curiously.

'Some of them left Southwark either before us or after us with their wheelbarrows and carts.' He shrugged. 'Now you know what those carts contained. They will be rewarded, which brings me to one important point. The Holy Inquisition will take care of the four corpses. We shall have them sheeted, coffined and carted to some lonely cemetery in Kent. All their possessions, their clothing, their weapons, documents and property are forfeit to the Holy Inquisition to use and sell as my masters think fit.'

Thibault glanced at Cranston, who just shrugged.

Enrico got to his feet. 'You have no objection?' He bowed. 'Gentlemen, you have a pilgrimage to make and I have certain tasks to complete . . .'

Athelstan sat in the small, ornate pavilion overlooking the rich flower and herb gardens at the Sign of Hope. Order had been imposed, harmony assured, serenity maintained. Master Enrico and his cohort, with the assistance of Sir John, had commandeered a cart and two dray horses from the tavern to take the four corpses, now coffined and sheeted, together with a considerable pile of baggage loaded onto another cart. Enrico had rigorously searched Giole's chancery satchel and pronounced himself very pleased at what he had discovered: information which would be most useful once he returned to Castile. The '*Miles Christi*' had eventually left in a clatter of wheels, the snap and crack of harness, horses snorting, hooves scraping across the cobbles. Now they were gone: their destination was St Grace's Priory where, thanks to Athelstan's good offices, Prior Sherwin had promised to bless the corpses and bury them in the Poor Man's Lot of the priory cemetery.

'More than they deserve,' Athelstan whispered to himself. He was at peace. The effects of the violence earlier in the day had now receded. He felt tired and sleepy, but he had one last task to complete. He stared at the greenery – the herbs rich and full, the flowers in full glory – yet he sensed this splendid summer was beginning to die. The first brown tinges stained the luxuriant glossy green; petals were weakening and falling; the breeze in both the morning and evening had lost some of its welcoming warmth. Autumn was beginning to creep in. The trees would shed their leaves and the glory of an English garden would dull, provoking more sombre thoughts. Athelstan closed his eyes. Tomorrow they would leave for Canterbury. They had delayed enough at the Sign of Hope and his parishioners were becoming restless. Athelstan looked forward to reaching their destination. He would guide the pilgrims around the city, down St Dunstan's to the majestic West Gate, and let them wander the Butter Market before taking them into the glory of the Cathedral, across Almony Yard and along Hogg's Passage. They could marvel and pray before Becket's gorgeously decorated tomb as well as stare at the most beautiful diamond in the world, the Regal of France.

'Brother?'

Athelstan opened his eyes. Cranston, Thibault and Master Matthew Gaddesden had entered the pavilion. He indicated they should sit on the turf seats around the heavy, wooden table and asked if they wanted refreshments. Thibault and Matthew refused, but Cranston plucked out his miraculous wineskin and took a deep gulp. He offered it around, but the others declined.

Athelstan stared at Matthew Gaddesden, his podgy white cheeks all tear-stained, dark shadows under his red-rimmed eyes, hair greasy, mouth and chin poorly shaved and peppered with cuts and scabs. A movement caught Athelstan's eye, and he glanced to his right. Albinus, as Cranston had advised, stood guarding the entrance. Athelstan stared across at Matthew.

'You are very frightened and so you should be. Hand over your dagger.'

'Why?'

'Hand it over!' Cranston roared.

Matthew jumped and hurried to obey, dropping the knife to clatter on the floor.

'Brother Athelstan, what is this?' Thibault asked softly.

The friar pointed to Matthew. 'You are a traitor and a spy.' He glanced at Thibault. 'You have told him about what has happened?'

'I have.'

'There were gaps in my indictment.' Athelstan tapped the table with his fingers. 'I wondered how Azrael knew so much, so quickly. I mean, for a foreigner in London, charming and persuasive though he could be . . .'

'He was Mephan's personal physician,' Matthew spluttered.

'Nonsense!' Athelstan retorted. 'At one time I thought the same, that Mephan told Giole everything. I was wrong. Mephan was hunting Giole. He knew something about the Spaniard's secret affairs, or thought he did. He would be very careful what he told Giole.' Athelstan breathed a small prayer to himself and hoped the bluff would work. 'Giole is dead and gone to judgement, but we have been through his manuscripts.

We have evidence he paid you for information.'
Matthew moaned, lips opening and shutting.

'You came back to London after the revolt,'
Athelstan continued. 'Your brother Mark
had been barbarously executed by the rebels
because of his allegiance to John of Gaunt,
being one of his henchmen, his clerk and a
member of his household. You were approached
anonymously by someone who offered to pay
you liberally for information. I suggest that
you, bitter and eager for profit, agreed. To be
fair, at the time you did not know it was Azrael,
but once you sup with the devil, you cannot
leave the table.'

Athelstan used his fingers to emphasise his
points. 'You handed over the following information
about Mephan, what he said, what he did, where
he went. You probably gave the names of Gaunt's
secret supporters, those merchants who advanced
him monies. You also told Azrael about the Secret
Chancery and where its clerks went to relax and
what they did; be it your brother Luke or Empson
the courier. You told him about the pilgrimage.
Only late in the day did you realise who you
were dealing with, but by then it was too late.
Azrael could either denounce you or he could
kill you.'

'I don't . . .' Matthew spluttered.

'Like any fish caught on a hook, you wriggled
and twisted. Only after Mephan had been
murdered did the full horror strike home, but
there was nothing you could do to stop what was
happening. You gave information about me, my
parish, even my cat Bonaventure, and, of course,

334

the pilgrimage. Azrael would ask you about Sir John here, perhaps even Brother Gregorio. A warning was left in the Tower on the door to the council chamber but Azrael never infiltrated so deep as trespassing through the royal chambers in the White Tower. You did that! In addition, when we reached the Sign of Hope and realised Master Chobham here had been threatened, we also discovered that Azrael wanted to know where John Gaddesden would be lodged, but there was no mention of his brother. Why was that? Because you were protected, you were needed.'

The clerk's head went down, shoulders shaking with sobs. Athelstan glanced quickly at Thibault and nodded. Thibault understood the message. He tapped his clerk gently on the shoulder.

'You have been punished enough, Matthew. Confess and face immediate exile. Persist in your treachery and you must face the consequences.'

'Of course it's the truth.' Matthew lifted his head. 'I returned to London with the rest, I was bitter after poor Mark's death. One night I was returning to Westminster by myself. I was going down to King's Steps when a hand seized my shoulder and the tip of a dagger pricked the side of my neck. I thought it was some felon, then a purse of silver was thrust into my hand. A voice hissed that it was for me, that there would be more if I handed over certain information. I was told to make sure that I left the Chancery offices by myself on a Tuesday and Thursday. If I was needed, I would be stopped as I had been then. Of course I took the silver. And so it began. Occasionally, the hand on the shoulder, the tip of a dagger against my neck and then the questions about Mephan, the Secret Chancery, adherents of my Lord of Gaunt. At first I saw no real danger. I confess, I gossiped like a sparrow on a branch.'

He paused, wiping the tears from his face. 'My mysterious visitor was very interested in Master Mephan. What was he like? What did he do? I told them about Empson's visits to the Lute Boy, and that Brother Luke also went there. Then Mephan was murdered, followed by Empson and Luke, and I was caught in a trap. I had no choice but to keep handing over information about the pilgrimage and what I knew about taverner Chobham. I was given a number of those wretched cords with their mocking greeting and ordered to place them where Gaunt and Master Thibault would see them. I never, even in my worst nightmare, believed that when it began, two of my brothers would be murdered. I didn't know what to do. I still don't.'

Thibault raised his hands and snapped his fingers, beckoning Albinus to come in. The Master of Secrets pointed to his former clerk.

'Let him take what he has, provided he writes a full confession. He must be gone within the day. If you see him again, have him hanged as a felon.'

They watched in silence as Albinus, dagger drawn, dragged the hapless clerk to his feet and pushed him back up the path towards the tavern.

For a while Athelstan and his two companions sat in silence.

'Evil begets evil,' Thibault murmured, turning to Athelstan.

'Aye, and their name is legion for they are many.'

Author's Note

A Pilgrimage to Murder is of course a work of fiction, yet it reflects accurately the aftermath of the Great Revolt in London. John of Gaunt quickly emerged as regent and keeper of the kingdom to continue his lifelong search for a crown for himself and the powerful House of Lancaster. England's ties with Castile did stretch back centuries and the two kingdoms were closely entwined. The prospect of an English army crossing into Spain was a real and strong possibility. Castilian merchants certainly played a prominent part in London's trade with the Middle Sea and further east to Outremer. The novel accurately portrays this, as it does the emergence of professional assassins who, over the next few decades of English history, played a prominent part in the mysterious and sudden deaths of some of the great players on the political scene, from Gaunt's minions to great earls and dukes such as Humphrey of Gloucester. Gentle reader, rest assured! Sir John Cranston and Brother Athelstan will have their hands full in resolving the murderous mayhem which became a hallmark of their time.

Paul Doherty OBE, June 2016
www.paulcdoherty.com